Enchan

Mind Forged

Book One of the Enchanters of Xarparion

By T. Michael Ford

Table of Contents

Acknowledgments

I wish to personally thank the following people who helped me in this, my first book. I would like to thank my father most of all. Without his assistance, I don't think I would ever have gotten as far as I have. He supported me in my writing and was there to listen. I would also like to thank Betty for her work as my editor and the many hours of work she put in. She has earned many hours of assistance for future remodeling projects! A special thank you to Jenny Hentges for her outstanding work on the cover. It looks great! And last, but not least, thank you to my beta readers, Tammy, Cathy, Bob, George, and Kaitlin, who provided constructive feedback on the book in its many reincarnations.

Thanks again, everyone, I couldn't have done this without you!

Prologue

"Mommy, will you tell me a story?" the little girl asked. She was already in bed but was in no way ready to sleep. Her mother smiled warmly and sat down on the bed next to her.

"And what kind of story would you like?" the mother asked.

"I want a scary story!" The girl was bouncing with excitement. "With princesses and dragons and unicorns!"

"Hmm, all right, I believe I have just the story. But are you sure you're old enough?"

The girl frowned, "That's not fair! You and daddy face scary things for real all the time, so I think I can handle a story."

The mother began, "Long ago, in the age of the sword, there was the kingdom of Wereia. In that kingdom was a huge fortress on a mountain; in fact, it was this very keep."

The girl wiggled deeper into her covers, ready to listen. "Wait! Is this a short story or a very long story? If it's long, I need a drink of water first."

"Well, daughter, which would you prefer?"

"The long story! Please, we don't have anything going on tomorrow. It's rained for the past two days, so I won't even get to play in the forest because it will be muddy!"

"Very well, but I will need to retrieve a book from your father's library. Go get your drink and come right back." The little girl nodded and scampered to a nearby nightstand that held a pitcher and a small handled cup. Concentrating, she poured her drink and sipped it.

The mother got up and left the room, returning with a large leather-bound book with a golden design on it. Her daughter slid over past the middle of the bed as she had done so many times. The mother folded her large, feathered wings in close to her body and carefully lay down on the bed, inching closer to her little girl protectively. Giving her a hug and a kiss on the head and pulling the blankets up over their laps, she began.

"Now, this is a special book that has a princess, dragons, and even unicorns. It tells everything about the events leading up to the final battle with the evil necromancer, who was really scary, and the brave people who defeated him. The book can tell the story better than I can." The girl nodded eagerly and snuggled into the soft feathers of her mother's wings as she opened the book and started to read.

Chapter 1

Alex

It's a lovely spring morning. The birds are singing, the sun is in just the right spot, and there's a nice warm breeze coming in. All in all, it's a perfect day. But am I out enjoying it? No, of course not, I'm doing chores for my dad. See, he's the local blacksmith in town, but not the impressive kind who make excellent and powerful weapons or armor. No, we're the type of shop that fashion pots, pans, and farm tools.

In reality, I love this work and I get along great with my dad. Well, most of the time. There are some days he can be a real ass. Anyway, today is just one of those days, you know? First nice day of spring after a long winter and all you want to do is be outside, but that's not going to happen today.

Getting back on track, my name is Alex. And before you say it, yes, I know it's boring, but hey - son of a blacksmith here! I'm nineteen years old, brown-haired, brown-eyed, six feet tall and that's about it. I like to think that I'm a decent enough looking guy, but I never seem to have much luck with girls. Yeah, I'm strong and in pretty good shape, but no one in this town wants to date the blacksmith's apprentice who works long hours and always seems to smell like smoke, hot metal and sweat. Not when you can find yourself a real live wizard who will most likely be rich some day.

Foalshead is your typical farming community, nestled in a backwater area where two gentle mountain ranges meet. The ground is fertile and the weather is generally pleasant, although winters can be difficult, especially for the smaller farms higher up into the hills. The main purpose this town fulfills is to support the only magic school in the known world. So naturally, it's not unusual to see wizards and want-to-be wizards all over the place. And the girls love them.

Of course, the wizards who come here are always acting very mysterious and secretive about what goes on in the mage tower in the middle of town. But believe it or not, farmers and townspeople are not stupid and, in fact, many are very well-informed. It also helps that the town has been doing business with the wizard school, Xarparion, for over three hundred years, and the locals have built up some knowledge about what goes on behind those walls.

First, the tower in Foalshead is not the school. It's not really that big, just a small stone keep with high walls and a gate. If you walk three hundred paces in a circle, you can go all the way around it. It's just a doorway of sorts; wagonloads of grains, horse feed, vegetables and even chickens and pigs drive in, are unloaded, and then drive out, and no one ever sees a trace of the stuff again.

Second, not everyone who comes out of the tower is a wizard. Some are apprentices or acolytes, but most are just staff who work for the various "towers" at the school, or staff of the school itself. These are the individuals who broker most of the purchasing from the farmers. The farmers and townspeople will tell you that dealing with the academy staff is sometimes nerve-wracking, but at least they can't fry you with a fireball or evaporate all the water from your body. But occasionally, full wizards will come into town and then it's advisable to pay attention to the color of their robes, or better yet, avoid them altogether.

The most common wizards in Foalshead are the healers, and for the most part, they are very well-liked in the community because they can save a leg that had been savaged by a boar, assist in childbirth or even save the town from an outbreak of disease. They dress in dark gray robes with red arms.

The next group is the earth wizards, in green robes, of course. They can move rocks, excavate caverns, shape crystals, and summon elementals. A few earth wizards are talented enough to be called druids, who are also very popular in Foalshead. They can encourage the crops to grow and drive off pests. It's rumored that they can even talk to the plants and animals, so all-in-all, a very useful person to have around in a farming community.

From there it tends to go downhill in the popularity department. The water wizards (blue robes) and the wind wizards (light gray robes) are either mostly neutral or can be downright pains in the ass. Normally, they don't have any real business in our town, so the ones who come through typically are young mages feeling their oats, looking for an adventure, a no-strings fling with the opposite sex, or a fight and they don't care which one they find. I'll give you a hint, Foalshead is chronically low on adventure at all times!

The final group is the red robes, the fire wizards. They have similar motivations for visiting our small town as the water and wind mages; however, in their case, they are almost always looking for a fight. Most townsfolk, when they see a full red robe, turn and go the opposite direction. I've even seen some of the very few businesses in town hang up their "closed" signs early if there is a fire wizard in Foalshead. They are the quintessential jerks of our little world.

Fortunately, or perhaps not from the standpoint of earning any coinage, the wizard community seems to have adequate blacksmithing wherever they come from so they rarely bother our tiny shop at the outer edge of town.

I live with my mother and father in a decent wooden and thatched-roof house on the outskirts of town, where we've lived for a few years now. We have a small garden and an airy stable out back where we can board a few horses, or house them pending a shoeing, etc. We were forced to move here after the situation in our old village got...complicated. But now things are going well. My mother used to assist the local healer at our old village, but since there are usually healing wizards in Foalshead, those skills aren't needed any longer. Now she works as a cook in one of the local inns, The Sleeping Hedgehog. Generally, someone my age would have already left home and be making their way in the world, but Dad is getting old and a life of constant toil and injuries from heat and the occasional recalcitrant farm animal has taken its toll. Besides, I don't think mother could handle me leaving. So I work the forge on a daily basis, and like most young people my age, dream of better things to come.

Today's client, Miss Stal, is the headmistress of the orphanage. She is a harsh, middle-aged woman with a beak of a nose that a vulture would envy. She had again brought in her largest pot; it was leaking again and she was furious. As usual, she is blaming us, saying that we do poor work. But really, it's the fact that she habitually soaks verbena root in the pot overnight and the acids that leach out of the plant destroy the iron. Most reputable farmers won't even feed verbena root to their hogs as it will cause them to grow sickly and underweight. It's really just a noxious weed, not even a food crop, and this horrid woman was feeding it to orphans. Just thinking about it makes me angry! I know a number of those children and they deserve better from life.

"Alex, I need that order!" I heard my father shout from outside. I blinked and the world spun for a second as I recovered from my daydream. I really need to snap out of this. It seems that since my last birthday, I have been daydreaming more and more. Usually, it's just about people and friends in the village where we used to live, or thinking about some great adventure I could be missing out on living in Foalshead. But other times, like now, I've actually gotten steaming mad just thinking about things I can't change. Dammit! Looking down, the pot I held in my leather gloves was steaming and glowing faintly, but it was a bluish tint and not even hot. I don't even know how long I've been holding it.

"Alex!"

"Be done in a minute." I plunged the pot into a nearby vat of water and watched the color fade. Once it looked normal enough to handle, I quickly tossed it into a large hemp bag along with the rest of her order and ran outside. I shook my head doggedly wondering what that blue glow was all about, but I had no time to ponder it further.

Miss Stal was around front complaining to my father like she always does when anything with ears is around. I jogged the rest of the distance and handed her the bag of goods. "Here's your order, Miss Stal."

She scowled at me. "About time! I've had to feed the children with expensive food from the inn. That place has no idea what good gruel is!" I winced slightly and thought, *"You're right, they don't know how to make good gruel, probably because there is no such thing as good gruel. The inn actually makes food!"* Those poor kids are probably praying right now for me to melt her cookware back down to the ore it came from and feed it to a stone troll.

"This better be the last time we have to fix that thing," she huffed. As always, the abrasive woman had succeeded in getting on Dad's nerves. Thankfully for me, she just spun around and marched off to take her anger out on her cooking, and sadly, those poor kids. "I hate that woman," my father growled under his breath.

"I think everyone does. I feel sorry for the kids every time we give that damn pot back to her."

He nodded. "I know, but don't worry; I delayed her long enough that your mother could run over some real food."

"Speaking of food, remember Mom is working late again tonight so I'm done for the day."

He grumbled as I started to make my way to the house, "Men shouldn't know how to cook." And then he expertly slid a bar of cheap stock iron into the forge for the next day's order of barrel rings.

I laughed, "If I didn't know how to cook, you would have starved to death long ago."

"Fine, but she didn't have to teach you all that other crap." The "crap" he was referring to was one of his favorite old grudges. When I was too young to help my dad at the forge, I spent my non-school days helping my mother. That meant following her around, helping her cook and even watching her work with the village healer. A good portion of it actually sunk in, so now I'm pretty good at both cooking and herbs. I've got tons of potions written down in one of my notebooks.

I chuckled and shook my head, stopping to pat the old family dog sleeping next to the corral fence as I went into the house to get started on dinner. I wasn't going to tell my dad, but I actually liked cooking. It felt good to see someone happy when they ate my food. The kitchen was the main reason my mother made dad buy this place. You could open a bakery in here and still not use all the space available. As I started assembling ingredients, I suddenly felt totally drained, like I had run a long race or had been putting up hay all day. Torn between exhaustion and hunger, I went for a quick stew made from last night's leftovers. That's not to say my mother didn't teach me to make leftovers taste great too.

With the stew going, I took the time to sit down in a chair at the table and relax...I don't remember the last time I felt this tired. I must have fallen asleep because the next thing I knew, my dad was in my face. "Son, what are you doing?"

I shot up from my flopped over position and nearly fell over from a bout of vertigo. I grabbed the chair arms and steadied myself. "For some reason, I'm exhausted all of a sudden."

Concern flashed across his face for a second but quickly vanished and was replaced with minor annoyance. "I'm sure you just stayed up too late last night reading those ridiculous adventure books of yours."

"Yeah, you're probably right," I agreed, but mentally I counted it as just another instance of weird Alex phenomena that had been occurring with increasing regularity lately. My appetite was way up; a growth spurt, my Mother assured me. My sleep was irregular, and I had taken to gazing at the stars a lot recently in the middle of the night. The overall effect was a desperate feeling that I needed to be somewhere else...soon.

"Come on, let's eat and get you to bed early tonight," my father groused, interrupting my thoughts.

We ate our slightly overdone stew in silence. Dad even offered to do the dishes tonight and sent me off with a curt command. With things in the kitchen under control, I careened off to my room, hands pushing off the hallway walls to keep me on a straight course. I didn't even have the strength or willpower to get undressed before collapsing on my bed and crashing heavily into my dreams.

Maya

Maya crouched low in a fighter stance with one foot slightly behind and tensed like a coiled spring, small shield and thin engraved long sword at the ready. She sighed and surveyed the dead dark brown earth beneath her feet, her elf senses reaching out and detecting no living water or green foliage anywhere nearby. There was no breeze to ruffle her hair or cool her skin beneath the light, small-weave ring mail she wore. The pale, muted sun above was as lifeless as the plain on which she stood, dispensing light only grudgingly, but still heating up the atmosphere to a very uncomfortable level. Perhaps the warmth radiating up her soft leather boots came from somewhere below instead. Satisfied there was no immediate threat, she stood up straight and shook back her long curly silver hair. She briefly debated tying it back in preparation for battle but knew it would make little difference and at least her ears could be unbound for one last battle. She stood about five and a half feet high as humans reckoned size, and it let her see the rippling, shimmering effects of mirages across the plain in the distance. Her breath caught a bit as first shades and then full figures materialized out of the distortion, marching toward her. Swiveling slowly around, she noted the same from every direction, north, south, east, and west or what passed for them anyway in this place.

The thought of trying to run for it, possibly finding a seam in the line, briefly crossed her mind, but the tactical part of her brain knew that the trap was already sprung, and there was no escape. At three hundred yards, the approaching wall devolved into individuals rather than a single mass. Walking corpses, mostly wearing rags, probably former innocent farm folk, carrying whatever weapons came handily to their putrefying grasps. Mindless, some even eyeless and brainless, they plodded forward. To a child born of nature, this sight was more bone-chilling than anything else imaginable for there was nothing natural about this scene - it was sheer abomination. In addition to the zombies, here and there wights and ghouls bobbed in and out of the line, as if to drive the lesser undead forward faster. They were stronger and smarter than the simple zombies and skeletons. Maya knew they were also cowardly and usually content to have the corpses wear down their opponents to the point of utter exhaustion before moving in for an easy kill.

At a hundred yards, the circle was complete and the horde was fifty deep or more in all directions. The sounds of their shuffling feet battered Maya's senses like a gravelly rockslide. As if on cue, the first sign of life appeared in the sky above and she took a second to squint up at the black buzzards now tightly circling. Pulling her gaze back down, she inspected her battered sword. A gift from her father years before, it was still more of a practice weapon than a true champion's blade, but she kept it ruthlessly sharp nonetheless and its leather wrappings freshly tied. At thirty yards, the wave of rotting flesh smell hit her acute nose like an avalanche, and her ears could pick up the background sound of lip smacking and moaning above the dragging crunch of footsteps. Her eyes noted a trail of dark miasmal fluids behind some of the fresher corpses and she had to stifle a retch. Quickly putting that visual aside, she took a last deep breath and brought her weapon and shield to bear. As an elven warrior, she would fight in the proud manner of her people and die with dignity, if nothing else.

With a quick glance, she judged the left side to be the closest, bounded forward and swept her sword in a darting arc to that side, cleanly removing the heads of two corpses, who dropped like cordwood in their tracks. The next row moving forward tripped over the bodies and rolled clumsily to the dirt. Milling about, more went down as the zombies and skeletal warriors were not intelligent enough to avoid the obstacles. The left side was piling up nicely and Maya allowed herself a grim smile. As she felt a slight tug on the back of her armored shirt, she spun around and realized the undead on the right were closing in. Pounding the pommel of her sword into the dripping jawless face of a zombie practically on top of her, she followed with a savage kick to its torso that drove it back into its peers and toppled several, causing yet another pile up. The undead horde to the other two directions received similar treatment. Soon her sword and armor were caked with slime and foot space was becoming a very scarce commodity as the undead continued to press forward on her position. Maya's sword sang in constant motion and with every swing, black ichors splattered off the blade, but she was fighting an enemy that knew no fear, no fatigue, and no doubt.

Finally, even the best-trained warriors are subject to the vagaries of fate, and in another attempt to kick back a deep-chested, rag-covered skeleton, Maya watched in detached horror as her booted foot burst all the way through her opponent's ribcage and became lodged there. Having used most of her momentum and flagging strength in the jump, she was unable to withdraw her foot in time to catch herself. Maya went down hard on her back as the other sides of the undead wall swarmed over her. On the ground, she watched dispassionately what should have been her last living sight, a large rusty axe blade cleaving toward her face.

Suddenly, a large silvery-white object blotted out the sun and the zombies standing over her! Instead of the lull in the battle she was expecting upon her death, she heard a fierce renewal of metal on metal, actually more like thunderclaps on metal. As the booming sounds reverberated everywhere, the ground under her even seemed to shake and Maya felt herself pulled back to her feet.

As her vision cleared, she saw a knightly figure in glistening white armor next to her. He carried a huge tower shield, with no heraldry markings, that was taller than she was. The crest of his helm rose above the top of the massive shield by at least another two feet; he was a giant of a man. In his other hand, he wielded an enormous white war hammer similar to what she had seen some bands of dwarves use, only this one was twice as large. Without even a glance in her direction, he tucked her inside the protective area of his shield and continued to use the hammer to great effect, spinning their position to counter the threats from all sides. Maya watched in amazement as with every hit, the hammer sent out a wave of force that shattered not only the undead targeted, but those around it as well. Breather over, Maya slid out from behind the relative safety of the knight's tower shield and took up position at his back, her strength and courage renewed.

Out of the corner of her eye, she could see the undead being mowed down relentlessly by the knight. Even the ghouls and wights were no match for the hammer and splattered like rotten fruit against a stone wall. For what seemed like hours, they fought on until Maya dispatched one last shoeless peasant corpse, slicing through its spine and cleaving it in half. Spinning to help her benefactor, she found he was gone and she was again alone, alone in a sea of smashed and dismembered bodies - an undead army no more. Collapsing to her knees in tears, Maya gasped and pounded her sword on the ground. Tossing it aside, she beat with her clenched fists again and again against the bloody ground in despair, and finally, mercifully, she awoke.

Chapter 2

Alex

I woke up the next morning to the sounds of someone in the next room. Looking out my small window, I realized it was way past daybreak, the usual time I get up. I sat up quickly, still a little drained and unsteady. Clearing my head with a large drink of water, I cleaned up, got dressed and flew out the door to get to work. But when I got to the forge, I couldn't find Dad, and the fire hadn't even been stirred up. Confused, I went back inside to find it was my mother who was making all the noise.

"Why are you here and not at work today?" I asked her.

She looked up from whatever she was baking, plastered back her gray-streaked auburn hair and smiled. "I worked extra late last night so I was given today off and your father was called into town this morning. From the sound of it, Miss Stal is at it again." I snatched a handful of dried apple slices out of the bag on the counter that she was about to use for apple dumplings if my analysis of her readied ingredients was correct. Today would be a very good day!

"Mom, I don't want to worry you, but I had another episode like the others last night. I don't understand it; I've never felt like this before." My mother set down what she was working on and rushed over to feel my forehead. She shook her head as I continued, "Did your parents or Dad's ever mention something like this? Does this run in the family like normal crazy?"

A strange, puzzled sadness ran across her face as she leaned in to give me a hug. It was as if she was tempted to say something but then didn't. "Alex, your body is just going through some late growing changes; I'm sure it's nothing to worry about. It will probably go away on its own." She went back to the work counter and started tossing ingredients into a mixing bowl, but I could tell she was distracted as she wasn't her usual meticulous ingredient-measuring self.

Just then, there was a knock at the door. Mother stopped what she was doing, brushed the coarse flour off her hands, and went to get it. When she opened the door, there stood an older man in an expensive black robe. He had a smiling face accented with laugh lines and blue, sparkling eyes. Behind him stood a tall figure hooded in a white robe.

The old man spoke first, "Greetings, Mrs. Martin. I am the Headmaster of the Wizards Academy."

I thought my mother was going to faint as I saw her knees sag. I caught her arm to steady her as she spoke, "Um, hello, sir...Headmaster, what can we do for you?"

I watched as the figure in white, who was quite a bit taller than the Headmaster and quite animated, seemed to be trying to get around him and through the door. Just when it seemed like he/she was about to sneak under an arm and spring into our kitchen uninvited, the Headmaster abruptly dropped his arm, effectively blocking the attempt. He glanced back with a look of exasperation and then turned to face my mother with a renewed but strained smile.

"May we please come inside? This is not a conversation best held in public."

Mom looked like she was going to turn them away, but instead, fearfully stepped to the side and let them come in. The Headmaster and the hooded figure in white entered. Behind them, I could see an older woman wearing the green robes of an earth wizard waiting in the yard. A full wizard, not an apprentice or a tower staff buyer. Next to her, I recognized a young girl with long curly brown hair and blue eyes. I knew right away she was named Julia and was from Miss Stal's orphanage. Mom also spotted her. "Julia, what are you doing here, sweetie?" She knelt down and the young girl rushed inside and into my mother's arms, sobbing quietly, holding on for dear life. But if I was reading her expressions correctly, it appears they were tears of joy, not sorrow.

I've known Julia for a few years now; her parents owned a peddler's wagon that toured from village to village selling fabrics, tools, pots, and pans. One day, not far from Foalshead, their wagon was set upon by bandits on a wooded trail, both parents were killed and the wagon taken. A local woodsman found Julia sitting in a small glen in the forest, talking quietly to the squirrels and rabbits that circled around her. Some of the townspeople assumed she was a little "touched" and with no relatives, she ended up at the orphanage. She's actually fourteen years old, but due to Miss Stal's cooking, she can barely pass for twelve. Amazingly enough, even after all the emotional shock, heartache and horrible food, Julia was still a very bright, sweet girl always smiling, looking for fun and hoping for a place to someday really call home.

The earth wizard lady waited outside as we all moved into the sitting area. The Headmaster began to tell us why he was here. "Early this morning, we received a hysterical report from a Miss Stal, the headmistress of the local orphanage, that her favorite cooking pot was demonically possessed. It seemed that whenever she tried to add anything to it, the pot slid out of her reach. As you no doubt know, this is rather odd for a pot. Our expert on the subject here," he said, gesturing to the fidgeting person in white, "says that an enchantment was placed on it so that it would move if this Stal woman attempted to add any ingredients to it at all. Anyone else could use the pot normally. Naturally, we found the entire account very intriguing."

By this time, the figure in white was literally hopping from foot to foot, either he/she was very excited or had to pee badly.

Mother frowned at this display but was still confused. "That's…um…very unfortunate, but what does this have to do with us? And why do you have Julia?"

The Headmaster smiled, "Ah, you see, we found her at the orphanage during our investigation. I guess you could say I have a soft spot for orphans, so I test them every chance I get. She turned out to have some promise as an earth wizard, so at least I could save one of them from that life. As for you, it's not so much you or your husband…as it is your son."

Mom's eyes grew wide. "What about Alex?"

He raised his hand calmly in an attempt to settle her down. "He has done nothing wrong, Mrs. Martin, but he was the last person to work on the item. We just need to test him to ascertain if this pot anomaly is a result of some latent magic Alex might have." He took a deep breath and glared warningly at the figure in white, before he sighed and held out a small gray sphere to me. I looked at my mother, her expression was pained, but she nodded for me to take it. I reached out and accepted the orb from him. As soon it left his hand, it turned clear. After a few moments, the color changed to a smoky hue and then finally white, and not just any white, but a bright glowing light that lit up the room.

I didn't have long to marvel at the wonder I was now holding in my hand. The next thing I knew, I heard a piercing screech and was scooped up into a bear hug by the tall person in the white robe. Unexpectedly, I learned a few things while being tossed around like a little girl's dolly. First, the figure in white was a woman; second, she was incredibly strong to the point where I was in some pain; and last, she was an elf. How do I know? Well, I got a very pointy ear in the eye...

From what I gathered as I was being spun around, the rather embarrassed Headmaster stated he was leaving and this woman was to take over from now on. But I wasn't too sure, I was starting to feel sick. Just as things were beginning to go black, she released me. I remember thinking, what had I done to deserve this? And what does all this mean anyway? Instantly, she put me back down on my own two feet. "I am so sorry!" she said as she covered her mouth. "I just couldn't contain myself. You, my young friend, are an Enchanter! And I have come to take you to Xarparion!"

Huh? Regaining my breath, I finally got a chance to look over my polite attacker. She was tall, at least six inches taller than me and her hood had slid back so I could see her face. She had long blond, braided hair and calm blue eyes, and as I surmised, she also had long elf ears. From what I could tell, she wasn't that old either - thirty, thirty-five, tops.

She smiled, brightening even more. "Thank you, that's very sweet of you to say!"

Despite how very odd that was since I'm pretty sure I hadn't said anything, I had other things on my mind; and apparently, so did my mother. "Can you please explain what this all means?"

The white-robed elf opened her mouth to explain just as the door burst open and my father rushed in looking like a dark thundercloud on two feet. "What the hell is going on? Why is there a wizard in our front yard, and I just passed another on the road coming from here?"

Mom ran over to him and wrapped her arms around him. She placed her head against his broad chest shaking. "The day has come." His expression softened to one of concern and he draped supportive arms around her.

He turned to the elf and growled, "We'll talk in the kitchen." He then looked at me. "Alex, stay here with Julia." The three of them made their way to the kitchen and I got one last look at the elf. She looked like she was having the time of her life as she practically skipped into the kitchen; I had to give her big points for bravery.

This left Julia and me alone, she looked nervous, but also happy and excited. She came over and sat next to me gushing. "I don't know what's going on, and I don't care. The old guy in the robes told me I wouldn't have to go back to Miss Stal ever again!"

I knew she had a rough life, but I didn't know how bad it really was. "Was Miss Stal really that bad?"

She looked at me with astonishment. "She's an evil and cruel woman. She makes us work all day instead of going to school. She hires us out to farmers to pick weeds, usually verbena root, and then that's what she feeds us. We sleep huddled together on the cold floor with only two meals a day. And her food is so bad the rats don't even eat it." Her face lit up with a memory as she continued, "You should have seen her face, though; it was hilarious to watch her chase after that pot, she was so angry! I hadn't laughed so hard since before my parents died... I want you to know that we all really appreciate what you and your family do for us, you're the only ones who seem to know or care."

"Yeah, sorry about that. Food was all we could really do for you."

Her eyes widened in alarm and she grabbed my arm gently.

"No, don't be sorry, really. You guys are great. You and your mother are the best cooks in town. We count the days between your visits. And the days that her stupid pot is broken are the best days of our lives there. Since the old guy took it away from her, I guess the others have about a week at least before you can make her a new one."

"Yeah, a lot longer if I'm not able to help. It's not like we have pots that large on hand."

She looked down at the floor. "I'm truly sorry about this, Alex. What may be a blessing for me might be a nightmare for you; I know you are very close to your family. Every night I prayed for my life to get better, and we all thanked the gods for sending us your family. The other children will be sad if you end up having to go away, too."

We waited a bit longer in silence as I thought over my fate. Was I really going to be trained as a wizard? What was it like in the tower? What kind of magic can I use? My thoughts were interrupted by my parents and the elf returning. My mother was crying and was still trying to stop the flow of tears. Dad just looked like he was pissed off. My parents started to come into the room, stopped like they were going to say something, then abruptly stalked off into my room.

The elf, on the other hand, smiled brightly and bounded over to me. "Forgive me for smiling, please know that I'm sorry if this causes you pain, but we need to leave soon. It's actually a fair distance to walk and we should try to reach the school before dark."

Ok, what is with this lady, she hasn't even told us her name, and now we are going away with her?

Her eyes shot wide with embarrassment. "I am so sorry, I forgot to introduce myself. I am Primus Rosa of the Enchanters Hall."

She looked at Julia and winked." And yes, I really am an elf."

Julia was shocked. "How did you know I was thinking that?"

Rosa giggled. "For one, it's an obvious question, but I can read minds, so that helps, too."

She can read minds? Is that even possible? *Ok, lady, try this; if you can read minds, say "turnip."*

She nodded and winked at me. "Turnip."

Grapevine.

"Grapevine."

Volcano.

"Volcano."

Platypus.

"Do you even know what that is?"

"No, but someone said they look funny."

She laughed, "That they do, but I find them rather cute. But your parents are almost done, so before they come back, they don't know I'm an elf and I'll explain why later so don't tell them." How can they not notice? She has elf ears six inches long!

"Umm, Primus Rosa, I don't think I can just leave. I don't think my parents can handle the shop without me. Maybe if I had a few months to train someone."

She acknowledged my concern with a kindly but serious look. "Don't worry, Alex, we are not bandits or slavers to just barge into your home and haul you away without compensation. I have supplied your parents, and gladly I might add, with enough gold that they could retire and live out their days comfortably from this point forward. The same gold could easily hire extra help if they need it to run your blacksmith shop. I am sorry that they will miss you and you them, but you, my young friend, are destined for bigger things than Foalshead can provide. Besides, once your training has progressed far enough along, you can come back and visit as often as you like."

I could hear my Father's grumbling all the way from the other side of the house as my parents returned with two loaded shoulder packs. Mom came over to me and handed me one of the bags. "I doubt you will need much over there, but I packed your favorite books and some of your personal things. There is also water and a snack in there." She gave me a tearful hug. "Be safe, my son, and listen to the nice lady. She is a good person and will help guide you through your new better life."

I nodded, a little short of breath and my eyes burning. Somehow I had a feeling she knew this day was coming, just probably not like this. She turned to Julia and handed her the other satchel. "Sweetie, I packed you a few things you might need as well. But I know you haven't eaten, so it's mostly filled with food."

Julia jumped up in tears and hugged my mother. "Thank you for everything, Mrs. Martin, I will try and keep an eye on Alex for you."

Rosa placed a hand on Julia's shoulder and whispered, "Head on outside, and the woman in the green robe will take you to Xarparion."

Julia gave Mom one last quick squeeze before bolting out the door. I looked at Rosa to see if we had to leave as well. She nodded so I knew it was time to say goodbye. Mom came over to me again and gave me another hug. "I'm going to miss you so much."

I blinked away the moisture clouding my vision. "I think I'll be just fine, Mom. I'll try to visit as soon as I can," I replied still unsure how my reaction should be to all this, but this was painful. I briefly wondered if I should just refuse to leave my life at Foalshead behind, but a little voice in the back of my consciousness whispered that it was time for me to find the adventure that I had always dreamed about.

Dad gave me a stern look and a strong handshake, his anger gone and replaced with resigned acceptance and a concerned nod. Coming from him, that was a very touching goodbye. A last sobbing farewell and a frantic list of instructions on behavior and personal grooming from my Mother followed. Mercifully, Rosa quickly pulled me out the door and away from my home for the past seven years.

We walked silently for a bit until we were out of sight of the house before Rosa started to lose it. She went from calmly walking to spinning in a circle, giggling manically. I think I even saw a couple of awkward cartwheels like a little girl would perform.

"What's wrong with you?"

Instead of an answer, she grabbed hold of me again and spun me around. After setting me down and hyperventilating like a teenager, she finally started to speak real words.

"I'm sorry, but I'm just so happy! I've been alone for so long, and now I finally have an apprentice! Someone to share my life's work with! This really is the best moment in my life!"

"Not to be disrespectful, but if this is the greatest moment of your life, that's rather sad."

She didn't stop laughing. "I know, right? Seven hundred years I've been waiting for this! By the gods, I feel like a hundred-year-old little girl again!"

She took some deep breaths and slowly calmed down. "Ok, I'm better now." She took a few more breaths before grabbing my shoulders and turning me to face her. "Alright, let's get this formal stuff out of the way. As I said before, I am Primus Rosa, of the Enchanters Hall and you are now my apprentice. That means I'm also your teacher, advisor, and I really hope to be your friend."

We continued walking towards the tower at the center of town. As we walked, I took particular notice of the few wizard types in town, most of who glared at us as we walked by. "Um, Miss Rosa...so why does it look like they hate us?"

She winced. "You noticed that, huh? Well, you would have learned sooner or later. As an Enchanter, you will find that the other towers will look down on you. We can't cast spells like they can, so they feel that we are inferior and useless."

"Are we?"

She looked hurt. "Of course not! I mean, they're right, we can't cast fireballs and the like, but we can do lots of other things they can't."

"Like?"

She finally smiled proudly and put her arm around my shoulder as we continued to walk. "We are the crafters of magic. We are the ones who make the wondrous magical items that make Xarparion the place it is today."

"So...we make magic pots?"

She stopped and just stared at me. "I can't believe I forgot about that! You have already done your first enchantment! I'm sooo proud! But yes, we can make magic pots as well as much more interesting and useful things. One of my greatest achievements, we will be using shortly."

As she said that, we approached the familiar keep. I had looked at it many times in the past seven years, but never with the thought I would someday see the inside. It had high ivy-covered, gray stone walls, but no one in town could remember seeing any workmen repairing anything on the structure, nor were there any visible guards to be seen. A few paces around and we arrived at the front gate. The iron-bound plank gates silently opened with no one touching them when we got within a few feet. My mouth was wide open as I walked through and into the courtyard. I was expecting something grand, but there wasn't anything there, just grass with wagon tracks worn through it and an old wooden ramp leading up to a huge metal-bound door.

Rosa laughed beside me. "Believe me, I was thinking the same thing when I went inside my first tower. But in the old days, they were actually just warehouses to hold goods until a non-magical caravan arrived to haul them away. It was frightfully inefficient and slow."

I looked at her, puzzled and hoped that she would explain further.

She smiled and grabbed my hand, dragging me up the ramp to the door. "Later, now let's go!"

As with the front gate, the doors swung wide as we approached. This time, though, they were opened by two men, holding pole arms and hooded in black leather, standing guard at the door. The men nodded as we entered and vanished into dark corners a second later.

As my eyes adjusted to the gloom and my nose to the dank smell, I got a chance to look around and was confused by what I found. There were no classrooms or other things I would normally think were used in teaching; in fact, the whole tower was just one room. All I could see was shelving and wooden crates of every shape and size, some with slats for holding chickens and pigs, some with flour sacks lining them to transport grains, etc. There must have been thousands of crates in that tower, most of them appeared empty as if waiting to be filled and sent on their way. There were also two wooden platforms that looked like wagon bodies without wheels stationed to one side. At the center of the room was the only thing that I would count as magical. It was an enormous stone pool with a ramp leading down to it; the water was also glowing with an eerie foxfire blue light.

Rosa didn't give me long to look around, she was already dragging me towards the only other person I could see in the room. This man was in black like the others but sat behind a desk shuffling through a large pile of papers. When we approached, he looked up at us, but I still couldn't see his face. "May I help you?" he asked. His voice was very deep and the inflections were odd, like it really wasn't a language he excelled at speaking.

Rosa stepped in front of me. "Yes, I need to register Alex Martin for class as an Enchanter."

"Please wait a moment while I find the proper form." He got up and went to a row of shelving that looked to be used for filing.

Rosa sighed impatiently. "This could take a long time."

"Why is that?"

She waved a hand at the man. "As you have been thinking, these creatures aren't human. They're a form of construct, like a golem. They are used as staff for Xarparion, but they are limited by their intelligence. That one is going to look for a form that hasn't ever been used before now and was created over six hundred years ago. And he is going to search methodically, year by year to do it, so relax and have a seat."

From out of the shadows, two more of these servants showed up with two chairs for us. With us seated, they vanished as quickly as they came. "Ok, those guys are kind of creepy."

"Believe me, I know. When I first came to the school, they didn't have the hoods and they are hideous. I still don't know where they originated from, but only a handful will ever leave the grounds, even if ordered to. But they do function splendidly in this type of situation where a human guard would be bored to death."

"Is this the grand entrance to Xarparion then?"

She smiled at me and patted my hand affectionately. "One of many. Just hold the rest of your questions until we get this done, I'd hate to spoil the surprise."

I took the hint that she was having way too much fun to ruin it, so we ended up chatting about mindless things as we waited. I mean, who knew that Medusas have serious self-image issues? Or that there are several species of coconut that actually move about on a seasonal rotation? After about a half hour, the servant came back and sat on the other side of the desk. "I will now ask you some basic questions." I answered everything he asked, but they were all very simple; name, age, height, favorite color and so on.

Finally done with the paperwork, he put a stamp on the form and handed it to Rosa. "File this in triplicate at your tower and also at

Central. Have a nice day." He dropped his head back down to the papers in front of him as Rosa hopped up and grabbed my hand.

She led me over to the pool in the center of the massive room. She stopped at the edge of the ramp and turned to look at me with a mischievous smile. "Would you like to take a swim? It's a hot day, is it not?"

"Um, no, it isn't. It's actually rather nice out, so I'm good," I said, remembering how cold the ice water runoff made the lakes this time of year.

She clamped a hand down on my shoulder. "It really wasn't a suggestion." She shoved me into the pool, laughing. I was up to my waist before I could even react, but strangely, I didn't seem to be wet. I looked at her and she was smiling right next to me in the water. "Keep going, Alex, all you have to do is walk. Close your eyes if you would like, I'll guide you so you don't trip."

Somehow, I knew I could trust her with my life but I also wanted to see what would happen, so I kept my eyes open and continued to walk. The water rose around us until it was around my neck. "Are you sure about this?"

She smiled to reassure me. "Don't worry, it will be fine."

I nodded, but my body shivered in reflex as I took a deep breath before plunging in. I could feel the water around me, but I wasn't being buoyed off the bottom like I should be in water. After only a few seconds, I could feel the water receding from around my legs. Another few steps later I could feel warm air around my hands. Then finally, I was out of the water and in the sunlight.

I looked around in amazement as Rosa just beamed beside me. I stared in wonder up at the glistening pool of water that was now floating above our heads, supported by a few columns. A little disoriented, I drew my eyes back down to something more mundane, my feet. I found that we were standing on a platform at the top of a grass-covered hill, with the shimmering pool of water above us and a ramp leading up into it. Foreign scents assailed my nostrils, the basic livestock and grain smells from the Foalshead keep were still present but overlaid with the scent of pine forests, wildflowers and some others I couldn't identify.

I looked to Rosa for an explanation and she smiled and giggled. "I must say your thoughts are the most amusing I have ever heard. Most people are profoundly affected by the beauty of the experience, or just plain frightened by what they don't understand. But your mind is instantly questioning, 'What is it? How was it made? What forces drive it?' You have not only the magic of an Enchanter, but also the mind of one...impressive!"

My mouth was still open. "But what is it?"

"It's a transportation portal, one of my very best creations!"

I was even more amazed now. "You made this?"

"Yes, I did. Took me years to get it right, but this is an excellent example of the things that you can and will do one day." Her eyes changed color to a white shade for a second before turning back to normal, and she shook her head admiringly. "And from the looks of things, you will be very powerful indeed."

"Uh, what was that?"

"What? Oh, the eye thing. Yes, that's mage sight, a very useful tool for an Enchanter and one of the first things I will teach you. It's also something that we can do and the others cannot. But for now, I would like to show you even more; your thoughts are very entertaining."

She grabbed my head and turned me to face another direction.

"Wow."

We were on a hill at the top of a vast sloping valley ending at the base of a snow-capped mountain. Forests of old-growth trees lined the sides and were tens of miles deep in places. The valley floor itself was covered with prairie grass and wildflowers. From here, I could see one road led from the platform where we perched to the single grandest city I could ever imagine sitting in the middle of the flatlands below us. At the center was an exquisite tower many times taller than the tower we just came through. Around it, in a wheel shape, were five slightly smaller towers with massive flags in different colors; red, green, blue, gray, and the last flag was red and gray. Amongst the towers, I could see many smaller buildings; there must have been hundreds of these buildings. Nearly all the smaller buildings had red tiled roofs giving the entire place a cheery, festive appearance. Two sets of stone walls surrounded the city. The outer wall was much shorter than the inner wall, but both were wide enough for six men to walk abreast across their tops.

"Impressive, isn't it? Welcome to Xarparion, Alex, I hope you will like it here."

I ripped my eyes away from the view and back to her. "You know, I think I will."

She took a deep breath and wrapped an arm around me. "Come on, it's a long walk home and I'm starving!"

We set off down the road; as close as the academy looked from this vantage point, we were still several miles from the main gate. Walking briskly, I dug out the apple dumplings that my mother had packed in my shoulder bag, so she must have already been on her second batch when I woke up this morning. As I shared the delicious treats with Rosa, she told me more about this place. Apparently, the tower at Foalshead is one of many that serve as supply lines for the real academy. Farmers sell their goods to the staff at the fake tower who then send it through the portals and back to Xarparion. In exchange, Xarparion offers the services of a wizard to any person of the kingdom who has the money. The money was used to fund the school and support the huge infrastructure that surrounded it, with quite a bit of coin left over, so much so that Rosa was able to compensate my parents a very large sum for taking me from them.

I thought about that for a while, then came up with another question. "Rosa, why are the portals built so far from the city? Wouldn't it make more sense to have them open inside the walls somewhere?"

My new mentor coughed in embarrassment. "Sadly, Alex, it's like this, not only are the other wizard towers contemptuous of Enchanters, but they harbor a fair amount of suspicion toward the non-human races, as well. When I built the first few portal systems, some members of the ruling council were convinced that the gateways could be used as an access point for hordes of invaders to pillage Xarparion. So they decreed that the portals had to open far from the city. That was over five hundred years ago; since then, I have apparently earned their trust enough that they have started allowing the newer portals to be constructed inside the city. So basically, anything after portal twelve is within the walls. But they have special security features."

So they don't even trust their own? I knew some wizards

could be jerks… This led to the obvious line of thought that questioned, what had I gotten myself into?

"Oh, it's not so bad," Rosa said, picking up my thoughts. "There will be some obstacles to overcome true, but overall, I think I can safely promise you the adventure of a lifetime here. We're going to have so much fun!"

"So can all Enchanters read minds?" I questioned, my mind still processing all the information she was giving me.

Rosa giggled. "Sorry, but no, that was something I acquired at a very early age, before I even knew I was an Enchanter. Besides, it's sometimes more of a curse than a blessing. You, unfortunately, hear lots of things that people think, without it being filtered by the tenets of polite society. People can be very cruel at times; also, it doesn't work on everyone."

We arrived surprisingly quickly at the main gate; after all, it was all downhill and on a very good road. On the walls, I could see men in armor alertly manning their stations. Their gear appeared to be of excellent construction and well taken care of. They didn't have their weapons trained on us, but they did seem to have a great interest in me.

"Primus Rosa, it's good to see you again." My head swung down to focus on the guard that I hadn't even noticed approaching. He was in the same armor as the others but had a different design painted on his shoulder. He snapped a quick salute to my companion and then glanced at me curiously, following my gaze up to the men on the wall. "Don't worry; they're here to protect you."

"I'm sorry, sir, but I wasn't thinking that. I worked as a blacksmith, until a few hours ago, that is."

The corporal smiled. "Ah, so you're looking at our gear? Fine stuff it is indeed; here take a look at this." He drew his sword, flipped it over in the air, and handed me the hilt. Perhaps it was all this talk of magic or nervousness about being uprooted and sent away from home, but as soon as I touched it, I felt a surge through my body and a hot spark of light left my hand and momentarily illuminated the sword. Both the guard and I jumped back in surprise as I nearly dropped the weapon on the ground.

"What the hell was that!" he growled, with a curious look at Rosa. I had no idea what to tell him. Rosa, on the other hand, smirked at our reactions and calmly walked over and took the blade.

She looked it over, turning it over in her palm. "Not bad, Alex. It seems we found your affinity and you're not technically even in the city yet."

"My what?"

She looked up from the blade, nodding happily. "Your affinity! It means you are naturally better with metals than any other materials; mine is stone."

The corporal, on the other hand, wasn't too happy. After all, it was the weapon to which he entrusted his life. He took off his helmet, clipped it to his belt, and ran his fingers through his hair nervously. "With all due respect, Primus, what the hell did he just do?"

Carefully, Rosa handed him back his blade. "He flash-enchanted your sword."

We both looked at her questioningly. "I did what?"

She clarified, her eyes changing to a light gray or white color for a second. "Flash enchanting sometimes happens when you don't yet have the skills to control your powers. You send out a pulse into the item you're touching and your thoughts are transferred to the item. You did the same thing to that pot. You were undoubtedly thinking about how bad a cook she was and feeling sorry for the orphans. This time, you probably were thinking of how you would sharpen it. A large part of magic is organizing your thoughts precisely to fashion a desired outcome. Thoughts are power, my young apprentice. The result is that this blade will never need to be sharpened again. Really, it is quite fortunate and unusual that you got this good a result on the first try. When I was still learning, I had to be very careful what I was thinking about when I worked and, frequently, I didn't get nearly as good an outcome."

The corporal was still confused. "So he is a real Enchanter? I thought you were the only..."

"Yes, my first apprentice!" she interrupted nervously, and her voice rose an entire octave. "And I'm already very proud of him! A warning, however, Corporal; be very careful with that sword, it's a lot sharper than it was."

The corporal examined the edge of the sword up close and then tentatively ran a thumb across it, jerking back quickly as his eyes grew very wide. He whistled softly and looked from me to Rosa and back again, then bowed formally to me. "Many thanks, Apprentice. I'm Corporal Higs and I am in your debt. Please allow me to escort you through the rest of the process."

True to his word, we were ushered through the two walls. The open area between the two walls looked like it was used primarily for livestock and the storing of hay and other open-air farm products. But there were stalls for food sellers and other merchants in this area, as well. Once past the second wall, the scene changed dramatically as we finally walked into the central core of Xarparion. Corporal Higs wished us a good evening and returned to his post.

Looking up at the towers, they seemed immense from this angle. Still staring at the towers, I asked, "Which one are we in?"

Rosa hesitated for a bit. "Um...I have my own hall, of sorts."

I shrugged "That's fine, lead the way."

She smiled and took my hand. "You're a sweet young man. Let's go, it's getting late. By the way, you don't happen to know the recipe for those apple dumplings, do you? They were magnificent!"

She led me past many buildings and around the large central core area. Most of the buildings were made out of cut stone and looked old enough for the limestone to be weathering in place and many had ornately cut windows and doorways. Most had pretentious signs of some sort or another that held no meaning for me, but conveyed how much of an outsider I really was. Between the buildings were either stone pathways or, in some instances, nearly field-sized areas of groomed grasses. Here and there were small areas that appeared to be used for reflection and meditation, primarily small garden spots with stone benches and fountains. Even at this time of the evening, there were students in all colors of robes circulating back and forth between buildings. I noticed with some envy that most of them seemed happy to be here. But then, they probably hadn't woken up in their own beds in their parents' home this morning, either, and were now struggling to figure out what the future might hold.

We walked on past the towers almost to the back wall area, until we reached a long whitewashed, two-story rectangular building. It looked like an ordinary building, nothing fancy, just a whitewashed wood building. It could have easily been a warehouse or a stable. The only thing that made it stand out at all was a sign above the door that said "Enchanters Hall" on it.

"This must be the place."

She stopped abruptly and sighed as if really looking at it for the first time in many years. "Yes, home sweet home. I know it doesn't look like much but it really is a nice place and it's a lot bigger than it appears. But come on inside, we have much to discuss."

She walked up to the wooden door and said something in a language I didn't understand. Immediately, small granite pins that I hadn't noticed before retracted down into the stone threshold releasing the white-painted front door. We breezed on through into the main hall; as she had promised, the inside was very nice. In fact, I hadn't seen a place so clean or fancy before. There were paintings of outdoor scenes on the walls, overstuffed chairs arranged around a fireplace and thick rugs on the hardwood floor. Tables and bookshelves lined the walls and there were lanterns placed around the room that didn't smell of burnt oil or waver with any lit flame I could see. All in all, I felt like I was in a comfortable old manor house.

"Welcome to my reading room." She pointed down the hall. "Down that way is the dining room and the kitchen. Upstairs are the living areas and in the basement is the lab where our classes will be, but for now please take a seat."

We both sat down in the chairs by the fireplace. Rosa stoked the embers and they burst back to life as the room was filled with warmth and crackle of the fire. She settled comfortably in her chair and looked at me expectantly.

"Now that we're here and comfortable, why don't you tell me about yourself, my dear sweet apprentice?" So I did and for some reason, I didn't hold anything back, well almost anything. I must have talked for hours, but she just sat there smiling the entire time, nodding every now and then. What surprised me most of all was that I actually could talk for hours! In retrospect, I guess, there may have been more to my life than I had realized. When I was finally done, I felt pretty tired and my throat was raw, but it was also like a load was taken off my mind and it was a very pleasant feeling.

Rosa leaned forward and smiled. "Thank you for sharing everything with me. Now, since you were very honest with me, I will be with you. This place is not called the reading room just because I like to read my many books here. It's also been enchanted so that people in the room feel more relaxed and will tell their true feelings and not hold anything back.

"Now I'll tell you a little about myself. My name is Primus Rosa. You may call me Primus, Master, or Rosa, whichever you chose. As you know, I'm an elf; technically, a green forest elf. I was born a little under seven hundred years ago. When I was still an infant, about the age you are now, my family's farm was torched and sacked by an Uri-pai war party. I was playing near the river when it happened, and my older sister placed me on a log and pushed me out into the current to save my life. I never did find out if any of my kin survived. Separated from my family, I drifted for what seemed like days, too terrified to move. Out of the blue, I heard a sweet woman's voice commanding me to get off the log, and I waded to the shore and walked a few hundred yards until I smelled food cooking. I was found by a little human girl who was playing in the forest, not far from where her parents camped. I can still remember her face and the song she would sing to me. The family took me in and raised me as one of their own until I was twenty-seven. As I was living in a human village when the wizards came, I took the same test you did this past evening. Like you, my orb turned white, but the elders of the time had never seen that happen and didn't know what it meant."

As she told her story, I found a teapot and tea leaves by the fireplace. Mother always told me that at times like this, it's always good to have something warm to go with your memories. She continued, "The masters put me through every one of the five towers' curriculum to see if I could do any of them. And in some ways they were right, Enchanters are not restricted by type as the others are, but finding that out was a long hard task. I could see the flow of magic, I could channel it in myself, but I could never get it to manifest like the others could. The teachers in the tower of fire thought that if they put me in a duel where my life was on the line then maybe it would work. It didn't work; time and time again they put me in that ring knowing I couldn't fight back and each time I woke up in the healers' tower some time later." She grimaced, remembering the pain.

The tea was ready so I got up again and poured two cups of tea for us. I brought them over to the table between us and handed her one of the cups and then returned to my seat. She sipped her tea and finally smiled again.

"Thank you, you're very kind. No one has made tea for me in over five hundred years." She took another long sip and continued her story.

"After many years of trying, I finally found out what I was good at." She smiled and chuckled to herself. "It's funny looking back on it now, but I didn't find my powers in battle or in the classroom. No, I found them at lunch! I still remember that I really didn't like what the school served for food and I remember wishing that my lunch would taste good. I was sitting at a table in the corner alone thinking of the home-cooked meals that I had with the family that saved me. And silly me, I was mixing the stew around with my finger.

Then, suddenly, I smelled something really good! I looked around for the source of the smell and realized that it was coming from my bowl. So I tried it and discovered it was the best tasting thing I've ever tasted. I even went up for seconds! I found out that any food placed in the bowl came out delicious. Soon, I was doing all sorts of things and my life had meaning once again. Many years later, they gave me this place to call my very own hall. And now I finally have someone to share everything with." She looked like she was about to cry. "For almost seven hundred years, I've been alone thinking I was the only one." She couldn't hold it in any longer. As the tears started to fall, I got up and walked around the table to sit with her. She cried on my shoulder for a few minutes, and then attempted to force herself to cheer up.

"So you're telling me we are the only two Enchanters to be born in seven hundred years? Who makes all the magic weapons that the great heroes carry and the bards sing about? What about the magic wands the wizards use?"

She put down her cup and tucked her feet under her. "I'll answer the last question first. Wands, staves, beads, etc. are just focus items, the power still comes from the wizard. The wand merely aids in casting a spell; certain items can be temporarily imbued with minor magic, but they are lesser works. Some races, like dwarves, gnomes and, to a lesser extent, elves are capable of creating relatively powerful magic items that work reliably, given the proper materials and exceptional skill of the crafter. These items utilize what Xarparion mages would call "wild magic" and are beyond the abilities of humans to duplicate. These make up the majority of the enchanted items in the world today. Most scholars do not believe the legendary weapons that heroes of past glory carried were created by mortal creatures at all, but were gifts of the gods, their agents or some other powerful benefactors." She grew very solemn.

"There is also another category, which I hesitate to even mention, but the enchantment on this room works on me too. Items of magic can also be formed by the practitioners of death magic, by enslaving demonic entities and sealing them into the item. Needless to say, these are very, very dangerous pieces and should be avoided at all costs."

"Well, where does that leave us then...humans, I mean?" I wondered.

"When humans and the human-minded races began to specialize in elemental magic - fire, water, wind, earth, they suddenly lost much of their ability to craft items. It's like the part of their brains capable of imbuing an item shut down. Some claimed that the gods never intended for mankind to keep that gift and simply withdrew the ability until it is needed again for some future calamity or age of heroes. Without regard to the reason, you and I are the only known human-style Enchanters in the world right now." She yawned and sagged tiredly in the chair. "We should probably get you to bed, we have a lot of work to do tomorrow."

I got up and helped her to her feet, feeling drained physically and mentally as well. We slowly made our way upstairs to the sleeping areas.

"Rosa, you are not what I was expecting from an elder mage."

She laughed. "Sorry, I'll try to act more like the old elf I am, but to be honest, I don't really know what that is. I have only met a few other elves in my life and they weren't that trusting of me. Besides, as you may know, wizards live a longer life and even at seven hundred, I haven't even hit the midpoint of my life. From the ancient records, Enchanters seem to live even longer than the other wizards, too."

"So you act young because you still are?"

She smiled. "Why, thank you! And yes, I have to act like this because if I didn't find a way to have fun, I would have gone crazy years ago."

"I guess I can understand that."

"Your room will be the one on the left. No one is in the other room and it's just storage at this point. My room is the big one at the end there. So unless you have any questions, I'm going to sleep."

"No questions. Goodnight."

"Goodnight, my apprentice."

I hit the bed and I think I was dead asleep before she closed the door.

Chapter 3

Alex

I woke up to the sun streaming in through my window. From what I could see from my bed, it was close to noon so I decided it was time to get up. Glancing around my room for the first time, I noticed it was not that big of a room but had everything I would need. I had a desk in the corner, two dressers, one with a basin of water and a towel. In the corner was a small closet already filled with white robes. Not wanting to be in my smelly smithy clothes anymore, I washed up, brushed my teeth, and changed into one of the robes. As soon as I had it on, it adjusted to fit me just right. From then on, I knew it was going to be a good day.

I exited my room and followed the hallway back downstairs to see if Rosa was up. But when I thought about her, I somehow knew she was still asleep; I even got a mental picture of her half hanging off her bed and still in a deep sleep. After a few minutes of exploring the main level, I found a small kitchen, complete with well-made pots and pans, a wood stove, dinnerware and a minimally stocked larder. From the looks of things, however, it didn't appear this kitchen got a lot of use.

I was starving, but thanks to my mother's tutoring, I knew what to do. After some digging, I found a dozen eggs, four extra thick strips of bacon and the ingredients needed to make griddlecakes. Once breakfast was cooking, I reasoned that Rosa would be hungry too. So I added two more eggs and the last two strips of bacon. Once everything was done, I loaded up two plates and set them on the table. After more searching, I found cups and a strange green juice that smelled wonderful. Still getting the feeling that Rosa was asleep, I grabbed a tray and loaded the food onto it. She was going to get breakfast whether she asked for it or not.

After carefully carrying the tray of food up the stairs and through her door, I found her right where my vision said she would be, halfway off the bed and snoring. It looked like she hadn't changed before falling asleep either. Rosa's room was slightly larger than mine, a bigger bed and some bookshelves dominated the room. She also had space for a small table with two painted wooden chairs in one corner.

"Master Rosa, it's time to get up," I said as I gently nudged her shoulder.

"…Fool…I have an apprentice now…and rabbits." She muttered, I had no idea what she was dreaming about and I'm not sure I wanted to know either.

"Master, please, you need to wake up." Her eyes fluttered open and she smiled at me, leveraging herself into an upright position.

"Hello, Alex, I'm so glad yesterday wasn't just a dream! And how are you this fine morning?"

"I'm doing very well, Master, but it's no longer morning."

"Is that food I smell? I see that it is!" If she wasn't awake before she was now. She sprang across the room, and was seated at the table in an instant.

"Did you make all this? I didn't know you knew how to cook." As I walked over, she had already removed everything from the tray and was ready to eat. By the time I was seated and started, she had almost half of her food eaten already.

"And it's good, too. Where did you learn to make these sweet flat cakes?"

"My mother taught me how to cook when I was a kid and still too small to help my dad work the forge."

"I see, and is this unusual for boys your age?"

"Of all my friends, I was the only one who knew how to cook. My mother always said that if I'm going to make a pot, I best know how to use it." She smiled slowly, paused as if thinking of someone else, and then went back to her food.

"Today is going to be a good day for us, but we have got a lot of work to do." She moved her empty plate to the center of the table and leaned back in her chair. "Lesson number one, make more food! As magic users cast spells, they use a large amount of their own energy. So to replace it, the body needs more food. I'd say by the end of the week you will be eating twice as much as you usually do. Now, before we start with the day's basic lessons, do you have any questions for me?" She was looking at me with one of those smirks that just scream, "I know something you don't know."

"Um, this morning when I woke up, I could sense that you were still asleep and I got a quick flash image of this room." I thought she was going to say I was crazy but instead she just smiled even more.

"And you feel relaxed around me, too, is that correct?" I was starting to get a little nervous now. But the more I thought about it, the more I realized she was right. Since our talk last night, I've felt no need to return home; in fact, I just want to stay here with her. That thought made me feel a little guilty, as if I was already turning my back on Foalshead and my parents, but something again told me that this was where I needed to be.

"Don't be afraid," Rosa continued encouragingly. "I was secretly hoping something like this would happen, but I didn't think it could happen this fast. You see, sometimes over time, a master and an apprentice will form a bond. Not from a spell, but just from their individual magics being so close to each other for so long. What happened is that last night our magic merged together and formed one of these bonds. You must have an enormous amount of magic for this to happen so quickly."

"Is it going to be dangerous?

"Oh, heavens, no! In fact, this will make life very easy for both of us. Not only will we always know where the other is, but as the bond gets stronger, we should be able to communicate through it. It should also let me show you how the magic is weaved in enchantments. No, I think we are going to be a great team!"

"Do other masters bond to one of their students?"

"None of the other teachers can. They all have at least five students each. In fact, most of the other teachers don't even have apprentices. But as there are only two of us, you automatically get an immediate promotion." This raised more questions for me to ask later, but for now I'll try to think basic.

"Now, come on, we have a lot to do today. You're like a toddler just learning to walk. You have spellcraft to learn, materials, incantations, and most of all, we need to teach you to eat!"

"Hey," I protested, "I've been eating just fine since I was a baby!"

Rosa laughed merrily. "No, I mean you need to learn to eat like a wizard! Like a pig! Like a dachshund loose in a sausage warehouse! A ravenous beast in starchy robes!" she giggled hysterically. "Seriously, as I explained earlier, it takes a lot of food to provide the energy to cast spells, and the more you cast, the more you need to eat. So you will train to increase your caloric intake and storage capacity. Beware the fat wizard!" She slapped me on the back and herded me out the door, still chuckling.

....

Far in the east, a dark tower settled uncomfortably on a rock promontory along a savage rock shore. Crumbling with age and ridden with decay, the smell alone inside the tower would have killed most heroic men, but these halls were filled with only the dead. One such creature dragged itself through the putrid antechambers until it entered what had been a throne room in a much earlier and more pleasant time in the long life of the fortress. He drew himself up and spoke reverently to a dark figure barely outlined by moonlight on the large chair in the center of the room.

"My master, our spies believe the prophesized one has finally appeared!"

"WHERE?" boomed a rough voice that dislodged dust from the empty torch sconces that still protruded from the walls throughout the room.

"Xarparion, my lord, which is also the current location of the girl!"

A loud grumbling sound filled the unlit stone halls. "Is that so? It seems they could not protect the children forever. Now is the time! Our caged canary in the coal mine has done her job and she is no longer useful. Send my best assassins, I want her dead without fail." The creature bowed and then ran off to fulfill its orders, leaving the room silent once more. After a long pause, the voice from the throne growled once more to no living ears, "The Child of Darkness and the Child of Light, at last. Let's see what they're made of."

Chapter 4

Alex

Two weeks have passed and I have gone through more books here than I had ever even seen at home; thankfully the history of Enchanters is not a long one. Master Rosa has taught me a lot about what separates us from the other wizards. To start with, the description the Headmaster gave me at the test was that only wizards have magic. After about ten minutes with Rosa, I found that to be utterly false. Everything and everyone has magic, it's one of the many building blocks of the world. What the orb test really does is find the ones who can channel magic.

From what I have learned so far, a wizard can collect magic from either themselves or the runoff magic from the area around them. They can then channel the collected magic through their bodies in what appears to mage sight to be magical veins or conduits. With this, they can bend the magic into almost any shape they want.

Enchanters, on the other hand, don't have the same system. We are unable to project magic like the others do. Instead, we shape the magic that's already in an object. When we do this, ordinary things can take on new qualities or even magical powers of their own. I seem to be naturally gifted with items made of metal, but with other materials, stone, wood, etc. I always seem to have more trouble.

Mind you, that does not mean that I haven't had my fair share of problems with metal. In fact, the first week was a nightmare for me as I was trying to learn how to control my magic. Rosa had me perform enchantment after enchantment to no avail, not even matching the one I did on the pot. I don't know how many practice rods I destroyed, but she was forced to order them by the hundreds. It wasn't until I learned how to use my mage sight that I could even start to get them right. Once I learned that, I could just watch her and do my best to copy what she was doing. Working with my mother, I learned to memorize from watching her tend to the injured. But even with what she called a "natural talent" for enchanting, I still have a very long way to go before I can hope to do what she can.

Rosa also took the time to teach me about the world, more precisely, about the kingdoms of the world. She had me sitting on a bench in front of a large map she pinned to the wall, using a long stick as a pointer.

The stick landed on a ring in the center of the map. "This is Xarparion. You will note that it does not show up on maps that are not made by us, so average people don't know where we really are. You might be surprised to learn that much of the world's human population consider Xarparion to be a fanciful myth." She pointed to a jagged area shaded in green a fair ways from Xarparion. "This is Anshea, your home kingdom. We have never really had problems with them so our relations are stable."

She pointed to another area shaded in orange. "This is Ocance; they don't really like our kind, so try to stay away from there. But even though they look down on us, we still have a trade agreement that is very profitable for both sides."

The next area was in blue and bridged the gap between the two others. "This is Elcance; they are a good people who are very fond of magic. In fact, that's where almost all wizards reside if not in the tower or on assignment. In reality, that's not more than a handful at any given time but still, most own land there."

Those three kingdoms only took up a third of the area around Xarparion, the rest was in black. She pointed to the black area. "This land has been lost. It used to be the great kingdoms of Normount and Wereia but is now controlled by goblins and the undead as the seat of power for The Lifebane. But even with their close proximity on this map, it would still take them months to march here."

She talked some more about the world's history, but I could tell that something else was on her mind. She must have heard that because she quickly wrapped things up to speak with me about it.

"Alex, we need to talk about something." Oh crap, what did I do? Did I track mud in or ruin something?

"No, it's nothing you did, but let's go sit upstairs and talk for a bit." I quickly settled into the same chair that I was in the first night I came to her door, and she did the same.

"I can't tell you how much I have enjoyed these last two week with you as my apprentice. You're like the son I've always wished for; however, I know it's not fair for me to keep you cooped up in my hall all your life. After listening to your thoughts as you worked, I have written a new lesson plan for you. Starting tomorrow, I'm giving you two more classes; well one is starting tomorrow and the other three days from now. Anyway, your mornings will be spent on my 'surprise' class until noon. You will also need to interact with your fellow students and apprentices; if you hang out with old elves too long, you'll start acting like one! To fix that, you will now go to lunch at Central every day that you have class. Even though I will miss your cooking very much, it's for the best. After lunch, you will go to your second class and be back for dinner. At this point, you're mine and we will continue your Enchanter training."

"If my first class is a secret, then what is my second?"

She smiled brightly, showing each and every one of her teeth. "I thought you would never ask! Your second class is weapons and armor smithing!" I thought I was going to die right then and there. She was not only going to let me learn about magic, but smithing as well. This was like a dream come true for me.

"I don't know what to say," was all I could think of. What do you say to someone who made one of your wildest dreams come true and did it out of love?

"You don't have to say anything. Remember, I can hear your thoughts. But don't get too excited, you still don't know what that other class of mine is."

"I don't care if it's advanced mathematics; I'll gladly do that and much more for you. It must not have been easy for you to get me into that class."

"Well, actually, it's not a class; I just know the master smith here rather well and called in one of the many favors he owes me. But do you really want to repay me for this?"

I nodded eagerly. "Yes, I'll do anything!"

She gave me an evil smirk. "Well, in that case, you can clean the lab today." All the enthusiasm I had was drained away in seconds. I should have said anything but that!

By mid afternoon, I had most of the lab cleaned up; that is until Rosa came in to check on me. The rest of the evening was spent with her running all over the room rediscovering all the things she presumed lost, but that had been, in fact, buried under a large pile of clutter. And I would have to put it all back, again. We finally finished our little dance of cleaning and re-cleaning just before midnight.

"I can't remember the last time the lab was this clean!"

"Probably six hundred ninety-nine years ago," I grumbled under my breath, but even at that low a volume, I forgot the mind reading. She spun around and punched me in the shoulder. "Hey, now that hurt!" I complained. "Remember I don't have a magical boost to strength yet!"

"Yeah, well, you deserved that one," she said self-righteously. "And I have cleaned the lab before."

"Really? When? And don't count the times where you tricked someone else into doing it for you."

"Um...well, there's that time the cockatrice eggs hatched early and I had to hose it all down to clean up all the...Crap! Fine, you win! I don't clean, ok? I just don't."

"Then who cleans the main floors?"

"Oh, I have housekeepers for that."

"And how many times did you try to get them to clean the lab, too?"

"I've lost count. They always give me some lame excuse about something blowing up and being too dangerous for humans. I think they were just trying to get out of it; you're human and you're still alive after cleaning the place."

"Ahuh, I'm going to bed." Goodnight, crazy lady.

"I heard that!"

The next day, after my usual routine of cooking and tidying up for the seven-hundred-year-old elf who can't cook or clean, we headed out the door for the first day of class. Rosa insisted that she come along to the first class to verify that everything was alright. Somehow, I didn't think that was the case; she was acting like a mother who was about to send her child out on his own for the first time.

I could smell the forge before we could see it. It was located out between the first and second wall, much closer to the first, because the wizards complained about the smell and the noise. Personally, I liked it; it reminded me of home. The building wasn't so much a building as it was a giant stone cone with the largest forge I've ever heard about. There looked to be ten complete stations all surrounding one grand kiln. Smoke from the wood burning to charcoal was roaring out the top, and I could see the heat distortions making everything below the cone look wavy. Currently, only one of these stations was in use by a dwarf in full swing. The sound made a dull comforting din of activity, so different than the quiet reflection time in Rosa's library, and I found it all very exciting.

"Darroth, it's good to see you again!" Rosa shouted. The dwarf put down his hammer and removed his gloves. He was stouter than most of the dwarves I had seen in Xarparion, with his reddish beard plaited into stubby braids to keep it out of the coals. A worn leather jerkin and copper armbands completed his outfit.

"Rosa, it's good to see you, too. So what can I do for you today?"

"You know that agreement we made last week? Well, today's the day."

"Already? Then this is him?" She nodded and Darroth walked up to me and gave me a onceover, paying particular attention to the size of my biceps and the calluses on my hands. "Rosa tells me that you were a blacksmith before you came here, correct?"

"Yes sir, I worked with my father."

"Cut the 'sir' crap, I don't believe in that stuff. Well, let's get you doing some good honest work and see what you know. From now on, anything you learned about how to treat the metal is to be forgotten. Steel is much different from the farm grade iron you worked with. Understand? Good." I followed him inside to the workstations, and he handed me a wrought iron bar. "Now, I know you have never done this before, but I need to get a sense of where your skills are. Today, your job is to turn that raw iron into the semblance of the blade of a long sword. I don't care about the hilt or guard at this point, just the blade. I know whatever you end up with won't hold an edge worth a damn or be pretty, but I'm not having you muck up a bar of good steel for an entrance exam. Get to work." Turning his attention back to Rosa, "I'll send him back to you when he is done with my test."

"If it's all the same to you, I think I'll stay and watch."

With that, I set to work at one of the open stations, quickly setting things up the way I liked them. I rammed the iron bar into the hottest part of the coals and was soon ready to work. After cutting the basic pattern and an hour of hammering and reheating, I started to notice changes in the bar and myself. I had a general knowledge of how to build a blade; after all, a harvesting scythe has a blade of sorts. Methodically, I concentrated on creating the bevel and that work formed a rhythm to which I was completely lost. Time meant nothing to me. I didn't even feel the heat, flatten, fold, sand, repeat, and finally quench in the barrel of oil behind the kiln. My mind noted indifferently that the blue glow that I had last seen on the magic pot at home had found its way into the metalwork, but still I continued to plow effort into the blade. Suddenly, as if a candle were snuffed out, I came out of my daze, a bit unsteady, but curious. I looked down at what a few hours ago was just a long strip of iron and was now a finished blade, hilt, and guard, too. I stood there dumbfounded, how was this even possible? My brain and limited experience knew that there are many steps that need to be done to a sword before it is complete. It needed to be cooled slowly for hours, and then hardened and tempered so it won't crack, then sharpened. But here it was, a sword in my hands, a nearly finished product, in less than a day. And I did it all with just a hammer and some sanding blocks? Something was very much wrong with the world as I knew it!

"Well, that's something I wasn't expecting." I jumped at the sound of a deep voice right behind me. Turning around, I spotted the dwarf stroking his braided beard with a very puzzled expression. "Now I was told that you've never made a sword before, but somehow, you made one in a few hours when it should take days. Care to explain this?" My mouth dropped open and I'm sure I did a reasonably precise imitation of a carp out of water. I didn't know what to tell him, do I say that I fell into some sort of trance and just did it?

"I'll take that question, Darroth." Primus Rosa got up from her chair in the corner and walked over to us. "You see, it's rather simple, he's my apprentice. And I couldn't be more proud of him."

"Hold on just a darn minute here! Are you telling me that the boy you wanted me to train is your apprentice? And when were you going to tell me that he was an Enchanter?" He huffed a little, then picked up the blade I made and looked it over. "This is excellent work you did here, even more so seeing that it's just iron. Of course, it will probably bend like a green twig the first time it strikes something unless you somehow found a way to magically normalize and temper it in an afternoon. But hey, I told you to fashion a sword and you more than passed. This could get interesting if we gave you some steel to play with and taught you some real bladesmithing techniques."

"Thank you, Master Darroth, and I'm sorry, but for some reason, I am suddenly very tired." I tried to brace myself on the anvil, but there was no point, my body felt like every ounce of energy had been leeched out of it. I vaguely remember the sky spinning lazily as I slumped to the dirt. Too tired to even open my eyes, I could still hear.

"Is he going to be ok?" Darroth said as he lifted me off the ground.

"He will be just fine. He just hasn't used that much energy before. Did you notice that he wasn't even reheating the last half of the forging?" The dwarf grunted in affirmation and carefully handed me over to Rosa; she had no trouble with the weight.

"After all these years, Rosa, you finally found another Enchanter. You must be happy."

She smiled warmly as she looked down at my head on her shoulder. "Yes, deliriously so! Teach him well, Darroth, I have a feeling his future is going to be amazing." She started the walk home with my body limp in her arms and a bright smile on her face.

Chapter 5

Maya

"Greetings Forge Master Darroth!" I grinned and bowed as I unceremoniously dumped a pile of bent and damaged practice swords on a table under a small overhang next to his monstrous cone-shaped forge. "It's a lovely morning, don't you think? I think so, the bees are buzzing, the birds singing!"

"Humph," the dwarf grunted, roused to wakefulness. He lifted bleary eyes up to meet mine. "What's gotten into you? You're usually grouchier than me in the mornings...you sound as bad as Rosa!" He was sitting at, or rather leaning heavily on, a large worktable that I had seen him use to pattern out projects in the past. But instead of pieces of armor or parts of a weapon, there was a single shining long sword resting atop a portable anvil in the center of the workspace. There were several broken steel hammers on the ground below him, as well as a disconcerting number of empty ale jugs. Shaking my head, I walked briskly over to the food stand across the street that catered to tradesmen in the non-student sector. I purchased a large mug of double strength Serro tea and a sausage roll, and brought it back, setting it just under the sleepy dwarf's red bulb-shaped nose to wake him up again.

"Darroth! Tea! Drink!" I barked and helped him wrap his stubby digits around the mug and lift it up to his bearded face. I'm pretty sure most of the first gulp just soaked into his scrubby, braided beard and would eventually drip on his shirt. And probably make the shirt smell immensely cleaner than it did at the moment. "How late did you stay up last night? By the way, that's a nice looking blade you're working on."

He growled and took a few more gulps of the beverage

before speaking. "Aye, it's a beautiful piece of work, but it's nothing I'm working on. In fact, I spent most of last night trying to figure out how to destroy it!"

"You lost me, why would you want to destroy it? If you hate it that bad, give it to me, and I will have the recruits turn it to scrap like they did those," I said, motioning to the swords on the side table.

"Ha! A couple of them would probably lose arms or heads if you gave them that sword to practice with. It's sharp enough to cut shavings from a block of standard steel without dulling, and I broke three of my best hammers trying to snap it in half last night. And guess what the best part is; it's not even steel, it's just ordinary wrought iron... or at least it was!"

I pulled up a wooden stool and sat down across from him, pushing the food toward him and taking a closer look at the sword. "May I?" He waved an affirmative and bit into the roll. I looked around, adjusting my dark-hooded robe so that I could see better, but still would have my face hidden from people passing by. Picking up the sword, I examined it, checking out all the essential points exactly as my father had taught me years before. "Well, it seems to be well made, it has decent but not fantastic balance. Still, probably worth more than a couple years of my pay just for the sharpness enchantment alone. Where did you find it?" I said, carefully setting it back in place.

"Maya, I know you're going to think it's the drink talking, but that new apprentice of Rosa's made it from scratch in an afternoon! Right here at this forge, and the last couple hours he wasn't even heating up the metal. I've never seen the like, I might as well pack it in and grow turnips for a living!"

"Ah yes, the new wonder apprentice who's been keeping her

so busy she hasn't even been coming to the dining hall to eat. Imagine Rosa not eating!" We both chuckled at the thought. "Well, I will get to meet him soon. She threw in a bunch of favors to entice me to give him private weapons training, but I can assure you, I won't be as easy to impress as you are."

Darroth finished eating, jiggling his beard to shake out the crumbs. "I appreciate the breakfast, Maya, and I'll get right on those practice swords for you. Say, you might want to give this boy, Alex, a chance. I think there's something special about him. Must be, only the second Enchanter to come along in how many centuries? Hey, weren't you going out with the lads on perimeter patrol today? I thought they were going to check out your favorite view up by portal seven."

I got up to leave and went around the table to give the smith a goodbye hug. "Not this time. For some reason, I feel like I need to stay close to Xarparion for a while...and I have a ton of paperwork to get through."

....

Alex

The next day, or more precisely, when I woke up, I found that when I overdid it at the forge, I slept for an entire day plus a few hours. Muzzy-headed and sore, not to mention enormously thirsty, I was motivated to hit the bathhouse, drink a couple ladles of lukewarm water and pull on one of my fresh white robes. I tried not to think about how I got out of the old one. A much more urgent thought, however, was hammering in my mind - food! Not finding Rosa anywhere, I reached through our bond and generally sensed that she was near the main gate. Suddenly there was a familiar voice in my mind.

"I'm sorry I wasn't there like I should have been when you woke up. I am also sorry if this causes you any pain; this is the first time I've tried sending my thoughts to you. But for now, go to the dining hall and eat! I can feel your hunger from here, and I'll see you this evening after your class."

I didn't care in what form that request came, I was more than happy to comply. And if I left now, I could get there before the midday rush. I quickly put on my boots and ran out the door.

The dining hall was not what I expected. From the outside, it looked like another boring hall tucked into the large tower that was Central. Wizards, as I found out, at least non-Enchanters, like to gather in groups and announce to all who will listen how wondrous they are and how amazing their feats are. I thought there would be at most fifty tables and some sort of line for food. Instead, there were at least a hundred tables, each set for five to eight people depending on the shape. Nearly every table was set up family style with mountains of food. From the looks of things, they didn't even have the same things on them. Some had sliced cold meats and breads, some had pots of hot porridge, cheeses, pastries...pretty much anything you were hungry for was someplace in the room. I slowed up as I rubber-necked through the entry area, hoping no one could see me salivating as I decided which table to attack first.

There were also more people here than I was expecting. About half the tables were occupied by at least one person. I started for one of the vacant round tables loaded with eggs and breakfast ingredients, when I heard my name. Looking around, I spotted a green-robed figure with huge brown curls. Julia, the girl from the orphanage in Foalshead, was jumping up and down from behind a pile of sweet rolls to get my attention. She dashed my way and gave me an enthusiastic squealing hug.

"Alex, come sit with me! You gotta, I haven't seen you in forever!" Hurriedly grabbing food off multiple tables and shoving the lot on my plate, I allowed myself to be dragged back to her table.

"Julia, you look great, school really seems to be agreeing with you." And it had, she looked like she had gained weight and height, and the listless look that seemed to characterize all Miss Stal's wards was gone, replaced by a vibrant young woman. I had a little bit of a homesick twinge when I thought about how happy my mother would be to see Julia thriving.

"Where have you been?" she asked. "I've been trying to find you for weeks now but you're never here!" As soon as I sat down, I tore into an enormous plate of small breads with ham and cheese fillings.

"Working and learning a lot," I said in between frantic bites, all the while trying not to look like too much of a pig. "Sorry, I moved in with Primus Rosa and she has her own kitchen so I've been eating with her." Then I dived back into my food.

"Wow, she must not feed you very often!" She shook her head ruefully. "So what's it like to have a master? I have a teacher, but I'm told it's not the same. I have also heard stories about your primus being mean, evil, and crazy." Hearing that last part made me almost choke on the pastry I was wolfing down.

"What? Where did you hear that stuff?"

"Mostly the hot air apprentices. They like to show how mysterious and in-the-know they are...you mean it's not true?"

"No! Primus Rosa is the nicest person I know, and she really cares about me. In many ways, she is more protective of me than my mom. True, sometimes I think she's crazy, but never a bad crazy; and evil, never!" She frowned, but seemed satisfied and went back to her own food.

Changing the awkward subject, I asked, "So how are your studies going? Do you like it in your tower?

Julia's face lit up, literally radiating happiness. "It's hard, but nothing like the orphanage! For once in my life, I don't feel like a castoff and I'm actually good at something. My teachers think I will make a great questing druid someday.

"What's a questing druid?"

She giggled. "Sorry, I forgot for a moment that you weren't an Earthie. Have you ever seen a kangaroo or heard of mangos grown near our village? Of course not, someone had to venture out into the world and discover all these wondrous things and bring the knowledge back. Sometimes, if the plants are similar, a druid can even convince a plant that grows locally to repurpose its production to a fruit or vegetable that normally only grows far away. It really helps in food production."

"You mean like growing figs on an apple tree?"

She smiled a brief, condescending grin and patted my hand. "Yeah, something like that, but not exactly."

"I just assumed that there were portals to all those places and it worked like food and animals coming from Foalshead."

Julia's pretty face clouded. "Yeah, well, it used to work that way, but more than half of the portals open up into dead lands now, so they have been closed permanently. At least from the other side anyway. It would be so much fun to see other places and animals."

After a few minutes of quiet eating, I looked around and

asked, "So why did you pick this table?"

She smiled again. "Because this is the table with the most sweets, silly!" She held up a large platter with all kinds of goodies on it, most of which I didn't recognize, but they looked magnificent. "And the best part is you can eat all you want. I love this place! I am starting to make good friends now and no one picks on me; well, no one from the Green tower, at least." Her mood shifted at the last part; now she seemed scared for some reason.

"You said no one in your tower picks on you. Are there others who do?" She nodded and I could feel anger rise in my chest. "Who?" She motioned behind me at four red-robed fire wizard students who were headed straight for us. They halfway surrounded our table before one of them pointed at Julia.

"Hey runt! What are you doing way over here? Trying to hide from your weekly beating behind some buns?" The leader, who was also the jerk talking, was skinny but a little taller than me with dirty, curly red hair and a baby face but hard contemptuous eyes. The others just looked like run-of-the-mill schoolyard bully-wannabes. Julia was already shaking with fear, and to make things worse, this jerk was calling a fireball to his hand. My anger had reached its limit; I put myself between him and Julia, getting right in his face.

"Who the hell are you? Did the laundry peasants screw up and bleach your robe?" He snickered, "Don't tell me you're friends with this farmyard runt? I'd stop trying to play the hero unless you want to get hurt."

"Leave her alone," I snarled. I had little use for bullies in Foalshead and here was no different. I did note that he had begun gathering magic as a bit of flame started to form in his palm.

"Or what?" Instead of answering, I used a trick Rosa taught

me a few nights ago. I reached my left hand out and grabbed the fireball he still had in his hand. Instead of letting it burn me, I transferred all the magic through my body and used it to power a heat enchantment that I put on the fork still in my right hand. I didn't break eye contact the entire time. Once the enchantment was complete, I could feel that the fork couldn't take the heat and was now running through my fingers onto the floor. I would have been fine, but the molten metal dripped on my boot and I felt the sizzle as it bit into my foot. I couldn't hop around like an idiot and maintain any sense of decorum in this situation, so I settled for narrowing my eyes in what I hoped was a menacing squint and glaring at the wizard. Thankfully, the pain subsided quickly, but I would have a burn to treat later.

"Who the hell are you? And why aren't you wearing the robes of your tower? What kind of newbie are you?" Absorbing his fireball seemed to make him mad; I'd remember that for later. I had a feeling we were destined to be at odds.

"These are the robes of my craft, I am an Enchanter."

All four looked surprised, immediately breaking out into laughter and not the feel-good kind of laughter either.

"Idiot! You're only a stupid Enchanter and you think you can take me on? Me, Naton Rad, a fire wizard! I could kill you with a single spell."

"Doesn't matter who or what you are. You have no right to threaten anyone, let alone a fellow student."

"We'll see how noble you are when you're a pile of ashes. An Enchanter, what a joke," Naton spat as he readied two more fireballs, his cheer squad stepping back to give him room. "Any last words before you die?"

"That's enough, Naton! You've had your fun, now leave before you really get hurt!" The voice came from a shorter, genial looking student a little older than I was who had approached silently from the rear of the hall. He had a strong earthy presence and I could tell he was a good guy just by looking at him. He was a leader and behind him were five other earth wizards and they all looked ready to fight.

"Stay out of this Hons; this is not your fight!"

"You made it my fight when you threatened Julia with your fire magic. And from what I hear, this Enchanter stepped up and protected her. So from the way I see it, you mess with him, you mess with us." Hons and the other earth wizards readied their own spells, lifting large chunks of stone from the floor.

Naton growled, "Damn, that fireball was only powerful enough to give her sunburn, or maybe burn some of that curly rat's nest she calls hair!"

"Your last tantrum like this ended with a wind wizard at the healers for over a week, now leave!"

"Fine, I'll go, but don't think that we're done yet, Enchanter! You better watch your back!" He stormed off with his buddies to the other side of the dining hall, well away from us. Hons sighed and then offered his hand. "My name's Hons."

"Alex."

"Good to meet you, Alex. And thank you for helping Julia for us. That jerk will bully anyone smaller than himself." I looked over at Julia. One of the other Earth Tower girls was hugging her while she was sniffling on her shoulder. Hon's sighed, "That's Lin, she and Julia have gotten close, being the two newest to the tower and all. Lin tells me she cries a lot in her sleep. I take it you knew her before she came to the school, do you know why?"

I felt all my accumulated anger at Naton drain off and I looked down at my feet, not entirely sure if it was my story to tell. "Hons, she had a really hard time before she got here. Her parents were killed when she was little and she had no one so she ended up in an orphanage, a pretty bad one at that. This place is the first good thing that has happened to her. She may be afraid that this is all a dream and she's going to wake up and be back there."

"I wish she would have told us that, but now, maybe we can help her heal. Has she said that she's working to become a druid?"

"Yes, she's so excited to have finally found friends and a niche in life."

He nodded warmly. "We'll do everything in our power to help her along; druids are especially precious to our discipline. We sometimes go years at a stretch without having even one qualify. This year we are fortunate to have two, Lin and Julia." He looked around as if gauging the time from the level of activity in the dining hall. "Alex, it was good to meet you. I think you are one of the good guys. But you better get a move on if you're going to make it to class on time. And don't worry about Julia. I'll make sure she at least has Lin with her here at all times. And try not to fret about Naton, if any of the earth wizards see him messing with you, we'll back you up." All the others murmured their approval; Lin was by far the most supportive.

"Thank you. It was great to meet you all, but I gotta go; Darroth will have my head if I'm late."

Running all the way to the forge, I found Darroth already at work and in rather high spirits, the beats of his hammer sounding like massive drums on the anvil.

"Glad to see you're still alive, boy! I thought you would never wake up." After a hard slap on the back, he led me over to the anvil he was working on at the last session. "See that, boy? Look what happened to my anvil!"

I was shocked; there was a split in the face of the anvil that ran all the way through. If it wasn't bolted to a plate in the ground, it would probably be flopped apart into two pieces.

"What did you do to cause this?" I asked, eyeing it warily.

"Me? No, this was your doing; well, that cockeyed sword's doing, really."

"Really? My blade did this? How? It was only iron, not even steel!" He laughed and took a long pull from the wineskin at his hip. He pulled out his pipe and stuck it in the corner of his mouth. I knew from watching him visit with Rosa that he was about to launch into a story.

"Well, you see, I had to test your work, you know, but none of my hammers would even dent the dang thing. And believe me, I tried! Broke three of my best hammer shafts, too! Anyway, I got a little bit irritated in doing so. I might have imbibed a bit too much ale and well...I sort of slammed it on the anvil and, well, just look! Rosa told me that all you really did was a simple spell of hardening, but when you kept folding the iron over and over again, it somehow folded the enchantment. You made a blade that only your own creations could destroy! Ha!"

At first I was surprised, but that was soon washed away by a flood of new ideas. If the folding of the metal strengthened the spell, would it work on other enchantments? Could I apply multiple enchantments with this method? And maybe even double the effect...my daydream was interrupted by Darroth tossing a chunk of steel at my head.

"Now we have work to do! Today, I'm going to work steel and you're going to assist me, but no magic stuff. I don't need to lose more tools. You just watch and learn."

The rest of the afternoon went by fast and the two of us got along great. Apparently, Darroth liked having a trained assistant, and from the stories he had to tell, he had been a forge master for a very long time and had traveled halfway around the world. But all too soon, it was time for the evening meal and lessons, and tonight was my night to cook. After getting a large pot of stew going, I was setting the table when Rosa breezed through the door.

"Hello apprentice! I think I smell some of your excellent cooking!" She walked into the dining area and stretched her arms above her head before taking her seat. "It's been a long day and my legs and shoulders are killing me."

"Well, dinner will be a short while yet, so just relax for a bit." She was still trying to get the kinks out of her neck.

"I wish I could. You don't know any home remedies that help with soreness, do you?"

"Just one." I grabbed one of my books and paged through it. After a little searching, I found what I was looking for. I quickly tossed together one of the potions that I had mixed with my mother many times. After a few minutes, I handed Rosa a glass of the green liquid.

She sniffed it. "What's this?"

"As you could probably guess, as a blacksmith, we have our

days where we are extremely sore after a big order. So my mother and the healers she worked with invented this for sore muscles and strains. It doesn't taste too good, but it works, and works fast."

She shrugged and took a sip, cringing slightly. "What's in it?"

I smiled. "If I told you, you wouldn't drink it, and I recommend you don't read my mind to find out."

She held her nose and downed it in one gulp. "Ok, that's really gross."

"Yeah, it is. But you'll feel like a new elf in a few minutes, and you'll sleep better, too. But for now, the stew is ready. I made an extra large pot since I could feel your hunger all afternoon."

"Thank you, thank you! You have no idea how hungry I am. You should have seen me an hour ago when I sensed you were planning to make your stew; the woman almost killed me, the she-devil!"

"Who were you with all day?"

"You'll meet her tomorrow," Rosa said airily, with a wink. "And I really think you'll like her."

Knowing that she wouldn't give me more than that, I went back to stirring my stew. Several quiet minutes passed, too quietly. I could sense a storm cloud of discussion speeding toward me. Rosa leaned back in her chair and absently picked up a piece of carrot root off the counter and popped it into her mouth.

"So do you want to talk about what happened this afternoon?" Oh-oh.

"You were listening in on that, huh?"

"Yes, and I think you did very well. Transferring that fireball was quick thinking. I'm also proud that you stood up to him. But what I really wanted to talk about was what happened before and after your chat with that fire boy."

"Before? You mean my talk with Julia?"

"Yes, your little friend from Foalshead." She poured us some table wine and passed a glass over to me. "You said some very nice things about me that are already circulating around Xarparion. But what really hit me was how much you truly meant what you said." Rosa's voice caught as she paused and looked away briefly, but I could tell a few tears were streaming down her face. I couldn't imagine what it would be like to be almost entirely alone for hundreds of years. Finally, she wiped her eyes and cleared her throat, turning back to me with a tentative smile. "Anyway, only you and that she-demon really care for me, and she doesn't always have the nicest way of showing it. But she's going to be in for a surprise soon enough," Rosa chuckled as if savoring an especially delicious conspiracy. "And that other thing, your talk with the earth wizards...I think you opened a new door for us. Earlier today, one of their teachers stopped by to explain what happened and to ask if I would help to upgrade their tower and equipment. This could be the start of a more significant role for us. If only I would have known how much having an apprentice would change my life! Now let's eat and get this cleaned up, we still have lessons tonight."

Chapter 6

"Where in the world are we going?" I said, nearly tripping over a stray cat in the dark as Rosa hustled me along.

"You'll see."

"Getting me up way before the sun is even thinking about rising and that's all you're going to give me?"

"Hey, I don't want to be up either, but I was told to have you there at sunrise and not a second later." Rosa was now almost dragging me, making full use of her longer legs as we raced to her mystery location.

Toward what would be called the rearmost section of the round academy, between the inner and outer walls, was an arrangement of small worn buildings not much bigger than sheds. The largest one looked to be a worn-down stable, and in the center of the building was a series of circles on the ground made of colored sand, getting smaller in size as they progressed. The area was dimly lit by lanterns in the four corners. As we approached, I could see five people in the largest ring, four large men and one woman, all in full armor and weapons.

From the looks of things, the men were set up and dueling as a squad against the woman. The group exchanged formal dueling bows and drew weapons. Suddenly the action started, and I briefly remember thinking this wasn't at all fair, four against one. But then she moved! She swiveled, ducked low and advanced spinning in one fluid motion, the flat of her sword blade slapping the first two fighters' helmets so quickly that it sounded like one loud hit. Whoever she was, she fought with such an inhuman grace that it looked more like a dance than a duel. It was like she knew where every blade edge would strike and effortlessly avoided them all. One of the men aimed a wicked, two-handed slash at her head while his partner dived low to hack at her legs. She leaped above the low cut like she was playing jump rope, glided sideways to avoid the overhand, and landed for the briefest of instants before bouncing head-over-heels and landing behind the surprised duo. Two sharp raps on the seam between their helmets and hauberks and they signaled surrender. In the span of a dozen heartbeats, all four opponents were on their butts in the sand, thoroughly defeated. I was instantly captivated. Rosa smirked and reached out with a long finger and pushed my jaw closed.

"Ok, there's the she-devil. Now, if you want to live through the day, be polite and try not to stare too much."

"I heard that, Rosa." The woman's voice was very pleasant and smooth, she wasn't even winded. Somewhere in the deepest recesses of my mind, I found the fortitude to dispel Rosa's nickname of she-devil, and I vowed to start out with a clean slate. She was striding over to us. I looked over at her opponents and saw they were all getting up slowly. None of them appeared angry or put out, more like schoolboys who had gotten the switch and were now happy the punishment was over. As she approached, I got a good look at her and the armor she wore. She moved with the silent grace of a jungle cat, if a jungle cat was encased in full steel.

As I couldn't see anything but her eyes, which were a startling shade of green, by the way, I concentrated on her armor. It was very well made - breastplate over chainmail - and looked like it had seen some heavy use. Despite the distractions, the metal-working Enchanter part of my brain was confident that I could make some needed improvements if she let me.

She must have noticed me staring because she changed her

stance in an attempt to only show her profile.

The deep green eyes flashed with irritation. "What is with you men? You're always drooling over a woman's body!" That caught me by surprise; in fact, I looked between her and Rosa, hopelessly bewildered.

After Rosa recovered from almost laughing herself to death, she finally helped me out. "I'm sorry, but he wasn't thinking anything like that. He was looking over your armor and wondering if you would ever let him fix it for you."

"Hmmm...anyone but you, Rosa, vouching for that line and he would have been missing parts. And what's with you, anyway. Last night you looked your age and were about to die from all the cleanup we did, and now you have a spring in your step that you didn't have even before we started."

"Oh yes, you see, last night I found another wonderful skill my apprentice has that you simply must try!"

"Really?" she said dramatically, and it sounded like she was really struggling to choke back a suggestive comment! "Well, for now, I'm more interested in his skills, if any, in the realm of combat." She turned to face me.

"All right, newbie! I have all morning to whip you into shape; combat training class shall now begin!"

Combat training? Master Rosa really did listen to me that night.

"Ok, where do I start? Swords? Armor?"

I couldn't tell with the helm covering her face, but I was pretty sure that she was smiling under it. And I think I even heard a snicker of evil intent!

"See that shed? Inside you will find an eighty-pound training pack. Go put it on and give me ten laps."

I did as I was told. After grabbing the pack, I quickly belted it on - this thing was heavy! I started to run but even after only one lap, I had rivers of sweat flowing off of me. By half way through, my legs were on fire and my chest was about to explode, but even with the pain, I didn't want to disappoint Rosa or the woman in armor. With new-found determination, I blocked everything else from my mind and pushed on. After the tenth lap, I collapsed in a heap at her feet still wearing the backpack.

"Not bad for a first run," she purred and handed me a ladle of cool water from a wooden bucket. "That pack you're carrying represents one half the weight of the full plate that Rosa wants me to train you in, and ten laps around my track is only a mile. So before we go anywhere with teaching you to use a sword, you're going to run five miles with that pack and then move up to the full-weight pack. Now get up and do it again!"

I take back what I said earlier, she is a she-devil!

During the next few weeks, I fell into a sort of pattern. Mornings were spent with my masked teacher, she insisted that I didn't yet deserve her name or to see her face. Then lunch with Julia and her friend, Lin, followed by work at the forge with Darroth. Thanks to hard work, he was now letting me work steel unsupervised for my own projects. In the evening was dinner with my master and more enchanting lessons. Tiring as hell, yes, but I kind of liked it. It felt good to have something to look forward to every day.

The lady in armor intrigued me. After the first day, I couldn't bring myself to think of her as the she-devil like Rosa. She never showed her face or any part of her body to anyone; when she wasn't in full armor, she wore a full-length robe with a deep hood. The one time she caught me trying to catch a glimpse of her face earned me twenty extra laps. After that, I regretfully decided that her privacy was her own and I had no business prying. Although it didn't stop my active imagination from trying out scenarios. One of my favorites, she was actually a runaway southern princess, hiding out from her father so that he doesn't haul her back to his kingdom and force her to marry a wealthy old baron. Or a witch cast a spell on her that prevents her from ever showing her face except to her one true love. Ok, hokey, I'll be the first to admit, but I read a lot of adventure stories growing up.

Eventually, even as hard as she worked me, and without the aid of facial cues to go by, I got to know her quite a bit better. She had a sharp, surprising sense of humor, and she tried her best to keep my mind off things (like the pain) with it. I also learned that she was honorable and had a fair sense of justice...very quick to correct me if I was doing something wrong, but at the same time just as quick to compliment if I was doing it right. She was very smart and apparently one of Rosa's only friends, although my master would always clam up whenever I would (ever so innocently) inquire about how they came to meet or where she was from. I soon found my daily goal was just to hear her laugh. Of course, when you are stumbling around a dirt running track with 160 pounds of weight on you, the inevitable trip and calamitous face plant into the dirt will occasionally take place. Let's just say I heard her laugh frequently.

At the end of training today, she motioned me over. "Good work, Alex! You can finally run five miles with a full pack and not be useless when you get there. Tomorrow, we start the real training. Oh, before I let you leave for lunch, Rosa left this note for you."

I opened the folded page and all it said was to expect an extra hungry mouth for dinner tonight.

"This is odd, why didn't she just tell me?"

She shrugged. "I don't know, she stopped by to ask for my help when you were still running. I guess she didn't want to distract you. So what does it say?"

"It just says that there will be another hungry mouth at dinner."

"That's odd, she never has company over. In fact, I didn't even know your Enchanters Hall had a kitchen, we always just go to the dining hall."

"Must be someone important then. Well, I think I know what she's getting at so I better get going. My thanks for today's lesson." I bowed out formally and took my leave.

I ran to the dining hall kitchen to ask for some things I would need for dinner that wasn't stocked at the hall. The cook staff there was very kind and even offered me a fresh voskk roast to make for the meal. With my bags of food and now a fresh roast wrapped in leaves and tucked in a bag, I returned home to get everything ready to go into the oven. I also put the roast into an enchanted clay pot that my master created. It was meant to cook food slowly without spikes in temperature that you can get with fire and without risk of burning down the house if no one is home to watch it.

With everything done, I grabbed a quick lunch and headed for the smithy for another day of practice. But no matter how hard I tried, I just couldn't imagine who would be joining us for dinner. I even asked Darroth, but he said he didn't even know we had a kitchen either.

Of course, the day dragged on, each hour seemingly like three. The work day finally over, I raced home to get everything started. As I walked in, the smell of the roast hit me and my mouth started to water. I could feel that Rosa had also caught the scent; she must be trying to find out what's for dinner again. Quickly rinsing off the day's sweat and throwing on a clean robe, I headed back to the kitchen to ready the side dishes.

After half an hour, Rosa opened the main door and stuck her head through and took an enormous whiff. "Mmm, that smells good! I knew that note would make you step up the cooking!"

"So where is our guest? Who is our guest?"

"Don't worry; she just went to get changed. She shouldn't be more than a few minutes." And as if on cue, there was a knock on the door.

"That must be her! Be a dear and go let her in, will you?" Rosa called mischievously from the other room; I could tell she was up to something.

Nodding, I opened the door to see the familiar helm of my weapons teacher. But that was the only armor she had on. She was in what I would call regular clothing: leggings, shirt, and soft boots, but her shirt had a high neckline and she wore gloves, so still no clue about her appearance.

"Teacher, welcome! I wasn't thinking you were our guest tonight; why didn't you tell me this morning?"

"Because that devious Rosa over there played a trick on me. She claimed that your previous company couldn't make it and that I still owed her a favor, so here I am."

"Hmmm, she's definitely been up to something lately, but please come in, the food is almost ready." I stepped to the side to let her pass and heard her take a deep breath of the smells coming from the kitchen and utter a little sigh. As we crossed the threshold, we found that Rosa had been busy in the last few minutes. The table was set, the bread was out, and she even had a bottle of wine open, a vintage that I didn't even know we had. She bustled around the table humming merrily.

"Rosa, you made all this just for one guest? I can't imagine what you would do for a party."

"Me? Cook? I can't cook to save my life! Alex made all this. He's the reason I've been eating so well lately, so I thought I would show off his talents."

Teacher turned to me. "You did all this?" I nodded. "Ok, so not only are you a smith, Enchanter, soldier-in-training, good looking and all around nice guy, but you can cook, too?" She turned to Rosa, "And how did you deserve this? And where can I get five more of him for the barracks?"

Then she did something that surprised me. She took a deep breath and removed her helm. As the headgear cleared her face, I was stunned by what I saw. She was about my age and had smooth dusky purple skin. Her hair was silver, neatly tucked into a practical bun. Solid white tattoo spots, almost like a galaxy of small stars, started under her eyes then swooped to the sides of her cheeks and narrowed as they ran down her neck. She had soft-looking lips that seemed naturally darker than the rest of her skin, a smooth jaw line, high cheekbones, long delicate elf ears and, of course, the emerald green eyes I had been fixated on for so long. I had seen many dark elves before, but none like her, she was just too beautiful.

Of course, she misinterpreted my awe-stricken silence as the fear or hatred that she was accustomed to seeing from ordinary villagers.

Looking very vulnerable without her helm to hide behind, she spoke quietly, "I know you won't trust me anymore since your country is at war with our people, but I hope you will come to see that not all of us are bad." She looked away from me and Rosa sadly. "I should probably leave, this wasn't such a good idea."

Pain, shame, and desperation shocked my turncoat tongue back into action. "That's not what I was thinking at all," I blurted.

She looked back at us as we both shook our heads. Rosa stepped closer to her and put a gentle hand on her elbow. "I promise you that is the furthest thing from his mind, my girl."

She gave Rosa a searching look, and the old elf nodded reassuringly and smiled.

She looked at me before allowing herself a shy smile. "Very well, my name is Maya, daughter of Faeron Talmin, leader of my clan," she said softly, melodiously, with a formal bow. Somehow that name was nagging at the back of my mind, like I'd heard it before somewhere, somewhere important. But I wasn't going to spend my time on the past; we had a guest to entertain.

The mood lightened and I helped the ladies sit down, then readied the roasted voskk and brought it to the table.

"A roast! Alex!" Rosa chortled, "You have never made me a roast before, or any of these side dishes." I barely got the platter to the table before she was cutting herself a large chunk and dropping it quickly on her plate. Maya seemed to be a bit more dignified with her food, but I could tell she was eager to dig in as well.

"Teacher, we aren't all that formal here, so please just dive in. If you don't, Rosa will eat the entire roast by herself."

"Thank you, Alex; I'll take your advice. And please, call me Maya. I hope we can be friends, when we aren't on the training field, that is." Then she attacked the roast with the same enthusiasm as my master. Maya, such a nice name, I like it. I still couldn't believe the lady in the mask was so beautiful, so perfect. Rosa must have been listening to my thoughts as she nearly choked on a mouthful of potatoes. I resolved to concentrate on my food and perhaps some safe conversation.

"So what did you two do all afternoon?" I asked nonchalantly, taking extra care in buttering a piece of bread.

Maya was the first to stop eating and reply. "Rosa wanted revenge for the other day when I made her help clean up the training grounds that we're going to be using."

"It wasn't revenge. You said months ago that you were going to clean that storage building out to store your stuff. I just reminded you of your obligation."

"Yes, but back then the place was empty, not loaded with all your magic junk! What did you have in those crates anyway, rocks?" Maya grimaced, remembering the weight and pointing a fork at my master.

Rosa huffed, "If you must know, just a few magic rocks, and all of Alex's iron and steel practice rods, and possibly a few fossilized Swernarth teeth in crates, but that's it."

"Hey, don't drag me into this; I had nothing to do with it!" I started clearing away the plates and empty platters; there were no leftovers to worry about tonight.

"Well, I don't care whose fault it is, you both owe me a new back," Maya interjected archly, apparently enjoying the banter.

Rosa smiled innocently at me. "Alex, why don't you make Maya one of the drinks you made for me?"

Maya eyed me suspiciously. "Yes, why don't you? Rosa wouldn't stop talking about how well she felt the next day after drinking one." Rosa motioned for her to follow her to the reading area where the comfy chairs were located.

I pulled my book out again and went to work. Since she is a dark elf, I'll have to use a different recipe. I just hope that she doesn't see what I was putting in it, most people run away when you tell them it has dried bugs ground into it. While I was working, I could hear them giggling down the hall. In short order, I presented her with an orange version of the drink I had served Rosa.

"What's in it?"

"Nothing you wouldn't find in your forest."

She tilted her head and seemed to be pleased that I knew where her race lived. She drank about half of it in one go. "It's not too bad." Then she finished off the rest and set down the empty glass, smiling. "How long until it wo… wor…" She slouched in her chair and began to inhale in soft, slow breaths, sleeping gently. I was struck by how different from the hard-as-nails combat instructor and lethal swordswoman she was as she sat curled in the chair like a cute little girl. Suddenly a wave of self-doubt washed over me.

"Oops."

Rosa jumped up and checked on her. "What do you mean 'oops,' I don't like 'oops.'"

"I forgot to ask her how long she has been off the normal dark elf diet. Her body has purged the common herbs that she would normally have in almost every meal so that drink hit her harder than I wanted."

"That's not all," Rosa snickered, examining the last dregs of the glass with mage sight. "I think you were so focused on creating the perfect drink that you inadvertently added a wee bit of enchantment into the mix, giving her what she desires most!" She snorted and looked at the dark elf affectionately. "A good night's sleep is always a blessing for her." Rosa stroked Maya's hair. "Well, help me get her in my bed so she can sleep it off." I picked her up carefully and was astonished at how light she was. Her hair smelled like the forest near the sea, and I kicked myself mentally for being the cause of the evening ending so abruptly. The inevitable retribution that would fall on me tomorrow in the practice ring would be brutal. Still, the thought occurred to me that if I died right now holding her as I was, I would go a happy man.

We got Maya settled in Rosa's big bed upstairs, then continued our usual nightly instruction. Rosa was acting squirrelly all evening, bursting out in random fits of laughter. As the night got late, Rosa left me with plenty of reading to do and went to bed. After finishing my reading, I stopped by Rosa's room to check on things and found them both asleep in the big bed. Shaking my head, I went back to my room.

The next morning, I decided to let the elves have their sleep and went about the work of making a grand breakfast for the two of them, also as a way to apologize. Six eggs, four slices of bacon, and ten griddle cakes each should do it. Even with the noise from the cooking, I could tell both were still fast asleep; looks like the ladies needed breakfast in bed! By some incredible feat of skill (probably granted by the gods only to idiots who stupidly drug their weapons instructor), I somehow got both trays of food upstairs and into Rosa's room without dropping anything.

When I set the trays down and went to wake them, I stopped. I could barely hold myself together. In the night, Maya had somehow thrown her legs around Rosa and the two of them were now a tangled mess. Having pity on what Rosa might do if she was the first one to wake up, I started with Maya.

"Maya, it's time to get up," I whispered; dark elves have excellent hearing. I was careful as I tried to untangle them.

"Don't go, Alex. Can't we stay here a bit longer?" Ok, I might like this dream.

"...rabbits...fish...unicorn!" Or not.

"Come on, Maya, I have food." That did the trick. Her eyes shot open and she was instantly alert but still couldn't move.

"What happened? And why am I in bed with Rosa?" she demanded. Hearing her name, or more likely smelling the food, Rosa snapped out of it as well.

"Why hello, my dear, sweet Maya! Did we have fun last night? I can tell you're already feeling better from Alex's drink!" Then Rosa planted a big, wet kiss on Maya's cheek.

"Ack! Old lady slobber!" Maya cried as she made a show of wiping it off her face. But I couldn't stop laughing.

Maya looked at me somewhat embarrassed and a little cross. "So is this how you treat all your female guests? I guess I shouldn't complain too much, I do feel wonderful! But you are definitely going to pay for this on the training field." I gulped, but then I caught the merriment in her eyes.

"Ok, you two, your food is getting cold so sit up and I'll hand you each a tray." After giving both of them their trays piled high with food, I sat down with my own breakfast at the small table in the corner.

"You made the same thing for me our first morning! Maya, you have to try those cake things; I don't know what they are, but they are to die for!" And as her usual self, she crammed her food in as fast as she could.

"Thank you, Alex, for the food and for last night. I do feel fantastic. That was the best night's sleep I've had in a very long time; you are a man of many talents." Things got quiet as everyone was eating, but everyone was happy, you could just feel it.

"Well, ladies, I need to get going to class; you both slept past noon. Just put your trays downstairs and I'll take care of them when I get back."

Chapter 7

Alex

Maya and I were in her private training circle, one that was not easily viewed from the outside and where she felt comfortable not covering her face. As usual, dawn had just barely broken and the only creatures awake were some night birds that snatched the moths drawn by the lanterns hung on poles. Maya was wearing light leather armor and had a well-worn metal vambrace on her off arm. We faced each other with wooden training swords.

"Today, we're going to start training with the sword. To start with, we will be using these wooden practice swords. Your task is simple; all you need to do is hit me and the lesson is done for the day. But every time you fail to hit me, I will hit you. This will go into the night if needed, so don't hold back if you don't want something broken. Now begin."

We started circling in our arena. I knew this was going to be a long and painful test. I tried two swift cuts to her left and right side that she easily blocked and was quickly rewarded with two painful hits to my legs.

This is not going to be an easy lesson. I kept on the attack, trying different directions with each awkward attack, hoping to get one through. But each time, I was met with the sharp pain of her practice blade and a cocky grin.

"You're going to have to try harder than that. This isn't even a warm up yet!"

This went on for hours. Every now and then, she would call a break claiming that this was a test of skill not endurance.

Fortunately, it was an off day and I didn't need to be at the forge in the afternoon. Finally, she sighed and motioned for me to sit down in the sand which I did gratefully, while she paced a few minutes as if rehearsing a speech before delivering the bad news.

"Alex, I don't think I can make you a swordsman," she said quietly. "A blade is an instrument of elegant precision, quick strikes to your opponent's vulnerable areas like joints, eyes, or seams in armor. A sword is never used as a club to beat your foe into submission. You, of all people, being a blacksmith, must have had to repair swords used as such; it's not proper."

She lost me at, "I don't think I can make you a swordsman," and it must have shown on my face as she frowned and moved closer. Sitting down cross-legged in front of me, she lifted my chin and drew my eyes to hers.

"Alex, with a lot of work, you could probably rise to the level of competency of the city guard with a sword, but that isn't going to be good enough for you, is it?"

"No," I said bitterly, thinking I was doomed to a life of making weapons I couldn't use.

"Good!" She smiled brilliantly. "That's exactly the right answer!"

"Huh?"

"I said I couldn't make you a swordsman, because the sword is all wrong for you." Maya poked me in the chest playfully. "Look at you, Alex! Those tree trunks you call arms, along with a strong back and legs; you're more like an elongated dwarf than a sword dancer. Ok, a cute elongated dwarf," she added with a slight blush.

"So where does that leave me?" I wondered, confused.

"Come with me." She hopped up and jogged excitedly toward one of the nearby sheds. I followed slowly wondering what this was all about. She darted back and grabbing my sleeve pulled me along impatiently. Opening the rickety wooden door revealed racks upon racks of practice weapons. They were mostly swords, but axes and pole arms were scattered in the mix, as well.

Maya started perusing the assorted axes. "I think something like this may be more your style - less finesse, more ogre bash!" Watching her bend down to examine each weapon from top to bottom was definitely causing a pounding, irregular heartbeat in my chest, the practice leather armor was formfitting and...

And the voice of reason, not to mention self-preservation, was strongly warning me that it would not be healthy to get caught looking at my weapons instructor in such a manner, but she was just so damn beautiful! Taking a deep breath and feigning nonchalance, I walked over and checked out the items in the farthest corner. My eyes were drawn to a dull steel handle and leather-wrapped grip that was sticking up out of a dusty old wine barrel. I glanced back, satisfied that she was still axe shopping, and reached into the barrel and drew out a war hammer. An old, beat-up war hammer to be sure, but it was still a formidable weapon. I took a few practice swings and, somewhere in the back of my mind, there was a sigh of sublime satisfaction...this would do nicely.

"Hey, what about this one?" Maya and I said simultaneously, she holding up an axe and me my war hammer. I pivoted to look at her and she was standing stock still. She had dropped the axe on the floor and was staring at me like she had seen a ghost, her face turning nearly as pale as her tattoos.

"Where did you get that?" she stammered, wide-eyed.

"It was in the wine barrel in the corner over there. I kind of like it, it feels right."

"That's impossible! I inventoried this shed myself two days ago and there was no war hammer here!"

"Well, mistakes happen," I said, following her back out the door with my new prize. Once outside, she stood facing away from me, and seemed to be hyperventilating slightly, this from a woman who could run five miles without breaking a sweat! Finally, she turned and stood, hands on her hips and watched me curiously as I got the feel of the weapon. She seemed to be having a heated discussion with herself in elfish, but I couldn't catch what she was saying. Finally, apparently having won or perhaps lost the argument, she smiled faintly, sighed and ventured back into the shed, returning a couple minutes later carrying a buckler.

"So what is the buckler for? Do I have to learn two new things?"

"Hell no," she laughed. "The buckler's for me! You might actually get lucky and hit me with that monster!"

Actually, I did end up using a buckler, too, as it is very difficult to spar with just a one-handed hammer. The weapon doesn't lend itself to the polite clashing of blades as in a sword duel, and being slower than a blade means the wielder is left vulnerable to the obvious effects of inertia. But when it does connect, the hammer is a nearly unstoppable force that can easily break a blade or knock it out of an opponent's hand, and the spike end was developed to pierce heavy armor.

We began to spar; the results were more satisfying but still mostly the same. I still couldn't touch her with my weapon. It was now well after dinner time, and I could sense my master was impatient and hungry.

"There is magic in a duel as well, remember that."

"Thanks, Primus,"

"Who are you talking to? Now is not the time to daydream," Maya growled.

I backed away from Maya and concentrated on trying to visualize the flow of magic between us. And there it was, just as my master had said. Even with my eyes closed, I could feel where she was and where her sword was going to be. I stood there with my eyes still closed taking in all I could from what the magic could tell me.

"Well, if you're just going to stand there all night, I'm going to come after you!"

The flow of magic in her body shifted and contracted like the muscles in your arm. I could see her moving and where she would stop. I could feel the presence of her sword, and I could react to it. I moved my buckler into her path in a decent block.

"How did you do that? Your eyes are closed!"

She started to attack again, but I could see what she was going to do before she did it. I easily blocked most of her half-speed probing strikes and even got close enough with a few hammer swings to cause her some concern.

"What the hell? You close your eyes and now you can somehow fight? Were you just toying with me?"

She was getting mad; her speed increasing. Even knowing where she was going to strike, I didn't have the speed or skill to keep up. My defense failed and she knocked me on my ass in the dirt. She then stepped on my chest forcing me further to the ground and held her practice blade to my neck.

"Ok, start talking, Magic Boy. What did you do?" She was really mad. But you know, I kind of liked it; she's gorgeous when she's mad.

"I just closed my eyes and used my mage sight. Doing that, I can see the magic in you and predict what you're going to do."

"You're full of it! And you just came up with this idea on your own, in the middle of a sparring match?"

"Well, not really, Rosa told me to try it."

"That's fine, but she is not here, so I ask again, who told you?"

"I'm telling the truth, we bonded when I first got here. Now she can listen in on anything I hear and talk to me over any distance."

"Prove it. Ask her for something only she would know.

"Tell her she had a wolf puppy named Fluffball and her favorite color is dark pink."

"You had a wolf pup named Fluffball and your favored color is dark pink."

She looked shocked, looking around furtively to make sure Rosa was not hiding nearby, and she let the sword fall away from my throat. "How did you know that?"

"I told you, she can talk to me."

"Oh, I got a good one! Tell her that I'll tell you what she was dreaming about last night."

"What?! No, Master, she would kill me!"

"What did she say now?" Maya demanded, bringing the blade back up.

"She said she would tell me what you were dreaming about last night." Maya gasped and the skin on her neck and cheeks turned three shades darker.

"If you do, Rosa, I swear I will kill you! Fine, you two have proved your point, but you still didn't hit me. Then again, there for a bit, I did have to work to hit you, so I'll be nice and say lesson passed." A wave of relief washed over me as she helped me to my feet. "With one condition."

"What's that?"

She smiled and playfully punched me. "That you make me dinner again tonight. The dining hall's closed and I'm starving. No potion shenanigans tonight though, I'd like to keep my virtue intact a bit longer, thank you!" We both were laughing as we started the walk home. Dirty, sweaty, battered and sore, I didn't care.

"You know, I already made dinner this morning. We're lucky Rosa didn't find it and eat it all without us."

"Wait, you mean to say that I didn't have to starve waiting for you? Why didn't you tell me? Where did you stash dinner?"

"Uh-oh, she's looking for it now; we better pick up the pace." We were jogging now.

"With her nose, it won't take her long to find it either," Maya ventured.

"Found you, the delicious bits!"

"She found it!"

We looked at each other with mock horror and concern. "RUN!" and stormed off towards home with the hope that Rosa would at least take the time to heat it up first.

The next day after breakfast, I set off for the training grounds. But I couldn't find Maya there; instead, I found a note saying that class was canceled and to practice on my own. How do you practice with a war hammer by yourself? After swinging the weapon aimlessly for over half an hour, and feeling idiotic doing it, I decided to take a different approach. Thinking about the previous evening when I was watching Maya spar with my mage vision, I realized that if I could master this technique, it would enhance both my weapon and enchanting skills. But to be effective, I would have to be able to rely on it in any situation, regardless of distractions.

Thinking the best place to be would be an area with lots of people, I headed for Central. Finding a nice, vacant seat with lots of foot traffic, I set to work. Bringing up my mage sight had almost the same effect as it did in the practice duel with Maya. But with some concentration, things became very clear. I could focus on things and see them from angles that I shouldn't be able to see from my bench. I could look behind me without turning my head; my mind was mapping the area around me. After some time, I no longer needed to concentrate; this was soon as natural as my own eyes. Colors were becoming more of what they should be; stone was now gray again instead of the green color of the magic inside of it.

I reopened my real eyes and found that I could see normally, but now I could also still sense things around me that were out of my eyesight. Like that there was a bumblebee on the flower ten feet behind me, or that there were three students on my left and one on my right, or that there was someone stealthily creeping up behind me.

Wait a minute! Creeping up on me? Focusing on the person, I could tell that she was wearing black leather and a full hood. By looking at her magic, I could who it was.

"Nice try, Maya, but that's not going to work."

"Crap! How did you hear me coming! A dark elf can sneak up on anyone, we're totally silent hunters," she complained as she rose up to her full height and slid gracefully onto the bench beside me.

"I didn't hear you, I could see you."

"You weren't looking at me and I checked for anything that could reflect my shadow, too. There is no way you could see me."

"You know yesterday when I closed my eyes and was able to block your strikes? Well, I've been practicing that skill a bit today, and I've gotten pretty good at it. Now, I don't even have to close my eyes."

"So now you can predict what everyone is going to do?"

"Not really, at least at the moment. I think the reason why I could in practice was because we were in battle and I was sharply focused."

"You're saying that your mage sight has a passive and an active part?"

Thinking for a moment, "Yes, I think that's exactly it."

"So in passive, you can see things without your eyes that are all around you, not just what's in front of you?" I nodded. "Can you see through things, too?" I nodded again. Now she stopped and thought for a bit. "I think we could use this to our advantage at a later time. But for now, you still stink at sparring, so it's practice as normal."

"So what were you doing today, anyway?"

"Ugh, part of my contract to stay here mandates I help train the local constables four times a month. It wouldn't be so bad, but I can't let the wrong people, especially wizards, see my face. They would be the first ones to accuse me of being a spy. Then I would get dragged past all the halls for everyone to see on the way to the Headmaster."

"But why would they do that? You have permission to stay here."

"Yes, I do but old habits die hard for some, and I'm not a wizard, so my status here is already barely that of a servant. Wizards being wizards love to show their superiority. After seven years of that game, I just avoid most people now. You have no idea how much I enjoy being able to lose this disguise once in a while, like the other night at your Enchanters Hall. Thank you again by the way"

"So why do you stay, then? Surely with your skills, any number of kings would welcome you with open arms to train their troops."

"Perhaps...I don't know," she whispered wistfully. "Something has kept me here these years, and until I find out what that something is, I will stay. It's not like I can go home."

"Seven years? I thought you were close to my age."

She slid closer on the bench next to me, closer than I would have thought she would, but I didn't mind at all. She adjusted her hood so people walking by couldn't see her face, but I could. "Well, I'm thirty-two, but in dark elf years, I'm nineteen. We don't live as long as green elves like Rosa, but we still live about four human lifetimes."

"Great, so you two will still be young when I'm an old man."

"Not true. How old do you think the Headmaster is? He is over five hundred and is still a human. You will possibly outlive me." That idea didn't sound so great either.

"Um, you don't have to tell me if you don't want to, I'll understand, but why did you leave home?" I asked tentatively.

She eyed me harshly, but her expression softened immediately and she nodded to herself. "I don't know why, but I feel strangely comfortable around you...I suppose there's no real harm in telling you some things. Our clan was one of the few that got along with humans, as well as the other races. But seven years ago, we were forced to join with a much larger and more powerful regional clan. I did not approve of their methods." I could tell from the pain in her face that she was not giving me the whole story, but I think she was still trying to decide how much to open up to me. "I couldn't live with what they were doing, so I left. Not long after that, I stumbled into Rosa on one of her laboratory ingredient restocking trips and she took me in, adopted me really, so here I am." She sighed sadly. "In truth, I would love to see my family, but that isn't going to happen anytime soon...so this is my home. How about you, Alex," she said, changing the subject. She pulled out some strips of jerky from one of her pockets and offered me a piece.

"How about me, what?"

"Well, a few weeks ago, you were just a village blacksmith-in-training. Now you're a full Enchanter apprentice and managing to astound your primus on an almost daily basis, and we shouldn't even mention poor Darroth. You've got him talking to himself and drinking far more ale than is good for him. Even when I say you stink at sparring, I don't really mean it; actually you improve way more rapidly than most of my students. Most people learn in fits and starts, two steps forward and one back. They have to fail occasionally to make progress. But you seem to somehow always move forward. It's like you're naturally good at everything! Were you born under a lucky star or something?"

I chewed slowly and considered what she said. "Maya, I don't really know what's going on with me. If you had known me six months ago, there is no way you could have claimed I was good at everything, barely adequate maybe. Perhaps this place brings out the best in me, or maybe it's just that I have the best teachers in the world. It's like I left the old Alex behind in Foalshead. I keep expecting to wake up and find out this was all a dream."

She frowned slightly at the word "dream" and her eyes showed me that she was momentarily somewhere else, but she snapped back instantly. "Well, you do have the best teachers in the world." She smiled and gave me a soft nudge with her elbow. "But I'm pretty sure I would have really liked the old Alex, too. In my experience, people don't change their spots that quickly; you probably just needed a change of scenery and some confidence."

I took the last bite of my jerky. "Hey, this is pretty good. What is it?"

"Rock marmot. I practically lived on this before Rosa found me and brought me here. I'll show you how to hunt them someday if you like. You need a shiny bauble to lure them out into the open.

They are masterful at hiding but shameless thieves; their greed always gets them in trouble."

I grinned. "So what, you don't just sneak up on them? I thought dark elves were completely silent hunters! By the way, what were you planning to do to me once you snuck up on me?"

She smiled a mischievous smile. "Well, you will just have to wait until I do to find out now. But I think you would have liked it!" She got up and walked away, and I watched her disappear gracefully into the crowd. A stiff breeze was coming up, and my peripheral vision caught a glimpse of something blowing across the commons area. Sailing aimlessly and tumbling, it landed on the bench beside me where Maya had been sitting. Grabbing it for no better reason than trash control, I examined it. Back in Foalshead, real paper was so expensive that it wasn't uncommon for people to use it over and over until it completely wore through. But here in Xarparion, it was just another base commodity. Examining it, I saw it was a handout for something called The First Day, apparently a social event of some kind. The date at the bottom set this party for three days from now at the field between the Earth and Water Towers.

There's a celebration in three days and I haven't heard anything about this? Well, I know two people who would, and I headed off to the dining hall.

Once there, I surveyed the usual tables covered with sweet edibles until I spotted my objectives. I grabbed a seed bun and sat down across from them, tearing off pieces while I tried to look nonchalant.

"Julia, Lin, so what's with this 'The First Day' thing?" As one, their eyes bulged, their mouths dropped open and both dropped their food, looking at me with pure shock. Lin was the first to recover.

"Alex, we all know you live under an enchanted rock on a deserted island, but seriously, you don't know?"

"No," I gulped. "No one ever delivers our news, and we don't have a newsboard anywhere close to us...and I've been really busy, and..."

Julia interrupted with a snort of disgust, "Ok, even I know what it's about! And I'm too young yet to really do any of the fun stuff!"

"What she is trying to say," Lin added, "is that it's a party to celebrate the first day Xarparion opened its doors. There's a big feast and lots of shows and shops brought in from the outside, all manned by our staff, though. Best of all, there is also a huge formal dance, so it's now a sort of a romantic holiday."

"And who are you two going with?"

"You think we have boyfriends? Ha, you're funny. No, Julia and I are going together for our first time. It should be fun even without boys." The two of them hugged and giggled hysterically for a bit, hamming it up. "But really, Alex, you need to get yourself a girl. You're too old to go by yourself and too good looking not to have a date."

"I'll think about it. I think I might know someone I could ask."

Lin frowned. "Ha! Good luck with that! Anyone remotely pretty has probably been asked already, and three days isn't enough time to sew a dress. If this mystery girl is taken, let us know; I know a few older girls in the Earth Tower who would gladly stitch together some banana leaves for a chance to go with you."

"Thanks, but I'll handle my own matchmaking," I said, feeling my face start to redden and wondering how I lost control of this conversation so quickly.

"You didn't tell him about the rule. That's the best part!" Julia squealed excitedly.

"Oops! That would have been bad. Sorry, I almost forgot the guy rule. The rule is that the man must bring the girl a gift to wear and show off that he made himself, emphasis on himself. You just can't go out and buy something. Halfway through the night, they will make an announcement telling all you guys to present your gift to your lady fair. Afterward, if your girl wants, there's a contest that they can enter to see who received the best gift."

"And what kind of gifts are we talking here?"

"You know, bracelets, necklaces, that sort of thing. Last year, an Earthie from our tower presented his girl with an albino yak that he raised himself. It was so romantic! Seriously, you should have the easiest time since your job is to make wonderful items. Speaking of wonderful, Julia, could you go find some of that really good juice? I think I saw some at the far table where the air slingers sit." Julia nodded and ran off to find some. Lin quickly slid over to my side of the table and whispered conspiratorially. "Alex, could I ask you a favor? You see, the guy rule is mostly for the guys, but I went and made a necklace for Julia anyway. See, neither of us had any friends before we got here and I just want her to have a good time."

"Sure, Lin, what can I do to help?"

She pulled a very nice river stone necklace from her pocket. "Could you enchant this quick? Just, you know, to give it some shine?" I smiled; I could do that and more.

I carefully took the necklace from her and set to work. First, I had to get a feel for the stone like I have to do with everything that is not metal. I noticed that Lin had used her own powers to shape the stones, which left plenty of pulsing residual magic in them. This made it very easy to mold the flow of magic in the stones to do what she wanted. It didn't take much to shape them into something that resembled a pearl; I also had enough energy to do a little something extra.

"Wow, what did you do to them? I was only thinking to shine them up a bit," Lin said breathlessly.

"I did that and also gave them a small glow, and there's more. With the extra magic that you put into them, I was able to make it so that whoever is wearing it will never get cold."

She slipped the stones back into her pocket and gave me a hug. "Thanks, Alex, you are the best. I can already feel the warmth in my robe."

Just then, Julia came running back empty-handed. "That was a mean trick, Lin; you know they don't have juice at lunch." We both burst out laughing. "Quit laughing, you two, I know a pigeon that will do my bidding, you know."

Chapter 8

Alex

After lunch, I went on with my day. But as the day went on, my thoughts were on a certain silver-haired warrior and not on my project. I couldn't think of a way to ask her to go with me or a gift that she would like. Setting down my hammer, I went over to Darroth for help.

"What can I do for ya, lad?"

"I could use some advice."

"On steel? Hell, kid, you know almost as much as I do."

"No, not about steel. I need advice on girls."

He tried to stand up, but he did it so fast that he lost his balance and both he and his chair fell over. "By the god's, kid! Why didn't you start with that? Come with me."

I followed him to one of the nearby buildings that doubled as his office and showroom. He took a seat behind his desk and I took one of the human-sized chairs. He reached back and grabbed a dusty tankard of ale from a shelf behind him. It looked like it had been sitting there for a while and I tried not to gag thinking about what was probably floating around in its depths. After making an offering gesture, which I quickly declined, he took a huge gulp, ignoring the liquid that dripped off his facial hair and began.

"So what's got your filly's beard in a knot then?"

Definitely not the issue! "Umm, no knots involved Darroth. I don't know if you know about it, but in three days there's a party. One of the rules is that the guy has to make a gift for the girl. The girls then compare gifts to see who has the best."

"I see, and you don't know what to make for her, right?" I nodded. "Well, girls like jewels and pretty things, unless we're talking dwarf women, then it's ale and beard combs. But we're not talking about a dwarf woman, are we?"

"No, we are not."

"Your loss. Oh well, leaves the field wide open for me," he chuckled, with a far-off look in his eye. "So what's the problem? With your skills, you could make the best damned bracelet in this academy."

"The problem is that I don't think she would like jewelry."

Darroth slammed his hand down on the desk in triumph. "So you're going after Maya, then? Rosa told me you two were hitting it off. She's a sweet girl, and she sure deserves a lot better treatment than what she gets around here. Of course, I'll help you out. So what were you thinking of making then?"

"I don't know."

We sat there despondently for a bit, both trying to come up with a first-class gift for Maya. I got the feeling that Darroth wasn't a real deep thinker as the longer he thought, the more ale he drank, and the fewer ideas he came up with.

"*Alex, make her a sword,*" said Rosa in my head, but that didn't sound like a bad idea.

"What about a sword?" I said. The dwarf looked at me appraisingly, came to some sort of decision, and then started rummaging furiously through the papers on the desk.

"I like it! And that's the only thing that would suit her. But if you're going to make a sword for that young lady, then you're going to have to make one hell of a sword! But time is short." Finding the elusive paper, he ran to one of the many heavy cabinets lining the back wall. "I got this shipment in a few days ago from a friend of mine in Ocance. I ordered it in to see what you could do with some real quality materials."

He held out three ingots of a dark gray metal that was far lighter in weight than they appeared and one block of an unusual metal that was almost white. I could feel serious magic flowing through the white block. Smiling broadly, he handed them all over to me.

"These are for you. That gray stuff is pure dwarven steel smelted in the deepest part of our underground capital. It's several times harder than ordinary steel so be careful. The other we call starlode, smelted from a meteorite quarry, that only we dwarves know the location of. It's also one of the very few ores that are naturally magical. If you do it right, any weapon you forge from them should be worthy of royalty.

I set to work, starting with the steel. My plan was to get the shape of the blade done as well as get the starlode folded into it before I had to leave for the day. As usual, once I found myself at the forge, time became irrelevant. My hands knew what to do and the metals sang softly to me. With time running short, I put the half-finished blade into the flames and headed home. After a long and rather quiet dinner, I could tell Rosa wanted to say something but kept holding it in.

"What's wrong, Master?"

"Oh, it's nothing, don't mind me. But there is something I

would like to ask."

"And what would that be?"

"Alex, do you know how to dance?"

Aw, crap! I must have stupidly let my mind wander to the party and my project. Most of the time, its fine letting Rosa run rampant through my thoughts; this wasn't one of those times.

"Um...where did that come from?" I stalled.

She smiled. "Don't play dumb with me. You already know that I know that you are planning on asking Maya to the party, right? So if you're going to be taking Maya to a dance, then you best know how to dance. See my point?"

"But I don't know how to dance; I've never danced in my life!"

"I know, that's why I'm going to teach you."

"And how exactly did you learn to dance?"

Rosa drew herself up to her full regal height. "I'll have you know that in my mid-three hundreds, I frequently danced, and became quite good at it. I want to help you because I love both you and Maya very much. If I can get her out of her shell by getting you two together, then I won't stop until it happens."

"You want us together that bad?"

"Alex, I'm not giving you two a choice anymore. Now, come on, let's dance!" She started humming a lively tune.

We danced long into the night, until she deemed that I knew what I was doing. I managed to only step on her foot twice. Close to midnight, I was sure that this was no longer practice for her and was now just for fun, but I let it slide - I could tell she didn't get to do this often. But a few hours past midnight, she finally collapsed into a chair, exhausted.

"I think you will be fine now. You should get some sleep, you have a long day tomorrow. I think I'll take a small nap here. Oh, and I need to start a new dress tomorrow, too," she slurred and was out. I grabbed a blanket and did what I could to wrap her up in it so she wouldn't get cold, then went to gratefully to bed.

The next morning bright and early, Maya took me out into the forest just outside the walls to another of her private training locations. It was just a clearing where she had set up a few practice dummies and a shed. The morning light filtered through the trees, birds sang and even though I was running on next to no sleep, all was right in the world...at least until she whacked me for the first time.

"Ok, Alex, today we are going to practice basic footwork," Maya said. "I am not an expert in war hammers, but my people have had enough altercations with dwarves to acquire a good bit of lore regarding attack and defense measures. We will be starting off slow and stepping it up from there. Now I know you're getting good at the mage sight thing, but try not to use that unless I tell you to."

We practiced for hours, she showed me the proper forms that I should use for strikes and blocks. As the day went on, she loosened up a bit, too. It seemed that she was having fun teaching me and that made it fun for me as well.

"You appear to be having a good day today," I grinned, as my shield caught another of her sword flicks toward my torso. She stopped the pattern she was following, lowered her weapon and stepped in closer, wiping a bead of perspiration from her forehead.

"You know, you're right, this is a lot more fun when you don't have to worry about your students grabbing pitchforks and torches. And you seem to have a talent for this. It's nice having a student who actually listens."

"You mean that we're almost done with the basics?"

"Basics! You blew past basics hours ago. I give you a week and you will be as good as any dwarf you are likely to encounter. I would already hate to meet you on the battlefield. I've never seen anyone take to any weapon as quickly as you have...it's like you were born for it.

"Well, I do have the best combat teacher in Xarparion."

She smiled primly, "Yes, you do, and you better not forget it!" We practiced for a bit longer, and I waited for our last break before I worked up the courage to ask. We stood together next to a bucket and shared a copper dipper of cool sweet water.

"So do you have any plans for two nights from now?"

She stopped to look at me with a puzzled face. "No, why do you ask?"

"Well, if you don't have plans, I would like to ask you to go to the dance with me."

There was a long pause as she got a stricken look on her face. "You want me to go to The First Day dance with you? This is not some kind of sick joke?"

"No, I really would like you to go with me."

She took two steps back, and I could feel a sense of fear from her. "Why?"

"Why, what?"

"Why do you want me to accompany you? I'm a dark elf, everyone hates us, and you deserve a girl of your own race. You would be hated as well by everyone there, just for being seen with me."

I took a few steps closer. "I don't care about them. I'm not the most popular guy as it is, so don't worry about them. And I'm not asking any of them, I'm asking you."

"You really want me to go with you?"

"Yes, I do. You're my best friend here and I want to take you."

She eyed me a bit longer and began pacing back and forth nervously. She started to say something and stopped, looked away, then back at me with a frown like she was going to tell me off. Talk about warring emotions, this was an epic battle! I must have made a pathetic face or something because just as she was about to explode, she stopped and just looked at me with a bit of concern in her deep, green eyes.

"Ok," she said, "Before I decide anything, a few things have to be cleared up. I would have to wear my hood the entire time and that wouldn't look good at a party."

Sensing a slim chance of success, I brightened considerably. "Don't worry about that. Rosa said she thought of something that would help you to look human and, of course, she will outfit you in a dress that will help you fit in and stand out at the same time.

She winced at the "look human" comment and I felt my chances plummet. Now I know how the rock marmots feel when they almost reach the shiny bauble and instead get the arrow!

"But I'm not human, Alex! Are you sure you want to do this?"

I reached out and took her hands gently. "Maya, the hood is just a tool, so is Rosa's enchantment. And there is no one else I would even consider taking to the party, so please do me the honor of being my date."

More silence as she thought things over. "I take it she has been helping a bit?"

I think I blushed but knew I had to tell the truth. "Yeah, and Darroth, too"

She nodded, "I've never been to one of these, so I don't know what to do or how to act."

"Neither have I, so we're even on that ground."

"Ok, just one last thing, a dance for you doesn't mean...well, it's different for..." She stopped and tilted her head as if listening to an emotion long forgotten. "You know what, that doesn't matter right now. Right now, if you want me to go with you, then we're going to spar for the remainder of the lesson."

So we sparred, and this wasn't like last time either. No strikes were made on each other, just sword on shield and hammer tap on shield. In a sense, we had been dancing like this for weeks, and we loved it. Maya was even happier than she was earlier, and I was literally walking on air. We just enjoyed each other's company as we dueled until it was time to leave.

Rushing through lunch, I dashed back to the forge to finish Maya's blade, even more determined that it would be absolutely perfect. But when I got there, I couldn't find the dwarf anywhere. Not having time to worry, I set to work. Retrieving the half-finished blade from the embers, I could hear some sort of buzzing. After looking around, I couldn't find anything that would make that noise but I could still hear it.

"So you're the new Enchanter, huh?" queried a small female voice and it was close, but I still didn't see anyone. "Down here!"

I looked down at my anvil, and sitting there with her legs crossed was a six-inch tall girl with dragonfly wings and long elf-like ears. She had braided red hair that hung down to her waist and enormous green eyes. She wore a patchy yellow dress that looked to be made from a flower. All in all, she looked kind of cute, for a six-inch tall girl anyway.

"Um, hello...who and what are you?"

She got up and bowed to me. "I'm sorry, I forgot to tell you I was coming. My name is...probably unpronounceable by a human, and we little people have this rule about giving out our real names to outsiders since that whole Rumplestiltskin fiasco, but you can call me Nia and I'm a pixie."

"Ok, well...very nice to meet you, Nia. Is there something you need? I am really busy right now."

She looked at me funny with her head tilted to the side. "You didn't read the King's letter," she accused, then a look of horror spread across her face and she dropped down on the anvil in a pitiful ball, drawing her knees up to her chest. "Of course you didn't! I forgot to send it to you! Bad Nia!" And she started to cry.

I have no natural defenses against female tears, even if they come from a six-inch little slip of a girl. I reset the sword into the embers, set my work hammer aside, and wiped off my hands on a rag. Crouching down, I looked at her at eye level.

"Wow, calm down, Nia, we'll get this figured out. You can call me Alex. Now, what did the letter say?"

She stopped and looked at me with tears in her eyes. "At least, I found the right human. Mr. Alex, I was so very lost in this big place, and then I heard you humming, and you were so happy that you stood out like a beacon in all these people. Once I smelled the forge, I knew you were the one."

"The letter, Nia," I reminded gently.

She stood up, wiped away her tears, and pulled out a tiny piece of paper less than an inch wide. "It says, 'Dear Mr. Alex, a pixie will arrive in your home by my orders. It has come to my attention that you will someday be important to the magical kingdom and will have a large impact on it as your life continues. As an offering of good will and to barter for further cooperation with our people, the pixie bearing this letter will now belong to you.'" Nia stopped and did a double-take. "Wait, what? The king made me your servant? That can't be right."

"What else does it say, maybe there's a reason?"

She continued reading, still flustered, "This pixie has been chosen to be your servant and bodyguard for the remainder of her natural life. If you are killed and your guard is not, then she will no longer be welcome here at home. But I do respectfully ask that you take good care of your pixie. Our people are few and growing fewer every year, and all are valued by me. With respect, signed Austinopfellius, the Pixie King." Nia slumped down and fell flat on her back dejectedly. "Well, that sucks. Now I can't ever go home. Then again, that may be a good thing."

"Why would not going home be a good thing?"

She sat back up and hung her head. "I was never much liked at home. You see, I have way more stupid magic than a normal pixie, but I can't control it, and that made some problems for me."

"What sort of problems?"

"Well, when I try to light a candle, I start the hut on fire, or if I attempt to sprout a seed, I get a full-size tree, that sort of thing."

"I don't see what's wrong with that, you just need some practice."

"But I've tried practice, I'm just too stupid to do it!" And she started hitting herself in the head. "Stupid Nia!"

"Hey, stop that." I used two of my fingers and held her small arms still.

"You don't think I should be shunned or punished?"

"No, I don't."

"But I'm so stupid!"

"I don't think so. I think you're just being hard on yourself. Besides, you're at a school for magic. If you're going to learn, then this is the place to do it. I'll help you."

She smiled and wiggled free of my fingers. Once free, she flew up, her silver dragonfly wings buzzing vigorously, and the pixie girl happily darted in close and quickly hugged my face.

"You're a nice master; maybe this won't be so bad after all. So what are you doing with that thing anyway?" She let go of my face and sat on my shoulder and pointed at the dull gray blade still in the embers.

"First, call me Alex. I grew up a blacksmith's son, and I am certainly no one's master. And to answer your question, I am making a gift for the girl I'm taking to the dance coming up."

She looked at it for a bit and her eyes got bigger. "Um, I may not be a good judge of things size-wise, but I don't think that's going to make a nice shiny bracelet or shiny anything for that matter."

I laughed and she flashed me a grumpy look. "Don't laugh at me! I may be a pixie, but I am still a girl, you know. We know fashion, and that's not it!"

"No, sorry, I'm not laughing at you. It's just that the girl I'm taking to the party doesn't favor jewelry."

I thought she was going to die, her wings went straight up and started to vibrate. "DOESN'T LIKE JEWELRY! What kind of girl doesn't like jewelry? What's wrong with you? Oh, you're not courting a dwarf girl, are you?" she asked, waggling a finger at me.

"No, Maya isn't a dwarf, she just isn't the kind of girl to wear a lot of flashy adornments - she really doesn't need them to look great."

"So what kind of girl is she then?"

"She likes swords."

"Swords? What's a girl to do with a sword?" She perked up and buzzed around some more, and then snapped her tiny fingers. "I've got it, she is a warrior princess! And instead of a silly bracelet, you're making a magic sword to protect her so that your true love always comes home from the battlefield!"

I was embarrassed, but you know she had a point; I did always want Maya to come home. "You are exactly right, Nia! See?

You are a very smart pixie after all."

She grinned and obviously felt better. "Well, if that's what you're going to do, we need to get started and you will need some help."

"You can help make a magic sword?"

I remembered from my reading that pixie magic was considered a "wild" form of the arcane disciplines and its effectiveness entirely dependent on the force of will of the caster. Nia was examining the blade from every angle seriously; finally, she looked up and back to me. "With the two of us, we shall make a blade the world has never seen!"

And with that, we set to work. I hammered and folded as Nia helped to set the starlode in place so it was folded into the blade correctly. Again, I dropped into the focused rhythm that ate up the hours. It was starting to get dark when we were finally done with the blade and it was perfect! But the hilt and guard would have to wait until tomorrow. After cleaning up, an exhausted pixie and I went home to get dinner ready.

"So this is where you live? It's huge, I'm never going to find my way out. I'll be lost for months," Nia yawned as she sat perched on my shoulder.

"It's really not that big, it only has nine rooms. Just be glad we don't live in one of the towers."

"Towers? What towers, and who is this 'we'? Do you already live with the warrior princess?"

I pointed to the six towers of Xarparion. "Those towers. The big one in the middle is called Central and the others are named by what type of magic they teach in them."

"Those are buildings? I thought they were mountains. Ok, I'm glad you live in a huge house and not the mountains."

"And as for who I live with, this is my primus' house and I'm her apprentice. Since we're the only Enchanters at Xarparion, we don't get our own tower."

"Well, that's not fair; you should have your own tower just like all the other colors."

"Yeah, but they don't see us as real wizards, so we don't get a lot of respect. In fact, the only ones who will even talk to us are the Earth Tower folks."

She slumped and looked sad. "Mr. Alex, it's like I was at home."

"Don't worry, I like it like this. If this place was any bigger, I wouldn't be able to keep it clean. Now enough moping! We have to get dinner ready, Rosa is on her way, and I can feel that she's hungry."

She brightened up quickly at the thought of food. Now that I think about it, good food seems to make all the women in my life happy. Nia was rather useful in the kitchen and stronger than she looked; she could carry and fly with everything but the flour.

"You're a real help in the kitchen, do you do a lot of cooking?" She flew over with the last egg I needed for dinner and cracked it open into the mixing bowl.

"No, I never did the cooking at home. Pixies don't actually cook. Fire isn't something 'good respectable pixies' use much. That's another reason I was an outcast, I like flame...at least when it isn't getting me into trouble."

"So what do you do for food?"

"We just eat things raw mostly. But I like cooked foods better so sometimes I would sneak into a human house and steal a little. The problem is that when a pixie takes food, they are supposed to do a service to pay for it. Like shine the shoes or something like that. One time I tried to rid a farmer's cottage of ants and accidently turned their pigs into aardvarks. Ever try to make bacon from an aardvark? Pretty soon I was unwelcome everywhere and I went hungry a lot.

"Well, you don't have to do that anymore, you will be eating with us now."

She sat down next to the now empty mixing bowl and pulled her legs to her chest. "I think I will like that." She looked up shyly and smiled at me. Then suddenly her head turned to the door. "Someone is coming!"

"Calm down, it's just our primus."

The door flew open as Rosa charged in with a big grin on her face. She ran over to the frightened Nia, who was now cowering in the mixing bowl.

"Hello, Nia, and welcome to our home!"

Nia was holding the mixing spoon and shakily pointing it at Rosa like a lance, ready to defend herself from the evil monster. "Mr. Alex? Who is the giant elf lady?"

"My name is Primus Rosa, I'm Alex's teacher. And I must say that you look rather tasty covered in breading!"

"Breading?" She looked down at herself and realized that when she jumped into the bowl, she got herself coated in the extra batter that was stuck to the sides of the bowl. She was almost completely covered, and then a large glop fell from the spoon and landed on her head.

"No! Mr. Alex, don't let her eat me! I don't want to be a pixie puff pastry!"

Both Rosa and I were having a hard time trying to breathe from laughter. I still laugh to myself when I picture her in the bowl, covered in batter.

"I'm not going to eat you, Nia, I promise," Rosa crooned.

"Well, ok, then." She put the spoon down and tried wiping some of the batter off her face. She must have gotten some in her mouth because soon she was eating the rest that was left in the bowl. When she was done with her "pre-clean," she looked back up at us with a smile, rather proud of herself. I readied some warm water in a basin, knowing someone was now going to need a bath.

"Well, now that you made a complete mess of yourself, we need to get you cleaned up."

She tried to use her wings but found that she couldn't due to the large amount of batter still stuck to them. "I can't fly!" Before she could do anything about it, I gently picked her up and dropped her with a plop into the warm water I had ready in the dish basin. "Hey, don't put me in here. I am not a dirty dish you know!"

"Yes, but you were just in one, so this seemed appropriate."

Rosa put a hand on my shoulder. "I'll take care of this, she may be six inches tall, but she is still a woman." She turned back to

Nia, still in the bowl, with an evil grin on her face. "We will have lots of fun; I'll get you cleaned up, we'll make dresses, and do each other's hair, paint our nails, and make a pie…"

"Yeah, hair and nails and…wait, what pie? Mr. Alex, please don't leave me with her!"

"Have fun you two! Just don't take so long that dinner gets burnt." I walked out before Nia could protest anymore. I sat down in the reading room with one of the enchanting textbooks and tried to relax a bit. Generally, that would work, but I could still hear shrieks and yells coming from both Rosa and Nia. After fifteen minutes, I had to set down my book because dinner needed to be turned. I knocked on the door to the kitchen.

"Rosa, is it safe to come in for a second? I need to turn over dinner."

"One second, sweetie." I heard a loud slam from the other side of the door. "Ok, now it's safe to come in."

I opened the door and found that Rosa was sitting on an overturned pot. I could hear faint tapping coming from the inside along with what I would assume was yelling.

"Just taking a quick rest from all the hair combing," Rosa said innocently.

"Uh-huh." After seeing to dinner, I returned to my chair and book for the remaining time until it was done. There was a lot less yelling this time around. With dinner almost done, I went back to the kitchen. As I opened the door, I was greeted with something red flying straight into my face.

"Mr. Alex! Look at the pretty dress Rosa made for me!" Sure

enough, she was wearing a new red dress. It only had one shoulder strap and went down to her knees. The dress itself was made from what looked like silk with a flower pattern stitched into it. Nia, herself, also got a makeover. Her hair was straightened and cut to shoulder length and all the caked-on batter was gone, too.

"You look beautiful. I take it she used magic on the dress?" She nodded. "Well, you look great, but I'm afraid that you will have to ask her for any new ones, I'm not so good with dresses."

"Don't worry about it, I have tons of ideas," Rosa giggled. "All those years wasted trying to get Maya into one and failing. Now, at least, I will have someone I can make dresses for, even if they're super extra small petite ones."

"Well, dinner's ready, so let's eat."

Rosa and I sat down at our regular spots, but Nia just hovered where she was. I patted a spot on the table.

"Well, come on, Nia, you can eat with us, you know."

"You really want me to eat with you guys? No one's ever actually voluntarily shared a meal with me."

Rosa reached into her bag and pulled out a mini table and chair, complete with plates and silverware, all made for someone of Nia's size.

"If we didn't want you here, would I have made all this for you?"

She set the tiny table up and motioned for Nia to try it out. As the small pixie tested her new furniture, tears began to fall. "My own people shunned me, but you two have given me more than I have ever even hoped to have at home. You don't hate me, you even made me nice things and a dress and you're sharing your meal with me. I don't deserve your kindness, but I will do my best to repay it."

I poured us all juice and passed them out. "We already talked it over; you're staying with us now."

"Talked it over? When did you do that? And how did you know my size to make this table?"

Rosa put down her spoon of potatoes to respond. "You see, Nia, my sweet apprentice and I can talk to each other in our minds over any distance. In fact, I was listening to you read your letter from the pixie king. Now enough chit-chat, let's eat. What did you make for us this evening, Alex?"

"Well, my mother called it 'pocket dinner.' Basically, it's a bunch of meats, cheeses and vegetables wrapped in dough, then breaded. You can also make small ones for a lunch or for traveling."

"What's cheese?" Nia asked.

Rosa and I looked at each other trying to hold in the laughter, and for the most part, we succeeded.

"Well, try it and find out." I served her a nice big piece - well big for her size - which she immediately attempted to eat in one bite. "Wow, slow down! You don't have to eat like Rosa." And I received a savage kick to the shins under the table.

"Sorry, if you don't eat fast back home, someone might try to take your food. I'll try to be more human lady-like."

And that's how the night went. We went about our evening lessons, with Nia there asking her own questions. She was trying her best to learn about her new home quickly and to learn as much as she could about us as well.

Morning was fast approaching and Rosa had already gone to bed. I was on my way up to my room for some much-needed sleep; tomorrow was the big day. "Um, Mr. Alex, would it be alright if I slept in your room tonight? I won't be in your way, I promise."

Then I remembered that we had never talked about Nia's sleeping arrangements. "I'm sorry; we forgot to get a room ready for you. You can stay in my room until we make a place for you, but I'm afraid we haven't made a bed yet either."

She flew into my room and landed on the windowsill. "That's alright, I think I'll just sleep right here. It's wood like my hole back home, and I can see the stars from here. Don't worry about me."

We both soon fell asleep, but I couldn't stay asleep. I didn't feel right just leaving her on the windowsill without even a blanket. I looked over to where she was and in the moonlight, I could see that she was asleep but was shivering. I quietly got out of bed and went downstairs. I found a small pillow to use as a bed and some cloth from the lab as a blanket. After some quick enchanting to make them both soft and warm, I headed back to my room. I carefully picked the chilly pixie up and placed her softly on the pillow. It may have been a small pillow, but it was still twice her size. Then I wrapped her in the blanket, careful not to hurt her wings. Confident that my work was done, I went back to my bed and was quickly asleep.

Chapter 9

Alex

The morning of the dance came around, and I could feel that today was going to be a fantastic day. I rolled out of bed and got dressed in my leather sparring armor. Looking over at Nia, I found that she was still fast asleep and tangled up in the blanket I made. I went over to her and tried to get her free, but she was bound up pretty good.

"Nia, it's time to get up. Come on, girl, we have a lot of work to do today."

Her eyes opened and she looked up at me with a smile. "I had the most incredible dream. I was so cold up here, but then you brought me something that kept me warm."

"Not a dream, I'm afraid."

Now realizing where she was, "Hey, when did I get this? It's so warm and soft; also I can't move."

I laughed a little and grabbed one of the exposed corners of the blanket and lifted it into the air, dropping Nia comically on her pillow.

"So much for asking for a few more minutes. So, Mr. Alex, what are we doing today?"

"Well, for starters, we're going to make breakfast and then I'm going to class. You're free to come if you would like."

She smiled, showing all her rather pointy teeth. "Yes, I think I will. Now, let's eat."

The morning went by quickly. Nia was a big help in the kitchen again so the cooking was easy. Rosa spent her time thinking of more dresses to make for her; I was starting to think that she was having too much fun with this. A short while later we were on our way to the training grounds.

"Now, Nia, I need you to be good for my teacher and try not to get on her nerves."

"Don't worry; I'll be a good pixie."

We arrived at the private training ground and Maya was already waiting in her usual spot. She was leaning against a post with her arms crossed and looked unhappy with me.

"You're late, Alex."

"Sorry about that, someone had a hard time getting out of bed this morning."

Nia peeked over my shoulder from where she was hiding. "Um, hi." She climbed into full view on my shoulder to get a good look at Maya. "Master, is she the warrior princess?"

I nodded. Nia flew up to Maya and did a few loops around her to get a better look. "Wow, Master, you picked well, she's gorgeous! Long curly silver hair, perfect pointed ears and beautiful skin! And that's a figure that would make a wood nymph jealous!"

"Ahem!" I interrupted. "I'm sorry, Maya. She gets like that when she's excited."

Maya cupped her hands together; Nia landed on her palms and looked up at Maya.

"It's fine, I'll take most of what she said as a compliment. But for now, you must tell me how you got yourself a pixie. I was told that there is only a handful left in the world."

"Well, it's more like they found me, actually."

"Then you definitely have to tell me." Maya tapped her foot impatiently and gave me a look that said she was going to hurt me if I didn't talk fast. Wow, some girls are testy until they get that first sword battle behind them in the morning! "Nia, this is your story, I'll let you tell it."

So she did. The three of us sat down in the shade as the pixie retold her story. Maya loosened up and calmly asked some questions, too. A few hours passed, Nia was done with the original story long ago, but Maya wanted to know more about pixie life. To be honest, I couldn't really understand what they were talking about. Then I realized they were talking in elfish. Now I'm pretty good at the elfish language, but they were just a little fast for me to translate everything; it had been seven years since we moved from our old village.

What I did pick up was that Nia really isn't that old. From what I could tell, she's barely two. She was also an outcast, due to her lack of control over her magic, and that she was abandoned by her parents. I thought about that for a bit; many of us here have a similar story to tell. It makes you feel grateful for the loved ones you still have. When they finished talking, Nia looked much happier and she even flew in close and gave Maya a hug and a kiss.

"So, Alex, you're not going to be late tonight are you?" Maya rose to her feet and grabbed my hand, pulling me up firmly with a coy wink.

"No, of course not!"

"Good, I'll see you at the festival. Don't worry about finding me, I'll find you first, I promise. And Nia, have a good day and keep Alex out of trouble for me." She favored me with a shy smile and slipped away. I didn't realize I was staring after her until Nia finally flew up and rapped me smartly on the nose.

"Wow, you got yourself a great girl there. Mind you, if you mess up, she will kill you. I mean it, dead, as in burnt-to-a-crisp dead."

"I know and I don't have any plans to do that."

"Good, because I don't think I could stop her. Don't think I'd try either."

"Some bodyguard! Come on, let's go eat."

Lunch went very well. Lin and Julia absolutely loved Nia, even invited her to visit the druid grove whenever she wanted. I've never even been invited there, although I'm told it's just a bunch of glowing trees, you know, underground. How cool could that possibly be? Anyways, with lunch over, we headed back to the forge to put the hilt and guard on Maya's new sword.

By the end of the day, we were finally finished. The blade was sharp, the guard was on, and the wrapping was perfection. We were both very pleased with the way things turned out. Now it was time to put our work to the test and let Darroth take a look at it. We found him in his office going over more paperwork.

"Arggg, I hate paperwork! You would think that a smith wouldn't have a need for it, but you can't order anything in this damned academy without it. So what can I do for you and your lovely assistant?"

Nia preened a bit with the praise, she still hadn't quite gotten used to being treated nicely by others yet. I shook my head and smiled before answering.

"Well, Darroth, we would like you to look over the blade we made for Maya, if you don't mind."

"Certainly, my boy, I would be happy to. In fact, I was looking forward to seeing what you made. I even mostly refrained from peeking when you were making it. So hurry up now, let's see it." He drew a monocle from his vest pocket and put it in his right eye, squinting just enough to hold it in place.

I unwrapped the sword carefully from its protective cloth and held it out for him to see. He was speechless for many minutes, checking the length of the blade with a measuring string and examining the thirty-degree grind. He glanced up at me, "Finished weight?"

"Two and one-third pounds as she sits now," I supplied, and he grunted appraisingly.

After studying the blade still in my hand, he reached for the hilt, but I pulled it away before he could touch it.

"Sorry, Darroth, I wouldn't do that if I were you. You see, I made this blade for Maya, and only Maya, and it knows it, so if anyone else picks it up, they will get a nasty burn."

He looked rather confused. "If you can't touch it, then how you did survive making it?"

"Well, when I was still forming the blade, we had an understanding with each other. I knew what I was doing and she allowed me to continue until I was finished and her requirements were met."

"You're saying that it can think? That it can talk?"

"She," I emphasized, "can think, yes. As for talk, it's more like talk in your head."

"And so 'she' has her own view of what she should be?" Darroth asked incredulously.

"Yes, and after tonight, she will have a name."

"Meaning?"

"Meaning that the blade won't be complete until Maya holds it for the first time."

"You know, with your skills, I would have thought your masterpiece would be more artistic. This just looks like a standard sword; mind you, one of quality that I've never even thought possible from someone of your years, but still normal in appearance."

"Tomorrow, ask Maya to show it to you. I promise it won't be normal."

I then rewrapped the sword and headed home. I had a party to get ready for and there was no way I was going to be late!

"Ow, Rosa, that's too tight!"

She had me in some kind of formal wear that was popular for nobility from Maya's homeland. It was a cross between what would generally be called a dress shirt and light armor. I'm told that the reason for that is often there would be duels at these kinds of events in her land and the nobles would need to wear something both stylish and functional.

I conceded that the shirt could possibly protect you against a nasty cat scratch, but it was just too thin and form-fitting to stop any kind of a decent blade. It was rather slimming and didn't hinder my movement in any way, so I didn't fight wearing it too much; especially after catching Rosa's thought that Maya would adore it. It came with long pants made from some material I didn't recognize. And, of course, everything but the shoes was white.

"Oh, quit being a baby. Now hold still while I fix your hair." Finished with my hair, she stepped back to get a final look. "You look wonderful. I know she will love the shirt, it shows off every one of your big muscles." She wiped away a tear that was forming. "I can't believe that I'm doing this, you two are like my children. I'm so proud of both of you."

I walked over and gave her a hug. She seemed surprised at first but soon was hugging me back.

"I should get going, I still have to help Maya. I promise I won't keep her too long. Oh, and before I forget, here take this." She handed me a beautiful pelt pouch. "It's a small bag of dimensions; you know, so you don't have to carry her sword in plain sight until its time. Gotta keep it as a surprise. And don't worry about Nia; I'll have her helping me."

"Thanks, Rosa, you're the best."

"I know," she sniffed.

The festival looked like some other planet. There were lights all over the place, some mundane and some magical, row after row of fancy cloth-covered tables, and booths selling all manner of things from candy to perfumes to puppets. Just from where I was standing, I could see five stages for performers. Jugglers, fire-eaters, knife throwers, tightrope walkers, and a mind-reading act were already attracting large crowds. Dozens of food stands were all expertly positioned to make a sort of trail through the outbuildings of Xarparion and the delicious scent of popped corn wafted on a warm evening breeze. I couldn't believe I walked across this same field on a daily basis, and to see it transformed into a spectacle of this magnitude was numbing. Judging from the crowd, almost everyone in Xarparion must have been there. I tried to see if I could spot anyone I knew, but that could take all night. So I decided to find a place to sit by the entrance and hoped to see Maya's arrival. Rosa had steadfastly refused to tell me anything about the dress she crafted, so I didn't even know what color to look for.

After a few minutes, I spotted Julia and Lin and waved them over. They both looked great; they were wearing matching green dresses with the druid symbol of a tree used as a pattern around the hem. They also had what looked like living white orchids growing out of their manicured hairstyles, Julia's a long mass of curly brown, and Lin's a shorter, straight blonde style. When they got close, they each did an exaggerated spin, letting their dresses fan out completely. Julia was very excited and asked the question first.

"So what do you think?" Girls will always ask that.

"I think you both look very lovely tonight and shouldn't have any trouble getting a guy if you want one."

"Thank you!" Unable to contain her excitement, Julia started jumping about. "Tonight is going to be so much fun!"

Lin eyed me up and down. "You know, you look pretty fine yourself. So when does the lucky mystery lady get here? And there better be one or you're a dead man!"

Before I could answer, a voice from behind us responded, "Oh, there's a lady, and I would have to say that she is very lucky indeed."

I turned around and found the most beautiful thing I've ever seen. There was Maya in a long and slender silver silk dress. The dress hugged her body perfectly and showed off everything that counted. Her hair was let down and combed straight with a little lock in front of her left eye. She also had a white flower in her hair and lipstick to match. She was also smiling shyly, which was the most beautiful thing about her.

"I...you...just, wow."

She blushed and looked at the ground. "You like it?"

"You're beautiful, absolutely beautiful."

She looked back up at me with a smile and even more blush. "I'm glad. You look very handsome, and I really like the shirt."

Reminding me that they were there, Lin and Julia walked closer to us with jaws dropped.

"You're the girl he's going with? Alex, where did you find this goddess and why have you been keeping her a secret?"

Maya chuckled nervously, but I laughed. "I didn't keep her a secret; this is my combat instructor."

"Your what? She can't be, she's way too pretty."

Maya smiled graciously, "My name's Maya. It's nice to finally meet you two." She leaned down and drew both of them into a brief hug. "Julia, Alex is so proud of your progress here. He has told me a lot about both of you."

This seemed to finally jog Julia from her trance, and she gave me a conspiratorial wink. "Come on, Lin, let the lovely lady have fun with Alex. We have a whole festival to see!" Julia pulled Lin away by the arm. Lin still had a hard time believing what she was seeing, even as she was being dragged off.

"But, but how? Three days ago he hadn't even asked her yet," was the last thing we heard from her as they skipped out of range.

With them finally gone, I turned back to Maya. "You look...well, I will be the envy of every man at the dance tonight!"

"Good, because you're never going to get me in a dress again." Ha, we will see. "And I'm pretty sure these shoes are going to kill me before the night is over."

"By the way, they didn't seem to notice that you're a dark elf."

"Rosa enchanted this dress to make me look as people expect me to appear, so if they expect to see a human girl, they see one. And when I am on the arm of the handsomest man at the party, they expect to see a beautiful woman, so it enhances that effect, too."

"Well, then I'm honored that I get to see the real you. Now let's go have some fun. I'm sure you must be hungry, and I smell something fantastic."

We took off into the evening, trying food and visiting shops, even catching a juggling show. But as the night wore on, I noticed that Maya was looking a little uncomfortable.

"What's wrong, are the shoes still bothering you?"

"All these people in one place, I guess I'm not used to it. All the stares and attention, people coming up to me who wouldn't give me a second glance in my trainer's outfit. I feel out of place and a little lost here."

I didn't say anything, just reached out and held her hand as we walked. She smiled and didn't say anything or try to pull away. We stayed like that for a long time, and the uneasy feelings she was having seemed to have gone away as well.

About an hour later, it was announced that it was time for the guys to present their gifts to their girls. I led Maya to a more private location behind some pine trees as I assumed it would be bad form to pull a sword out in the middle of a festival.

"What's going on?"

"One of the main events of this festival is where the men make a gift for their ladies. After the gifts are presented, the girls will often have a contest to see who has the best gift. But the rules say that you must make it yourself, you can't just buy one."

She looked down at the ground. "Oh, I see."

"Would you like to see your gift?"

She looked up at me in surprise. "You made me a gift?"

"Of course I did!"

"But why? I'm not a human girl, so why did you make one for me?"

"Because you're wonderful and you deserve one."

She nodded eagerly, and I opened the dimensional pouch and drew out the still wrapped sword. She looked at it oddly for a second before unwrapping it. Once the hilt was exposed, she stopped as if frozen.

"You made me a sword?" she gasped shakily.

"Before you say anything, please hold it for a second, please."

Breathlessly, she gripped the hilt. Once firmly in her hand, the wrappings fell away and the blade was exposed to the mild night air. The metal started to glow, the edges shimmering and distorting the view like heat off a winter campfire.

"Alex, I can hear a voice in my head, she's so calm and peaceful."

"Maya, close your eyes and listen to her, she will guide you." She brought the sword into an upright position, leaning the flat of the blade against her forehead and calmly drew her eyelids closed. A range of expressions crossed her beautiful face, with the most common being wonder and awe. For a frozen minute, nothing happened, and then suddenly she thrust it out into the night sky above her head.

"Winya Coia." When she spoke the words, the blade flared white hot in color, and I had to look away. Once the light faded, I turned back and her blade was now complete. Maya was turning it over and over, admiring the lines of the weapon and its new appearance. The blade was now sparkling polished silver instead of the gray it was, with a sharp accent line of pure white running the length of the blade down the fuller. The guard was now also white and curved slightly upwards, and the pommel featured a large emerald the same color as Maya's eyes. The leather windings of the hilt matched the color of her skin. But the most noticeable thing was the words "Winya Coia," meaning "new life" etched into the blade; the words seemed to glow and pulse.

"Maya, your gift is complete; I hope you like it."

She stared blankly at the blade in her hand, finally shaking her head and whispered something in elfish that I didn't catch as a tear started to run down her cheek.

"She's beautiful, Alex! Winya feels like a part of me already. I don't know how to explain it."

"Then I will. This sword is now a part of you, she is you. She is also a living and thinking entity. The voice you heard? That's your sword, like a baby's first words...and now that you gave her a name, she has gained her personality. No one else can ever use her, can't even touch her, only you. She will serve you faithfully for the rest of time."

She was full out crying now, but they were tears of happiness. "Thank you, Alex. She's perfect and so beautiful. I can't wait to try her out in the ring, although she belongs in the hand of a duchess or queen rather than a dirt-poor weapons instructor."

"You know, there's a contest you could enter to show her off if you would like."

She drew a finger under each eye to wipe away the tears and mustered a smile. "No, I think just us seeing her will be fine." She stroked the blade a bit, looking over everything. "She's perfect, but I think she should be put back before someone sees her. Thank you!"

She gently wrapped her sword back in the fabric and slipped it back into the pouch.

"I'm glad you like her," I whispered, leaning into her ear as we walked out and rejoined the celebration. Maya was seemingly lost in thought, but she clung to my arm like a lifeline to a drowning man.

Close to midnight, I drew her to the dance area that was in epic full swing. Students, staff and teachers, all in their finest apparel, were having a great time. I even saw Lin and Julia out on the floor, spinning in dizzying circles to make their dresses poof out. The dance floor was decorated with streamers that hung from the sky, and magically gyrated in lockstep to the melody. The music was pretty exotic by Foalshead standards, with lofty, lilting swirls of pipes, strings, and soft drums that seemingly twirled the energetic dancers around like puppets on gossamer strings. I stopped and stared for a moment, unsure if Rosa's last minute dance instructions had prepared me adequately to enter this fray. But it was now or never.

Without warning, I veered into the dance crowd, pulling Maya with me. I quickly turned to face her and formally bowed as Rosa had taught me.

"My lady, may I have this dance?"

"Alex, what are you doing? I don't know how to dance!" She looked around in genuine panic.

"Don't worry, just follow my lead. It's not unlike the patterned footwork that you teach every day." I placed one hand in hers, and wrapped the other around the small of her back, which was bare to the waist, save for some thin straps. At my touch, she took a ragged breath and stared up at me with a startled expression in those emerald eyes. By mutual consent, we began to move with the smoky backbeat of the music, tentative at first, with the voice in my head shouting, *"Watch her toes...watch her toes!"* Of course, I didn't, leaving the poor toes to fend for themselves. I was already lost in her now trusting gaze and the oh-so-smooth silky skin where my hand touched her back. Her clean woodsy fragrance affected me far more than the hundreds of stray perfumes that had assaulted my nose throughout the evening.

She must have read my thoughts as she smiled and was sneaking looks at the other dancers. Quickly she started to loosen up and have fun. I snickered at the thought of how terrified she had been a few minutes before, and now she looked like she was ready to try some of their moves, and even surpass them. What can I say? The girl has a competitive streak. A few more dances and we were both enjoying the event as it was meant to be enjoyed.

She and I completed the dance, and then the music changed flavors and spun way down, allowing some dancers to depart and even more to jump in. Finally, a slow dance! I pulled her much, much closer.

"What are you doing?" she whispered, looking a bit scandalized.

I switched to the elf language and dialect that I had grown up with in my old village and answered. It had been seven years since I've used it on a daily basis, so I hoped I still remembered. "This song is a slow dance, and this is how it's done...I think you'll enjoy it." The words had come back to me like a long-ignored faithful hound, and the syllables rolled in the correct sequence and tone.

She stiffened and leaned her head back away from my embrace, her expression bordering on exasperation. "You know the language of my people," she returned in the same tongue.

I nodded and gently placed her head back on my shoulder. "I picked up a little in my youth." She hugged me and then continued in the same dialect, but avoiding my eyes and talked into my shoulder instead.

"Alex, what if I wake up tomorrow and find out this was all a dream...you...me...us? I don't know how much of all this to trust. It's like my senses have abandoned me and I'm walking deaf and blind here."

"Maya, this is no dream and tomorrow will a good day, and the day after that, and the day after that. I promise."

She shifted and sighed ever so slightly as if savoring that thought as we moved slowly to the beat of the music. "I think I could get used to this dancing thing."

"I never gave it a lot of thought until tonight here with you. Now it's my new favorite pastime, but I needed the right dance partner."

Surprisingly, that resulted in a throaty growl under her breath, and I felt her hands tighten up, and her nails dig in slightly. "I swear you are trying to drive me insane, Alex Martin! I am so going to kick your butt on the training field tomorrow, and the day after that, and the..."

"What did I do to upset you, my lady?" I smirked innocently.

She looked up at me, finally tracking me with those big eyes. When she replied, it was in a soft, dangerous tone. "Am I your lady? What is all this? The party, the dancing, the touching, Winya Coia, your constant smelling of my hair, about the only thing you haven't done is..."

I drew her back in close and let the music and soft lights wash over us. The dance floor was crowded, but as we were the only two speaking elfish, it really seemed we were in our own little world. Finally, Maya seemed to mentally put away her anger and frustration and sighed fatalistically. She took a deep cleansing breath. "You know, Alex, there is one very important thing that I've been trying to tell you. For my people, if a man gives a woman a gift, it's a sign of love. But if that gift is their personal weapon then…well, damn it, it shows a desire to court her, dancing like this, this close, means much the same. Now, I understand if you weren't intentionally trying to…"

"I know."

"You know?" Maya stopped abruptly and put both strong arms on my shoulders and pinned me with a look that took no prisoners. "What do you mean, you know?"

"I mean, I would be extremely honored and happy to court you, Maya, if you will have me."

Her eyes widened, and I had to catch her as it looked as if she was going to wobble off her high shoes. She quickly regained her balance, and with an iron firm hand, dragged me off the dance floor to a quiet area behind a wine stand. After a quick glance to assure we were alone, she put her hands on both sides of my head and pulled me down to meet her searching eyes, her chest heaving with deep emotions.

"Do you really mean that? Dark elves have very strict courting customs. We would have to get permission from both our fathers and sometimes there's even worthiness testing and bloodshed involved. My father can be…daunting. Tell me do you really want to pursue a dark elf girl, even knowing that?"

"Yes, more than anything."

She stared at me in confusion for a second, a wide range of emotions crossing her lovely face, happiness, self-doubt, relief, fear, and sorrow all present. Finally, she managed to summon up speech and it came out husky and filled with wonder.

"You're a brave fool, Alex Martin. But it so happens I have a serious weakness for brave fools this week." She nestled closer to me and whispered, "I accept your offer of courtship."

I really wanted to kiss her. I thought that now would be the proper time, so I sought out those lips that I had been dreaming of all evening. Maya stiffened at first, but soon relaxed. As we were both inexperienced, it took us a little while to get the hang of it. But soon, we got a feel for one another and Maya started to get a bit more eager. I don't know how much time passed for us and I really didn't care, her lips were so soft.

"By the gods, breathe, you two!"

We pulled away from each other and found Lin standing there with her hands over Julia's eyes. A wave of embarrassment washed over both of us.

"You two do know that this is a public dance, right? I swear, if I didn't stop you, poor Jules here would have been scarred for life!"

"Sorry, Lin," I explained, switching back to the common spoken word of Xarparion.

"Nah, I'm just messing with you guys. Actually, we thought it wouldn't take nearly this long for you two to start kissing."

Maya blushed and turned away. "Alex, it's late, I think we should head back now."

I shot a playful scowl at both Lin and Julia before taking Maya's arm and leading her toward the exit. We walked silently almost all the way back to the Enchanters Hall, lost in our private thoughts. The stars in the sky above us almost seemed to be winking in approval as I contemplated the cosmos. But no astral light show came close in beauty to the woman walking next to me. I took a deep breath, savoring the moment. Outside the door, Maya swiveled and faced me.

"I had a wonderful time tonight, Alex - ok, a little more than wonderful," she whispered with a shy smile and caressed my ears slightly with her hand. I mused over her comment for a few seconds and finally shook my head, nothing I could say would be adequate. I lost myself in her deep emerald eyes until she broke off with a sigh and practicality intruded. "We can't stand out here all night Alex."

"You don't need to go. Rosa said she won't be back 'til morning so you can have her bed. It's probably a lot more comfortable than yours would be."

"You have a point, and I do have to return this dress and pick up my own clothes. Wait, do you think Rosa knows about us, you know, during the dance?"

"I didn't think of that. Yeah, she knows all right, no way she wouldn't."

Maya grinned. "Well, in that case, we might as well make this as scandalous as we can."

I opened the door and held it for her. She ran in and sat down in one of the broad chairs in the reading room and took off her shoes. I put some wood on the embers and got the fire going again. Turning back to her, she was trying to massage her own feet.

"Grrr! The most uncomfortable shoes ever made! Mean, spiteful little monsters, they are."

"Here, let me."

I sat down on the small bench in front of her and started to massage her feet and ankles. She closed her eyes and just enjoyed the sensation.

"Mmm, that feels good." After a few minutes and an equal number of yawns, she was feeling much better. "Why don't you come and sit here with me?"

So I did. We sat in that chair for a while, just watching the fire and enjoying the closeness. Maya leaned against me but ended up with my elbow in her back. "This isn't going to work." She pulled me down to the floor and had me rest my back against the chair. She then sat down in front of me and leaned back so she was resting on my chest. "Much better, I think I could learn to love this treatment," she relaxed with a very contented sigh.

"Well, that's good because I intend to…" My next words were forever lost to posterity as I was interrupted by gentle rhythmic breathing coming from the dark elf leaning up against me. At least, she had fallen asleep with a smile on her face. I took one more indulgent whiff of her hair, knew that (at least for the moment) all was right in the world, and drifted off to happy dreams myself.

Chapter 10

Alex

When I woke up, we were still where we were last night, dawn hadn't quite broken, and the fire was down to mere embers. Maya was still asleep in my arms, using me as a pillow. And I loved it, she looked so beautiful there.

I stroked her hair a little and brushed across her ears. When I touched them, she stirred and without opening her eyes, purred, "Hello, handsome."

"Hello, beautiful."

"Could you please stop stroking my ears now?" she asked, finally looking up at me.

I stopped. "Does it hurt?"

She blushed and looked away. "No, quite the opposite. It's extremely…motivating, and I'm just not ready for that yet."

"Oh, sorry."

She smiled and stretched up, kissing me on the cheek. "Don't worry; I'll let you touch them someday soon."

"Oh, that would be fun to watch!" That was Rosa's voice, uh-oh.

We looked behind us with fear in our hearts. And there she was, reclined crossways in the chair that we were leaning on. She was smiling and leaning her head down to our level.

"I'm so proud of you two! I knew you would be perfect for each other the first time you met, but I wasn't expecting it to happen so fast."

Maya and I looked at each other with pained expressions. "I think I'm going to die now," I winced.

"Quick, hand me my sword, I would like this to end, as well."

"You two are so funny, but I just love it!" She planted wet kisses on each of us. "When I watched you lovebirds dancing, I thought that Maya might finally have opened up to someone, but the proposal and the kissing were completely unexpected."

Maya was getting more embarrassed by the second. "Well, within the customs of my people, his actions meant the desire to court me."

Rosa chuckled, a wicked light in her eyes. "Yes but you didn't have to accept so quickly."

"I know, but with all the time we have spent together, I already know what type of man he really is. Besides, he reminded me of the way my father courted my mother."

We both looked at her, trying to urge her to tell the story, and she seemed quite happy to tell us. She took a deep breath and started in.

"When my father was a young warrior, he fell deeply in love with a spear maiden by the name of Renalla, daughter of Mingt, a shaman of a nearby friendly village." Ok, now I have definitely heard that name before, but from where? She didn't give me time to think as she continued her story. "Renalla was young, smart, very beautiful and already an accomplished hunter; she was the absolute pride of her village."

"My father was beyond smitten, but even at that headstrong

age, he was already very wise. He knew that if he were to have any chance of courting the fair Renalla, he would have to somehow prove that the depth of his intentions was far and above any other suitor. He needed to make a statement, and that statement would be to present her with a courting weapon like no other."

"As my people are wood folk and not great workers of iron, my father first sought out a dwarf forge master who agreed to fashion a spearhead if, and only if, my father agreed to chop enough wood to fill the huge barn that fed the forge. For a full month, my father labored in the forest, removing dead and dying wood, chopping it into the proper size, and dragging it back to the storehouse. Over time, his hands grew calloused and his back strong, but his determination never faltered." Rosa sighed happily, getting into the story.

"Despite having little to no affection for dark elves, the dwarf was impressed with my father's efforts, and the two even became good friends. The dwarf gifted my father with some of his carefully hoarded special metals to make the spear point truly unique. And by the end of the month, the weapon was ready for the final tempering. My father removed his belt knife and cut deeply into his own wrists. He still has the scars - I've seen them. And he bade the dwarf to do the final quench of the blade with his own blood. Whether it was the dark elf blood, stray magic, or the result of the smith's skill, the spearhead forever took on a blood red hue and was imbued with incredible sharpness and durability. The two agreed to call it 'Gwiwence' or 'Huntress' in the dwarf's language. To this day, it is still known by that name."

"When father presented the spear to Renalla, now complete with a beautiful white oak shaft, Renalla said she felt it sing to her and the song was a ballad of love written in her heart by my father.

From that day forward, Renalla would have no eyes for any but him, and she became his wife and my mother."

She turned to Rosa. "Rosa, I grew up with the story of Gwiwence and I always believed it was the height of romantic dreams that all girls have in their youth. There was no greater gift in any elf village that I have heard of, and I have held her many times and felt her magic. But last evening, Alex gave me Winya...and she surpasses my mother's treasure in every way! When I held her for the first time, she spoke to me. As clearly as I hear you now, we exchanged thoughts, emotions, and even dreams. Instantly, she was the sister I always wished for, a life friend, confidant, and protector, guardian of my soul. And do you know what she told me, Rosa? She said a maker like Alex can't hide anything from his creations, the process is too personal, too consuming for deception. His very being has a connection to Winya nearly as deep as my own. She knows him well, and when Alex made his proposal, do you know what she said?"

Maya shifted around and grasped both of my hands as she looked romantically into my eyes. "She said, 'Meh...you could do worse!'" Maya grinned and launched herself at me to plant a quick kiss before jumping to her feet in an instant and running away cackling down the hall.

She called back over her shoulder, "Yes, Rosa, it was a very quick decision to accept Alex's courtship but, somehow, I think it was the right one!" We all laughed a bit before Maya came back down the hall, and her eyes fell on something behind me. "By the gods, Rosa! What did you do to poor Nia?"

I looked behind me and all I could see were Nia's feet sticking out of a goblet. I quickly got up and checked that she was alright. Thankfully, it looked like she drank almost everything in the goblet so she didn't drown in wine, but she was out cold.

"Rosa, how could you?"

"What? She only had one."

"Yeah, but its volume is four times her size!"

"She will be fine. Now I'm going to bed before the wine really hits me."

"What do you mean? How late were you two up?"

She started for the stairs. "Oh, we just stopped drinking when you two woke up." Then she was off to bed. Looking around, I saw five empty wine bottles around the chair.

"She is going to have such a hangover."

Maya snickered, "Well, I best be going. It looks like you will have two patients to care for today, so no practice. Besides, I would like to get out of this dress and into some real clothing."

"Just promise me you won't destroy it once you get it off. You do look wonderful in it."

She smiled coyly. "I won't shred it if the next time I am in a dress, we can dance together again."

"The next time you're wearing a dress, I'm not letting that chance slip by."

"Fine, then how about this; someday you make me armor to go with my beautiful blade?"

"Now, that's even better, I already have a few ideas. But speaking of your blade..." I removed my pelt pouch and handed it to her. "You should take her with you. Just promise me that you won't use her on anything until I teach you how tomorrow."

She gave me a snide look. "Do you really have to teach me how to use a sword when I'm the one who is supposed to be teaching you?"

"She's not just a sword, so yes, I do."

She looked puzzled. "I know she's sentient and I love her, but not just a sword? Show me."

I smiled and watched her remove the sword from the pouch. She held it in front of her, unsure of what to do.

"Winya, Maya seems to have doubts about your abilities, would you be so kind as to give a demonstration?" Winya quickly changed her shape and the wrappings fell to the ground revealing a small, but lethal, serrated dagger. Maya was so surprised that she almost dropped her.

"How did you do that?"

"I didn't do anything, that was all her."

Maya looked over her new dagger and gave it a few quick swipes through the air. "But why did she listen to you? I thought she would only obey me."

"And she will, but she still has her own thoughts and personality. She was just trying to prove to you her worth, show off her strength a bit. She very much wants to be your friend and especially your protector."

Maya smiled at her blade. "You don't have to prove anything to me, girl. I already know you will be with me for all time."

"Take her with you, have a talk with each other. Get to know her more."

"Thank you, Alex. This is the finest gift I have ever received, and I will never forget this night!" She kissed me on the cheek and went out the door. "Have fun with the drunks!"

"You know, you could stay and help."

"Not a chance!"

Turns out, I had several hours before I would have to deal with my patients. In that time, I finally got some bookwork done and even learned a few new tricks that might help with my upcoming problem if I could do them correctly. But I, thankfully, had some luck left because Nia was the first to regain consciousness...well, sort of.

"Ugggg, flyswatters are not nice to use on pixies!"

"Glad to see you're alive."

She clamped her arms around her head. "Oww, Mister Alex, please don't talk so loud."

"Sorry."

I had her washed up and in her bed hours ago, but recovery was apparently slow going.

"So, do you remember last night?"

She looked around the room and shook her head.

"Well, then, what do you remember?"

"I remember going to the party with Rosa and all the good food and the people."

"What else?"

"I remember something at the tavern...wait, Rosa gave me

something to drink, but it was way too big for me to even lift."

"Well, you drank it."

She looked horrified. "All of it?"

"From the looks of things, I'd say, yeah, all of it."

"I'm never going to drink again, I feel like I'm going to die!"

"Here, let's see if this will help."

I put a finger on her stomach and started one of the new enchantments that I just learned. This one was meant to speed up the body's reaction to poisons, so it should work on a hangover...I hope.

"There, you should feel better soon, just try to get some more rest, ok?"

"What did you do?"

"It was an enchantment, but enchantments on other people's bodies don't last very long so the effects will wear off soon. Try to sleep if you can."

"I will try." She nestled back down into her blanket and was asleep in seconds.

Two more hours passed before she woke up again, but this time, she was looking rather well.

"I see that you're feeling better."

She crawled out from under the covers and stretched out her arms, wings, and back.

"Yes, I'm feeling much better, thank you. I'm really sorry for doing all this to you, Master. You have been spending more time taking care of me than I have of you."

"Don't worry about it; I just hope you had fun."

"Yeah, the sad part is that I don't remember if I did."

We both laughed. "Now let's go see if Rosa is awake yet, and don't mention what I did to help you, she gets to deal with all the pain."

She giggled and agreed not to say anything. When we got to her room, Rosa was about what we expected, a sick mess. She was pale and moaning in pain with her arms around her head. One good thing was she couldn't read our minds in her present state; believe me, I tested that theory.

"Well, don't we look incredible this fine afternoon?"

She pulled the covers over her head. "Alex, please let me die in peace."

"Not going to happen. We need to get some food in you and get you up and about."

"How many did I drink?"

"Well, how many did you have before you got here?"

"I think I had five glasses of wine...I think."

"Well, how many glasses are in a bottle?"

"About five. Did I really drink an entire bottle?"

"No."

"Well, that's good."

"You drank six."

"What? Gods help me, that means this is going to get much, much worse."

I turned to Nia and she looked at me with concern in her eyes. She turned back to Rosa, who was clenching her stomach in pain. "I can't watch this."

"Neither can I."

I placed my hand on Rosa and performed the enchantment. I also used one that Rosa taught me and put her to sleep. Once she was out, I repositioned her on the bed and covered her with the blanket.

"What did you do to her, she looks happy?"

"I did the same thing I did for you, but I also put her to sleep. I hope she doesn't make a habit of this."

A few hours later, Rosa came downstairs and, as expected, was starving. After getting some food in her, she seemed to be doing alright; the worst of the hangover was gone. By now, it was getting late, so I got Rosa back into bed and used the same sleep enchantment that I had used earlier. Once done with her, I got myself and Nia into bed as well...I could use a good night's sleep.

The next day, I met up with Maya for our regular practice. But before I got there, I stopped by the forge and picked up a few of the sword "seconds" that I had practiced my enchantments on. When I got to the training grounds with my bag of loot, Maya was already there, dressed in her leather training armor. But with it being early and one of the more remote training circles, she had her training mask tied to her belt, so I could see her face. At the moment, Maya's face was locked in concentration as she practiced strikes and blocks with her new sword, getting a feel for her. As usual, Maya moved quickly, with long-practiced precision, a sight I knew I could never emulate, nor get tired of watching. Finally, she acknowledged my approach and bounded up to me like an excited child.

"Alex, she's perfect! The balance is incredible and I'm not feeling the least bit tired from swinging her and I've been doing this for a few hours now."

I slid the bag off my shoulder and dropped it on the ground with a clang and a puff of dust. "So excited you couldn't sleep, huh?"

She stuck out her tongue at me and grinned. "Well, I did as you asked and we talked a lot yesterday, but we were just so excited about this lesson that neither of us could sleep."

"I'm glad you two are doing so well together. And, Winya, I am proud that you haven't tried to teach Maya yourself. I know how tempting that would be."

Maya held the sword in front of her. "Wait, you could have taught me everything? Why didn't you? Because 'he' asked you not to? Really, you're going with that excuse?" Maya's face suddenly darkened and her green eyes widened with surprise and embarrassment. "Now, that's a low blow, and I'll thank you to keep your observations about my boyfriend's physique to yourself!" The glow of the writing on Winya pulsed with what I could only guess was mirth.

Really? Do I need more elongated dwarf comments? "Well, where would you like to begin? Or do you already have a question?"

Regaining her composure, she coyly walked closer to me. "Yes, she has already told me about how she came to be and all that.

But what I would like to know is, why a sword?"

"That's easy, because you wouldn't have been happy with a bracelet."

"Ok, fair point, but why one of Winya's unique quality? I would have been very happy with any of the beautiful swords you make."

I looked down and shuffled my feet for a few seconds. "Perhaps, but I wouldn't have. You are a special woman, so only a special sword would do."

She took in a shallow breath and looked away from me. "But this is still too much. I don't deserve a sword like her. Alex, there are kings who would ransom their entire treasuries for a weapon like Winya!"

I walked over and gently put my arm around her, moving her chin so she would look at me. "Yes, you do deserve her, and so much more. Ask her yourself, she would serve no one else. And I don't want to be with anyone else."

She kissed me quickly on the lips. "All right, enough you two. I don't want to melt right here on the ground." She wiped away a tear that was forming.

"Besides, I already made you a bracelet." I said smugly.

"You what? When?"

"Look at your wrist."

She looked down at her right wrist and found a beautiful white and silver bracelet with an emerald at the center. She stroked it a few times. "Alex, it's gorgeous...wait...where is Winya?" I pointed at the bracelet. "You're kidding me! Girl, why didn't you tell me you could do that?"

"Why do you think I never made you a sheath?"

"I was wondering about that. So why didn't you?"

"Because I thought that if you were seen with her on your hip, she would draw a lot of unwanted attention. This way, you can have a regular sword on your belt for all to see, but really have Winya when the need arises. She also won't hurt anyone who touches her as a bracelet; well, accidently, anyway."

"I can't believe you thought about all that."

"What can I say, I listen to what you say to me and, in this case, I also listened to what Winya's desires were, too."

"Hmmm, a man who listens, I'm a lucky girl. Now tell me what else she can do."

I leaned against a post. "Well, for starters, she has four different forms that she can take: sword, dagger, bracelet, and the last one we will get to later. But for now, let's work with the sword. To get her to change back, all you need to do is mentally ask her to."

Winya quickly changed back to a sword right in Maya's hand. I went over to the pack that I brought and selected a sword that Darroth had made.

"Ok, this is a regular sword, nothing magic about it. Now, I'm going to hold it out and you are going to strike it with Winya." She nodded and I held out the sword with a firm grip. With a gleam of light, Maya slashed Winya at my blade and the metal parted, the front half of the blade dropping cleanly to the ground between us.

I smiled and whistled, "Wow, you are going to be expensive to spar with from now on!"

Maya stared at the ruined sword in disbelief and dropped to her knees to cautiously pick up the sword part from the sand and examine the edge. "I cut it clean through, the edge is as smooth as glass. How is that even possible?"

"That's one of her enchantments, but don't worry; most of the time, she will behave like an ordinary sword. When you need her to, though, she can cut through almost anything that isn't magically protected. Just destroying an opponent's weapon can result in a battle being avoided."

She nodded understanding and hopped back on her feet.

"Now, as a dagger, she won't be able to do that, but she can adjust her color to match any background, making herself almost invisible. Good for when you are all dark elf stealthy."

"That could be useful, so what's the fourth form?"

"A crossbow. "

She seemed a bit confused. "You're serious - a sword that turns into a ranged weapon?" But Winya had already turned into a small hand crossbow. Within seconds, Maya was bouncing around with glee. If I had known she would have this reaction, I would have told her when she was still wearing the dress!

"One-hand crossbow bolts not included."

She calmed down to look over Winya in appreciation and to line up a few practice shots. "So I need to carry bolts with me, now?"

"Yes, and not just any bolts; they have to be my bolts."

"Why?"

"Regular bolts would explode." She looked surprised, and then I glimpsed a bad idea forming in her mind. "Explode in your face, not at the target." That idea was forgotten in a hurry.

"Not to doubt your warning, but I'm curious why would they explode? It's a hand crossbow."

"Another enchantment...even at her diminutive size, she has the force of a heavy crossbow. Normal wooden quarrels this size aren't made for that kind of stress. But don't worry; I brought some special bolts with me."

I handed Maya a small pouch of bolts that was meant to attach to her belt. The belt pouch could hold fifteen bolts, which should be more than enough for most situations. If she needed more for a full-out battle, I had some other ideas for her armor to help with that.

She quickly loaded a bolt and took aim at a twelve-inch thick training pell about fifty feet away. When she released it, there was almost no sound from Winya, but the bolt blasted right through the solid oak beam and buried itself deep into the hill behind...no getting that one back without a trained dachshund and a bag of cookies! I had a feeling that I would have to volunteer to make her new targets that could stand up to her new toys.

"Winya, you are perfect. I've always wanted a crossbow."

"Well, she will take some getting used to; she isn't like a normal crossbow in operation and she re-cocks herself automatically."

"That's great, but I guess I need to practice with her now."

"Speaking of practice, I brought some of my other blades that should stand up against Winya for a little while, so what do you say, practice duel with your new sword?"

She smiled, "What, no war hammer?"

"I thought I would take it easy on you and use a sword today. Besides I have a whole sack of swords," I grinned.

We sparred for over an hour, and Maya loved it. I could tell that the two of them, Maya and Winya, were getting a lot better with each other because halfway through our session, I was forced to use my mage sight to predict her movements. Even then, I was almost always on the defensive. I also got the feeling that Winya was coaching my girl as there were a number of maneuvers that I didn't remember Maya ever using that popped up in our match. During the course of our session, Winya broke three of the swords I made without even augmenting her sharpness. I was using the last one, and it wasn't looking so good.

As my last sword disintegrated under Winya's final onslaught, Maya laughed and taunted, "Ha! So much for your paltry weapons, Sir Knight...do you surrender? Or shall I leave your broken body on this hallowed field of battle?"

"My lady, I surrendered the first time I saw your face in my kitchen," I bantered back. I started to clean up the broken sword pieces thrown all over the place. But as I was cleaning up, Maya marched right over to me, grabbed me, pulling both of us to the ground and kissing me deeply. Time slowed down as we had our arms around each other, exploring each other. A few minutes passed before I came up for air, and she nuzzled me softly.

"Well, if this is how you intend to treat my broken body on the field of battle, my new motto is 'never surrender'!"

"Oh, I think you will." She winked, got up, and pulled me back to my feet. "It's time to get you back on schedule." As we were heading back to the main training area, Maya donned her usual trainer gear with mask.

"Alright, where's the bloody sword!"

We both looked in surprise at the very annoyed dwarf marching across the training fields. I looked down at Maya with a mischievous smile, and she patted me on the back in agreement; we had an idea. When Darroth finally got to us, we were standing side by side, looking casual.

"Alright, let's see it. I was promised that it would look completely different the next time I saw it, so you had better make good on your promise."

Maya held out her wrist to show off the bracelet. "Look at the wonderful bracelet that Alex made for me, isn't it simply stunning?"

"I don't care about a bracelet. Where is the sword?"

Maya slipped her arms behind her back and brought out Winya as a dagger, but used her powers to make it look gray. "How about this magic dagger he made for me?"

"Yes, that's very nice, but the sword, woman!"

She brought the dagger behind her back again and put her free hand on her chin to make it appear that she was thinking hard. "Sword? He wants a sword, huh? Oh, you mean this sword!" She pulled Winya out as a crossbow.

"That's not a sword!"

"Yes, it is."

"No, it's not!"

"Yes, it is."

"No, that's not a bloody sword!"

Winya changed to her sword form. "Yes, she is."

"By my rock-headed ancestors! What is that?" I wish I could have captured the look on his face at that instant. Darroth's eyes had become the size of saucers and I'm pretty sure he stopped breathing momentarily. Maya and I doubled over with laughter, even Winya joined in.

"My eyes must be getting weak or did that crossbow just become a sword?"

"Darroth, I would like to introduce you to Winya Coia, she was all the items that Maya showed you."

"You made a shape-shifting weapon?" he stated incredulously, looking at each of us for verification.

"In a way, yes, and each form has its own powers."

"Like what?"

Maya reached down and picked the first sword that she had sliced in two out of the bag and handed it to him. "Like doing that."

Darroth took one look at the cut and dropped the sword half and stared at me accusingly. "What the hell are you? Who are you? No one should be able to make something like this! Even the hallowed ancient dwarven masters couldn't make a weapon that could change shape by itself!" He stood there for a few seconds, his mouth was still moving but nothing was coming out. Then he rushed over to me and grabbed me in a crushing bear hug. I could feel my bones starting to crack.

He finally released me and all the oxygen rushed back into me. Feeling a bit light-headed, I started to stagger a bit but, thankfully, Maya held my arm and let me regain my balance.

"Sorry about that, son; forget my own strength sometimes." For those who think I'm a wimp, you try getting squeezed by a dwarven smith, it hurts!

"No worries, I have Maya for support."

He turned to Maya and gave her a flustered bow of profound respect. Straightening up he nodded.

"For a smith to give away his first masterpiece is a monumental honor, young lady."

I couldn't see her reaction under the mask, but she reached up and gave one of my ears a playful caress. "I know, and I will honor Winya for as long as I breathe. As for the gift, I'll make it up to him someday."

After a few seconds of trying to figure out what she meant, I gave up. What good is a surprise if it's not a surprise? But her body language as she melted into my side wanting nothing more than just to be close to me, made my chest hurt more than Darroth's hug. After a few more minutes of casual talking, we all parted ways and went on with our day.

Lunch wasn't quite what I was expecting; Julia and Lin were at our usual table with their arms crossed and annoyed looks on their faces.

"Where have you been?" they shouted in unison, attracting the attention of the rest of the dining hall.

I apologized to the people around us and then sat down to face the wrath of the two druid girls. "Both Master Rosa and Nia had way too much to drink, so I spent yesterday tending to two very sick women."

They didn't seem too happy with that answer, waving it away with a flick of the wrist. "We don't care what you were doing; what we want is for you to tell us every detail of what happened at the dance and to tell us now!"

I was extremely puzzled at the moment; I had no idea that girls get so worked up about dances. "Um, well, we had a wonderful evening, and Maya seemed to really enjoy the dance."

Lin looked like I had just said the stupidest thing on the planet, and Julia just stared at me. Thankfully, she had a bit more kindness than Lin and helped me out a bit.

"No, Alex, tell us about Maya and how you got her to go with you, and about the gift you made for her."

"Yeah, what did you make for her? All throughout the dance I was trying to spot a necklace, or ring, or something," Lin countered. "And how come I've never seen her around here before, not even at the food hall?"

"Well, she works with the guard force primarily, so she wouldn't have a lot of contact with students. Rosa pulled some strings and convinced her to train me, so she really is my combat instructor. We have spent a lot of time together and became good friends."

Lin snorted, "Just friends? Seriously? I've never seen just friends lip lock like you two were going at it. And, Jules, did you see what she was wearing in her hair? A white Gardenia!"

Julia snickered, "Oh, yes, tell us more about being 'just friends,'" she said, rolling her eyes.

Now I was really confused, but I tried to explain. "When you spar with someone every day, you learn more about them than words could ever say."

"Like what?"

"Like she's strong, smart, honorable, caring, and has a terrific sense of humor. I fell for her very quickly, and I think she felt the same for me."

They both stared in silent judgment of me. "So by beating someone with a metal stick, you fall in love with them? Men!"

"No, that's not what I meant. By dueling each other, our true personalities and beliefs are shown to each other. We both just liked what we found in each other."

"So you can't put on a fake face and try to act like someone you're not in a duel?" Lin pressed.

"Correct - not for long, anyway."

"So to know if the guy is right for us, we have to fight him?"

"Well, no, but that's one way to do it."

"I see, and the gift?"

"I made her a sword."

They were both scandalized and it showed. "Ok, you have serious issues. Why didn't you make her some lovely jewelry or something?"

"Because Maya wouldn't have liked it as much."

"And she liked this sword?"

I smiled. "She cried over it."

Julia put down her sweets and nudged Lin with her elbow. "Trouble, Lin."

I looked in the direction she was facing, and sure enough, trouble was indeed coming. Marching across the room in our direction was Naton and his two favorite goons. He looked as though he was out for blood.

"Enchanter scum! What's this I hear about you having a girlfriend?"

"That's none of your concern, Naton."

He laughed at me. "That's where you're wrong. At the dance the other night, me and my girlfriend were supposed to be voted the best couple. Instead, the idiots at the party voted for you and your mystery girl. Then, you didn't even have the guts to show up yesterday to face your punishment for humiliating me!"

"Well, that's not my problem, so don't blame me for others' opinions."

"From the way I see it, it is your problem. All you had to do was find an ugly girl to take, and I would have been king of the dance. But no, you found a hot one instead...bad mistake." He smiled again with an evil look. "I have an idea, how about we pay your girlfriend a visit and make her ugly. A few burns on the face should do it."

I snapped. The next second, I was up from the table and in his face with a grip on the haft of my hammer.

"You foolishly go anywhere near her, and you won't live to regret it."

He sneered at me. "Or what? You going to do the same trick you did with my fireball? Well, guess what? My teacher taught me how to keep you from ever being able to do that again."

I smiled this time. "I won't need to. By the time you even start to cast a spell, you'll be a dead man. You fire wizards are so arrogant because you can do a lot of damage, but the downside is that it takes you so long to cast a spell that you would be the first to die on the battlefield. And it's not me that you have to worry about, it's her. She doesn't have my patience for things like this; if she were here, you would already be dead."

Apparently, he was too dumb to get the point because he immediately tried to conjure up a fireball. But with my mage sight, he didn't even have enough magic ready to make a spark before the spike of my war hammer was tickling his Adam's apple, and not in a good way.

"I suggest you leave now so only your pride gets hurt."

He snarled but backed away. "You'll pay for this! Someday, I'll see you killed!"

With that, he and his two goons left, trying to make the most of the situation by looking tough, but failing miserably. Everyone in the dining hall had seen what happened, and they all knew that the big bad fire wizard was beaten by the lowly Enchanter.

Once the jerk was gone, I returned to my seat at the table with my good mood ruined. But Lin and Julia were just staring at me, not eating or moving, just staring. It was kind of creepy.

"What?"

"I can't believe you did that!"

"That was so cool! He was totally scared of you; that was awesome!" Then Julia jumped up from her seat and ran around the table to hug me.

"Hey, what did I do?"

"You kicked that bully's butt, that's what you did."

"Yeah well, that still won't be the last of him."

"We're not worried," Lin piped up. "The spitting cockroaches living in his room and I have a plan for revenge."

"We have cockroaches on campus?" I sputtered, choking on a grape.

"Nah," she returned with a sly grin, "just in the Fire Tower."

I was so astonished and proud of both of them, I could barely ask my final question. "Umm, Jules, before you go, tell me something. What is the significance of a white gardenia?"

She leaned in close, giggled softly, and breathed in my ear, "It means secret love, silly. And she was wearing it before the dance even started."

That night after dinner, Rosa sentenced me to a night of reading. The sun was starting to go down when the hall shook with an explosion. What the hell is going on? I rushed to the lab, which was where I thought the sound came from. When I opened the door, a cloud of smoke rolled out. "Nia, are you all right?"

I heard coughing as both Nia and Rosa appeared out of the smoke, grabbing onto the door frame for support. "We're ok...nothing to see here."

I took one look at them and started laughing. Their hair was blasted almost straight back and they had layers of soot on their faces. They looked confused, so I pointed at a mirror on the nearby wall. As they looked at their reflections, there was a long, open-mouthed pause, and then they turned to each other and burst out in hysterical laughter.

After getting cleaned up, they joined me in the reading room. "So, what happened?"

Nia shyly tried to hide herself, but Rosa told me anyway. "Well, as you know, I've been working with Nia's spells for a time now, and she has made excellent progress." Nia beamed from her hiding place. "But we have made some interesting discoveries. It seems that she is incapable of casting normal pixie spells. Instead, she excels at mindless destruction." Rosa grinned, and Nia performed a mock bow. "As well as illusions and scrying."

"Pretty sure that boom and all that smoke from the lab wasn't a mere illusion," I countered.

Nia peeked out from around the corner of a bookcase. "Sorry, Mr. Alex, that was my fault. It takes so much magic for me to get a normal spell to even go off, so I used the same amount on a test fireball and well...that happened. It won't happen again, I promise."

Rosa was still beaming. "I watched her closely, and from what I saw, she can cast fireballs all day without even breaking a sweat. I'll have to test her more, but I think she could be stronger than most fire wizards. Nia may be a throwback to an earlier age when her people's magic was primal and much more powerful."

Nia smiled happily, flew over and landed on my shoulder. "Huh, who knew? Guess I'm just an old-fashioned girl. Well, I say we celebrate with some sweets," she giggled, obviously trying to change the subject.

Rosa and I laughed. "Sounds like a good idea to me, the lab needs to air out now anyway."

Chapter 11

Alex

Thankfully, the next few days were rather peaceful. Darroth started me on plate armor and Maya added heavy shields to our training. In fact, the only one who was concerned about the fire wizards was Nia, who was sticking close to my side. We all fell into a comfortable routine, with one exception. I now lived for the one or two minutes a day I could spend alone in the arms of my dark elf girl. Life was better than I could ever have imagined at Foalshead.

Four nights later, when both Nia and I were fast asleep, I heard something. At first, I thought I was dreaming, but as I listened, I could hear an urgent voice shouting frantically in my head.

"Alex! Please wake up! Something has happened to Maya and I can't stop it! Please, I need your help!"

"Winya, is that you?" I was fully awake now at the thought of Maya in danger.

"Yes, of course! How many other swords talk to you? Now please hurry, we're in Maya's room!"

"I don't know where that is!"

"I'll guide you!"

I quickly threw on a robe, then woke up Nia and explained what was happening. I briefly thought about waking Rosa, but Winya said there was no time, so we raced out the door. Thankfully, Nia had been to Maya's room several times with Rosa, so she knew the way, but it was still a long way to go. Winding our way at high speed through the warren of towers and buildings, I would also have to get out past the inner wall, and it wasn't something you could just jump over.

"Alex, hurry, I think there's someone at the door!"

I pushed even harder. "Hold on, we're almost there."

"He's in the room!"

Darting past the astonished guards, I burst past the gatehouse and used my mage sight to find Winya and Maya. They were in a section of long, worn wooden buildings that probably stabled overflow horses in time of need. Across the narrow alley, nearer to the training rings, were equally rundown troop barracks. Maya had a small one-room apartment at one end of the first building that looked like it had been a tack room in better days, but now just contained a cot and some meager amenities. Focusing, I could see that a man in dark red, almost black, robes and a hood was standing next to her with a dagger. If we didn't go faster, we wouldn't make it in time. I put everything I had into my legs, both strength and magical. But it was like hitting a wall and not being able to go any further. Then the man brought the dagger up to make a thrust. For a second, distance meant nothing to me, I was already there and through the door!

The red-cloaked figure had a wicked-looking dagger in one hand and a hooded oil lantern in the other. He spun around in surprise as shards of wood from the shattered door bounced off the walls near Maya's small cot. Flustered, he cursed, dropping the weapon. It clattered off the rough floorboards and skittered under the bed frame.

Furious, I charged him, but I didn't make it. Suddenly, icy blades stabbed sharply into my chest muscles, then contracted into a fist. I was lifted off the ground and slammed into a heavy support beam, pinned like a fly on a wall.

Shaky, but still working, my mage sight showed me my attacker - a tall, gaunt man dressed as a noble who came out of nowhere. He had sparse white hair, an amused expression and the largest canine teeth I had ever seen - vampire!

He turned his head casually and addressed the assassin.

"It's our lucky day, Rast. Both young lovers just dying to meet us. Won't the Master be pleased?" He looked back at me contemptuously. "Although, I fail to see why my lord Duke Pharmon considers you and your unconscious doxy over there to be of sufficient threat to warrant our high level of services. Perhaps, by some total unfathomable travesty of nature, something marginally exceptional is destined to spring from the fruit of your loins and become a pain in the ass to him in the future. Oh well, that's irrelevant, I suppose, as neither of you will see the light of day again."

The assassin, apparently named "Rast," was busy searching for the lost dagger. Finally, he retrieved it. Holding his lantern back up to eye level, he spotted the glittering bracelet on the arm of his intended victim. Pulling it off, he slid it on his own wrist and held it up to the light, admiring it.

"Nice little bauble, it would be a shame if it melted when I burn this place to the ground. Are you sure you wouldn't like a taste of the pretty bird here before I slice her, M'lord Ascott?"

I struggled against the grip holding me to the post, but I had nothing. Neither magic nor physical strength were recovering fast enough to give me a glimmer of a chance to escape. I glanced around desperately for a weapon of any kind, knowing full well from my studies that vampires were immune to nearly everything, especially the old ones, and this one looked very old to my admittedly untrained eye.

The vampire grinned, his blood-red eyes boring into my own. "Tisk, Tisk, now quit struggling, it sours the blood. And you can stop looking around for a silly weapon to pursue your last valiant attempt at being a hero, it won't work on me."

"Who is this Duke and what does he want?" I croaked through the pain in my chest. The vampire sighed in an angry, bored fashion and waved his hand indicating Xarparion.

"Is this place not supposed to be an institute of higher learning? Do they teach you dolts nothing in school anymore?" he spat angrily. "Duke Pharmon, the Lifebane, is the powerful lich who controls more than half of the dirt on this world. His armies of undead are legion; wights, ghouls, zombies...if it's undead, he controls it. As far as what he wants, it's simple enough for even a bumpkin like you to understand. He wants to control ALL the dirt on this world, idiot!"

"Why?"

"It's always 'why' with you humans, isn't it?" he sneered. "How do I know, maybe his mother didn't cuddle him enough as a child or a marmot stole his peanut brittle. Perhaps he just has an enormous itch that can only be scratched by complete and total world domination. If the payment is right, I really don't care."

He turned back to the assassin and ordered, "Finish the wench, her blood is tainted anyway! I think there is more than enough liquid in this husky young mage to satisfy me."

He switched hands and held up one of his talons coated in my blood.

"Perhaps a taste before I enjoy the main course is in order."

I watched as he licked his fingers like a cat lapping cream. In my peripheral vision, I saw Rast moving Maya's head to the side to present the best angle for a cut to my love's carotid artery.

"Hmmm," the vampire purred, "an odd taste to be sure. You're not really altogether human, are you my inquisitive friend?"

Suddenly his eyes grew wide and he convulsed slightly once, then more violently again and again. And that's when his eyes began tearing up uncontrollably. An expression that had probably not been in the vampire's repertoire for over five hundred years - fear - crossed his face. He let go of me and dropped to all fours on the floor gagging, smoke wafting out of his mouth like someone who had just taken a deep draw on a pipe and was now breathing it out.

"What are you?" he demanded, looking from his hands to me. "Your blood burns like acid, I can't regenerate! Rast, kill her! And help me, you fool!"

I finally found my strength, and feet. Shoving off the beam, I lunged for the man in red.

"Winya, now!"

The assassin raised his knife over Maya, and on the fatal down stroke was extremely surprised to see the arm holding the weapon and wearing the pretty, sparkly bracelet flash brightly and turn to formless gray ash. A radiating effect continued up through his torso and finally erased his astonished expression completely. Winya clunked heavily to the floor, as did the oil lantern, which promptly shattered and sent flames flowing in all directions. My momentum carried me far enough to allow me to snatch up the bracelet from the wood planking just before the flaming oil carried over it. The old tack room was as dry as tinder, and the oil-charged flames fed ravenously.

In a few seconds, the room was seriously aflame, with a great deal of smoke accumulating near the ceiling. I turned to find the vampire bearing down on me with a sword of his own. He didn't look so good, but my rational mind estimated he was still probably stronger and faster than me.

"Winya, I could use a little help!"

"*Anything to help Maya, but you must hurry! The flames, Alex!*" Instantly she was a sword in my hand, and I barely parried his first slash. He jabbed viciously at my midsection, driving me back toward the flaming half of the floor. Damn! This guy was no slouch as a swordsman either, but it made sense if he was a noble in his breathing days.

"I don't know what you are or what that shit you call blood is, but you will still die by my hand tonight," he wheezed and took another swing. I was saved further monolog from him by the fact that, even though he didn't need to breathe to survive, he did need to pump air through his lungs to talk. Judging by the acrid smoke still leaching from his mouth, he couldn't have much lung tissue left. He backed me right up to the edge of the fire less than five feet from Maya's cot. With both of us running out of time, he gambled on a risky Fleche move, which Maya would no doubt have disapproved of had she been conscious. I managed to sidestep, and failing to connect, his lurching charge carried him into the burning flames on the floor. The oil-stoked fire immediately ran up his expensive pant legs and took hold. For a few seconds, he failed to notice and struck at me again, which I barely managed to deflect. He was still as strong as Rosa, if not stronger! I took a cut at him, more to keep him occupied and unaware that he was on fire. He hissed and scored a shallow furrow across my shoulder, my shortcomings as a swordsman becoming more pronounced. Unfortunately, I didn't create Winya with a war hammer option.

It's an interesting phenomenon that a person engaged in the heat of battle can ignore a lot of pain and still function, but for us guys there is still a spot that always gets our attention. As we battled, the flames on the vampire's clothes finally raced higher than his knees, and he stopped. His sword arm dropped to his side, and he looked down shocked and dumbfounded.

"Winya, I need your best," I coughed and swung. Winya's ultra sharp blade moved across his bloodless neckline, leaving hardly a trace. His eyes lost focus, but he still brought his sword arm back for another thrust, the act of which unbalanced him slightly. It was at that point that his head and body parted company forever, the sneering skull rolling further into the fire and the body dropping in a flame-licked heap. Regenerate all you want, but you're still dead without a head!

By this time, the flames and smoke were awful, and Maya's cot was a small pitiful island in a full sea of fire. Coughing up what I was pretty sure were actual parts of my organs, I asked Winya to return to bracelet form and slipped her on my own wrist. I painfully hot-footed it over to the bed and scooped Maya up gently then ran for the door.

Without considering any alternative, I began to carry Maya back to the only safety I knew - the Enchanters Hall. My lungs and chest felt like they were burning as hotly as the stables. When we finally bumped into Nia still flying toward the fire, she looked out of breath and exhausted.

"Mister Alex, are you ok?" She looked as if she was about to faint when she saw the blood covering the front of my shirt.

"I've been better, but we need to get Maya back home, Winya says she was poisoned. But you need to take a break as well. Sit on my shoulder and catch your breath."

She plopped ungracefully on my shoulder and took a few deep breaths. "How did you move so fast? I could barely even see you move."

"What do you mean?"

"When we were about halfway there, you blurred out and left me in the dust." Well, that's something to ask Rosa about. I wonder if it's like her enchanted strength.

"Maya was in danger, so I guess that pushed me over the edge. But I really should not have worried so much, Winya was still watching over her."

"I'm sorry, Alex, I should have been more careful. I almost failed at the task you gave me and still might if that poison takes her. I'm sorry, Maya; I hope you will forgive me." I don't know how but I felt she was crying, and it was making me tear up as well.

"It's not your fault, Winya. Besides, you were the one who defended her, I was just a distraction."

"I know, but when she was hit by the dart, I tried my best to heal her in an attempt to stop the poison from spreading, but I couldn't. What I could do was make damn sure that the bastard would never get another chance again!"

Even as a bracelet, she was starting to feel hot my arm; it was actually beginning to hurt.

"Um, Winya, could you please cool it down a bit? That's starting to hurt...and what dart?"

"*Oops, sorry, sir!*" She cooled back down to a normal temp. "*The dart is still in her left shoulder.*"

I motioned to Nia and she flew to the dart and had a tough time pulling it out. It was lodged deeply and had sliced through Maya's leather training armor. The assassin must have darted her as she entered her room after training and she collapsed on the bed shortly after. When he knew she was unconscious, he entered her room to finish the job. The vampire must have been there to supervise and take care of any loose ends. Nia finally strained and carefully pulled the dart out. She then sniffed the barbed end. "This poison is made from red nightshade, I recognize the smell."

"Red nightshade is fatal to most humans," I whispered, automatically looking down at my unconscious girl, my healer training kicking in."

"*Then I have failed in my mission again.*"

"Calm down, both of you. In case you have forgotten, she is not human. Red nightshade will kill a human, that is true. But it only has a small chance to kill a dark elf and it won't kill Maya. I know something that will help her, so don't worry, she will survive."

"*Thank you, Alex; I am forever in your debt.*"

"Ok, I can tell you two are having an important conversation here, but this one-sided talking is making me crazy!" Nia complained.

"Sorry, Nia, but we need to pick up the pace."

I shakily jogged the rest of the way home and since Maya was fully a dark elf at the moment, I was careful to not pass too close to any of the scores of people who were attracted to the sight and noise of the fire. On the way, I did my best to send my thoughts to Rosa in an attempt to wake her up. After a few tries, I finally got her out of the deep slumber she was in and into the now really panicked reality. By the time we got there, she was dressed and waiting at the door. When she saw us, she ran out into the night for us.

"Alex! What happened, is she ok? Who did this to her? By the gods, you're both bleeding!" She was in full motherly panic mode. If I wasn't so concerned and lightheaded, I might have found it rather funny.

"Red nightshade poison. Don't worry, it won't kill her, but she may wish it had when she wakes up."

Relief hit her for a brief moment but was quickly replaced with anger. "Who did this to her and you?" she said, probing the wounds on my chest and shoulder as she walked alongside.

"I got a good look at their magic, so I know one was a fire wizard and apparently an assassin, but I've never seen him before. The other, who seemed to be in charge, was a vampire."

She shuddered. "A vampire? But how did it get past the wards and walls? How did you escape it?" She paused for a second, "Never mind, I don't need to know." Even though I'm sure she just read my mind and found out. "Why would a fire wizard do this, why use poison?"

"It was probably an attempt to shift the blame to someone in the Earth Tower or someone who isn't a wizard," I guessed. "Good idea, but the execution was sloppy, and he didn't count on Winya...neither of them did."

Rosa's face took on a hard, determined look, one that I was

not used to seeing from my usually jovial master.

"Alex, if you are positive you can save Maya, I recommend we keep her with us. I'm not sure who we can trust anymore, even the Healers Tower." She grimaced but then her resolve set in stone. "And where are the assassins now?"

"They're both a pile of ash in her now burning home."

"You killed them, then?"

"Winya killed the wizard assassin, and the two of us defeated the vampire."

"Thank you, Winya! If her home is on fire, then there are some things that she will need in there. I'll go try and save them, you tend to Maya. We will chat more about this later. For now, I'll use the link to read your mind to learn the rest so I don't distract you." She reached out and gently stroked Maya's silvery hair. "Save her, Alex, I don't know what I would do without you two anymore, and I'm not the only one!" With that, she ran off into the night.

With help from Nia to open the doors, I gently carried Maya into the reading room in front of the fireplace. Nia and I then carefully removed her bloody leather training armor and got her into a warm nightgown of Rosa's. I tried to keep my eyes closed throughout the process, with Nia guiding my hands. We got several blankets ready and the fire going strong. Nia even brought her bed to use as a pillow. Once that was all done, it was time for the hard part.

"Ok, Nia, I'm going to need your help." She nodded determinedly. "A sick dark elf is a funny thing compared to a human; they're almost like two separate beings when sick. Right now we need to keep her head cool, but the rest of her body warm. So I'm going to work on that. What I need from you is to make the medicine."

She looked panicked and flew up, her wings all abuzz. "But I don't know any dark elf medicines! I don't even know pixie medicine!"

"But I do, and mixing medicine is just like following a cooking recipe. I need you to go to the kitchen and mix milk, black ginger root, orange juice, and apple juice together, and some of Rosa's special herbs that she keeps in that black glass jar. I'll call out the amounts when you are ready."

"Eww, I thought milk was bad when you were sick."

"Not for a dark elf, it calms their stomachs. Then I need you to grind up some rosemary, lavender honey, and oil shale powder; mix it together in a different bowl and bring it all to me. Rosa uses it in her enchanting so there should be plenty in the lab."

"I'll be fast, Alex!"

With that, she darted off into the kitchen. In the meantime, I found a small bowl and filled it with cool water. Grabbing a few small hand cloths and bandages, I returned to Maya. I moved some of the chairs around so I could lean back on one and could still prop her up on my lap, similar to the position we were in after the dance. I placed a moistened cloth on her forehead and slipped Winya on to her wrist as a bracelet. Now ready, I channeled the same enchantment that I did for Nia's and Rosa's alcohol poisoning to help her fight the effects of the nightshade. I could feel Winya doing what she could to mimic the effects of the enchantment and give her strength, I was very proud of her.

Nia came flying back with the bowl of honey mixture and set it down next to me. "The other stuff is ready; should I bring it?"

"Yes, please, and a spoon, as well, if you can still carry one."

"That will be no problem." She zipped off again and soon returned with the other bowl and a spoon. I took one of the clean cloths and carefully cleaned the wound where the dart had hit her. The barbs had done more damage than I thought. Once clean, I scooped some of the honey mixture out and smeared it on the wound to draw out the remaining poison, then wrapped it loosely in the bandage, then did the same for myself. Nia helped me wrap her tightly in the blankets I brought; I could see she was barely holding back the pixie tears.

"So what do we do now?"

"Now, we try to get some of that milk and juice in her and wait for the eventual fever to start."

"Will this stuff really cure her?"

"Actually, all the real work is being done by my enchantments and her body, and Winya is a big help. This will help her recover faster and make it less painful, but sadly, this will still hurt like hell for her."

After only getting a little of the medicine in her, she started running a high fever. I stayed where I was with her head in my lap, keeping her forehead cool. Nia wrapped herself in her blanket and sat on the end table next to us to watch. We sat there for over an hour before Rosa finally came home. She had a large bag of smoky smelling stuff and wasn't happy. But when she saw us, that anger was replaced with motherly concern.

"How is she doing?"

"She will be fine in a day or so. She'll probably be waking up soon."

She relaxed a bit and walking over to us, sat down on the floor. "That would be nice."

"So, did you find everything you needed to?"

She nodded.

"The fire had burned most of the old stable and had jumped the alley to the guard barracks by the time I got there. Apparently, the other headmasters decided to let it burn without even trying to put it out. She shook her head. "Thankfully, she stored most of her special things in a trunk that I made for her so not much was destroyed."

"That's good. When are they going to rebuild the buildings?"

She sighed. "That's one of the things I'm mad about. They aren't going to rebuild them because the Tower's opinion is that the buildings in that area are ugly and should be razed and turned into a garden anyway."

"But if they do that, where will the staff and guards live?"

"Underground barracks."

"You're joking, right?"

"Sadly, I'm not. They were planning on doing it in two years, but now with a large portion already burnt down, they're going to start the process now."

"So this fire and the loss of people's homes is just an advantageous turn of events?" I was starting to get angry.

"That's not even the best part! I went before the elders, and none of them will support an investigation of her assassin to see who he was working for. The only one who supported us was the Headmaster, but even he was out-voted."

"So they're going to do nothing?"

"Correct, and we are forbidden from doing anything either."

That pissed me off. "Why the hell not?"

"Maya is listed as staff for the Enchanters Hall and not a student. And since she is not a student, Xarparion is not responsible for her safety. They actually wanted to put Maya in jail pending their investigation into the death of this probable fire wizard/assassin because the life of a wizard is apparently more valuable than that of a mere weapons instructor. I had to explain that Maya was unconscious when he died, and so was not responsible. Then they wanted me to turn over Winya for study."

"I'd like to see them try and take me away from her!" Winya said in my mind, but Rosa must have heard it through me, too.

Rosa chuckled a little. "Relax, Winya, it was a stupid statement on their part. If they did take you, they would have had to give you over to me for study. None of them can even figure out how the training orbs function...let alone you."

"So what are we going to do?"

"Well, as much as it pains me to say, we will just have to wait and see. But don't worry; I have a few ideas that may expose the rat. I have always suspected one of the elders to be a traitor, several of them are very adept at blocking my mindreading, but now I have the tools to sniff him out."

"What tools?"

She smiled and motioned at Maya and me. "You two are going to shake the foundations of those towers soon and see what falls out. But that's not important right now." She motioned to my patient. "What is important is Maya. I know dark elves don't mind it underground, but I still don't feel right making her stay down there, especially now with assassins lurking on the grounds."

Then Nia had an excellent idea. "Why doesn't she stay in the other bedroom upstairs?" We both stared at her. "What? If they already count her as Enchanters Hall staff, then she should be able to stay at the Enchanters Hall, right?"

"Use their own asinine rules against them - I like it!" Rosa chortled, and then she gave me a playful look. "But I don't know about having you two young lovers so close together, I don't want to be kept up all night."

I smiled, "As long as we refrain from saying the word 'food,' I'm sure we could have a tavern bard performing in here and you wouldn't notice."

She punched me in the shoulder, but oddly, it didn't hurt this time. "Smart ass. But I would like to keep her here from now on. This is one of the safest buildings in Xarparion; I enchanted every inch of this place personally."

And with that, Maya started to stir in my lap. I gently put my hands on her shoulders to keep her from rolling over on her bad arm. After a few seconds, she stopped trying to move and slowly opened her eyes as she struggled to focus, her breathing coming in short searing bursts.

"Alex? Rosa? What are you doing in my room and why do I feel so strange?" Then her eyes grew wide and panicky as she lurched forward in an attempt to vomit. I held her down on my lap.

The last thing I needed was for her to ruin all the hard work Nia and I did to get that medicine in her in the first place. She calmed down, too weak to escape my firm grip. I could see how much pain she was in, and I hated that there was nothing I could do to take it away.

"Alex, what's happening to me…where am I? The Enchanters Hall?" she gasped weakly.

"Maya, you have been poisoned, so please try not to throw up. You need to keep that medicine down."

She nodded, but I wasn't sure how much she really comprehended. She lurched again as her body did its best to expel its contents. I started to softly rub her neck, arms and shoulders with the goal of relaxing her and as a distraction from her pain. It worked for a short while and she was a bit more relaxed now, but I could still feel her stiffen up in violent spasms regularly. The best thing I could do for her would be to put her back into a healing slumber.

"I'm sorry, sweetheart, but I'm going to put you to sleep now." Then I placed the enchantment to have her sleep. Soon, I would need to wake her again to drink more of the juice, but the kindest thing at the moment was to let her slip into dreams. After a second, she was out. The clenching of her muscles continued, but at least she wasn't consciously feeling the pain any longer.

"Where did you learn to do that?"

I looked at Rosa in confusion. "Um, you taught me to do that a few weeks ago?"

"I don't know how to do that," Rosa said flatly.

I was really confused now. "I could have sworn you taught me. Oh well, it's a nice trick; I used it on you already."

"If I couldn't read your mind, I would say that you were lying. But no matter, for now we need to worry about Maya. Is she truly going to be alright?"

"She should be, as far as I know. She is in no danger of dying from the poison anymore."

She was shocked for a second. "I thought you said that dark elves don't die from red nightshade poison?"

"No, I said *she* wouldn't die from it. About one in four dark elves who are untreated die from most natural toxins, red nightshade included."

"But how did you know she wouldn't?"

I smiled down at the sleeping dark elf in my arms. "Because I won't let her."

Rosa accepted that and even looked a bit proud of my response. "You should try and get some sleep."

"I can't. She still needs as much medicine as I can keep down her, and I still need to keep the fire going and her head cool. No, I won't be sleeping much tonight, but I can't think of a place I would rather be right now."

She smiled and patted me softly on the head. "Well, in that case, I'll get you something to help keep you awake. And in the meantime, I'll start cleaning up the spare bedroom."

"Wow, Rosa cleaning...the concept!"

"Hey, watch it. Just because Maya is sick doesn't mean you are free from a future beating. Now be a good boy and take care of your true love."

"I will."

"At least you will have someone to talk to...where is that sprite anyway?"

"Yeah, you may want to rethink that last part." I motioned over to where Nia was sitting on the table. She was wrapped up in her blanket and was using an unlit candle as a pillow. It was really cute and I had no desire to wake her from her sleep. She worked hard tonight and she earned it.

We both chuckled as Rosa headed upstairs. A few minutes later, she returned with a hot mug of something that tasted a lot like dirt, but oddly, I kind of liked it. Once she was gone, I finally had a few moments of quiet to reflect on the past night. There were still some things from the story Rosa told about the elders that didn't add up. Then there was a fire wizard using red nightshade poison in the first place. The only ones at the school who should even know how to make it would be the earth wizards and I don't see any of them giving it to a fire wizard. So that would point to outsiders. The assassin claimed to have been sent by the Lifebane himself...why? Why would either Maya or I be someone the necromancer would specifically target?

My thoughts were interrupted by Maya stirring again in my arms. She wasn't shaking like the last time she woke up, so I counted that as a good sign. Her green eyes opened slowly and she looked up at me.

"How are you feeling?"

"I hurt all over, my head is killing me, my stomach is tied in three knots, and I keep bouncing from feeling like I'm on fire to freezing to death. And worst of all, the man who I most want to appear beautiful for has to see me as a ragged, puke doll all night. So very romantic…"

"I'm so sorry."

"Don't be." She reached up with an overly warm hand and caressed the side of my face. "Winya has been talking to me in my sleep and told me everything that happened. I owe her and you my life."

"No, you don't. You will never owe me anything. And I hate to have to put you through this, but it's time for you to drink your medicine."

I reached over and picked up the bowl and held it so she could drink without having to hold it herself.

"What is in it?"

"If I told you, you wouldn't drink it."

"Great, that's the part that scares me."

She brought her lips to the bowl and took a quick sip. Once the mixture touched her tongue, she tried her best to spit it out. But I could see that coming, so I quickly covered her mouth with my free hand so she couldn't.

"Swallow." After a hurtful look, she finally did. "Good girl." And I removed my hand.

She looked like she just tasted something extremely sour. From the look on her face, it must have been the worst thing she had ever tasted.

"Alex, if you are determined to kill me, at least have the decency to use a sword," she coughed. "What in the world is in that awful stuff?"

"Well, most of it you would have no trouble with, but the part you hate so much would be black ginger root."

Her eyes shot wide in alarm. "You know I was kidding about the determined-to-kill-me part, right? So your idea of curing one poison is to feed me another?"

I shook my head. "Unlike what you have been told, black ginger is not poisonous to dark elves. In fact, it's very good for you and will help cure many of your ills. The reason you were told it's poisonous is because the shaman and healers in your society are the only ones who know the proper dosages and what it will and won't work on. They don't want anyone using it unsupervised. I'm not sure why that is an issue; as you can tell, most dark elves find the taste of black ginger to be extremely offensive."

"It is repulsive! And disgusting! And almost as bad as the noxious potions my grandfather concocted to give me dream-free sleep, and they didn't work. That was another reason I took up the sword and ran away to the forest."

"Remind me to thank him when I see him someday. At least you being lost in the forest all the time kept the handsome elf-boy suitors away. Now you have two choices, you can impress the hell out of me and drink the rest voluntarily, or I do it the hard way. But either way you're drinking all of it."

She scowled at me. I was taking a chance with that challenge, but if I knew her like I think I did, then this should be easy.

"I hate you so much right now," she growled and grabbed the bowl from my hand, gulping down the rest of the medicine in a few large draughts. I would have liked to have administered it in small sips, but hey, she drank it.

"That stuff is incredibly foul! I never want to get sick again. But if I get to sleep like this all night, it might not be so bad. As long as you never feed me ginger again and no, I don't care that it's good for me."

I smiled. "Glad to see that you're feeling better." Some color had returned to her face and she didn't feel so feverish.

"A little, yeah. Oddly, that stuff made my stomach stop hurting."

"That would be the milk."

She gave me a puzzled look. "How do you know so much about dark elf medicine?"

"That's a story for another time."

"No, that's a quick way to brush away the question." She groaned.

I chuckled and brushed the sweaty damp hair away from her eyes. "Either way, you're not getting that one just yet. For now, the best thing would be for you to get some sleep."

She yawned and snuggled down into a more comfortable position. "Fine, but I'll get that story out of you one day. And you are staying right where you are; I have no desire to give up my best pillow."

I wrapped my arms around her shoulders. "Wouldn't even dream of moving."

"Good."

In less than a minute, she was sleeping peacefully.

Chapter 12

Alex

I stayed up all night; whatever that brew was that Rosa gave me, it definitely worked. Maya was very cooperative in the night and never tried to roll over in her sleep, not that she had control over something like that. But never once did I want to be anywhere else. I was very content to sit there and hold her for as long as she needed. The smell of her hair alone was enough to make me happy.

Nia finally woke from her slumber and stretched luxuriously, looking as though she had completely forgotten the night before.

"Um, Mr. Alex, why was I sleeping on a candle?"

"You tell me, I didn't put you there."

She must have remembered where she was then. "Oh no! I must have fallen asleep when I was supposed to help you take care of the warrior princess!"

"Don't worry about it, Nia; you were exhausted and only one of us needed to go without sleep. Besides, when this potion of Rosa's wears off, I'm going to fall asleep and then it will be your turn to watch the warrior princess."

She thought it over for a second and then smiled. "I can do that."

"Do what?" I turned to see Rosa coming down the stairs. She looked like she was up all night as well, bags under her eyes, messed up hair, the works.

"Couldn't sleep?"

"Of course not, I couldn't stop worrying about you two. All I could do was lay there and think about the assassins and what life would be like if she had died."

"Yeah, I did some of that, too," I said grimly.

"How is she?"

I smiled the best I could. "She is doing great. Winya and I have been pumping her body full of magic all night; she should feel almost normal when she wakes up."

Most of the tension in her posture was released, and she looked a lot better. "Well, that's a relief."

"Just to warn you, she is going to be wildly hungry, almost feral, when she wakes up. We need to get some food going, actually a lot of food going," I corrected. "But if I move, I'll wake her and I don't want that to happen until we are ready."

Rosa was horrified. "You want me to cook? I can't cook!"

I smiled. "I know you can't, that's why Nia is in charge. Just follow her lead."

Nia was beaming as she led the still protesting Rosa into the kitchen to start getting the food ready. It wasn't long before the smell of cooked eggs made it over to us, and my stomach reminded me all about what a night of enchanting does for the appetite. Much to my surprise, Maya didn't seem to notice the smell at all. Normally, if you bring food anywhere near her or Rosa, you would be in danger of losing a finger or two.

Over the course of the night, Winya and I had a lot of time to talk after recent events. She will freely talk with me now, even about unimportant things. But the main thing we did was help her gain more control over the new abilities that she has as a magic user. She has grown a lot in one night; I would easily say that she had doubled in strength due to this past evening.

I thought about waking Maya, but Winya volunteered. *"She is in a deep healing sleep, Alex. I know you are familiar with many dark elf foibles having lived among them; however, I doubt you know just how very rare it is for a dark elf to relax anywhere but their forest clan home. That is why solitary or isolated dark elves rarely thrive and usually sleep literally with one eye open and a dagger in their hand. Yet even injured and totally vulnerable, Maya feels comfortable and safe enough to sleep here without any concern, and her dreams are always good ones when you are nearby."*

"I'm sure she knows that you are here guarding her and it makes a world of difference, Winya."

"As much as I would like that to be true, Alex, it's your presence that eases her mind and heart, not mine. Would you like me to start bringing her awake?"

"Yes, please do, Winya. I would like her to have some time to adjust before we feed her."

"I understand."

It only took a few seconds for her eyes to flutter open. Even seeing her at her worst, she was still able to take my breath away with those green eyes.

"Hello, Magic Boy," she whispered dryly, her voice still not back to its usual melodious tones. She struggled to sit up straighter as I gave her a sip of water.

"Hello, warrior princess."

Maya smirked up at me. "You are going to pay for that one!"

"Oh, I think after last night, I'm enough points ahead to poke a little fun."

"Hmmm...maybe," she purred. "But from what Winya just told me, you were stroking my ears again."

Guilty or not, I could feel my face turn bright red.

"Ha, caught you! So you were touching my ears! I asked her but she avoided the question, the steely minx! Apparently, the two of you bonded thoroughly while I was asleep?"

"But how did you know to ask?"

"Because you don't have dreams like the ones she had without help," Rosa supplied. She and Nia had returned from the kitchen with a large platter of food.

"Rosa, I told you never to look into my dreams again!" Maya was blushing from ear to ear. She covered her head with a blanket to keep me from seeing her face. "I swear, Alex, it's not what you think."

I looked over at Rosa and she mouthed "yes it is" to me. It took all I had to keep from laughing. I had a feeling that I might get hurt if this conversation went on any longer. I slid the food tray closer to us. Even from under her blanket, she should be able to smell the food.

"Alex," Maya whispered, "please, could you take Nia and Rosa with you out into the hall while I eat? I am hungrier than I have ever been before and it's taking all the strength I have to maintain control...now, please!"

Grabbing Rosa by the arm, I motioned for Nia to follow and we retreated to the kitchen. I leaned up against the wall and faced them.

"Once, when I was twelve or thirteen, I was with my mother working with the village healer at our old home, and there was a villager there that had been bitten by a venomous lizard. They had no choice but to put him into a coma of sorts to slow the spread of the venom before it reached his heart. For three days, we fed him potions and the local shaman put healing spell after healing spell on him. By the end of the third day, the effects of fighting the poison and all the magic had caused him to lose a quarter of his body weight. He was literally skin and bone, and when he did wake up, he was like a ravenous wild dog. He snapped and fought with the people trying to feed him, his own wife among them, totally oblivious to everyone attempting to help. He only knew the pain and the hunger and defending his food against everyone he imagined was trying to take it away. The funny thing is, he was one of the kindest, nicest people you could ever meet normally. Finally, after devouring enough food to feed a family of ten, he settled down enough for the healer to go back into the hut where he had to immediately stitch up a large wound on the fellow's arm. He had gotten so out of control that he had bitten himself.

"Are you saying that Maya would have been like that?" Nia asked in disbelief, looking between Rosa and me.

"No, Maya isn't in as bad a shape as that villager, but her first instinct is still self-preservation, and she might say or do something that she would regret later. At the very least, we would make her very uncomfortable while she was eating, and we need her to eat in order to recover.

As if on cue, Maya glided into the kitchen carrying the tray of empty dishes, and set them gently down next to the wash basin. Sighing, she grabbed me by the arm and rested her head against my shoulder. "Thank you, Alex, you always know how to make me feel better."

Nia buzzed around us a bit, paying special attention to Maya's arms, and finally landed back on my shoulder with an all clear sign. Rosa smiled and hugged us all gently.

"Now that you're feeling better, Maya, I think we should all have a nice chat. But first, you need to go and take a quick bath. And then we are going to get comfortable as we are all having a nice long talk."

Maya scampered stiffly off to the bathhouse and returned in a short wearing one of my white robes and smelling fresh and fantastic. She smiled shyly at me and curled up in a chair with her legs under her.

We all sat down in our own overstuffed chairs, well, all but Nia. She made her way to a half-burnt candle that melted away into a perfect chair for her. She even stitched some fabric onto it somehow.

"Before you start your thing, Rosa, I would like to ask an important question of you, Alex," Maya said levelly. Uh-oh, I don't like where this is going. "Winya keeps saying that she is getting more used to her new form. My question is, what was she? I asked her several times, but she keeps saying that she doesn't remember."

Crap! That was the last question I ever wanted to hear. I knew this would come up at some point, but I was hoping I would have a few years to really learn about what I did and how I did it. But what I really dreaded was that Winya made me promise never to tell them who she was.

"I was hoping you wouldn't ask that."

"So you won't tell me?"

I sighed, "No, Maya, I will tell you. I never want there to be secrets between us, but you may not like it or, for that matter, me after I tell you."

"I need to know, Alex. Winya is a part of me now," she said firmly.

I hung my head and stared at the floor. This was the one time that I didn't want to look at her. "I'll try to explain the best I can, to make things simple. Winya was not her first name. It's her real name, but not her first, if that makes any sense. She died some time ago and her spirit was set adrift to wander until her task was done. I could feel her and bonded her to the metal to forge your blade."

I didn't have to look up to know she was reeling with anger as she digested my words, but I also promised Winya that I would keep her past a secret. And I would suffer any punishment as long as Winya was always there to keep Maya safe.

Maya launched herself out of the chair and confronted me. "How could you do such a thing? You robbed her of her afterlife; you are literally using her soul! You're no better than that filthy necromancer! I thought I knew you, Alex!"

I didn't know what to say, there wasn't anything to say. "I'm sorry." She slapped me hard across my face, holding nothing back and raced for the outside door.

"Maya, stop!" She froze in place halfway out the door, tears in her eyes. *"Please return to your seat, Alex has done nothing wrong."*

"But you heard what he did to you!"

"That's not what happened. I asked him to leave my past out of his story, but as you can see, without it, Alex is portrayed as an evil man when he is really my savior."

She slowly made her way back to her chair, pulling her legs up to her chin defensively. Pointedly, she still wouldn't look my way.

"Now I will tell you my entire story. I cannot divulge my old name for I cast it off long ago. I died about four hundred years ago. Rosa, you may remember the stories of my death. I was the leader of the Wereia royal guard with the task of protecting our queen and princess, but I failed them and our kingdom died with them."

Rosa gasped and covered her mouth. "The battle of Sky Raven Fortress?"

"Yes, our queen's favorite place, it really was once a beautiful place. Now, it's just a haunted shell of its former glory. But to this day, the walls still stand strong."

"But if you were the captain of the guards, then you must have been the leader of the Steel Maidens!"

"Yes, I was. We were an all-female force that had the best training and weapons of the time. We were also the only wholly female fighting force as well. The queen had never liked the idea of so many men too close to her and her daughter so she asked us to be her royal guard. At first I refused; we were only fifty strong, hardly a guard force for a queen. But she insisted. The next thing we knew, we were in the mountains at her fortress. Many years passed and things were going very well. There were only a few small skirmishes in the area to deal with and we even had time to train a few new girls. But then that changed."

"Without warning, our neighboring kingdom attacked the fortress. Our army was not mobilized and was too far away to make it in time. To this day, I still don't know how such a large force got so close without us noticing, but assumedly foul magics were involved. But that doesn't matter anymore. There were less than eighty of us to defend her majesty and the princess. I knew we had no chance against the fighting force on our doorstep. I sent the queen and her daughter out a secret underground tunnel with ten of my best girls and told them to join up with our army. The rest of us were to stay behind and buy them time. I still remember the queen begging me to go with them, but I couldn't leave the rest of my girls to die alone and without a leader."

Maya was sobbing, cradling Winya in her hands in an attempt to comfort her. I found that I was crying as well; hell we all were. I slid into the chair next to Maya and she threw her arms around me and cried on my chest. "Why didn't you all run, you never stood a chance against that many."

"Sweet one, someone had to buy them the time to run. I knew that we would fall, but I also believed in my girls. They may have had the numbers, but the fortress was far more than a castle. Seventy of us had no trouble manning the walls. It was a brilliantly conceived stronghold; there were cliffs on three sides so they only had one way in, and we were located on the peak of the mountain. There is a river that runs down the main walls. The beings that built Sky Raven were very good at their task. In the end, they redirected the river to split into a 'T' shape in front of our main walls. If you fell in, the current would quickly pull you over the falls to your death. Without the river, we never would have lasted as long as we did. We lasted three days. Three days and four thousand of their men dead. But I was down to seven of my girls."

"Then the army retreated. I thought we had one more round in us before we would fall, but it never came. Hours passed, then a day, and nothing came. Our army should have been there long ago, but there was no sign of them. The eight of us used the same tunnel that we sent the queen out in hopes to find them again safe. But I was never ready for what was at the end. We emerged into the sunlight to be met with a blood-covered battlefield and the heads of my sisters on pikes."

"The duke responsible for this had captured the queen and princess and took them to our capital, where he forced the queen to marry him and named himself king. I gave my last girls a choice, try and start a new life or help me gut that pig. They all voted to join me without a second thought. We fought our way back into our city by using underground tunnels that are only known to the guard. I didn't take long to retake the keep, even with our few numbers. But we were too late; the duke had already killed the queen and the princess before we arrived. Naturally, we still killed him for it, as well as all his staff. But we had failed, the queen was dead, the princess was dead, and the city was still under foreign control. Even if we did leave, we had nowhere to go. Most of us only knew battle. So my last seven girls did the only thing they knew how to do. They marched out and took as many of those bastards as they could with them to hell."

"I was not so noble. I could not bear what I had done, the heavy burden of failure weighed on me like an anchor around my broken heart. If I hadn't sent them out that tunnel, the queen might still have lived. I promised her that I would protect her daughter at all cost and that I would die before I would ever let her be taken. But I failed. I had no one left to protect and, therefore, no purpose. I prayed to the gods that they send me a second chance in the afterlife and I vowed that I would not pass on until I completed my task, but they did not answer. Finally I took my own life because I could no *longer bear to live."*

Maya has run out of tears, but I could feel her shaking; she still hadn't lifted her head from my chest.

"I haven't told that to anyone in hundreds of years. I'm glad you can't see me in the state I'm in, I look worse than Rosa."

"But what about Alex?"

"Sorry, I'm almost there. Death was not quite what I was expecting; no molten lava or angels, no, just a lot of gray. It was like being in a big gray room with no walls, you just walk for miles. There were a few people there, as well; some were even my girls. But as time went on, they all gave up their desire to return and moved on. Many more years passed and I was starting to give up as well, but then I saw something odd. Lots of people were gathered around a glowing blue portal. I watched as a handsome young man talked with all the people around him, asking questions, and dismissing them one after another upon hearing the answers. After a few minutes, everyone had moved on and I was the last one left. He beckoned for me to come over to him and asked me what my dream was, and I told him 'to protect a princess for all my life.' The strange boy just smiled and offered me his hand. To be honest, I was baffled. He turned down several men who were far greater warriors than I ever was, yet he wanted me? I later learned more about Maya and happily agreed to take the responsibility. So from the way I see it, Alex has given me everything I ever wanted in return for having to live in a sword. I could like that, he gave me a new life and with it, my new name Winya Coia."

"But why did you agree to protect me, I'm not a princess?"

"No, but you are a queen, that worked fine for me."

"I'm not a queen! Where did you get that idea?"

"Not yet you aren't. But a kind female voice once told me that I would serve the queen of my land once more someday. She was talking about you, and here we are."

"And you told Alex all this before he bound you?"

"Yes, I did, and then some. We also made a deal that he has already honored. I would also guess that he knew about you being a queen, as well. He didn't look at all surprised when I said it."

Everyone turned to me, expecting some grand plan or something. The truth was that I did know, but I don't know why I did. My memories were oddly fuzzy, but I chalked it up to my being in one of my blacksmithing/Enchanter trances at the time.

Rosa must have been reading my mind again because she stepped in. "Yes, he knew, but that's not important right now. Winya, I feel awful for what happened to you in your past life, but I'm glad you're with us. You already saved Maya's life once, so I have no doubts about you. And I am also sorry, but I must turn this discussion around. Maya, with your quarters burnt to the ground, you will be staying in the third room upstairs."

"Also, I have started a plan to find the traitor in our academy. For a long time now, the Headmaster and I have been looking into a few things. It appears that someone here is moving a lot of supplies and other equipment needed to train wizards."

"What do you mean?" I asked.

She sighed. "From what I have gathered, someone is trying to open another school."

That caught us all by surprise. "But why? What would they

need another academy for?" asked Maya.

Rosa shook her head. "No, this one will be nothing like our school. Based on what I have found, the new school's purpose will be combat and only combat. I have found boxes and boxes of copied books being sent to this new place and not one of them is for healers, research or anything that doesn't have to do with killing. Whoever is making this new place only wants wizards for their power. And if they only see wizards as weapons, then I would say they intend to use them for war."

Maya nodded. "And if they are going to do that, then they will need to get rid of the only people who could stop them, and that would be the wizards of Xarparion."

"Exactly. But from what I know, they still need a lot more funding, and the best way for them to get it is coming up soon. So I will need you to do something for me, Alex. I need you to win the tournament coming up."

"Win the what?"

She smiled. "It's a duel, of course. Wizard versus wizard in one-on-one combat."

"How am I to beat wizards in combat if I can't cast spells?"

"Don't be silly, I know you can't cast spells. What you can do is bring any gear you want as long as you can carry it in with you."

That got me thinking. "So you want me to fight wizards with hammer and shield?"

"Yes, and some excellent armor, as well."

Maya seemed to like the idea the most; the thought of

kicking wizard butt seemed to get her spirits out of the dumps. "That would be amazing! I could have fun with this!"

"I'm sorry, Maya, but you can't enter; you need to be a wizard. So for now, we need to step up the preparation, starting the day after tomorrow. The rest of today you recover - Rosa's orders."

"Why not tomorrow then?"

"Alex, you silly boy. Tomorrow is your birthday!"

I had completely forgotten. It's funny how time flies.

Rosa quickly left, saying that she was late for a meeting with the Headmaster, leaving the three of us alone. Well, more like two of us. Nia had flown off in search of food when Rosa ended her speech. I turned back to Maya and hoped she wasn't mad at me anymore.

"Can you forgive me?"

She didn't say anything, just looked at me with her incredible green eyes. Then she nuzzled me with her face against my throat and whispered, "As long as you forgive me for not trusting in you. It will never happen again."

"I already have. I knew that talk would be a hard one for you to accept from the start."

"Hmm, then tell me about this queen thing."

"I really don't know anything about it."

"That's not what Winya said, and she hasn't lied to me yet."

"Ok, I had a dream that you became queen of a new kingdom."

She looked hard at me. "And where were you in this dream? Are you sure it was a dream? Not some magical vision of the future?"

"Well, you were in white and silver armor with a red cape and riding a unicorn. As you rode along a causeway, you were being saluted by golden angels."

"Ok, that sounds like a dream to me."

Chapter 13

Alex

The next morning I was in for a rude awakening, literally. The sun was nowhere to be seen, yet Rosa busted down the door and rousted us anyway.

"Get up! We have a big day today and we have to hurry or we will be late." She marched over to Nia's bed to shout at her, as well. "Nia! Time to get up!" She yanked the blanket off the poor pixie, sending her spinning like a sleepy top off the side of her pillow bed.

"What's going on, Rosa? Why are you even awake? How are you awake?"

She smiled. "It's easy to get up early if you never went to bed. Now, both of you get dressed. Nia, you can pick out a nice dress if you would like. Hurry up!"

The door to Maya's new room cracked opened and she stood there half asleep in her nightgown, holding Winya in sword form at the ready. I must admit that I was now suddenly interested. Even half asleep, she was gorgeous; oh, and did I mention in a nightgown?

"What's with all the noise, are we under attack?"

"Ah, Maya, I was just waking Alex so we can get on the road in time."

Personally, I don't think she heard any of that because her next statement was, "Oh, good, I thought the bunnies started their assault on Carrot Mountain." I looked at Nia and we both just shrugged. What do you say to something like that, "sorry, the radishes had reinforcements"?

She turned to head back to bed, but Rosa slipped between her and the door. "You're coming, too."

"Oh, fun…wait, what?"

"Get dressed. We're going on a trip."

Rosa dragged Maya into her room and slammed the door, leaving me and Nia staring at the door with no idea what was going on. She turned to me and asked "Alex, you have any idea what she's planning?"

"Nope, you?"

"Not a clue. But we better get dressed before she comes back. At least I get to wear a dress today," Nia said cheerily. I washed up and threw on a clean robe, then pondered a few minutes before deciding to bring along my war hammer and a small buckler, just in case. A half-hour later, we were being marched through the silent streets of Xarparion. Rosa told us to leave the talking to her and keep quiet until we were outside the walls. A funny thing happened when we got to the guards at the south gate. They took one look at me and opened the gate with no questions. They even escorted us past the second wall without any questions or stopping either. Once past the final wall, we were free to talk again.

"Well, that was weird."

Maya was walking beside me in her long cape with the full hood up. "Not really, you're kind of a celebrity among the guardsmen." She said lightly.

"I am? What for?"

"Well, for starters, you are a smith, and that's always a good thing to them. Second, you're an Enchanter of weapons." She smiled proudly. "And third, you're the only one who can match me in a duel. You have no idea what it was like when they found that out. I had to order extra laps to get them to stop asking me to bring you in to show them."

"I wouldn't mind if you ever want me to."

"Really? I mean, I never thought you would want to help me train a bunch of recruits."

"I have no problem with that, but I will say that the main reason would be to spar with you more. Have you noticed that the more we duel, the more it feels like an intricate dance rather than a fight?"

She smiled saucily and gave me a hip check, which accidently hurled Nia off my shoulder. Thankfully, she was just awake enough to recover before hitting the ground.

"I am so sorry, Nia, I forgot that you were up there."

"Don't worry about it, Maya. I'll just sit on his big head from now on, and then you can beat Alex all you want," she said, yawning grumpily.

We walked for an hour or so before we got to the same portal that I came through the first day I came to Xarparion. It looked so strange back then, but now I know how it works, and that Rosa was the one who made them so many years ago. Maya seemed very relaxed and happy being out of the city and even commented that this was her favorite area when she joined the guards for perimeter patrols.

"Alright everyone, this is it. Maya, you may want to keep your hood up for now and, Nia, you should stay in Alex's pocket until we reach our destination," Rosa commanded.

Nia climbed into one of my pockets that was big enough so she could stand up and still look out if she wanted. Maya raised her hood back in place and took my hand.

"So we're going through that?"

"Yes, it's a portal to my home village."

"I've been almost up to it many times but never this close before. We have to jump into a pool of water to get there?"

"Trust me, it's not as bad as it looks. Didn't you use one to get to Xarparion?"

"Of course not, I had to walk." Ouch, we were weeks away from anything that even resembled a village!

I placed my hand on her head over her hood and then did the enchantment that I learned from watching Rosa so that she would look human.

"What was that for? Not that I don't like a pat on the head, but still..."

"I copied the enchantment Rosa used on your dress, only this one only works when your hood is up."

"That will be nice to have, thanks."

I heard the end of a sigh from Rosa. "You know, sometimes I feel that you're getting this enchanting way too easily. That one took me months to learn and you got it instantly from just watching me do it once."

"I can't help that I have the best teacher in the world. If

anything, you should blame your excellent mentoring skills."

She smiled, "You're darn right. Now come on, it's time for a swim."

We started to wade into the pool. I had Nia stay in my pocket so she wouldn't freak out; scared hyper-powered pixies are not fun. Sadly, I couldn't do the same for Maya. She had a death grip on my arm and looked in no mood to be here.

"Would now be a bad time to say that I never learned to swim?" she whispered warily.

"No swimming needed, just walking."

"Good. I also don't care if I hurt you; I'm not letting go. If I get sucked down a whirlpool or swallowed by a giant fish, I'm taking you with me," she gritted.

I smiled, "That's entirely fair from my standpoint."

We passed through without any problems. Nia apparently didn't listen and poked her head out to take a look. Strangely, she seemed to love the experience and demanded to do it again. Maya looked like she was going to be nauseous.

"Let's never do that again."

"Well, unless you would enjoy walking back, we kind of have to," I countered mildly.

She thought that over for a second and made a decision. "Walking it is. I'd say we would get back in about six months, but it could be fun, just the two of us. By the way, what are we doing in your village anyway?"

Rosa clamped her hands down on each of our shoulders.

"Come now, Maya, even Alex has figured it out. We're going to visit his family for his birthday."

Maya froze in place. The look on her face was one of pure horror. "You're taking me to his parents? But, Rosa, I'm not ready for that! What am I going to say to them? How do I convince them that I'm not a monster?"

Rosa wrapped her in her arms and whispered in her ear, "There is nothing to worry about. I have looked into Alex's mind, and I think you will be surprised at the reaction you get."

"But what if they don't like me?"

"They will love you, just wait and see."

Coming out of the gates of the keep, we walked through town. I noticed that the townspeople I knew were keeping their heads down and ignoring me, most even seemed somewhat afraid. I could hear a number of them whispering questions about what kind of wizard wore white. I was starting to think that something was wrong, but then I remembered I was seeing the odd, symbiotic relationship that Xarparion had with Foalshead from the other side of the aisle, and it was a sobering sight. We arrived at my old house on the outskirts of town to find that it had changed drastically. It was now larger, recently painted and had new windows. All in all, it was now one of the nicer-looking houses in Foalshead. The shed for the forge out back was even rebuilt and expanded.

I anxiously knocked on the door, hoping that my parents were home and that this trip was not a waste. I also felt like I needed them to meet my master and friends. But those fears vanished when my mother opened the door. She looked a little more gray-haired than my mind's eye remembered, and the laugh lines were deeper, but she still wore the same simple work dress and sweater as always. She stood there with no expression at all, just stared at me.

"Um, hello. Mom, are you ok?"

"It *is* you." She wrapped me in a hug. As much as I wanted to hug her back, I had to keep my arms between us to protect Nia from getting squished. "You have no idea how much I missed you. I was starting to think you would never come back!"

"Can we come inside so I can introduce my friends?"

She then realized there were, in fact, others with me and started fussing with embarrassment. "I am so sorry; everyone, please come inside!"

She led us inside to the living room. Again, there were some improvements from the last time I saw it; some new chairs, the old cracked pine mantle had been replaced with a solid, new oak one. I found myself cataloging where everything was and what was new.

"Honey, come quick, Alex is home!"

My dad came in from one of the back rooms, wiping his hands on a towel. He looked me up and down with an approving nod and shook my hand firmly.

"You look good, son."

"Thanks, Dad. But please, let me introduce everyone." I stood next to Rosa and stepped her forward a bit. Through the link, I could tell even she was nervous. "This is Primus Rosa. You both met her before, and she's my master, teacher, adviser and stand-in over-protective mother." She elbowed me in the side.

"It's so nice to meet both of you again. I've heard so many stories of his youth, it's nice to finally be able to thank the ones who shaped him into such a fine young man."

My mother blushed and my father brushed the complements away like they were common facts.

"He is twenty now, and from the looks of it, I'd say he is a real man.

"Compared to me, he's just a baby."

The two of them looked confused, so I pulled her hair out of the way so they could see her ears. "She's an elf and about seven hundred years old. We will talk more about that later. Right now, I'd like to introduce someone else."

I undid the button on my pocket and carefully helped Nia climb out. Seconds later, she was sitting in the palm of my hand waving at my parents, trying to look cute and succeeding at it, too.

"This is Nia. As you can tell, she is a pixie. She is our friend, as well as my bodyguard."

My parents were stunned, but not because they had never seen a pixie. No, I could tell they just never thought they would see one again. My mother started firing off question after question so fast that I don't even know what she was talking about. Nia was even more confused than I was. She looked up at me in a plea for help.

"Mother, please calm down, there will be time for questions later."

"I'm sorry, you're right. But she's just so cute!"

Lastly, I turned to Maya, who was looking both confused and terrified at the same time. I put my arm around her to try and comfort her; I still didn't know why she was so scared of my family. I whispered into her ear. "Are you ok?"

"Alex, why aren't they afraid of Nia?" she whispered back in awe.

"My family has some experience with forest folk. Don't worry, I think you will find that they will like you even more than Nia."

She was even more confused now. I coaxed her from out behind Rosa and closer to my parents.

"Alex, don't tell them that you're courting her, she needs to do it herself," Winya whispered in my head.

"Mom, Dad, this is Maya."

She bowed formally. "I am very pleased to meet you both. I am Alex's combat instructor."

"There's also one more thing." And with that, I pulled down her hood and let the show begin. It was a dirty trick to play on Maya, but I knew it would turn out just fine. If they were stunned when they saw Nia, then I don't know what they were now. Maya was horrified and quickly tried to pull up her hood again to hide herself. My mother grabbed her in a hug with tears in her eyes. My father even joined in, and he is not the kind of guy to give out hugs lightly.

Maya was even more shocked than they were. She never considered receiving a welcome like this; tears for a complete stranger all because she was a dark elf? My mother pulled down the hood again to get a good look at Maya's true face. "You're a very beautiful woman; please don't hide yourself from us."

"Why aren't you afraid of me?" Maya stammered in confusion.

They were surprised. "Didn't Alex tell you? We lived in a dark elf village for many years. Alex was even born there and spent the first twelve years of his life there before we had to move here."

Maya and Nia were speechless. They both kept looking from my parents to me, thinking one of us was going to say it was a joke. Rosa wasn't too shocked, she being a mind reader and all. But I was surprised that she never mentioned it to me.

"You grew up around dark elves?"

"Yep. I'm surprised you didn't figure it out before now."

"And how exactly would I have anticipated that?" Maya said, her eyes narrowing dangerously.

"Haven't you ever wondered why you never have to worry about eating anything that would be distasteful or poisonous to you whenever you're at the Enchanters Hall?"

Her eyes widened. "Nothing ever was!"

"Or how I never asked you questions about your homeland or dark elf society?"

"And that you know about dark elf medicine?" Maya shook her head.

"That, as well."

"I can't believe I missed that...I must have been distracted." She arched an eyebrow in my direction, letting me know that there would be revenge extracted at some point in the future.

Everyone settled in the living room in the new chairs that my parent bought. Apparently, they spent half of the money they received from Rosa as compensation for taking me on the house and

Dad's business, and are saving the rest for if he ever stops working, but I don't see that happening of his own free will.

"So, son, tell us about life at Xarparion. What are your classes about and what do you do?"

"Well, Dad, as you can see, I'm wearing a white robe so that makes me an Enchanter, not that I expect you to ever know what we are.

"We are not so ignorant as to not know what a wizard is."

"That's not what I meant. You both have seen plenty of wizards in robes running around, right? Well, each color represents what type of wizard they are. Green for earth, red for fire and so on. But have you ever seen a wizard in white?"

"Now that you mention it, no, we haven't."

"That's because you have the entire Enchanters Hall and staff in your home."

"What? There are only four of you?"

Rosa stepped in. "That is correct. And to be more precise, only your son and I are Enchanters. As far as I know, the only two in existence at this time. Unlike other wizards, Enchanters can't project magic, we shape it. With our powers, we can make an ordinary item into a magical one, or shape an item's characteristics into something else, like making cloth hard as stone. Your son is really incredible as both an Enchanter and a young man." She directed her attention to my mother. "And I must thank you, Mrs. Martin, very much for the skills you gave him, especially his cooking and healing skills."

"His cooking skills?"

"Believe it or not, Mother, but in her seven hundred years, Rosa has never learned to cook. In fact, all of her household skills are terrible. Nia is only two years old, and even she can cook."

Rosa punched me extremely hard in the arm. She put enough force into it to overcome my new resilience so that her punch would now hurt, and boy did she succeed.

"Ow, Rosa, what was that for?"

"For trying to make a fool of me, and I had to make it hurt."

"Son, did you just get hurt by a woman? And here I thought you got tougher," my father groused.

"I have an idea, Dad. Why don't you challenge Rosa and Maya to a test of strength? Then we will talk about what hurts or not."

Rosa has happy with that, and Maya was happy with anything to get her out of the limelight. I hoped she would loosen up and have some fun today.

Turns out my father had just the thing to test their strength on - which contestant can carry the most iron. I already knew who was going to win this one. I watched from the sidelines as my father did his first lift of five ingots. My mother hugged my arm as she stood beside me, watching, as well.

"So who will win, Alex?"

"Rosa, by far."

"And here I thought you were going to side with your gorgeous girlfriend."

I turned to her. "You knew?"

She nodded. "A mother always knows. It's easy to see. When she looks at you, her eyes fill with affection and she can't stop smiling, even after you surprised her by not telling her about us. That was mean, by the way, and if she's anything like the elf girls back home in our old village, you will be paying for that when she gets you alone." Mom reached up and ruffled my hair a bit. "All the while she's been here; she keeps stroking that beautiful bracelet of hers. Did you make it for her?"

I nodded. "She is talking things over with Winya, asking for advice on what she should do and say. Maya has lived at the school for seven years, but in many ways, she is still pretty new to human society."

"Who is Winya?"

I smiled. "Winya is the spirit of the sword I crafted for Maya. I wanted to protect her. So I made her a guardian that will be forever faithful and never leave or abandon her, even if I am not there.

My mother's eyes danced with mischief. "And would I be prying if I asked if this magnificent sword is her personal weapon?"

Before I could answer, the others came over to us. My father was dumbfounded, but both Rosa and Maya were happy as could be. My father was still scratching his head, trying to wrap his head around what just happened.

"I don't get how I lost to a couple of skinny girls."

"I'd watch what you say to them Dad. All five of the ladies in this house could kick your butt."

"Five?"

"Rosa has magically enhanced strength, Maya is the best

swordswoman on the planet, Nia has spells and the natural pixie inclination for mischievous mayhem, and we both know you would never stand a chance against Mom."

"That's true, but who is the fifth?"

"The last class I take is a bladesmithing class. And I have gotten very good at it. Maya, would you like to show my parents Winya Coia?"

My father did a double-take as the bracelet shimmered and transformed dramatically into the silver and white shining long sword. Disbelief turned to professional anger in a heartbeat, and he grew red-faced.

"The Mage School taught you about weapons? I find that hard to believe, you were just a half-decent ordinary blacksmith when you left, and now you are trying to tell me that you somehow learned decades worth of skills in a few months and forged that showpiece? This is complete idiocy! I don't believe it! I didn't raise you to be a liar!"

Maya didn't like that, I could tell from the look on her face. She stepped in front of my father and held Winya sideways in front of her to display the masterwork in her full glory. The rays of light streaming in through the windows lit up the emerald pommel stone like a torch.

"Mr. Martin, your son is the best smith ever to walk this earth. Even Xarparion's dwarf Forge Master, and Alex's instructor, cannot match his creations. He forged Winya Coia and breathed life into her, solely to protect me. She has already saved my life twice, so please, never doubt his abilities or his word." Her eyes blazed brightly. "And one more thing, my full name is Maya, only daughter of Faeron Talmin, high chieftain of the Flint Bands of my people, and

I would like permission to court your son."

There was that name again, the recognition of which was right on the tip of my brain, but slipped away. As it looked like my mother was about to faint, she had obviously heard it before. Dad paused to look at both Maya and Mom for a second, and then focused on me. He just stared. I could tell he was getting madder by the second. I was just waiting for him to explode like I had seen a thousand times before, but this time he surprised me.

"He is not my son to give," he vented angrily and then marched off to the shed to work. The rest of us just stood there in shocked awkward silence. I was still trying to comprehend what he meant by that. I looked at my mother for clues, but she had gone white as a ghost and was clutching one of the chair arms like it was the only thing keeping her on her feet.

"Mom, what did he mean by that?"

"Please forgive him, Alex. We both prayed to all the gods that you would not come today. We just don't want to lose you."

"What are you talking about?"

"I'm sorry to tell you like this...but we are not your real parents." My head was swimming. Not my real parents? They were the only ones I remembered. How could they not be? And if not, what happened to my birth parents?

"Please explain."

She motioned for us all to take a seat. "On this day, twenty years ago, two strangers, a man and woman, showed up at the dark elf village. Both were hooded and we could not see their faces, but we could feel immense power flowing from them. It was terrifying, but at the same time, I could feel no malice or evil from them, just overwhelming sadness. They had with them many things, but the most important was the newborn boy that the woman was cradling. They asked the village leader for permission to leave the child. The elder objected saying that a child must have a family, not just a village. Your father and I had been praying to all the gods for the blessing of a child but it never came to pass, and we eagerly agreed to care for you until this day." She paused to steady herself. "They quickly departed, as if somehow pursued, but they left us with instructions, most of them very strange. We had to take a very heavy box with us that neither of us could open, and we had to keep a stable for horses, even though we never owned any. We were also told to give you these on your twentieth birthday, which is today."

She withdrew two well-worn envelopes with no markings on them from her dress pocket and handed them to me. "These are from your real parents; we've never tried to read them."

Then she ran off into the kitchen crying. I motioned for Rosa and Nia to go with her; they both knew what I needed them to do. This left Maya and me alone with the letters. I looked at them dumbfounded. Twenty years of memories proving to be some elaborate hoax; it was really too much to wrap my head around for the moment. Maya moved closer, trying to lend me strength through touch.

"I'm sorry, Alex, this can't be the birthday you were expecting." She massaged my shoulders gently as she looked at the letters in my hands and leaned down to kiss away the salty tear that was traveling slowly down my cheek.

"You have nothing to be sorry for. I suppose this could explain why I'm not normal," I gritted, shaking my head.

"I know you're feeling hurt and confused right now. But never forget you have people who love you for who you are, and no amount of revelations about your parentage is going to change that. Now, perhaps there are some answers in the letters. Are you going to read them?"

"I guess I have to."

I opened the first letter, but the page was blank. I turned it over and there was nothing on the backside either. Exchanging glances with Maya only revealed her baffled expression as well. She moved around and perched on the chair's arm. Then words started appearing on the paper. It was as if someone was invisible and just now writing a letter. I read along as best I could.

"Hello, Alex…Son… You have no idea how sorry I am for what we did to you, but please understand that we did it for your safety. If I could have, I would have kept you for all eternity. Your mother was beside herself with grief for years after we were forced to leave you. I am sorry to say this, as well, but we cannot tell you who we really are. Just know that we have been watching you for all your life and helping where we could. Soon we will have our chance to talk face-to-face and we will explain everything to you then. In the meantime, I understand that you have a wizards' tournament to prepare for, so I whipped together a small gift for your birthday. And don't think I have forgotten all the others I have missed, either. When the time is right, I shall give them to you as well. Until then, the box behind the shed is yours. From what I know of you, it should be a fine gift. Oh, and there should be plenty for two sets. And one more thing, tell Maya that she has my sincere blessings for your courtship. Good luck with her, she is something special. And I thought my wife was a handful. Good luck, son. Your Father."

"Well, he seems nice," Maya breathed out with some relief.

"And you're not alarmed that he knows all about us and who you are?"

She laughed nervously. "Well, yeah, I am, but I get the feeling that your parents aren't normal people. Maybe they are very powerful wizards or something. Hey, maybe they're gods!"

We both laughed, but I don't think my father found it to be a joke because the writing on the letter changed to *"WE ARE NOT GODS! THE GODS ARE COMPLETE IDIOTS!"*

"Sorry!" we replied in unison.

The writing changed again. *"I know, just having some fun with you two. The looks on your faces were hilarious. But really, we are not gods. Anyway, you need to read your mother's letter now. She is getting very impatient with me!"*

I opened the other letter and positioned myself so that Maya could read it, too. She seemed as interested in the message as I was, but I suppose that's natural when you are sort of meeting your future mother-in-law for the first time.

"Dear Alex, you have no idea how much I love you, and it kills me that you have lived your entire life not knowing it. But please understand that if your life were not in danger, I never would have left you. This was the only way for you to have a life. But one thing that your father and I could do was to see that you had the opportunity for a good life, one filled with glory and adventure. The moment you stepped into Xarparion, your life changed for the better. We have been shaping the world to be ready for you, even for the people around you. I'm sorry, Maya, if you ever hate us for shaping your life a bit as well, but you were the only one that my son would give his heart to. I know it's pitiful of us to try and buy your acceptance and love with gifts, but I don't care. Gifts were what got

me interested in your father before I knew what a wonderful man he is, so I say bring on the bribes! I have delivered to you two of my best creations. I know you will love them, Maya. Your best dreams are filled with you riding off into the sunset on one; well maybe not your 'best dreams,' there's that one…"

Maya's hand was covering the rest of what mother was writing. I looked at her and she was blushing furiously and plainly about to die of embarrassment.

"Alex! If you care for me at all…I'm begging you, please don't read that line!"

"I won't. Mother could you please not talk about Maya's dreams. They are private and she doesn't want me to know."

I carefully removed Maya's hand to reveal that Mother had removed that line; in fact, she started over at the top of the page.

"I'm terribly sorry, Maya, I already feel as if I know you, and affectionate teasing is part of my nature. I just forget that you don't know me yet, but we will have to fix that very soon. Maya, you are our stalwart one, and we owe you far more than mere gifts can convey. As I was saying, they're in the stables waiting; you need to take them with you. And don't worry; they are very smart and already trained. Well, we have to say goodbye for now. We will see you soon. Oh, and make sure you hold on to these letters so we can talk more. I love you both!"

"Ok, your mother is very strange…and does everyone we meet have to be a dream reader?" she muttered under her breath.

"Yeah, but I think they're both just new to the parenting thing. But for now, let's go see what they're so excited about. I vote we start with my father's gift."

"Ok, it's your birthday, but I have to admit that your mother's gift has me the most intrigued."

I held her hand and led her across our small farm to the back of the shed. Despite all the improvements that Rosa's gold had bought, the farm seemed impossibly small, almost alien to me now. For the first time, the realization hit me that this was no longer my real home. I glanced gratefully at the woman walking supportively at my side, lending me her strength.

And as my father's letter had stated, there was a large rectangular box that seemed to be carved out of a dark glass-like substance. It wasn't something anyone could miss, especially thinking back to the number of times I pulled weeds behind this very structure. I found it impossible to imagine that I'd never seen it before. But then surreal seemed to be the order of the day today. Sitting on that box was my foster father, just staring at the dirt. He looked over at us and I could see the sadness in his eyes.

"Maya, could you please give me some time alone with Alex?"

She put a comforting hand on my shoulder. "I'll be in the stables when you're done." And with that she left, although I could tell she really wanted to see what was in there.

He moved over to make room for me to sit with him on the long black box.

"I take it you read the letters?" he began gravely.

"Yes, they are interesting people."

"From what little I remember, that they are. Look son, I'm not the kind of man to dance around a problem, so I'll just say it. I'm sorry."

I looked him in the eyes, what was he talking about?

"I'm sorry we lied to you all these years. I'm sorry you were kept from your real family and your true birthright. I'm sorry we couldn't give you the life you deserved. And I'm most sorry for the way I acted today toward you and your friends."

"Dad, you have nothing to be sorry for. You and Mom may not be my birth parents, but you are the ones who raised me and taught me to find meaning in my life. Without you two, I would not be the man I am today, and I wouldn't change a thing, believe me."

He wrapped an arm around me. "I'm proud of you, son. No matter what I ever say, just know I'm proud."

We laughed the tension away between us, and things were back the way they always were. "I do have a few questions for you, though," he continued.

"And what's that?"

"Explain to me the roles of all your friends again."

"Well, Rosa is my primus or master and enchanting instructor. Nia is my bodyguard and a student; Rosa is teaching her to control her magic. Darroth is a dwarf Forge Master and my bladesmithing teacher. And Maya is my combat instructor, best friend, and well...quite a lot more. We're courting and someday, if I'm blessed, she'll be my wife."

"You have done well for yourself with her."

"More than well, Dad; she is beyond amazing."

"I can see that. It's hard to find a woman who has some

starch, likes to get her hands dirty, and can still act like a lady when the time is needed. Well, enough about that stuff, you need to open this box. I have been guarding it for twenty years and I'm dying to know what's inside."

We both stood up and I started looking for a way to open the thing. After finding no form of keyhole, I started looking for other ways to open it. On the lid was an outline of a hand. Having seen some similar items in Rosa's lab work by touching them, I figured it wouldn't hurt to try. Placing my hand on the outline, we heard a loud click, followed by the box lifting itself two feet off the ground. It just hovered there. Having also seen this type of enchantment before, I knew it was to lift heavy objects and allow you to move them around with ease. I tried to open the lid again and it moved. Shoving the heavy glassine cover to the side revealed the contents; rows of bricks made of pure white metal and many bolts of fine silver-hued chainmail.

"Wow, he wasn't kidding when he said there was enough for two. I could make a set of weapons and a shield and two sets of armor and still have some left," I whispered under my breath. I felt something stir within me, a reaction to the metals almost on an unconscious level. I was drawn to the contents, and they to me. The metal reminded me of the starlode that I crafted Winya from, but on an order many times purer and more powerful.

"What is all this?"

"It was in the letter. It's a gift from my birth father. I'm guessing that he somehow collected this for me to enchant with. I've never seen anything like it, even the special metal I forged Winya from was weak compared to this. I can sense the magic is barely containing itself within the walls of its current form. It yearns to be something else, and it needs me."

"But what is it?"

"I honestly don't know. But it will be fun to see what I can do with it."

"So you really are a master smith now?"

I shook my head ruefully. "Dad, I would never claim to have the years of experience at the forge that you or Master Darroth have, so the title "Master" wouldn't be fitting. It's more like I have a natural-born affinity for the metal. I know it sounds crazy, but it talks to me and I to it when I'm smithing." I eyed him. "I really did make Winya, you know."

"Yes, I know. Winya is amazing. Master smith or no, I've never seen such work, and it's a perfect courting gift, too. I really hope her dark elf father will be impressed enough to not try and kill you on sight." He grinned and punched me in the shoulder. "And speaking of your girl and her fancy sword, how long are you going to keep her sitting alone in an empty stable?"

I smiled. "Oh, it's not empty anymore, and somehow, I have a feeling that I'll never get her away from them again."

He was confused, and that didn't often happen. "Why...you know what, never mind. You go get your betrothed, and I'll go check on your mother. You all are planning to stay for dinner, correct?"

"That was the plan, but be aware that all of us eat a lot, and I mean a lot."

"Not to worry, your mother even knows some dark elf dishes she can make. You know, bringing Maya here brought back many good memories of our old home and the friends we left behind."

"That would be perfect. I don't think she has had anything

from her homeland in a long time. Thanks, Dad, for everything." We shook hands warmly and parted. He went into the house and I made my way the short distance to the stables. Out of curiosity, I put my ear to the door to see if I could tell what she was doing in there. I heard what sounded like a dog and Maya giggling. I opened the door and was surprised by what I saw. Inside, Maya was playing with two enormous blue-eyed winter wolves. The odd thing was, they were having fun, none of the typical trying-to-eat-you stuff. But as soon as they all saw me, they froze.

"Alex! Look what your mother brought us! She gave us our own hunting wolves, isn't that incredible?"

The wolves, on the other hand, did something strange. They sat on their haunches next to each other and stared at me, their tails sweeping the odd bit of dirt and straw powerfully from side to side. It was as if they were waiting for me to say something. I had a strange feeling that these were by no means normal animals. In fact, looking at their magic, I knew they weren't wolves at all.

I gently grabbed Maya by the arm and pulled her a few feet away from the wolves, and they made no move to stop me.

"Alex, what's wrong?"

"These really aren't wolves, Maya."

She looked as though she was going to question me, but the look on my face must have been a serious one. She, too, started to look concerned.

"Ok, please change to your true forms," I said addressing the canines.

The two wolves exchanged looks and then nodded to

themselves. After taking a few steps backward to space themselves from us, they transformed. Fur turned to scale, jaws elongated, tails lengthened a lot, claws bristled, body weight quadrupled, and eyes became saurian. They were young dragons! They were about twenty feet long and ten feet tall. They had to lower their heads to our level in order to stay below the stable rafters, and their tails had to wrap most of the way around their bodies. Both had dull silver scales and very long, very slender bodies. Large skin-covered wings folded gracefully on their backs. They were very beautiful, majestic creatures. But I could still see plenty of dagger-like teeth and very sharp claws.

Maya must have just been looking at the teeth and claws because she instantly had Winya at the ready.

I gently took hold of her arm. "Maya, Winya, please calm down. They aren't going to hurt you."

"But they're dragons, Alex!"

"Maya, listen to me! They are silver dragons, silver. Not red or green or black, but silver. Trust me, I know a lot about magic creatures now thanks to Rosa, and I'm pretty sure my birth mother wouldn't send us anything that wasn't wonderful."

She lowered her sword slowly and turned her glare away from the two young dragons and put it fully on me. I love to watch her when she's like this, primal beauty at its finest. It can make your blood run cold, as well.

"You know full well the history and what dragons did to my kind!"

"Yes, I do. But at any time in your history, did a dragon whose scales were metallic attack you?"

She thought for a moment. "No, I've never even heard of a metal-colored dragon."

"That's because metal dragons are good dragons."

"Then why have I never heard of them if they are so 'good'?"

I knelt down in front of one of the young dragons and stroked the smooth scales of its head. It purred in satisfaction; they really were gorgeous creatures.

"You haven't heard of them because they're nearly extinct. Aside from these two, I only know of one other, and she's a golden dragon that lives in the Elcanse capital."

"A dragon in the capital? You're joking; you can't hide something as big as a dragon!"

"Metal dragons aren't like the colored ones. They are talkative, honorable, and spend most of their time helping right the wrongs of this world. They can change form just like these two did to become wolves.

"So these two won't start breathing fire and killing everyone?"

I laughed a little. "No, they won't. In fact, they can't breathe fire."

"No breath weapon; well, that's a start." Maya exhaled, becoming a little more relaxed, and Winya reverted back to her bracelet identity.

"No, I said they don't breathe fire."

I pulled her down next to me so she was closer to the dragons. I took her right hand and looked her in the eyes.

"Do you trust me?"

She nodded, "I followed you into a magical pool of water over my head when I can't swim, didn't I?" I moved her hand so it rested on the crest of the young dragon in front of her. For its part, the young drake remained motionless. Its eyes were like multifaceted dark silver ornaments that radiated friendly, peaceful intent.

"It's cold."

"I would hope so."

"So tell me about them, then." She was stroking the head of her dragon and even scratching under its chin, which caused it to sigh happily and lean into her attentions.

"Well, these are apparently young silver dragons. They are also called shield dragons from time to time because of the shape of their crest. They grow to be the largest type of metal dragon, getting easily three times larger or more than they are now, their scales becoming so thick that they are practically indestructible. Silvers like to shape themselves into humans and often live among common folk, even making lifelong friends and taking human or elf lovers."

"Until they get hungry and eat all the farm animals!"

"Silvers' diets are the same as ours. They are fine with three normal-sized meals a day like your ordinary person. Thankfully, they don't have any odd tendencies like the others do."

"What do you mean?"

"The others, like copper, brass and bronze dragons, all have odd traits; like coppers are tricksters and brass never shut up."

"What about gold?"

"They are too good-willed to do things like that. In fact, that's why they are so rare. They like to give themselves quests to face the forces of evil...often alone and against great odds."

"So what can silvers do?"

"They can sleep on clouds."

"Uh, how does that work?"

"I don't know, you would have to ask one," I grinned.

"Like I'm going to be able to find a dragon that will tell me," she snorted.

Wow, she had already forgotten what she was petting with her hands. I nodded to Maya and to the dragon in front of me, hoping that it would understand.

"Then perhaps we could be of assistance, my lady?" The voice was not what I was expecting from a dragon. It was smooth and very feminine. If I didn't know where it came from, I would have said a young noble girl was in the stables with us.

Maya froze. "You can talk?"

"We apologize if we startled you." Both young dragons bowed their heads to us. "We also regret our late introduction, but we had to be sure that you two were the ones we seek. I am the silver dragon, Dawn. This is my sister, the silver dragon, Dusk." Dawn sat in front of me and Dusk was still purring under Maya's rubbings. "We are both extremely honored to meet you, Alex and Maya."

I nudged Maya out of her trance, and she recovered a little shamefaced. "Oh, um, thank you. Hey, I am truly sorry if I was rude at first."

The dragons smiled, their lips appear to be more nimble than I thought. "No, you two honor us with this chance. Alex's mother saved our lives when we were still in our eggs."

"What happened?"

Dusk pulled away from Maya and took over the tale. Her voice was almost the same as her sister's, just a bit higher. "Our story is not a long one. When we awoke in our eggs, we were driven by the need to get out. Normally, with the aid of our egg tooth, it would have been easy, but over the many years that we were in that cave, sand and rock had fallen around us, covering our shells. Unable to escape, we screamed for help as our time was running out. But when we were about to give up, we felt the debris shift away from us and a voice said, 'I have given you a chance, now you must fight for your right to live.' With the rocks and sand gone, we were able to break out of our shells to find the woman who aided us. She told us that to repay her, we must serve her son when the time came, and that you would grant our wish as payment once your destiny is fulfilled."

I sighed and turned to Maya, "Why does everyone else know more about us than we do?"

"I don't know, but it is pissing me off," she whispered.

The two dragons looked confused. "You do not know of what we speak?"

"No." I shrugged.

"Not a thing. Everyone just keeps calling me a queen," Maya complained softly, with a concerned look in my direction, and I could see a certain line of thought there that troubled her greatly.

"That's a shame. We were hoping you would be able to tell

us. Now all of us are confused," Dawn added.

"Well, no point in moping about it here, dinner should be about ready. We need to get inside before Rosa eats everything."

"No kidding! A tip for you two, if Rosa is around, eat fast," Maya advised.

"We will do as you say, my lady."

We started for the door with the two dragons following us. It occurred to me that having them in their true form and in the house would probably be a bad idea.

"Please, can you two turn human for this? I don't think my parents would like the house destroyed."

They both hissed laughingly. "We were hoping you would ask us. In truth, we would love to practice our human forms."

Watching them change forms is kind of creepy. It's just too unnatural, like a reversal of the wolf transformation, but now with obviously bare human skin and female skin, at that! Fortunately, shimmering dresses appeared shortly after to cover them. The two "girls" were now about our age, with brown wavy hair and tan skin. They had silver-colored eyes that matched their dresses exactly. Both had huge, if slightly confused smiles that didn't quite look natural. They were still learning facial expression and human movement, as well. They looked great, mind you, but they still had nothing on Maya.

"You two are twins?"

"Why, of course, we are from the same clutch."

"Well, let's go, I'm starving."

Maya fell in beside me. "Eyes front, recruit. We'll have no 'twins' fantasies on my watch," she grinned and poked me in the ribs.

The four of us entered the house and made our way to the new dining room where everyone else was waiting. As soon as we entered the room, I knew that Rosa and Nia had succeeded in lightening the mood for my parents. Dad and Rosa were at the table drinking the wine she brought. Mother was in the adjacent kitchen with Nia cooking up a storm and seeming to be having a great time with her, but even so, she was the first to notice us enter.

"Alex, your friend Nia is amazing in the kitchen. She has really been a great help."

Nia blushed and hid behind a pot in embarrassment. "Mr. Alex was the one who taught me everything I know."

"Who are your friends?"

I moved Dawn and Dusk up front. From their expressions, I guessed they aren't used to being in public or being around people at all. "Everyone, I would like to introduce Dawn and Dusk. My birth mother sent them to us."

Everyone introduced themselves and shook hands, and my mom gave them a huge hug, which they seemed to enjoy. Rosa gave me a knowing look to tell me she knew what they were, and I could sense she approved. Mom got them seated at the long table and, with help from Nia, set out plates and bowls for everyone.

"I really hope you like what we are making for dinner tonight, Maya. It's my best dark elf dish that I learned a long time ago."

Maya's smile lit up the room. "Really? It's been so long since I have had anything from my homeland. Not that your food is anything but excellent, Alex."

"Don't worry, I know what you mean."

"Well, you won't have to worry about that anymore. I will be sending some of my cookbooks home with you so Alex can make you any recipe you would like."

She hugged my arm. "Any recipe? Now that does sound splendid to me."

Mom laughed, "Yes, even those recipes!"

I looked at the now blushing Maya. "Huh?" Damn, another tantalizing insight lost. I really need to be paying better attention!

"Oh, nothing you need to worry about right now. I'm starving, so let's eat."

Maya wrapped her arms around Dawn and Dusk, much to their surprise. "Come on, you two, you can sit by me. I'm sure you're both hungry, and if Mrs. Martin's the one who taught Alex how to cook, then this is going to be extra special."

"Maya, please just call me Mom, I already know you and Alex were meant for each other."

Awkward timing on that one, Mom! But thankfully, Maya just nodded and brushed it off, returning to helping the young dragons to their seats. I had Mom find her seat next to Dad so she could visit with everyone, then went into the kitchen to help Nia finish up.

"So how is everything going in here?"

Nia was busy stirring a large pot of some form of soup that smelled familiar from my childhood. She was also working on bread and a huge chunk of terrific-smelling roasted meat suspended over the cooking hearth next to the stove. She turned to me and let out a sigh of relief.

"I'm sorry, Mr. Alex, but I've been stirring this pot for over an hour and my wings are killing me. But as for how dinner is going, everything should be done in a few minutes."

I patted my shoulder. "Take a break, Nia, I'll take over for you."

She slowly flew over and crash-landed noisily on my shoulder. "Thank you so much, my wings were starting to cramp up."

"You know our rule about you saying so when your wings are tired." I took over stirring the soup.

"I know, but your mother was so nice to me and I wanted her to be happy. I also didn't know if I would fit on her shoulder like I do with you."

"Why wouldn't you?"

"Master, you are huge compared to your mom; there's a lot of room up here. Oh, and it's time to take the dessert out of the oven."

I grabbed some padded mitts and removed the dessert that turned out to be my mom's famous blackberry cobbler. This evening keeps getting better and better. Setting that out to cool, I returned to the soup. "So what did my mom say this soup was?"

"She said it was a cave root soup, something that the dark elves seem to love. It's made from a root that tastes like a potato but with a strong butter flavor. Then there are bits of beef and bacon mixed in, as well, but the bacon was not part of the original recipe.

We just had it on hand and thought it would be good. I think it will taste wonderful, or it's just that I'm hungry and she hasn't let me lick out anything." I laughed.

"But really, Master, she hasn't let me lick ANYTHING! I'm starving!"

"Well, if your wings are up to it, I believe everything is ready to serve."

She sprang into action. "You bet! Sooner it's on the table, the sooner I get to eat it!"

A short while later the two of us carried the food to the table. I had the soup and other heavy stuff, and Nia darted in and out of the kitchen delivering sides and the toppings. Everyone was in high spirits, especially for the mood we were all in a few hours ago. The twins seemed uneasy for some reason, though, as I set the massive roast down on the sideboard to begin carving.

"Something wrong, you two? Is Maya not playing nice?"

They both shook their heads in embarrassment. "No, nothing like that. Everyone is being very polite to us. It's just that we don't feel right about you having to serve us, when we were sent to serve you."

"Don't worry about that, please just enjoy the food."

Nia buzzed between the two of them. "It's just the way he is. He has never been one to have others do things for him; in fact, he goes out of his way to make our lives better. You couldn't ask for a better master. Really, I know!"

Then she flew off to her spot on the table and started wolfing down on a chunk of bread that was cut for her. The twins seemed to believe what the pixie had said and finally joined in on the conversation with Maya and Mom. Dad and Rosa were still chatting away and drinking to their hearts' content. Somehow, I had a feeling that I would have to carry Rosa home tonight. Good thing I am a lot stronger now.

Once the bread and roast were passed around, I went around the table to serve soup to everyone. Having the big pot on the table would mean that no one would be able to talk to each other. Both Rosa and Nia dived right in once I filled their bowls, but I could tell Maya was doing her best to restrain herself. Once everyone was served, I took my seat, but those who weren't already eating were looking at me as if I had forgotten something.

"What? Go ahead and eat everyone."

Mom was the only one who seemed to know what was doing on. "Alex, it is a dark elf custom that the one who serves the meal should be the first one who eats. It's a sign of respect for the service of delivering the food. At least, that's what three of us are doing; I don't think your new friends know what to do."

I looked over at the twins and both of them were trying to use the wrong end of a fork on the soup. Thankfully, I was able not to laugh at their expense; it was clear to me that they hadn't had much time among humans.

"Maya, could you, please?" I nodded in their direction. She smiled and turned to help them, showing them what everything was for and how to use it. Once they were using a spoon, I finally started to eat. As soon as the soup touched my lips, Maya was downing it as fast as she could. The scene around the room must have been very strange to my parents, so I leaned over to them to explain.

"I'm sorry for all this. I know we must look like we have no manners. But please understand that all of us are either magical critters, wizards or both, and we all need a lot more food every day than an average person would."

"So that's why Primus Rosa said to cook for thirty?"

"Exactly." Having talked long enough, I dived into my food. Just like the others, I was starving. Maya finished her first bowl, and with the edge off her hunger, was finally able to talk again.

"This is wonderful, Mrs. Martin. It's been so long that I have almost forgotten what food from the villages tasted like."

Rosa and Nia both agreed with her in between mouthfuls of food. The twins also seemed to be enjoying it, but from the amount of roast on their plates, I would say that they prefer meat. The meal went on for almost an hour. Well, it went on until we ran out of soup, to be more precise. Everyone was partaking in conversation, and my parents were telling everyone stories from my childhood. Thankfully, they didn't fully get into the really embarrassing ones. At the end of the meal, Nia was flat on her back groaning from overeating. The twins seemed to be in a similar state; apparently wizards can out-eat dragons, who knew? Dad and Rosa were nodding off in their chairs after way too many bottles of wine. Mom, Maya and I were the only ones who didn't seem to be in some sort of coma.

"Who wants dessert?"

Groans came from the twins, but Nia made an effort to sit up, propping herself upright with her tiny arms. "If it's the blackberry cobbler, count me in."

"Nia, you can barely move."

"Yes, but I *can* move, so I obviously haven't eaten enough yet."

I helped Mom dish up cobbler for everyone, everyone who was awake, anyway. I decided to be mean and placed large slices in front of the twins and Nia.

"I think you're trying to kill me with food, aren't you, Mr. Alex? Oh well, I can't think of a better way to go." Nia sighed sorrowfully and did her typical excellent job of eating everything. I still have no idea how she can eat more than three times her body weight at each meal. "This is really good and made with berries found in the forest, not grown on a farm, I can tell," she moaned.

The twins only managed to finish off half of their cobbler, promising Mom it wasn't that they didn't like it, but that they had eaten too much as it was. The rest of us, who were smart, had remembered that there was dessert and had ample room in our bellies to enjoy the best cobbler in the kingdom.

Unfortunately, once we were all completely stuffed and nearly comatose, it was time to leave, and we had a long hike ahead of us. Thankfully, both Dad and Rosa woke up before we had to go. Mom said her goodbyes to everyone, breaking into tears. She even gave the twins hugs that they definitely weren't expecting, but they seemed fascinated by all the touching. Lastly, was Maya and myself; Mom was still crying.

"I can't believe we're doing this again. It seems like it was just yesterday that we were forced to send you away."

"Mom, being sent away was the best thing of my life. If I hadn't been, I would never have met any of my friends, become an Enchanter, or worst of all, never have met and fallen in love with Maya."

Maya pulled me down and kissed me, wrapping her arms around me. She stopped kissing me but didn't let me go. "You got that right, Magic Boy. But don't worry, Mrs. Martin, I'll keep him safe."

Dad gave us both a hug. "Be careful. Reports are coming in that there's an army of undead on the move out there."

"We will. We can all hold our own in a fight. I will come by again sometime after the tournament is over, but we have to get going or we'll never get home."

Everyone said their final goodbyes and we started down the road. Maya was hooked in my arm and Nia was on my shoulder. Rosa was stumbling along and seemed to be mumbling to herself like she sometimes did after drinking a lot. And the box filled with metal was floating along behind all of us. What struck me as odd was that the twins seemed to be having an argument, but neither seemed mad at the other. Suddenly, they walked ahead of us and stopped us. With their heads held low, Dawn was the first to speak.

"Alex, Maya, please forgive our actions. We had no right to do what we did and we are truly sorry for deceiving you."

"What are you talking about?"

"We lied to both of you. We told you that your real mother was the one who sent us, that was not true. She did save us as we said in our story, but we have already repaid her real price. The reason we told you that was we hoped you would accept us without question if you thought your mother sent us. But after you shared so much with us, we felt that we would never have had to deceive you. In truth, we replaced your real gifts with ourselves." Dusk bowed and walked off into the forest. "She is going to get them for you. I know that we lied to you, but we never planned to take her gift to you. We would have given them to you as gifts from us. It makes me sick to think of what we were going to do."

"But why do this, then?"

"We are dying. Not the two of us, but all the metal dragons. There are so few of us left that we have become desperate. We ask, no, we beg you to please help our kind. Soon, your true self will be revealed, and your mother said you would be the only one who could save our kind. So please, let us serve you both for the rest of our lives in exchange for sanctuary. Please, we only did this to protect the future of our species."

I looked at Maya's reaction next to me. Her face was stern, but I could read her eyes much better anyway. And as much as she hates dragons, I could tell she couldn't let them die either. "What do you think?" I whispered.

But before she responded, Dusk came out of the forest with two enormous white horses. They were perfect, completely white, and had more muscles than any horse I've ever seen. Dusk led them up to us and let go of the reins. One walked right up to me and one to Maya and then started to nuzzle against us. The shoulders of these two were as tall as I am, and I'm six feet tall. Their heads were almost ten feet in the air! Dusk walked around and stood between us.

"I am so sorry for what I have done. Any actions you want to take should be made against me, my sister never wanted to go along with this plan."

"That's not true and you know it. Punishment belongs to both of us."

I looked again to Maya. "Well?"

She nodded and stepped forward. "We forgive you. And we accept your terms under a few conditions."

Both dragons nearly passed out when she said that. They apparently thought we would kill them for what they did. At the same time, they both wondered what her conditions were.

"First, obviously, never do anything like that again."

"You have our word."

"Never again will anything like that happen, we swear."

"Second, Alex already has Nia, so you two are with me." She looked at me for approval, and to be honest, I was going to send them both with her anyway. We all started walking again as we talked.

"Third, over dinner, I could tell that you two don't have many life skills so we are going to fix that. From now on, you will be helping Alex and Nia in the kitchen for the morning and evening meal. You will also join Alex every day for lunch to help with social skills. Any other time, you're with me. Oh, and one more thing, you two are joining my combat training class. Consider that your punishment."

I thought all that was rather fair, since I have Nia do most of that with me. It should be fun to show off two dragons to everyone at lunch. But both Dawn and Dusk were crying. Now I know her combat class is grueling, but to cry about it?

"You're forgiving us and letting us learn how to better serve you. There is nothing more that we could ever dream of!"

Of course, Nia cried, too, the first time she came home. She wouldn't let me out of her sight for those first few days until it really sank in that her life had truly changed for the better. Speaking of Nia, she was tapping me on the ear. "Uh, Master, I think Rosa is walking in her sleep."

Sure enough, she was somehow walking and sleeping at the same time. I have heard that over long trips elves can sometimes do things like that, but I always thought it was a form of meditation. Well, at least we have two strong horses. I picked up Rosa and brought her over to the horse that seemed to gravitate to Maya. As soon as I was next to her, she did a sort of bow, lowering her back so that I could lift Rosa into place. Once she was safely on her back, we continued on our trip.

"They are very well-trained."

Dawn and Dusk smiled. "Of course they are; they're two of your mother's best warhorses."

"Somehow, I have a feeling that there are mounted combat classes in my future."

Getting through the portal took longer than expected, as Maya still wasn't very happy about it. Rosa was no help at all, Nia was passed out in my pocket, and dragons apparently like getting wet about as much as your average cat. Oddly enough, the horses took the experience stoically as if they were totally used to this sort of transportation. Clearing the portal, it was already fully dark on the Xarparion side and we still had a hike to go. The twins began to limp after a few hundred yards, something that I attributed to their lack of experience with human feet. Also, the slippers that formed with their shape-change clothes were not really hiking friendly, but neither girl complained. After nearly losing Rosa off the back of the mare for the third time, I called a stop and asked Maya to climb up and help keep the elf from toppling over. I called over the stallion, which had been trailing the group almost like a watchful guard dog, and he moved in obediently as if he knew what I wanted. He lowered himself and I lifted a very grateful Dawn and Dusk up on his broad back. I led the way through the rapidly chilling night air, glancing back at the two dragons. They were riding happily, seemingly not affected at all by the cold, and were whispering animatedly to each other.

Eventually, we all made it back to the hall in one piece, well almost. Nia had gotten warm in my pocket and crawled out and resumed sleeping on my shoulder without me knowing, so when I stepped over a log, she fell off. Thankfully, the big stallion right behind me reached down and deftly snatched the bottom of her dress in his huge teeth before she hit the ground. The remainder of the trip was rather fun. The twins really opened up to Maya and me about their lives. Sadly, they haven't been doing anything exciting recently, or ever for that matter. They just lived in the deep forest away from everyone, learning to be dragons, until they could defend themselves, and then my mother called for them.

We made our way around the hall grounds and Maya finally realized something was different as we entered the stables.

"Um, Alex, since when do we have a stable?"

"Since this afternoon."

"Huh?"

"You know that this place is probably the most enchanted structure on the planet, right? Rosa had hundreds of years with nothing much to do other than place enchantment after enchantment on these walls. After the first couple centuries, the level of magic in the place reached kind of an arcane terminal load where it became semi-sentient and self-directing. So the hall has the ability, among other things, to change its shape and repurpose internal spaces with just a request from one of us. Over the afternoon and dinner, the two of us added a few new things to the hall. For one thing, the twins need a place to stay. We need more room in the rest of the hall and a larger dining room and kitchen, plus a stable, among other minor changes. I also added a few things of my own. And yes, we did it with our minds."

"Why haven't we used that before?"

"Um, we forgot about it?"

"How does someone forget about something like that?" She stomped angrily and put both hands on her hips, giving me a disapproving glare.

"Sorry? If it makes you feel better, I made your room larger."

"You think a larger room will make me happy? After *you* nearly drowned me today, then without warning or sufficient preparation, *you* introduced me to both of your parents - twice? And in all the months we've known each other, *you* wickedly avoided telling me that *you* grew up in a dark elf village?" I winced each time she put an emphasis on the word "you" and I knew I had some making up to do.

"You have a private tub that always keeps the water in it fresh and warm…"

Maya paused, thought about it for a second, and then a broad eager smile crossed her beautiful face. "Ok…you're forgiven!"

As we were arguing, the twins put the warhorses away in the stalls with plenty of feed and water. With Rosa and Nia still asleep in my arms, I led everyone inside and showed the twins to their room. They were extremely happy and surprised that they had a room to themselves. I put Rosa and Nia to bed before checking in on the twins again. Apparently, they didn't know what the beds were for. They were trying to sleep on the hardwood floor and my explanations didn't seem to make sense to them.

After a lengthy discussion that was going nowhere, I gave up and went for the direct approach. I scooped them up one at a time and placed them in bed like you would do for a child. I even had to tuck them in. Dragons are incredibly smart, so seeing two that couldn't figure out a bed was rather funny. After making sure they knew where to find the washroom, and the kitchen if they got hungry in the night, I departed.

On my way back to my room, I found Maya in her silky nightgown leaning against the hallway wall, a smirk on her lips. "I love the changes you made to my room. But I have to ask, why did you add a double bed? Is that your attempt at a not-so-subtle invitation to share it with me?"

Crap. "No, nothing like that! Just felt you would like the extra room…"

She smiled one of her evil smiles. "Well, too bad, then. Seeing that it is your birthday, I was going to let you join me. But since you added it just for me, it will have to stay just for me."

Then she went back into her room, winked at me and closed the door softly. I began to mentally reconsider my long-standing contention that dark elves are not naturally evil and sulked into my room. Nia was snoring softly on the windowsill. She'd had a very long day though, so I didn't mind the noise. I had made my own room larger as well, with my own larger bed too. I cleaned up quickly, then dived under the covers and soon dozed off.

I woke to the sound of my door opening slowly. A few seconds later, someone slid under the covers with me. I knew right away it was Maya just from the smell of her hair, which was still damp and fragrant from trying out her new bath. Silently, she glided next to me and wrapped an arm around my chest. Her head rested on the back of my neck. I laced our fingers together and we stayed like that as her breathing slowed and she fell asleep. I could feel her breath on my bare back, and it felt good. With her there, I was completely comfortable and very contented...all in all, it had been a great birthday.

Chapter 14

Alex

The next morning, I woke up with Maya still wrapped around me. I really hope that one day soon we won't have to do this in secret; I love her being here with me. Although, if anyone else wakes up before we do, we're toast. Rosa has made this rule clear, even if we don't do anything inappropriate. I rolled over to face her, finding that she was already awake and smiling at me.

"Good morning, beautiful. I thought I didn't earn your company last night?"

"Well, it was your birthday, and I felt this was a good present."

"The best, thank you." We kissed briefly before agreeing that we needed to get moving so the others wouldn't notice.

Once Maya snuck back to her room and we were both dressed, we started our morning rounds. She went for Rosa and I woke Nia. Once done with my morning "unwrapping of the pixie" routine, we joined Maya in the twins' room. Maya was in her drill instructor mode, "Rise and shine! It's a great day for training!"

The two of them were wrapped in their blankets just like Nia always is, but Nia is much easier to pick up and shake free than they are. "Do I look like that every morning?" Nia giggled.

"Yes, but you're cute; this is just sad and pathetic. It looks like they are trying to strangle themselves with the blankets."

Maya stepped up to us after attempting to wake them. "Well, poking and yelling isn't working, any other ideas? Bucket of cold water?"

"That could work, but hot water would be better."

"Why?"

"Well, silver dragons are similar to white dragons, they like it cold. So hot water would be more of a shock."

I grabbed a vase of water and used an enchantment to heat the water. Once good and warm, I poured a little on each of the young dragons. The reaction was quite hilarious. Both of they screamed as though it was ice water and tried to get away from it, but wrapped as they were, they couldn't move.

"We're up, we're up!"

"Please, no more water!"

They were awake but still tangled in the blankets. Maya took the warm water from me and held it above them with her evil smile.

"Well, what do you two have to say for yourselves? Training starts today and you are still in bed."

They scrambled out of bed. "We're sorry, Mistress, it won't happen again. We just never slept in a real bed before and never had such a good night's sleep."

Maya smiled warmly. "I know, and if we weren't short on time for the next few weeks, I would have let you both sleep all day. But for now, it's time for you four to get to work in the kitchen." She turned to me and Nia. "And what are you making for us today, Master Chef?"

"I don't know yet. Suggestions?"

"Eggs, bacon, and sweet cakes, please!" Rosa interrupted mentally.

"Ok, never mind, Rosa picked for today."

"I am surprised she doesn't have a hangover."

I sighed, "Well, once she figured out that I could cure them, she probably never will again. But for now, Dawn, Dusk, please get dressed and meet us downstairs."

"Um, Mr. Alex, what should we wear now?"

"There are robes, staff clothes, undergarments, towels, and footwear for each of you in the closet. See you soon."

Reaching the kitchen, I stood back and watched Nia as she darted back and forth taking in the new changes with obvious delight. Oohs and aahs were replaced with squeals of delight when she discovered that there were even pixie sized perches over the cooking grates.

"Master, this is great! I have places to sit and still work."

I collected the bowls that we would need. "I thought you would like them."

"But, do I have to use them?" She was looking a little coy, and I could see something was bothering her.

"Well, no, you can still fly if you like."

"No, I mean can I still sit on your shoulder? I like it up there."

"Of course, you can. I only added the perches so you have a place to work from, not as a place you must stay on."

"I'm so glad." She then took her usual place on my shoulder. Less than a minute later, the twins arrived. They were both wearing white robes similar to mine but had black cuffs and neckline to represent staff of the Enchanters Hall. They spun around in a circle to display their new finery.

"Mr. Alex, we are ready to work."

"Glad to see you both. But the first lesson is that cooking is not work if you're doing it right."

They both nodded. "And today, I'm going to do something different. Seeing that Rosa wants a very simple breakfast compared to what she normally wants, I won't be helping."

All three of them were in shock.

"Instead, Nia is in charge."

Her jaw hit the floor. "But…but…but!"

"You can do it. This is practice for you as much as it is for them. Besides, you taught Rosa already. I got everyone up early so you have plenty of time, even if something goes wrong. So, chop-chop, Rosa is famished."

"Well, this is a fine way to treat your bodyguard, Mr. Alex! But then, I doubt you were in any real physical peril last night," Nia smirked and flew off giggling into the kitchen. Ouch! Pixie blackmail alert!

It took a little longer than we were hoping, and we lost a mixing bowl in the process, but that's fine. They all came out of the kitchen with smiles on their faces, flour on their clothes, food in their hands, and joy in their hearts. I would say that my plan to make them friends worked just fine. We sat down to a good meal with almost nothing burnt. The larger table worked out great, it was like having a large family gathering, and I think everyone felt the same sense of belonging.

After everything had been cleaned up, Nia and Rosa went to the lab to work on their stuff. The rest of us made our way to the training grounds. The twins were surprisingly athletic and were almost able to keep up with Maya as they did their run, for a short time anyway. I spent my time with the new warhorses to see what they could do. As it turns out, quite a bit. Their strength and size made them powerful, but their skills, training, and uncanny intelligence made them truly unique. I put the mare back in her stall but allowed the stallion to follow me around, just to see what he would do.

Once the twins were almost dead from Maya's exercises, I took mercy on them and rounded both of them up, along with Nia. I gave Maya a quick squeeze goodbye as she headed off to work with her guards. The twins stood there breathing heavy and soaked with sweat, looking generally pitifully bedraggled.

"Please don't make us run anymore, I don't think we can take it."

Nia and I started laughing. "Don't worry, I'm going to feed you guys." They both sighed in relief. "Don't relax yet, it's still a mile walk to the food." Their expressions went right back to the way they were. "But if you would like, we could ride there and I do believe the stallion can take all of us with no trouble."

"Yes, please!"

We got some strange looks on our way to lunch. Mind you, I would think that a man, a pair of identical twins, and a pixie riding a pure white horse would be odd. I couldn't tell who was having more fun, the twins or Nia. All of them were laughing and enjoying the trip through the crowd of astonished residents. Once we arrived at Central and everyone was on the ground, I sent my horse home, and yes, he knows the way.

"Who's ready for lunch?"

Really, I shouldn't even ask anymore. Whoever said girls don't eat much is insane. As always, they were starving, so I led them into the dining hall. But when the twins entered and saw all the people milling about, they froze in panic.

"Ok, you two, the reason you're here is to get used to crowds, so let's go." Nia and I each took one and practically dragged them over to our regular table where Lin and Julia were already seated. We sat the twins down with their backs to everyone else so they only had to look at our table. Julia was acting like her normal self and gave her customary greeting. Lin, as usual, was more inquisitive.

"Hello, you two. Who are your friends, new staff?"

"Sort of. This is Dawn and that's Dusk." I waited until they were done greeting each other. "They're dragons."

"Huh?"

"Dragons."

"Where?"

I motioned to the twins. "Right here."

The twins waved and nodded their heads. "He's right."

Julia and Lin looked at each other, and Lin snickered. "Really, Alex, you're not fooling us with a wild story like that, we're druids you know."

Dawn looked at me and smiled. The pupils of her eyes changed from the customary sliver-tinted human appearance to a vibrant silver and green vertical bar with a midnight black center. She reached out and grasped Lin's hand under hers and allowed just the skin on the back of her hand to change to scale.

Lin's eyes bulged drastically as she looked down at the hand holding hers and then up into Dawn's face. "Draconus Argentis," she whispered excitedly to Julia. "A real, live silver dragon. Our books say they are almost…" She was about to say "extinct" but caught herself beforehand, thinking it might be rude. By this time, both human girls were holding Dawn's hand and stroking the scales with great animation. Jules even leaned in to get a closer look at Dawn's eye pattern, and Lin flipped open a small sketchpad and started drawing purposefully.

Ok, this was not the reaction I was expecting, and poor Nia was laughing so hard she rolled herself off the table. Fortunately, she was quick enough to snatch a soft bun on the way down and used it as a pillow to break her fall. After a minute or so, the girls calmed down. Nia got off the floor and Lin and Julia released poor Dawn's hand, which they had trapped in the name of science.

They started asking the twins all sorts of questions, most of them silly. I could see that Dawn and Dusk had been elevated to the status of newest, most interesting friends in an instant. The dragons, on the other hand, were looking uncomfortable and scared. Hyper young teenage girls are apparently not in the wilderness dragon survival manual.

"Lin, Julia, please calm down, you're scaring them. Neither of them has had any real contact with humans, so this is all new to them. I brought them here so you two could help them to better understand normal life around here."

"What can we do to help?"

"Take them out with you guys, talk girl stuff; just be their friends." The twins were smiling cautiously, clearly not knowing what I was getting them into. Lin and Julia also seemed to enjoy the idea.

"We can do that!"

Lunch was going great. I stayed quiet and just watched as the girls had fun. Julia sat between the twins with Lin across from them. They were talking up a storm, and even though the twins probably didn't know half of what they were talking about, they seemed to be having a great time. After a half hour, they were even asking the druids questions. Sadly, our great time came to an end as my least favorite person made a visit to our table.

"Hey, scumbags! I hear you have more staff."

All our good moods went in the dumps. Naton and his goons were back again; they always show up when we're having a good time. Somehow, I was regretting not bringing my hammer this morning. But what was I worried about? I have Nia and two dragons as backup, let alone my own strength.

"Go away, Naton. There's nothing for you here."

"Ah, but you see, I'm in search of some new slaves. Sadly, my last ones died from burns, and then I heard that you registered two more for your pathetic hall. You know the Fire Tower has a rule that we take priority on all new servants, so I'll be taking these two. And, oh look, they're twins." Well, that wasn't going to happen. But he still continued, "So why don't you two come with me quietly, or I burn all your worthless friends." He reached out and cuffed the back of Julia's head.

Well, apparently the last time I beat him didn't sink in. This time when I stood up, his two goons tried to grab me and pin my arms - bad idea. They may be big bad fire wizards, but they weren't exactly big bad men. In fact, I don't think either of them weighed more than a hundred pounds. I grabbed the two of them and slammed them together hard. Dazed, my next move sent them flying over a table to land in a heap. When they got up, they didn't stick around.

"Get back here, you cowards! He's only one stupid Enchanter! Fine, I'll deal with him myself," he groused, drawing himself up like he was about to do something epic.

I stood in front of him, blocking him from the girls.

"You're going to die now, Enchanter!"

I had nothing to say to him, so I said nothing. As soon as I could see that he was starting to summon a fireball, I closed the short distance between us, grabbed him around the neck with one hand, and lifted him off the ground.

"Next time you try anything like this, or hurt anyone and I hear about it, I will end you." I looked around at the rest of the now silent dining hall. "Anyone mind if I take out the trash?"

No one said no; in fact, almost everyone begged me to do so, even one of the fire wizard teachers.

I whispered so the others wouldn't hear me, "I'll tell you what, Naton. I'm entering the tournament coming up, so why don't you enter when you wake up and we can settle this there. Deal?"

He stopped struggling and gasped. "Fine," he spat, "but why 'when I wake up'?"

I smiled and used my enhanced strength to throw him across the dining hall and straight into a stone pillar. The impact blew chunks off and spider-webbed the huge stone column. Naton kind of splattered and then slid down the column head first into a discarded food bin. I walked over and made sure he wasn't dead. As expected, the enchantment I placed on his robes when I was holding him worked. He wasn't dead, but he had a few broken bones and was out cold. After removing my enchantment, I quietly returned to our table with thunderous applause echoing from nearly every table in the place.

Unlike the rest of the dining hall, our table had continued business as normal. As I was walking back, one of the earth wizards nervously rushed up and fixed the column that I had damaged. I even saw a few of the smaller students kicking the bully and dumping more food on his head on their way out.

I sat down as if nothing had happened and, in fact, it felt kind of good. Julia was hugging Dusk, but I couldn't tell who was comforting who. Dawn placed a hand on my forearm. "Thank you for standing up for us."

"I always will."

Lin came over and wrapped an arm around me. "Yeah, I told them that, but they have never seen your fights with Naton. Well, fight is the wrong word, more like when you kick his ass all the time."

"Lin, could you and Julia do me a favor? Can you take them to Maya for me? I need to get to class. I would send them with Nia, but she gets protective after things like this happen. And if he ever bothers you guys again, just open a hole in the ground and crush the bastard."

"No problem! I am really going to enjoy doing that."

I took off with Nia on my shoulder and more cheers coming from the dining hall. More people hated that guy than I thought. I swung by the stable to verify that my horse made it back just fine and to collect my box. On second thought, I decided the horse should come as well. With box and warhorse in tow, I headed off to the forge to get to work. We got there a bit late, but I wasn't worried about time for today.

"Darroth, where are you?"

"Right here, you blasted idiot!" He came out from behind a weapons rack. "What the hell is so damn important?"

"We have work to do."

He huffed, "Tell me about it, all they have me doing right now is sharpening swords."

"No, I mean real work."

His eyes brightened as though he had won a prize. "Really? What have you got?"

"I'm entering the wizard tournament coming up so I need a rush order - a suit of armor for myself, of my own making."

"That should be fun, but you would need some good metal to work with."

"Got that covered." I placed my hand on the box to open it. Once it was open, his eyes gleamed with delight; the forge master was in dwarf heaven. He ran his hands up and down the rows of blocks. I'm pretty sure he would have been delighted to climb up into the box and take a blissful nap on the bars.

"Where did you get these beauties?"

"It's a gift from my birth father."

"Who is your dad, the smith god?"

"No, he doesn't seem to get along with them."

He stood there silently, as several conflicting emotions ran across his broad face. "That was meant to be a joke, kid."

"Yes, but it is close to the truth. I need to turn this into armor. Any tips?"

He tried to pick up one of the blocks but couldn't with his first try. Once he used both hands, he was finally able to lift one of the smaller blocks out of the box. "By the gods! What is this? It must weigh two hundred pounds. How would you even move in a suit of this stuff?"

I picked up one of the blocks and tossed it up a few inches and caught it casually. It felt like it was maybe three or four pounds and I wasn't using my extra strength. "Um, it feels lighter than steel to me. It must only work for me and Maya."

"Figures. So what the hell am I supposed to do?"

I smiled and pulled him outside. "I need you to armor our horses."

"You're just full of surprises today, aren't you?" He walked over and assessed the warhorse with a practiced eye, touching him here and there, inspecting bone structure and finally running his hand across his broad muzzle. "This is quite an animal."

"A gift from my mother."

He whistled thoughtfully. "You have some powerful family. So you want me to armor him?"

"Yes, him and his sister."

He stood there thinking. "Ok, I have some ideas. But are you sure that you want me to do this? When your armor is much better?"

"Darroth, I have no experience with armored horses - you do. Besides, I think you would have a lot of fun with a pair of trained warhorses at least five times stronger than normal.

He again stopped to think. "Warhorses, five times stronger, you say? That could mean five times the armor." He stroked his beard some more. "You know what? I'll do it! Should be fun, but I'll need some time to plan and to test how much they can safely carry."

"No problem, let's get to work then."

We went to one of the drawing rooms to start charting out plans for our own projects. As always, Nia was a great help; she has impressive drawing skills. The two of us had a design well-planned out with detail by the time we had to leave. I collected the papers, and Nia had her other roll of paper, which she had been hiding from me. After dinner, I caught her working on it a few times, but she still wouldn't let me see it.

Two days later, I started the actual construction of the armor. The metal that my father gave me was very surprising to work with. It seemed to mold itself into the shape I wanted without really any hammer strikes, which was fortunate since the hottest fire we could summon in the forge wouldn't even begin to soften it. All I really had to do was pattern it in my mind and will it to take that shape; I was making great time. Enchanting was easy too, every piece seemed to know what enchantment it wanted and no other. Needless to say, some were getting rather odd.

By this time, Nia must have finished her secret project. She's been spending most of her time on my shoulder again.

"So, done with your secret project?"

She sighed unhappily, "No, I just don't know how to get the measurements I require."

"Well, I can help you if you need."

She thought it over for a minute. "Fine, but I'm not showing you what it is yet. I need Maya's exact measurements and don't know how to get them."

"That's easy. All we have to do is have Rosa get them for you for some other reason, like another dress. Then when you're in there helping, Rosa can give them to you without Maya knowing."

She cackled. "Well, that should be fun!"

Several hours later...

"Rosa, I don't need more damn dresses! And you two, I can't believe you two are helping her. This is no way to treat a queen." Maya growled unhappily.

Rosa, Dawn, and Dusk were holding Maya down so Nia could take all the measurements she needed. I guessed that it would be best for my health if I wasn't involved. Thankfully for everyone, Nia was very fast and efficient, and all figures were recorded and double checked in a few minutes. Once she was finished, Rosa had Dawn and Dusk released her and they wisely dove for cover.

"Ok, Alex, come calm her down for us."

I knew exactly what to do, but I don't think that's what she meant. I signaled for Nia to do her thing and suddenly the room was filled with music. Maya looked at me strangely, confused about both my presence and the music. I smiled and showed her the glass of wine I had hidden behind my back.

"Alex, what's all this?"

"It's a celebration! Some of the staff gave all this to us for a thank you. Somehow, they feel that burning down the barracks was a good thing, because of the beautiful gardens the Earth Tower is putting in where the wood structures used to stand. They obviously aren't the ones having to live underground because of it."

Maya was still confused, but Rosa wrapped her arm around us and gave us a hug. Apparently that hug was not really for us...I looked at my hand and I was no longer holding my drink. By the time I turned around, she had already drained the glass. "Thanks, Rosa."

She smiled at me. "My pleasure!" And all of us burst out laughing.

I grabbed the crate I had stashed outside the door and brought it in. Inside were ten more bottles of different kinds of wine and ale. "Well, I guess it's party time, then!"

Everyone let out a cheer and joined me, everyone but Nia, who just stayed with water. But, either way, we all had a blast. The twins were great to watch, they had never had alcohol before and the effects on them were hilarious.

Apparently, in addition to loving bright, shiny objects, silver dragons are also very fond of good wine. Unfortunately, the more they drink, the more they lose control of their shape-shifting abilities. For the rest of the evening, it wasn't unusual to see a couple of bat/wolf/zebra/human/dragon hybrids greedily upending the last of a bottle down their throats.

After every bottle was empty, the twins and Rosa were out cold and Maya wasn't too far behind them.

"Why are you not tipsy like the rest of us?" she slurred.

"Because I planned ahead and only had two glasses."

She groaned. "Why? What nefarious scheme are you cooking up now? By the way, I am so going to hate you in the morning."

"No, you won't. I made sure you won't have a hangover."

She smiled and snuggled deeper into the chair she was in. "Ok, Magic Boy, thanks, but I think I'll take a nap now."

She was out in seconds, leaving me and Nia to do the cleanup. We got all of them into Rosa's huge bed and cleaned up after the party.

Only Nia and I were left awake so we decided to have a little fun of our own. We ended up in the kitchen whipping up a sweet-tasting nectar tart thing that Nia loved. But since she never bothered to learn how to make them, only knew what they looked and tasted like, this turned out to be a fun adventure of taste-testing. Our first few were nasty, but as we went along, they got infinitely better.

After a few hours, we finally got it right, having gone through all our baking ingredients. In truth, they were delicious, but it was getting late and we were both covered in flour. So we wrapped up the rest for later, cleaned up and got ready for bed. On our way, we swung by Rosa's room to check in on everyone. All four of them were in a big pile on her huge bed, tangled in a mess of limbs. Nia and I had to leave before we woke them with our laughing. We weren't going to risk one of them waking up before morning. So we threw a blanket over them and went to bed.

Morning was even better than the two of us could ever have hoped. We got up a few minutes early to get ready. After getting dressed, we silently slipped into Rosa's room so we had prime seats for the show. As if on cue, both Rosa and Maya woke up. It took them a few seconds to realize that they were tangled up with two dragons...as dragons. Dawn's left wing was twitching causing a pleasant breeze to flow across everyone. Even as massive as the bed frame and supports were, the entire bed surface seemed to be sagging precariously. Maya had her arms and legs wrapped around Dusk as though she was a pillow. Rosa appeared to be in the most uncomfortable position, on the bottom of the pile with a tail in her face.

Nia and I burst out laughing; the sight of them trying to work their way out from under two dead-to-the-world dragons was hilarious. What made things even funnier was when Maya finally got free, she started to help Rosa, but Dawn rolled over on top of her, leaving them both unable to get free. Rosa was still able to move her upper body so she could talk to us.

"When you two despicable jesters are done laughing your heads off, would you mind giving us a hand?"

Nia flew up in front of my face with one of her famous pixie smiles. Whenever she is like this, she is thinking of an evil prank, and pixies invented the art of evil pranks. I didn't know what she was thinking, but I was almost scared to find out. I nodded, giving her permission to do what she was planning. Smiling, she flew down the hallway, returning a minute later with a bowl of warm water and hovered just out of reach of Rosa. Seeing what she was holding, the color in Rosa's face drained away.

"Nia, don't do it! Bad pixie, bad!"

I heard the muffled sounds of Maya being pressed into the bed, "What's going on?"

"The evil pixie has hot water!"

"What? Nia, no! Please don't do it!"

In one fell swoop, she threw the bowl of water on the dragons. To Rosa and Maya's surprise, nothing happened. Well, except for me and Nia rolling around on the floor.

Rosa was utterly dumbfounded. "What just happened?"

Nia was still laughing but flew up to her. "You should see the looks on your faces!"

"But you threw water on them!"

"No, I didn't! The bowl was empty; I just used an illusion to make it look full!"

Now with both of them knowing that they had been duped, they struggled desperately to get out from under the twins so they could enact their revenge. After a half hour, everyone was awake, the twins spending most of it apologizing profusely. Nia and I presented the sweets we made last night as a show of good will. It's amazing how much goodwill can be restored with shared food, and the Enchanters Hall continued to really come together as a group to everyone's delight.

A couple days later, with Nia on my shoulder, I headed for lunch. After working heavy shields with Maya all morning, I was starving and my arms felt like lead. Yet my gorgeous combat instructor was still as fresh as when we started. I shook my head absently and grabbed some sandwiches and milk from a platform near the entrance. We made our way to our usual table which was, as always, piled high with tarts and other goodies.

Approaching the table, I found a very sad and nervous Julia sitting there. Lin had an arm around her, and they were talking quietly with their heads together.

I stopped abruptly, nearly losing Nia, and looked around for signs of a Naton visit. Nothing seemed out of the ordinary anywhere in the hall, so I slid in across from them.

"What's wrong with you two?"

"Hey, big brother," Julia smiled weakly.

I nearly snorted milk out my nose, "Big brother? Umm, Jules, should I be asking my Mom about something she never told me?"

Julia looked horrified and covered her face with her hands. "I'm so sorry, Alex - did I say that out loud?"

Lin patted her on the back and explained, "Alex, ever since you started standing up to Naton for Jules, the other Earthies in our tower have started calling you Julia's big brother, but not in a bad way."

"I will tell them to stop it right away, Alex," Julia vowed, "unless you don't mind so much." She glanced at me shyly, twirling some of her curly brown hair around her fingers. At least, she no longer looked like she was about to burst into tears any second. Lin was behind her and out of her field of vision, making exaggerated begging motions at me.

I couldn't help but smile and take Julia's hand. "Julia, I would be deeply honored to call you the baby sister I never had. We've been through a lot together, and it feels right. I'm pretty sure Mom would approve, too." I winked at her, and Julia came around and gave me a very sweet hug and a kiss on the cheek.

I felt a few tiny drops of water run down the back of my neck, and I didn't have to look to realize that Nia was crying silently on my shoulder. Pretty much any discussion about orphans hit her pretty hard. Time to change the subject and quickly.

"So you still haven't told me, why the sad face?"

Lin grimaced. "Reginaldo. Jules needs to take her test today and she's a little afraid."

"Who is Reginaldo?"

"More like, what is Reginaldo?" Lin snorted. "He's an ancient earth elemental that lives just outside the walls. One of the key tests for any earth wizard is to summon an earth elemental and make it do your bidding. Nothing major, just move a boulder from one spot to another or smash a tree trunk to smithereens...pretty basic stuff."

"But you two are druids; I would think your tests would be different."

"Sheesh, Alex, we may be druids, but we're still earth wizards, too. We just specialize and prefer our druid disciplines..."

I nodded and she continued, "Well, as you can imagine, living next to an earth wizard tower, Reginaldo gets summoned hundreds of times a year to move the same stupid rock and perform the same menial tasks, and he's sick of it. To make matters worse, the fire wizards have started firebombing his home for practice and to piss him off, the jerks!" She paused angrily and took a sip of water.

"Lately, when summoned, Reginaldo has been really scary and mean. Last week, he made a boy from our floor wet himself. He was so scared, the headmaster had to pull him out of the test altogether, and the kid has to start all his classes over again."

"What do your teachers say?"

"Not much they can do. Reggie is so unhappy he won't listen to humans anymore, not even the primus of our tower. They are saying he could go rogue and would need to be destroyed to safeguard the school."

"And Julia has to face this thing today? I don't like the sound of this; do you want me to talk to Hons?"

"No!" They both loudly blurted, and Lin continued, "Jules has to do this for herself, no interference, not even from a big brother. Besides," Lin smiled proudly, "you may not know this, but our girl here is the youngest student to be accepted into full druid training in decades. Very few earth wizards have what it takes to be a druid. We are actually almost as rare as you are. And all the teachers are saying that her powers are going to be awesome. She can handle one grumpy elemental."

Julia seemed to be buoyed up by the speech and was now smiling and nodding. I shook my head, not really knowing what to say. Before I finished lunch, we said our goodbyes and the green-robed girls took off, looking determined. Walking back to Darroth's forge, I noticed that Nia had taken off as well and I was alone.

Julia clung to Lin's hand right up to the entrance to the testing area. There was a small section of wooden rough-sawn seats built into the side of a small hillock on the sunward end of the field. Seated close to the bottom were a couple of faculty members and a handful of younger students. Hons gave her a confident wave, and Lin joined him on the bench. Closer to Julia was a chalk circle where the tested was to stand. Ranging out from the circle was the rest of the field, mostly flat and partly grassy with a number of large boulders and tree trunks scattered unnaturally about. Of course, it was only partly grassy due to the large scorched areas where fireballs routinely detonated, marring what would have been a benign pastoral setting. The druid part of Julia's mind hated it. As she entered the circle, her eyes caught a flash of small wings that rocketed up from behind one of the boulders and was immediately gone.

"I wish I could fly away from here as fast as you, little bird," Julia whispered with a sigh. Quickly, she set up her spell cast precisely as she had been taught, and with a glance and a nod to her teachers, she raised her arms and barked the command word.

Nothing happened for a few seconds. Finally, the ground shook, escalating into a decent tremor that actually jostled a few spectators out of their seats. Dirt, stones, and smaller boulders began to draw to one spot in the field very close to Julia. The effect was very similar to water being pulled down a drain but, in this case, instead of going down, the column of debris was rising to tower above the small curly-haired girl. Finally, it coalesced into a humanoid shape easily twenty-five feet tall, with a head as big as a wine barrel and boulders for articulated arms and legs. The being, Reginaldo, peered down at the diminutive human female.

Julia looked up in awe; she had never seen an elemental appear this size before. Even Reginaldo, when she had watched other students take the test, rarely bothered to produce an avatar taller than ten feet. And instead of the harsh, angry scream she was expecting, she heard nothing externally, but in her mind, a warm, mellow voice hailed her.

"I greet you, and I am yours to command, Lady."

Jules continued to gaze up at the featureless rock, but now instead of fear, she felt great warmth, like heat stored from a sunny day. She smiled as if seeing an old friend.

"I am druid apprentice Julia. But I am baseborn, an orphan and no lady."

He rumbled slightly, some rocks grating together. *"You are held as kin by the Ore Minder,"* he stated flatly as if that said it all.

"Ore Minder?" Julia rolled that name around in her mind and came up with only one possible conclusion. *"Do you mean Alex?"* An affirmative wave of sun-baked warmth pulsed across their bond.

"Lady, you have a powerful call and strong earth magic, but your human body is frail and you require protection to complete your role in the destiny of this world. The small spirit of the forest has spoken of this to Reginaldo."

On the hillock benches, Lin and Hons were watching in a growing panic. The rest of the spectators were murmuring nervously as well.

"Why are they just standing there saying nothing?" Lin demanded, grabbing Hons by the arm.

"I don't know. I've never seen him manifest that big before. Usually, he just appears, booms out a rude 'Command me and let me be gone!' Does what he is commanded and vanishes. Something's not right."

Hons stood up, pulling himself from Lin's grasp, and began readying a spell.

"Hons, wait," Lin gasped pulling his arms back down. "Jules is doing that twisty thing with her fingers in her hair...she only does that when she's happy."

Jules was indeed doing the twisty thing as she continued to listen to the elemental, losing track of time, her fears, and the presence of her friends and peers a hundred yards away. It was like she suddenly opened a window into another world, and the views and sounds were spectacular!

"Grave winds of change have begun to blow and even the hardest stone can crumble before relentless evil," Reginaldo intoned. Julia watched as the stones shifted and the huge figure went down to the equivalent of one knee before her, his giant head at her level.

"I pledge myself to you, Lady, and the noble path on which you are about to embark."

Back at the seating area, the small group watched as Julia put a firm hand on the head of the manifestation, and her hand seemed to glow as she patted him with seeming affection. He stood back up to full height and appeared to consider something for a moment, then carefully walked over and moved a large boulder. Then he smashed a tree trunk into several pieces before dissolving noisily back into the field as if he had never been.

Hons stood stiffly off to the side of the seating area and watched as Lin ran out and flung her arms around a beaming Julia. The rest of the spectators clapped mildly, and he had to wonder, "What the hell just happened?"

Alex

Two weeks went by smoothly, until I returned to the forge one day. It's not that something bad happened; I just had an astonished dwarf on my hands. As usual, I was working on my armor, and at the rate I was going, it should be finished on time. But as I was working, I fell into an odd (even for me) sort of trance. I was aware of what was going on but wasn't really in control of my body. Instead of swinging my hammer, I placed it on the anvil and sat cross-legged on the ground. Then the block I was working on floated in the air in front of me. In my mind, I pictured the shape I needed, and as I did, a small part of the block melted into liquid and took that shape before re-hardening to a completed piece.

This took me by surprise as Enchanters aren't supposed to be able to control things without touching them. But for now, I was more interested in what I could do with this new ability. I kept working for about two hours, making unbelievable progress. The work I had done in two hours would normally take me almost a week and a normal smith about a year. Now with time to spare, I tried to do the same thing with a chunk of standard steel, and sure enough, it worked.

I tried all sorts of things until something in my pocket felt warm. I reached in and found the letter that Dad sent me; I could have sworn I had left it in my room. Puzzled, I opened it up and watched the words again write themselves across the page.

"Hello, son. I have been watching you work, and I must say that it's very impressive. I know that giving you that gift was the right choice. Your mother and I feel that it is time to unlock some of your more...basic talents. As you have already discovered, you have the ability to control and shape metal from a short distance into any form you would like. This is something that you got from me. Your mother has activated two of the talents from her side of the family, as well. One you may have noticed a few nights ago with your sweetheart, the other she won't say - just that you will use it when you need it. Also, I want you to know that I'm proud of you, both of you. You and Maya are becoming everything we had hoped. I wish that the day we

can finally show ourselves to you was now, but it is not. But soon, my son, soon we will tell you everything. But for now, you seem to have a confused dwarf to deal with."

I looked up and there was Darroth, mouth open and pointing at me. "What in the world are you?" I looked around and realized that I was still shaping the metal around me. From the number of pieces, I would have to estimate that my suit was about done. But Darroth didn't seem to be concerned about that at the moment.

"Um, I can explain, I think."

"You're darn right you can explain!"

I told him everything I knew about my father and what he disclosed about these "talents". To my surprise, he took things rather well, only stopping me twice to ask questions.

"So let me get this straight, because of whatever your parents are, you now have the ability to control metals?"

I cringed, "Yeah, that's about right."

Darroth paused in thought and absently pulled his weathered old pipe out of his shirt. He lit it with a straw ember from the forge and puffed up a great cloud of smoke that temporarily hid his features. Waving it away, he leaned back against a post.

"Son, I've been around a while and I've seen some things: rare artifacts, legendary weapons, and metalwork from all over the known world. And I am not too hidebound of a smith to state that, in my opinion, more than a few of those relics were never made by the hand of dwarf or human." He took another draw on the pipe and motioned toward my pile of armor pieces. "Some of them looked a lot like that, however."

"It seems to me that every so often, the world gets out of round, like a broken grinding wheel, no good for anything. When that happens, certain beings, call them what you will, and mortal heroes are called upon to step up and make it right again. When it happens, the process ain't pretty, a lot of blood will spill, and a lot of good people will end up dying doing what's right. But for some reason, when the call is made, there are heroes who answer it."

He took another puff and smiled, "Of course, a wise person in these situations would run like hell. But I guess I'm too old to learn wisdom, and you used all yours up when you decided to court Maya."

Darroth put out the bowl of the pipe with his thumb and tucked it back into his shirt. "Now, if I were you, I wouldn't do this where people who are just passing by can see you." I was shocked that he took it so well. He then stepped past me to the assortments of parts behind me. "Looks like all you have left is to rivet everything together."

"No rivets required, actually I think I'm ready for my first fitting. I'll need your help with that."

I took off my robes and got into the leather gambeson that I made to absorb impact and for comfort. Once I was ready, I used my new ability to float each of the pieces into place, starting with my boots and working my way up. As more and more of the armor took shape, I was beginning to get a sense of the size I had become in it. Everything fell into place nicely. I fitted the pieces of the helmet together last and inserted the leather and cloth lining. I put my helmet on and turned to Darroth for inspection.

"Kid, you're a damn monster in that stuff."

"But how does it look?"

"You look great, but I can see some things that aren't fitted quite right. Here let me help you."

We ended up working a bit late into the night fitting everything properly, so I had full range of movement. I even added a few things that Darroth suggested would be useful. Later that night at home, Nia came to me after dinner.

"I take it you're almost done with your armor?"

"We actually got it fitted today."

She smiled, "That's great! I'm sorry that I couldn't be there to see it, I'm sure it is awesome."

"That it is. But don't worry, I'll be putting it on again tomorrow, and I'll need you there for that."

"Ok, Mr. Alex, but could I ask for some of your time now?"

"Of course."

She smiled and dragged me up to our room. She then shut and locked the door. Satisfied that we wouldn't be interrupted, she took her secret rolled up sketches out of their hiding place.

"I know I'm not a master smith like you, but I would really like you to look this over for me."

She unrolled everything on the table so I could look it over. I was very impressed with what she had drawn up.

"I knew you were up to something like this, but this is superb!"

Nia was beaming. She had drawn up a complete illustrated diagram of armor for Maya. Her design was very sleek and slender compared to mine. She even had notes on all the enchantments she felt were needed. This suit of armor was designed with speed in mind, but still offered protection that would be unmatched by any other armor but mine, even full field plate.

Nia must have been spending all her free time working on this. I had no doubt that this would be perfect for Maya.

"This is excellent! It must have taken you a long time to do this."

She blushed. "To tell the truth, I even faked going to sleep some nights so I would get it done in time, so you could build it as soon as you finished the tournament. Do you think it will be good enough for Maya?"

"It will be perfect! But there are some minor things that we need to put in that you wouldn't know about."

Nia listened intently to everything I said and made her own changes to her design. I was not going to take over anything. She worked so hard on this; it will be her armor design and hers only. Nia understood all the reasons I gave her for modifications and even changed some other things before I even said they were needed. After a couple of intense hours, we were done with the revisions.

"Nia, come here for a second, I would like to try something."

She flew over to me. "What do you want to try?"

I pulled a small piece of left over starlode metal from Winya's forging from one of my pockets. "Ok, I know this will be a bit strange, but just trust me. I need you to close your eyes, stand on this block with your feet apart and your arms and wings out, and don't move."

She did as instructed, and then I started to form the metal.

The liquid metal was not hot so I wouldn't burn her, but she still flinched a little. I had it climb up her legs and out to her arms, slowly hardening into the shape I was wanting. After about a minute, I was done.

"Ok, you can open your eyes now, and you're free to move."

Once I said that, she sprang into the air, away from the block in my hand. She was horrified by what she just saw. "Ok, what the hell, Mr. Alex? What is that thing?"

"This is a simple piece of metal."

"But it was moving...and on me!"

"That was me, a new ability from my dad. And I must say it worked even better than I hoped."

"What worked?"

"Look at what you're wearing."

She looked down at herself and realized she was wearing a suit of armor. She had on a suit of breast plate that looked to be made of pure silver. She had slots in the back for her wings to move, but even they had a super thin layer of silver around the edges of her wings. I also gave her twin long swords the size of toothpicks. Nia looked herself over with her mouth wide open.

"This is fantastic! I can fly in armor! Wait, why can I fly in armor?"

"It's made from starlode, with a few of my enchantments mixed in, so it's super light but still very strong. Due to your size, I would still try to not get hit with anything, but it will protect you from most magic attacks and help you control your own. I worked the channels of magic in the swords and gauntlets so they work like a wand would. So if you're in a fight, just point a sword at a bad guy and fire away."

She flew around a bit and then landed in front of a mirror to admire herself. "I look great! But do I get a helmet, too?"

"Do you want one?" She nodded shyly. I shaped a small helmet from the block that looked similar to the one she designed for Maya. "Here you go."

She snatched it away and put it on, then continued striking exaggerated martial poses in front of the mirror. She looked rather badass actually. There's just something about a pixie in armor that instills fear in everyone. Ok, not really, but it is really cool.

"I still can't believe I can fly in this!"

"As I said, it's very light and has a lot of magic pumped into it. I also have it set to a keyword phrase so you will need to pick one."

She thought for a moment. "Combat Pixie!"

"I like it!" I set that as the keywords to activate her armor. With that done, I carefully liquefied it again and turned her armor into a small cube that I held in my hand. "Now all you have to do is touch it and say the keywords, and it will do the rest."

"That is so…I can't explain! Thank you, Alex!"

"But you need to promise me that you won't tell the twins or Maya."

She made a sad face. "Oh, I can see not telling Maya, but why not the twins?"

"Because those two can't keep anything from her, so it's best if they just don't know."

"Got it."

The next few days were extremely hectic. Nia and I spent most of our time working on all three of our armor sets, much to the disgust of everyone else. With us two busy, most of the cooking responsibilities fell on the twins, and the only meal they were comfortable making unsupervised was breakfast, so the hall ended up with eggs, bacon and sweet cakes for every meal. Even Rosa began to get tired of it and threatened to eat at Central if something wasn't done soon. The dragons were perfectly fine eating the same food over and over as they had developed a special fondness for bacon, lots of bacon. At lunch one day with Lin and Julia, I even overheard two cooks complaining about the looming bacon shortage that seemed to be on the horizon at the school.

But the work needed to be done. Rosa and Maya were working out a plan to find the guy protecting the assassins, apparently that was going well. The twins even spent the day with Julia and Lin doing girl things. I asked Nia what that meant and she just said, "Boys don't understand girls." Someday I hope to understand them, but somehow I feel that isn't going to happen.

Chapter 15

Alex

The first day of the tournament had arrived and we were ready. Nia and I took the day before off and got to bed early so we were well rested. Nia has made it very clear to me that she doesn't trust the other competitors when I'm not in a match, so she will never let me leave her sight. She is taking this a bit too seriously...I hope.

After a good breakfast with lots of bacon and a pep talk from everyone at the table, we went over to the starting area for the opening ceremony. In the meantime, I took this opportunity to get a feel for the area. The layout was simple, broad stone steps were arranged in a giant "C" shape with the opening facing a row of tents. In the center, were five colored rings, one for each of the towers, arranged in a circle as well. Sadly, there was nothing representing the Enchanters Hall. Some of the pre-tournament favorites had banners hung up to cheer on their side, and of course reds, greens, blues and grays were represented proudly. I could see nothing that would give me the advantage; I also didn't see anything that would hinder, either. In fact, if both opponents have to stay in the circles, I would say this will be easy.

I decided to wear my leather undersuit so not everyone would know right away that I was an Enchanter. Looking around though, I probably did seem a little odd being the only one not in a robe. My pondering was interrupted by the loud sound of someone clearing their throat. Looking up, I could see that the Headmaster and the other heads of the towers on a raised platform in their finest robes were ready to get things started. The Headmaster used a spell to amplify his voice.

"Greetings, everyone, to the 607th Wizards Tournament!" Thundering applause and shouts filled the stadium. "It gives me great honor to oversee this year's tournament for the first time since returning from my research hiatus. But none of you want me to talk all day, you want duels!" More thunder from the students. "For those of you who are new this year, we have some rules to go over. First, every contestant has been given a tent. When you are not in the rings or in the stands, you will be in your tent. Second, when you are in a duel, there will be no fatal blows. Third, if you leave the ring, you're out. And fourth, you can use only what you can carry with you, no outside aid. Toward the end of the competition, the tower primuses will make changes to the rules if needed. But for now...let the tournament begin!"

Well, that was short; here I thought I would be standing for a long time. With the games started, the contestants began exiting the stadium to find their tents. From the number of participants, I would say this could take a long time to declare a winner; there must be over two hundred of us. I found my tent quickly; after all, it was the only white one. Inside, I found Rosa and Nia, along with the floating stone box which was now holding my armor. Rosa got up from a small table set up in the back corner and gave me a hug and a peck on the cheek.

"Don't worry about anything, you will do fine."

Through the link we shared, I could tell that she was the nervous one. "I'll be fine, Rosa, don't worry about me. You should go sit with the girls in the stands, I'll be fine here."

She wrung her hands. "I still don't feel right about this. I know it was my idea, but I don't want to see you get hurt."

Nia flew over to us and attempted to get Rosa away from me

and out the door. "Rosa, he couldn't get hurt in this armor if he fell off a two hundred foot cliff!"

Rosa gave the two of us a hard look. "And how is that supposed to make me feel better? Only you two have seen it, and I can't tell anything about it from reading your minds. Every time we mention it, all you two think about is measurements and improvements. It's driving me crazy!"

I slowly pushed Rosa out the tent flap. "I'll be fine. I have Nia to watch my back, so don't worry. Please, go have fun with the others today, your undercover work can continue tomorrow." She looked like a mother sending her child off to join the army, but she left eventually.

With Rosa gone, Nia let out a sigh of relief. "Finally! I thought she would never leave. Even I can only take so much melodrama in one day." She flew over to the table and grabbed a thin piece of wood with paper on it. She looked it over as she talked to me. "Ok, Champ, it looks like for the first day, you have three matches to compete in, provided you win, of course, and you will! The first one is in competition ring three, so we have less than an hour to get you ready. So get your armor on already!"

"Yes, Ma'am!"

A pixie with authority, who knew?

....

Maya

We had excellent seats, tenth row up and in the middle so we could see everything. I sat down wearing an Enchanters staff robe that Rosa had enchanted with the same spell as my party dress, so I wasn't standing out as a dark elf. The sun felt good on my face. Today was going to be a good day. The twins sat to my left and Lin and Julia on my right. The dragons seemed excited by the new experience, but the girls were going absolutely nuts. Julia grabbed my arm and then wrapped me in a tentative hug. She looked at me with those big blue eyes of hers.

"Maya, I thought Alex was going to be joining us."

"He and Nia are on their way." I could barely contain my excitement. Alex said he never told them about competing, so I was anxious to see the looks on their faces when he stepped out into that arena.

"Sad, he's going to miss all the fun."

"Oh, I think he will have plenty of fun."

She looked at me with a puzzled expression. She started to say something, but I put a finger on her lips. "No talking, they're about to start round three."

Lin and Julia directed their attention to the announcer who was calling the names for the third round. "In the blue ring, we have Turkel Hatst vs. Nitile Burs. In the green ring, we have Ranny Eose vs. Alex Martin."

I wasn't looking at the announcer, I was looking at the girls, just waiting for him to say that. Their jaws dropped and they slowly turned their heads to me. Julia looked stricken and started hyperventilating, but Lin was still able to find her voice.

"By the gods! Alex is competing? It's going to be a massacre, a slaughterhouse, a big boom and a pile of ash!"

I patted them on the knees and grinned, "I know, it's going to be so thrilling!"

They both stared at me, blinking like I had gone completely insane. "No, you're not getting it. Alex will be the pile of ash!"

Still smiling. "I don't think so. Have some faith, you two."

Just then, Rosa joined us, looking rather sad. Julia took the opportunity to go straight to the source of the information.

"Rosa, please tell us it's not true. Please say he's not actually competing!"

Rosa was actually shedding tears and wringing her hands in a mild panic. "It's true...all true. I just hope he doesn't accidently kill anyone."

The girls were speechless now as the contestants began entering the rings. I put a hand on each of their heads and turned them to look at the green ring directly in front of us.

"Whoa!" Winya intoned breathlessly in my mind.

This was the first time that I've seen the armor he made and just looking at it took my breath away. He was now a seven foot tall white and silver monument of perfection. The plates of his armor were so smooth that it looked like a white mirror, and with the shine of the silver chainmail peaking through the plates, he seemed to glow. He looked up at us, but there were no slots in his helmet for the eyes. I then remembered he no longer needs them. Aside from the massive armor, he was wielding a white tower shield that was as tall as he was and casually carried a large gleaming white war hammer that still almost seemed too small for him. From the viewpoint of someone who had seen battle and had sent many foes to the afterlife, I recognized the steely angel of death out on that field. I felt a panicked chill run through my body. I knew this armor...from my dreams!

....

Alex

This armor feels great. I have been in it for about half an hour now and I don't feel like I'm even wearing it. Nia has really cracked down on me, though; she had me at the stand-by area twenty minutes before I needed to be there. But time flew by and it was time to start the show. I walked out and took my place at my starting point in the green circle. An official came by and explained that I win by knocking my opponent out, making them leave the ring or forcing surrender. And when I say "came by" I really mean he had no desire to be anywhere near me, so he just shouted the instructions incoherently and ran for the hills.

My opponent, on the other hand, looked as though he wished he could run. I felt kind of bad for the poor kid. There he was, maybe five foot two, eighty pounds if he was lucky, shaking in his boots. I guess having your first opponent be a seven foot tall white and silver metal behemoth would do that to you.

The official on the sideline started the countdown, but the kid wasn't even readying a spell. The moment he said, "Start," I gripped my war hammer and crossed the hundred feet between us in the blink of an eye. When the dust settled from my sprint, the boy found the spike of my weapon an inch from his neck. He let out a small squeak before backpedaling out of the ring and falling on his butt in fear and staining his blue robes.

I turned to the official, but he seemed too stunned to move. Thankfully, he regained his wits before this got too awkward and signaled a victory. After winning my first match and setting a new record, I was asked to return to my tent. As I left, I looked up at the girls and found that Lin, Julia, Rosa, Dawn, and Dusk were all staring at me strangely without blinking. Maya was nowhere to be seen. Funny, I could have sworn she was there right up until the judge's decision. I walked over to the side of the arena closest to my friends and indulged them with a snappy salute. Then I left, grinning behind my helm.

I returned to my tent were Nia slammed into my face plate, hugging it, as soon as I stepped inside.

"You were awesome! You scared him so good that he wet himself!"

"I only did that to end things quickly so he wouldn't get hurt," I defended, still feeling a little guilty about scaring the kid that badly.

She released me and sat on her built-in pixie perch on the right pauldron of my armor. It's also where her armor was now located. "Well, Alex, we don't have another match until late this afternoon, and then they're almost right in a row."

"If I keep winning. That's fine, so I guess I should get out of the armor if we're going to get some food."

"I'd hold up a minute. Rosa said she would stop by after the match to see this armor we've been so hush-hush about. And I don't think the others will miss the chance either."

I took her advice and stayed in the armor, but I did the smart thing and put the hammer, shield, and gauntlets in my box. With that done, I stood in the middle of the tent and waited with Nia on my shoulder. Now, standing in the middle was not part of some plot for when they got here, it's just the only area where I can stand up straight without my head hitting the top of the tent.

The next thing I knew, a misty-eyed Maya charged into the tent, threw her arms around my head and leaped up into my arms like a small child. She put her head on the breastplate of my armor and squeezed her eyes tight, saying nothing.

"Alex, she needs you to just hold her for now," Winya advised sagely.

Rosa and the others rushed in a few moments later. Julia stopped abruptly and gawked at Maya's behavior, and then looked at me and gushed, "Alex, that was so cool! Your armor is huge and it's amazing it lets you run at those speeds, and you look awesome!"

"Thanks, but can anyone tell me what's wrong with Maya?"

Julia thought for a moment. "She was fine until she saw you come out in your armor, and then she gasped and mumbled something about this being a dream and started to shake like a leaf. Then she bolted."

I looked at Rosa questioningly. She shrugged, and finally Winya answered the question.

"Maya is ok with me telling you this, Alex, she just isn't prepared to say the words out loud. To make a long story short, she is experiencing a mental shock. Interwoven in this are strong feelings of love, hope, validation, joy and not a small amount of desire.

"You might say Maya had a haunted childhood. From her earliest memories, she has dreamed of a knight in shining armor very, very close in appearance to the armor you have on, who wielded a fearsome hammer to smite his foes. The knight never spoke or removed his helmet, but she still fell in love with this knight from her childhood. He was always there to drive away the horrible nightmares of undead that haunted her sleep nearly every night.

"At some point in our late childhood, we all come to the realization that our childhood's fondest dreams are just that - fantasies and nothing more. Maya cast off her dreams of the white knight and resolved that if she could not depend on him for protection, then she must become her own protector, a capable warrior in her own right. She vowed that no one would hurt her again, be it man or apparition. So she trained and trained until she became the swordswoman she is today, but still the awful nightmares continued.

"Alex, when she met you, the ghost of the valiant white knight resurfaced again in her thoughts, like a long forgotten melody, and the nightmares miraculously stopped. In her mind, she placed you inside that gleaming white armor and she fell in love all over again. In training, when she first saw you pick up a war hammer, swing it and become proficient with it so naturally, again the image of the white knight with your face came to her mind.

"Today for the first time, seeing you in the ring, in that armor, Maya realized that you are, and have always been, her knight!"

Maya's arms were moving now, but her eyes were still closed tightly, as she fumbled clumsily to try to remove my helm. I reached up with my free hand and removed it, letting it drop to the ground next to us. Immediately, her lips hungrily found mine, and after a few intense moments that elicited some gasps from the younger crowd, her eyes snapped open just inches from mine. I was instantly lost in those emerald green, searching, frighteningly fierce eyes.

"Just to make sure I'm clear on this," she whispered. "I am never letting you go, like ever! I don't care if there are a dozen crazy prophesies out there saying I will be a queen someday. If I can't have you and be a queen, then I will happily remain a simple weapons trainer forever as long as you stay by my side."

"No need to worry, my lady. I am your humble servant, always," I whispered back and gently lowered her feet to the floor.

She smiled, drying her tears with the cuff of her robe. "That was exactly the right thing for you to say."

We were brought back to reality by the sound of Julia trying to lift my helmet. It was kind of funny to watch; she didn't have a chance of rolling it over. Both Maya and I burst out laughing, much to the confusion of everyone else. Defeated Julia gave up and with a huff, kicked my faceplate and then hopped about from the pain in her foot.

"What the hell, Alex? How much does that thing weigh?"

I picked it up and held it so they all could get a better look. "Well, I would say somewhere around a hundred pounds or so when Maya or I aren't holding it."

The twins and druids seemed to be fascinated. They crowded around it, touched it, and lifted the face shield. Dawn was the first to notice something was wrong. "Um, as a dragon, human armor is not one of my strong points, but how can you see out of that if you don't have eye slots?"

"I don't need to see anymore, not normally, anyway. I can see things all around me, even through things. I can also follow the flow of magic and predict what people are about to do."

Maya grew serious and added, "It also enables him to use his tower shield unconventionally." Dropping naturally into her weapons instructor persona, she continued, "Normally a tower shield is a liability in single close combat. It's slow and heavy to move, and it's difficult to see what your opponent is doing on the other side. Alex doesn't have those issues. To him, the shield is as light as a training buckler and transparent as glass, and with his ability to anticipate his foes position, he can utilize even a relatively slow weapon like the war hammer to maximum effect. That makes him very hard to beat in our duels."

She stopped, noting the glassy-eyed stares from the mages in the group, and fanned herself vigorously. "Sorry, but weapons and tactics are so..."

Lin rolled her eyes dramatically and then shifted her attention to me. "Ok, so you're supposed to be an Enchanter. I thought you guys couldn't cast spells."

Rosa was kind enough to answer that one. "You would normally be correct there, Lin. But as you can probably guess, he is not just an Enchanter."

Julia asked next, "What do you mean by that?"

Rosa smiled and placed a hand on my armored shoulder. "It's simple really, he's not human."

I would imagine that most people would be shocked to find that they were not what they thought they were. For me, it was kind of a relief. I knew that my real parents were something much more than human, and the vampire I fought said as much, also. But my real question is, how much more?

The twins came over and started smelling me; in truth, it was a rather odd sensation. Dusk took a deep breath before shrugging her shoulders. "He smells human to me."

"Actually, he smells really, really good for a human," Dawn added with a soft sigh, which earned her a wicked glare from Maya. "What, Mistress? Some humans don't bathe often enough," she explained.

Still smiling, Rosa handed me a steel practice rod. "We shall see about that, not the bathing part," she snickered. "Alex, I would really like for you to show everyone your new power your father gave you. Nia is biting her tongue to keep from telling everyone."

I looked at Nia, who was indeed trying hard not to say anything. "Nia, you don't need to try so hard to hurt yourself." She relaxed and nodded. I turned back to Rosa. "What do you want?"

"How about a necklace?"

Well, that would be easy, a small chain is nothing compared to the complexity of a suit of armor. I didn't even have to try real hard to get a small amount of the steel rod to melt. Everyone gasped as the metal liquefied and spun majestically in the air, slowly starting to re-harden in the shape of a twisted chain necklace with the elf rune of magic as the pendant design. Once done, I slowly lowered it around Rosa's neck. She placed her hand on it and smiled.

"It's lovely, thank you. But, please, tell everyone what your power is."

I glanced around at all the looks that I was getting; most were of amazement, but Maya nodded calmly.

"One of the powers my father gave me is the ability to control metals from a short distance. I can melt and shape them into anything I want. I can even enchant them as I work. One of the things Mother gave me was my extra sight, another is much more control of the magic in the metals. Basically, I can do things with metal that no one else can."

Everyone seemed excited by that and wanted a

demonstration, and I had a great one. "I'll demonstrate. Rosa, would you please stand over there." She stalled for a bit, and I could tell she was trying to read my mind, but I have long ago learned that if I think about armor she can't get past it. Giving up, she walked to the far side of the tent. For safety's sake, I placed a fire proof enchantment on the tent and then returned to the center with the others.

"Nia, if you would kindly throw a fireball at Rosa, please."

Everyone's jaws dropped, but Nia looked like I just gave her a birthday present. She eagerly flew over to my shoulder and stood on her stand for support. She started a fireball spell, really hamming up the preparations like she was readying the biggest fireball of all time, and giving Rosa time for a few last words.

"Alex, please call off the pixie, call off the pixie!" She was in full panic mode.

"This is for trapping me under a pot!" Nia cast the fireball and it hit her right in the chest or, at least, it looked like it did. At the last second, the fireball splashed across a light blue shield that put itself between Rosa and the fireball. Realizing that she wasn't dead, Rosa removed her hands from her eyes and quickly patted herself down, looking for injuries, smoking holes, etc. There were none, but I'm pretty sure she was wise to me all along, as least as far as realizing I would never intentionally hurt her.

"That necklace will block most magical casts directed at you, but it can't stop everything and can be broken by a powerful spell. If it does ever fail, then you might as well throw it away because it only has one shield in it."

Nia was very proud of herself. She was the only other one in the room who knew of all my new tricks before now. She was sitting proudly on her perch on my shoulder gloating at Rosa. As soon as things looked safe, the twins ran up to Rosa and looked her over, then examined her necklace trying to find out how it works.

Lin came over to Nia and me. "So what are you?"

"I truly don't know. My parents aren't able to tell me yet."

She thought that over for a few seconds. "Fine, I'll accept that. But you still haven't answered why your armor weighs so much when you're not holding it."

I smiled and the others must have overheard that because they gathered around us again. "In truth, its weight never changes; it's just really light to me and Maya. In my full combat gear, I weigh over six thousand pounds. My shield alone is over eight hundred pounds. Thankfully, it seems that our horses were given the same gift that we were, so I don't crush them."

Rosa wrapped her arms around my waist and tried to lift me up. She grunted and strained her muscles but wasn't able to even move me. "Ugh, you're heavy. How can you even walk around without sinking or bringing the place down?"

I lifted my foot. "Enchanted boots. They stamp enchantments on whatever I walk on; it's really one of my cooler new enchantments."

Nia flew off my shoulder and got everyone's attention. "Ok, people! I know you all love Alex and his new abilities, but we have wasted over two hours talking, and I have two hours to get him out of that armor, fed and back into it. So with that said, EVERYBODY GET OUT! Except Maya, I'll need your help."

I laughed as the others left the tent, grumbling about a pixie with an uppity attitude. Rosa gave me the look that said we would be having this conversation again later; of course, she wasn't even out the door before asking questions through the link. But Nia was right, time was short and I didn't have time to talk her through all of them at this point.

I ignored the rest of Rosa's questions and turned to Maya and Nia. Maya was very happy, but Nia was in her drill sergeant pixie mode. "Alright, Alex, spread 'em!" I laughed but stretched out my arms and legs as ordered. "Ok, Maya, this is my gift to you; you get to unwrap Alex!"

I don't think Maya could be happier with any other present. She proved it by keeping her lips pressed to mine while her hands worked on removing the armor. Soon I found myself desperately short of breath, and my moral compass was flailing about like a drunken gnome in a pickle barrel. Finally, Nia tapped her on the shoulder and sent her on her way with a smile and a sinful saunter. With a deep cleansing breath, I headed to a late lunch with Nia.

I shouldn't have been surprised that people came up to me, but I was. Most of the people came over to wish me luck and to congratulate me on my first win. But three others had a different approach; they threatened me with humiliation and grave personal injury should I be impertinent enough to stay in the competition. Sadly for them, I could see how much magic they were capable of using, and I didn't think they would even last half way through the tournament.

But one visitor really surprised me. Ranny, from my first match, was being dragged over to me by a stern looking, older girl, also in blue robes. She stopped him right in front of me and pushed him forward with a dark look. He looked from me to her and back before offering to shake my hand. "I...it was a good match."

I shook his hand and smiled, trying to be friendly. The girl with him rolled her eyes and stepped forward.

"What my brother is trying to say is 'thank you.' He was forced into the tournament by his idiot friends, and I was afraid he would be killed. You beat him without hurting him and saved him from having to fight others, so again, thank you."

I shook her hand as well. "I'm glad this worked out for both of you, but I am sorry for scaring you."

Ranny shook his head. "Don't worry about it. Just do me a favor and win so I won't look like too much of a wimp."

We all smiled. "I plan to do just that, don't worry."

We said goodbye and they both promised to cheer for me in the rest of my matches. As the two left, I could make out the last few comments they made to each other. The sister asked her brother questions about me and Nia. I think I heard the girl ask if I had a girlfriend, too bad for her that I do and have no desire to leave Maya at any point in my life.

Once they were gone, Nia returned to forcing food into me and got me back to the tent as fast as she could. Finally back in the tent, I had about three seconds to rest before she had me suiting up again. And fifteen minutes later, I was back in the standby area.

When I was called to enter the ring, I was disappointed that I missed the name of my opponent. But after seeing him, I got the feeling that I wouldn't get along with him anyway. He was shorter than I was - but most people are - and was wearing the gray robes of a wind user. He reminded me of a diminutive version of Naton. Another thing that stood out was his obvious attitude.

"Hey, Enchanter, you ready to be blown away? I saw your last match and your speed won't help you with me! Ha, I'll be the one who puts you stupid Enchanters back in your place!"

Great, one of the high and mighty types. But I have a feeling that he might find that I am harder to blow away than he thought. The match started with him launching a blast of wind at me, kicking up a huge cloud of dust and dirt.

"Ha! Got him in one blow!"

The look on his face when the dust cleared was great. I am glad I don't have eye slots in my helm for all that dirt to get in. Normally, I would have fun with the jerk, but sadly, these things are timed and you get more points for speed. I calmly walked out of the dust cloud towards the guy. The look on his face was just as I expected - pure shock. Looking at his magic, I could see that first big blast was apparently all he could muster at one time, and I didn't even flinch in this much armor.

"How are you still standing? You should be flat against the wall right now!"

He was now desperately trying to knock me down with several weak wind blasts, but soon he was out of energy and his attacks were nothing more than a soft breeze. When I reached him, he was pale-faced, exhausted, and having a hard time standing.

"You should take it easy, you have reached your limit. If you cast any more spells, you'll burn out."

"Go to hell!"

Not really wanting to hurt him, I just grabbed him by the shoulders and tossed him out of the ring. He landed in a heap and didn't move. Two of the on-hand healers rushed over to him and after a brief examination called out that he over-exerted himself and would be fine. Quickly, the official declared me the winner and I was allowed to leave.

I got a lot more looks on my way back to my tent. Many seemed to be trying to figure out what I was. Ignoring them, I entered the tent to find Nia there with her list and a quill.

"Great job! A runner came by and updated me already. He seemed surprised that a pixie was acting as your manager."

"Oh, I'm sure it wasn't just that. So...anything else happen?"

She put her paper down and shook her head. "Nope, nothing. But your next match is coming up pretty quick, so you have about ten minutes to rest up."

I put my boot on a chair to transfer an enchantment before sitting down with her. "Well, to be honest, I don't really need to rest. Not to be rude, but he was easy."

She smiled. "I know he was. I was watching with one of my pixie scrying spells. They seem to be very useful for these events. But since you have some time, the twins dropped off some snacks for us."

We enjoyed our sweets and talked a little before I had to leave for my last round of the day. Approaching the arena, it sounded like there were quite a few more people in the stands than for my first two events. When I got there, I was shocked to find that my next opponent was a tall, very attractive blonde girl, and a healer! I didn't think that they had offensive spells. After entering the ring, the gray and red-robed healer girl smiled, approached, and was kind enough to enlighten me as to why she was here.

"You're Alex, right? I'm Alera. My friends say good things about you and your bunch of Enchanters, but sadly, I have never had a chance to meet you. You honor me with this match."

"It is good to meet you, Alera." I performed a formal salute with my hammer. The growing crowd for our event let it be known that Alera was a fan favorite, something she dismissed with a quick smile, and then refocused on me.

"Wow, you really are a traditional guy, aren't you? Well, I'm guessing that you may be wondering what a healer is doing here. My talents lie in summoning magic, as well as healing, so really you aren't fighting me as much as one of my protectors. I'm told you're pretty strong and not to go easy on you, so if you are ready, let's get started."

Well, you couldn't say she was a shy wallflower-type of girl. I liked her and her straightforward attitude right away. The match was signaled to begin and she instantly cast a circle in front of her. Out of the pink light came something that I wasn't expecting. It looked like a man but had a head like a golden bulldog and was wearing heavy plate armor and carrying a great sword.

"As you may have guessed, he is a nebulia; he is also my personal protector," she called out in a confident cheery voice.

I have read about them. They are defenders of good and fight for the weak in their defense. If he was really her guardian, then she must be a good person. No nebulia would ever voluntarily work for evil, and he was by no means restrained.

He saluted me with his great sword before charging the distance between us. The battle was joined with him using his two-handed weapon to try and batter me into submission. He was fast and very skilled. Normal armor would have been fractured, dented, or made otherwise inoperable in just a couple minutes of this pounding. But Maya's training and my armor made me the better combatant, and he wasn't really even touching me. Unfortunately, this put me in a quandary. If I were just fighting a summoned demon or even a natural animal, I would have taken it out in very short order. But this creature was a defender of good, and I couldn't kill him for a meaningless victory in a tournament. Consequently, our match lasted much longer than I would have liked as I was working for his surrender, not a kill. Our weapons clashed a number of times, and he continued to flail away at my shield to no avail. It must have been an exciting show for the audience as we were generating a lot of noise, but we were no closer to resolving the match. Finally, exasperated and with time running out, I activated one of the many enchantments on my hammer and the next time he blocked, my hammer snapped the great sword into pieces, leaving him with just an empty hilt in his human-looking hands. The nebulia stared incredulously at it for a moment, then seeing my hammer back in the ready position for a strike, he knelt, dropped the remains of the sword in the sand, and bowed his head to face his destiny, a defeated champion of good.

The crowd went absolutely stone cold silent. I looked over at a pale and stricken Alera, who had tears streaming down her face, probably thinking I would kill him.

"Alera, could I ask for your surrender?"

She was confused for a second before her face lit up with a relieved smile. "Yes, please, I surrender!"

I sheathed my hammer and offered my hand to the nebulia. He accepted and I pulled him to his feet. The stunned audience finally seemed to take a breath and there was a thunder of applause in appreciation for the show. Alera came running over and hugged the exhausted big guy, sobbing softly the entire time.

"I'm so sorry! I should never have entered this tournament. I never wanted to endanger your life, please forgive me."

He put a hand on her head and said something that I didn't understand, but I could tell they were words of comfort. Her tears died away and she looked up at him. "What do you mean?" More strange words were exchanged between the two before she turned back to me, with him by her side.

"He wants me to tell you that you are the best fighter and the most honorable opponent that he has ever fought. He also knows that you passed up many chances to kill him in favor of surrender, and he thanks you sincerely for your mercy, as do I."

"The honor was mine. I would be glad to fight beside you one day. But please, a warrior is broken without his weapon, so it's only fair that I fix yours." I pulled off my helmet and dropped it on the ground as I did my gauntlets. I quickly collected the pieces of his great sword and kneeling, sorted them in the proper shape in the sand.

"Alera, could I borrow the shawl you have around your shoulders for a moment? It won't be harmed." She pulled it off and handed it over, curious about what I was doing. I spread the shawl over the sword parts to hide them and willed the pieces of the blade to reform, stronger and sharper than they were originally. I sensed a small amount of innate resistance from the metal, telling me that this was no ordinary steel weapon. But the metal desired to be whole again and in a few seconds, it was. Sliding the cloth back, revealing the repaired weapon, and giving Alera back her shawl probably looked like some cheap parlor trick to the people still in the stands, but I didn't care. I picked up the great sword and presented it formally back to the nebulia. As a warrior would, he accepted it reverently.

Returning the sword to the nebulia produced interesting results. He took one look at the renewed blade and his canine face became very animated. Instantly, he dropped to his knees, spewing out words in a gush in his strange language. Alera had a hard time keeping up with what he was saying.

"Slow down, I didn't get all that. What's this about a prince?" His wide-eyed gaze found her face, and he quickly pulled her down to a kneeling position beside him. He slowed down a bit to explain to her, and as she understood more of what he was saying, her blue eyes grew enormous as well. She, too, was now bowing earnestly to me.

"Please forgive us, I had no idea you were…" The nebulia clamped a hand on her mouth; she was not supposed to say that apparently. He let go of her and she froze, framing her words very carefully. "Just know that we are forever in your debt and that we will come if we are ever needed."

They both rose and backed up respectfully, then turned and quickly passed through the portal that the nebulia initially came through, leaving me to wonder again just what did everyone else seem to know that I didn't?

Chapter 16

Alex

Last night had been an interesting one. Lin and Julia had come over for dinner to celebrate with us. Thankfully, Rosa had thought of ordering food to be delivered from the dining hall so Nia and I didn't have to spend the night cooking and the twins could have a break. Part of it was I don't think she could stomach any more bacon! As such, we all had an enjoyable time together. Just as dinner arrived, Darroth stopped by to join the party, bringing some dwarven ale with him.

Despite the fun we were having, we all knew we couldn't get drunk or stay up too late. The first day of combat had gotten rid of all but the best combatants. Only three rounds remained with about twenty opponents left, so we needed our rest. Rosa initially planned to lock both Maya and me in our rooms for the night, but then remembered that none of the locks in the house would stop me anyway. So she made Maya sleep with her, quoting obscure house regulations about a "dark elf who cares too much"!

The next morning after a large breakfast, Nia and I returned to our tent to get ready. When we got there, we found a new roll of paper with the new schedule. Nia swooped down and snatched it away before I could read it. After she had studied it, she told me what it said.

"Ok, we have today's plan. Looks like there's another short speech before the last rounds. Says something about 'judge's rules', whatever that means. Oh wait, here it is. Apparently, the various headmasters will have the right to pick extra rules at the start of each round." She looked concerned for a second. "Well, that's not good. We don't have anyone up there to support rules in our favor.

Needless to say, your opponents will have an advantage now."

"Well, not much we can do about it. Maybe Rosa will have some luck if she can find one of the primuses cheating. Although, to be honest, I still don't see how this will help her find the traitor."

She shrugged. "Don't ask me, I'm just your humble manager."

The headmaster's speech announced basically what Nia had said. From now on, the primuses will draw extra rules for each match to be voted on by them. So these next few matches should be fun. Unfortunately, I had no time to go back to the tent; my first battle was right after the speech.

Waiting in the standby area, I was read the new rules. This match was to be done in half the time and in a much larger ring. When I went out into the ring in my full armor, the stands exploded with applause. Nia had told me that my win over Alera had won me some support from the crowd and that she had asked her supporters to cheer for us, but I wasn't expecting anything like this.

Once out in the ring, I found that it was easily four times the size of the other ones and I was at a loss how this would matter. On a whim, I asked one of the judges if I could still use and change anything in the ring or the ring itself. He said as long as I didn't leave it, I could do anything I wanted.

My opponent turned out to be another nameless wind user. Rosa told me last night that they don't like to give out their names to others, something about them trying to be secretive and "like the wind," whatever that means. I don't know about secretive, but this new opponent looked almost like a clone of the first one, only a bit shorter yet.

Once the match started, I knew I would have to end it quickly, but that wouldn't be as easy as I thought. This wind wizard was apparently very skilled at illusions because I was now looking at about a hundred of him. This could be a problem from what I know of Nia's illusions. I won't be able to tell the fake one from the real one, even with my mage sight.

"What's the matter, Enchanter? Don't know who the real one is?" The voice seemed to come from all of them, and he punctuated it with an evil chuckle.

"Well, just so you know, I guess this means that I will have to cut down each and every one of you until I find the real one."

The color drained from his face. My best thought was to use my speed to do just that and it would be the best way to finish this; however, I had promised the girls that I wouldn't kill anyone. But my chat with the judge brought an idea to mind. I am an Enchanter and this arena is powered by one big enchantment.

I sheathed my hammer and dropped my tower shield on the ground, then sat down to concentrate on figuring out the enchantment. This one was done in stone, which is Rosa's specialty and not so much mine. As time slipped by, the wind jerk was apparently getting impatient, so he started throwing mild wind blasts in my general direction, probably wary about getting me mad, but wanting to look like he was actually fighting. Seeing that it wasn't working, he gave up and was happy to let the time run out. I was down to a few seconds before I finally broke down what Rosa had done to this place. A second after that, I had full control and shrunk the size of the ring down to a five foot ring around me, trapping him and all his illusions outside the ring.

The stadium was deathly quiet as people processed what just happened. My opponent dropped the illusions and kept looking around him and then back at me with an open mouth. I turned to the judge who was also shocked.

"You never make this easy for me, you know?" He was frantically flipping through the rule book before looking up at the headmasters. "Since we have never had an Enchanter compete, we don't have rules set for them, but by all established rules, he is in the right and the victor of this match."

The heads of the towers argued amongst themselves before coming to an agreement of sorts. The Headmaster stood. "Alex, since we don't have a rule against what you did, we will allow it. But from now on, there is a rule against it, so please keep the field the way it is. It would be unfair to the others if you did that for a win every time."

My opponent started to protest, "But, Master, he cheated!"

The Headmaster raised his hand to stop him. "The way I see it, Alex would have been forced to do what he said he would do. Not only would you have lost, you would certainly have been seriously hurt, if not killed. This was the only way for him to win without risking your life and the only reason we are allowing it this time."

With a wave of his hand, several servants appeared out of dark corners and escorted me back to my tent. Nia was there, and she wasn't too happy.

"What's wrong?" I asked as I entered the tent. Nia was sitting with several rolls of papers all over the table.

"Just so I make myself clear, I'm never going to work at a desk again. This is as crazy as a cross-eyed squirrel in fall!"

"So what's happening?" I sat down at the table, now spelled

to take the weight, with her.

She sighed and rubbed her eyes. "After I sent you off to the speech, several people came by. Most of them demanded that you step down immediately, claiming that it is an embarrassment for real wizards to have to fight a mere Enchanter. Others had the guts to even say that the wizards can't go all out for fear of killing you. This last hour has been so insanely stupid!"

"What are all these?"

She sifted through the papers. "From what I have been able to discern, there's a big betting game tied to these tournaments. This appears to be one of the main ways Xarparion makes its money. Normally, I wouldn't have a problem with that, but there's also a nasty underground game to this as well. Rosa came by with most of this, and from looking at what she found, I would say the Fire Tower primus has the most to gain if a fire wizard wins, and I mean by a lot."

"How much are we talking?"

She sighed and sifted through even more papers. "Well, according to what Rosa found, if a fire wizard wins, he will get a number that I can't read. It's a three with six zeros after it. But she thinks it would be more than enough to buy what he would need. Rumor has it he's not a fan of Enchanters or even healers."

"That would be bad for everyone but the Fire Tower. But what happens if one of the other towers wins?"

"He would get nothing and his backers would be pissed. One, in particular, has not been named, and he is putting up over half the money. We think it could be a neighboring kingdom or a very powerful duke. But either one is not good."

"So, basically, I have to make sure I at least knock out the rest of the fire wizards."

She slammed her tiny fist on the table. "NO! You're going to kick all their asses! It's the only way to make sure all the towers stay equal. If you win, everything goes to the general treasury, not an individual tower. That, and if I have to deal with more of this crap, I think I'll vaporize the messenger, and no, I don't care that it's not his fault!"

We laughed. "I'll do my best."

The next match was only a few minutes later. I was waiting in the starting area for a judge to come by with the new rules. Within a minute, the same harassed judge who overlooked my last match came over to me, looking like he hadn't slept in a week.

"Look kid, I don't know who you pissed off, but I suggest you quit now while you can. Your next match is a cage ring match against a fire wizard. Basically, you're in a ten-foot round ring that you can't leave with a fire wizard in a separate ring throwing spells at you. Don't get me wrong, I hope you win, but I just don't want to see you get killed."

I thought on this for a moment, Nia and I had actually planned for something like this. But not having mobility will be a problem, then again, it might not be. I had a plan, sort of...

"No, I'm staying in. I can still use my ranged weapons, and he can't dodge my attacks either."

"You're one gutsy kid. Alright fine, just make sure I won't have to sweep your ashes out of that arena."

With that, he left and started the countdown to the start of the match. My opponent happened to be one of Naton's buddies, so I didn't have any nagging moral problems with what I was about to do. We entered our rings which were about seventy feet from each other, just far enough for me. One of the other rules for this match was no time limit. You have to make your opponent surrender or nearly kill him, and it was easy to see by the look on my opponent's face which end game he was looking for.

Before the match started, I slammed my tower shield into the ground to make myself a wall; I would like to see him move that! One positive note, the guy I was facing was at least the quietest of the two goons, so I probably wouldn't have to deal with non-stop insults this time.

As soon as the match started, my shield was hit with a large fireball that splashed harmlessly off its surface. I sat down with my back leaning against my shield and waited. My waiting was rewarded with several more fireballs as well as a few boos from the crowd, though I don't know if they were directed at him or me. After a very boring half hour, I used my mage sight to look at the fire wizard, and he was well on his way to being out of juice. He also had a staff with him that I didn't notice before, that's probably what kept him going as long as he did. A half hour may not seem like a long time but in a duel, it's an eternity.

Deciding now was the time; I got back to my feet, stretched leisurely, and pulled my shield from the ground.

"You look like you're about out of magic, would you like to surrender?"

He snarled at me, "Not on your life! You can't reach me over here and my strength will come back. All I have to do is wait and watch you burn!"

"By chance, do you know what a loaded gauntlet is?"

"No, and I don't care either. Why does that matter?"

I held up my left arm. "Well, you see it's an armored gauntlet with a small crossbow built right into it, and it looks kind of like this." I fired the small bolt and struck him in the shoulder. He cried out in pain and dropped to his knees, clutching his wounded shoulder. "So would you like to surrender now? I have lots of those bolts, you know."

"N-never!"

I fired another one into his other shoulder. This time, his mind couldn't take the pain and he keeled over face first in the sand. I didn't have to wait long for the judge to call that match. As the healers were tending to him, the judge came over to me.

"Why didn't you start with that instead of taking all those hits?"

"Well, as you can see, I'm not hurt; in fact, my shield only has some soot on it." I brushed some of the black charring off the shield to show him that it just needed to be cleaned. "That, and if I did, he would have used a firewall or something to burn my bolts before they reached him. This way, I made sure he didn't have the strength to block them."

"That's...very good thinking. I have been refereeing these matches for years now and you're the first one who actually came in with a plan. Typically, all these contests are is a mindless slugging match to see who has the strongest spells. I think Enchanters are more powerful than everyone thought. You seem to be perfect for taking down wizards."

"Thanks, but I need to get moving, my manager will be mad if I'm late."

We shook hands and went on with our day. When I got back to the tent, Nia was done with all her paperwork and was treating herself to some fresh fruit. I sat down at the table with her and she silently slid the fruit bowl over to me before speaking.

"I have good news...sort of, and bad news. Which do you want first?"

I sighed, "Let's start with the good."

"Ok. You did great last round! That gauntlet thingy worked great, better than I thought it would."

"And the bad news?"

"Your next match is against Hons."

"Well, crap!"

This is not going to be fun. Hons is a good man; in fact, one of the best guys I know and a friend. He is the strongest earth wizard to come through the academy in a hundred years. He is also the next in line for headmaster of the Earth Tower. So a duel with him was not really one of the things I had planned on.

What made the situation stink even more was I only had ten minutes before I had to leave for the ring. So, with no time to spare for a plan this round, I scooped up a bunch of iron practice rods and brought them with me. I might be forced to trap him instead of fight him. And I still didn't know the wildcard rule for this match.

When I got to the staging area, the judge told me that I may have the advantage in this match. It turns out that most of the earth combat spells are fatal and can't be toned down, so I won't have to worry about being dropped in a hole and crushed. For this round, the new rule was a larger ring. I was expecting something terrible, but I could work with this.

I went out into the ring with my bundle of iron rods under an arm. Hons was already out there waiting, looking confident, but not cocky.

"Good to see you again, Hons."

"I still can't believe it's you in there, Alex. Lin and Julia were concerned when they first learned that you entered the tournament, and I had to agree with them. Now it seems you have made us rethink that. You have beaten all your opponents without even getting touched."

"Well, I guess I've been lucky."

He laughed. "I don't think luck has anything to do with it. You beat Alera's nebulia and she was thought to rank highly this year. Well, let's get this over with, but don't think I'll go easy because I count you as a friend."

Once the match started, I threw the rods I held around the ring. I had just enough time to get my shield up to block a large chunk of earth cast at me. It shattered off my shield but still had the force to push me back a few feet.

"Very impressive, Alex! That had enough force to punch a hole in Xarparion's main wall!"

"What can I say, I'm hard to move."

I rushed forward to close the gap between us. Using my mage sight, I could see he had a plan for that, but I didn't have time to react. At soon as I was within twenty feet of him, large stone spikes shot out of the earth. At the last second, I was able to dodge the spikes, but my maneuver had forced me to dive away from him.

Getting close to him was not going to work, and the spikes now blocked him from my ranged attacks. But before I could come up with a plan, more spikes shot out of the ground around me. I was entirely surrounded by rows of six foot tall spikes on all sides.

"Would you like to surrender now?" I shook my head. "Well, I gave you a chance." Hons moved in closer and was just on the other side of the spikes now. He then ripped a five foot round boulder out from deep beneath the ground and levitated it over my head. I could tell from my mage sight that he planned to carefully lower the boulder down on the spikes, trapping me for the win. If I tried to break through the side spikes, the trap would collapse, the boulder would fall and I would subject myself to a flattening that I wasn't sure even my armor could absorb. It was the perfect trap.

While I was pondering my predicament and watching Hons carefully maneuver the boulder over me, suddenly my mage sight detected a mote of magic zipping out of the section of the crowd that was predominantly red robes. In an instant, it impacted the middle of Hons' back and he flinched, losing concentration and, more importantly to me, control of the boulder still fifteen feet above my head. It dropped immediately like a deadly eclipse blotting out the sky!

With no place to escape, I only had one option. Just before impact, I planted the end of my tower shield on the ground and desperately aligned the top edge to catch the bulk of the weight of the rock. I swiftly crouched down next to the shield so that it would take the force of the drop instead of my head. Grabbing my hammer, I slammed the head into the ground and commanded the handle to elongate until it contacted the plunging boulder. Something like eleven tons of granite impacted the top of the shield driving it a foot or more into the ground. The momentum slowed, it teetered slightly, and then, fortunately, the boulder started to tip over to the side where I had placed the hammer. The entire colossus sagged to a stop with a groan and a cloud of dust.

To the casual observer in the stands, I had completely disappeared under the rock, with the stone spikes still hiding me from all sides. The crowd groaned and there were a number of screams of horror and dismay. The reality was that I was pretty uncomfortable but not quite dead. I had precious little room to move, however, in the precarious balance of boulder, shield, and inch thick hammer shaft. But my feet were still under me, which was about the only positive I could think of at the moment.

Using my mage sight, I saw a very concerned Hons run up to the spike wall and one of the referees sprint toward us, no doubt to call the match and allow Hons to recover my lifeless body. At this point, I think my brain went a little haywire, probably from lack of oxygen, and I decided the obvious course of action was to simply push the boulder sideways. Bracing myself against the inside of the spikes, I reared up, screamed, and pushed with everything I had. It's fortunate that my armor was built as strongly as it was, as the overlapping plates locking together kept my muscle groups and internal organs from blowing out completely and probably saved my life.

I managed just enough momentum to encourage the boulder to fall on the other side as I tipped the shield. It dropped the final six feet or so and crashed noisily through the side of the spike wall and rolled past an astonished Hons and the referee. I staggered clumsily through the opening and fell on my backside, facing the two, dirt and dust streaming off my smooth armor in rivulets.

Hons was looking wildly at me, and then the boulder, and then back at me again. My mage sight showed him standing almost on top of two of the metal rods that I had distributed across the field - it was about time I caught a break! The first rod coiled around his ankles like a pissed off anaconda, dropping the earth wizard to the ground roughly. The second steel snake slipped around his throat in slow motion and then shot down to his wrists and pinned them together. Trussed and tied, the earth wizard wasn't going anywhere.

"How in the hell did you live through that?" Hons gasped from the ground.

I painfully levered myself up using some still-standing stone spikes and limped over to him. The referee looked at me questioningly and, for convention sake, I drew my dagger and absently pointed it at my friend and earth wizard opponent. The judges signaled an immediate end to the match, and I sheathed the dagger wearily.

"I'm sorry about this, Hons, truly I am; you deserved to win." And with that, I collected my things and released the still astonished mage, then slowly made my way back to my tent. I almost didn't make it. The adrenaline rush of competition petered out, and I was beset by unrelenting pain in every joint, and most of my muscles were on fire. I think I drifted in and out of tunnel vision, concentrating solely on putting one foot in front of another. I stumbled into my tent to find that Nia wasn't alone. She was sitting at the table chatting with Alera. When they saw me enter, Alera got up and moved the chair to the middle of the tent and gestured for me to sit. Nia flew up to me.

"Alex! This healer girl came in and said you were hurt."

"Yeah, I think I overdid it a little."

Alera came over and walked around me, inspecting me. "That's an understatement. This is the kind of damage I would expect to find in someone who had been tortured on the rack for a week and then dropped off a cliff. Every bit of skeletal muscle tissue in your back, legs, and upper arms is either torn or damaged. You also have some bone fractures and a great deal of bruising." She put her hands on her hips and shook her blonde head. "By any measure of health that I am aware of, you should be completely unable to move right now."

"You can tell all that even with me in all this armor?"

She looked shyly away. "Um, I know I'm not supposed to know this, but you Enchanters have a power that lets you see magic. Well, some healers have a similar sight that allows us to see injuries. It's one of the reasons the other towers hate us; we both have unique sights and they don't."

Even sitting down, the burning pain in my back and legs was getting worse. I tried my best to remove my helmet, but raising my arms was no longer an option. Nia was starting to get concerned. "Is he going to be ok? Can you fix him?"

"I can heal him, but I need him out of that armor."

I sighed. "Well, I can't move much anymore, my body is locking up. So I'll have to ask that you stay calm and promise not to tell anyone what you see." She nodded, and I started to use my powers to float the pieces of my armor off and back into my box. It took longer than normal, but I got everything in place. Alera didn't even flinch. Nia and Alera helped me out of the leather undersuit. Nia gasped when she saw the bruises that covered my shoulders and back. "By the gods! Mr. Alex, your whole body is hurt. You must be in a lot of pain."

"It wasn't so bad in the ring, but now it's really starting to hurt," I gasped almost unable to even draw a full breath.

Alera placed her hands on my shoulders and almost instantly the pain began to fade. "Don't worry, the pain will be gone shortly." She was right, I was feeling better in minutes. She worked quickly and quietly. I could feel my body being repaired as she went. But it didn't feel like I thought it would. I was expecting a healing spell to feel good, but it didn't. It felt like things were moving under my skin, like snakes or something. Creepy! Thankfully, she was done very quickly, but I could see that the effort had cost her. She was audibly panting and looked much paler and tired than when I first entered the tent.

She bent down and looked me straight in the eye. "Alex Martin, you need to remember, you may be inhumanly strong, but you still have the limitations of human bone structure, tendons and muscles to contend with. You're not going to like this, but as a healer, I have to recommend that you do nothing strenuous for a couple days."

"But I thought you fixed him," Nia said.

"I have repaired the damage and he can move now, but his body's reserves have been severely depleted. The healing arts can only redirect and strengthen the body's natural repair mechanisms, but the energy to do so came right from Alex. He needs food, lots of it, and rest."

"Alera, I don't have the option of sitting this out, the final match is in...?" I looked at Nia.

"Less than an hour," she replied morosely.

Alera smiled sadly and nodded, she stood up and placed a cool hand on my shoulder. "Please be careful, Alex, the world cannot afford to lose one such as you." Then without another word, she bowed to me and left. Now it was just me and Nia.

"So what happened out there?" she asked.

"Well, that boulder was a bit heavier than I thought it was."

"You think? Your armor may be able to take something like that, but you can't! You're lucky your new friend is a healer. Alex, do you think we should take her advice and withdraw? It is just a stupid contest." Her big eyes reflected the concern she felt and her wings buzzed in agitation.

I shook my head vehemently. "No way, we've come too far, and I'm pretty sure me being out of the tournament would fall right into the hands of whoever's behind all this." I told her about the strange incident with Hons in the ring.

Nia, of course, became very agitated, as she now felt she had failed me in the protection department. "I am a horrible bodyguard," she sniffed plaintively.

"You are the best bodyguard anyone could wish for Nia. But I have to ask you not to mention Alera's advice to anyone else, especially Maya, and don't even think about it with Rosa close by."

We left to eat a quick lunch before having to return to the tent. I had a feeling that the final match was going to be interesting, and as Alera had predicted, I wasn't feeling all that strong. As I was just starting to suit up, Rosa and Maya stormed into the tent.

"I'm sorry I even mentioned it!" an exasperated Rosa was saying to a very grumpy dark elf.

"Mentioned what?" Nia said, looking up from her notes.

Maya shot me a glare and stalked around me doing a very thorough inspection; she even paused to sniff me thoroughly. "Mentioned why some lavender-scented, young, blonde human girl was running her hands all over my mate!" she hissed, showing some teeth at the thought.

"Like wow, Maya, get a grip," Nia buzzed. "Alera's a healer for petunias' sake! Alex was badly hurt!"

My dark elf's eyes softened and she laid cool, gentle hands on my shoulders. "I know, Alex. I heard you were in pain, but by the time I raced back to the arena, it was over and you were gone. Hons told me that you looked hurt but were still mobile. He was pretty shaken up and kept apologizing. I think he was far more upset about what happened to you than losing the match." She took another experimental sniff across the back of my neck. "But whatever she did to you, you better not have enjoyed it!"

"I didn't," I blurted honestly, and strategically tried to go for the quick change of subject. "How goes the investigation?"

Both women sighed and Maya sat down and dropped her head hard onto the table. "I hate paperwork! Tracking down this betting scam is excruciatingly boring."

Rosa placed a hand on her shoulder. "I know, sweetie, I know." She turned her chair to face me. "Well, it's going ok for now. We know it's the fire wizard primus who is trying to open a new school, but we don't have all the proof we need to have him imprisoned, or even removed from office. But we also know that his chance has passed. Your final opponent is a wind user, so even if you lose, he still won't win anything and, therefore, not have the money to finish it. But I am still concerned about his backer. We looked through everything we could find about the bettors and got nothing. As far as we can tell, there is not one duke or kingdom that has the money to fund him like this."

"So we have no idea?"

"I do have one thought, but I really hope it's not true. The only one who could fund him to that level is the Lifebane himself."

Duke Pharmon, the Lifebane, leader of the undead and all around bad guy, against everything with a heartbeat and a functioning moral sense. Many years ago, he forced many of the magic races: dark elf, troll, orc and the like, to serve him or die. The dark elves were the only ones that he ever feared, but he tricked them into a deal that they still honor to this day.

"So Duke Pharmon wants his own Xarparion?"

"We think so, and to make matters worse, his armies are definitely on the move."

"How much time do we have before they get here?"

She sighed again. "That's the thing. If they walk here, we have months. But if they have magical help, they could open a portal and be here tomorrow. That's why we're going to do what we can to prepare for the battle."

Maya raised her head off the table. "That's why I am stepping up the guards' training from now on. But that's about all we can do without permission from each tower's primus and the Headmaster and they won't believe us anyway."

Nia was getting impatient again. "Ok, this can all wait for later. Alex has to get going, and if you're both going to stay here, I'm going to watch this one in person."

Nia and I started to make our way out when Maya got up from the table. "If you two think you're leaving me behind, think again."

The four of us left for the arena. I split off from them and walked to the staging area. Once there, I was greeted by my favorite judge with his usual pained expression.

"Bad news again! Your opponent, for some reason, stepped down. Normally, that would make you the victor, but somehow your opponent vanished and was replaced before we could confirm that he stood down voluntarily. Now, it seems you're facing Naton Rad in this match."

I smiled, "That's fine by me. I was hoping to kick his ass again."

He threw up his arms and started to walk off. "You're nuts!"

I entered the ring and, not at all to my surprise, I found Naton there grinning evilly. Thankfully, I was saved from his typical comments by the voice of the Headmaster above us.

"Greetings, everyone! Welcome to the final match of the tournament! As you all know, this match is between the Fire Tower and the Enchanters Hall. The Fire Tower, the ultimate wielders of destruction, versus the best crafters of our age. This should be an exciting match. And without wasting any more time, I will hand things over to the Fire Tower primus.

The red-robed man stepped forward. "As the Enchanter delegation has been voted to act as the challenger in this match and the Fire Tower as the defender, I claim the right to choose the rule! And for this match, I choose a five-wizard team match, of wizards from the same tower. Five fire wizards and five Enchanters, but they must not be teachers or other staff." The spectators remained strangely quiet as the rules sunk in. Shortly thereafter, a number of boos and catcalls started erupting from the crowd.

Well, crap. There are only six of us even if you count staff. But the ass continued speaking.

"But seeing that the Enchanters Hall is so small, I will allow you to fight an uneven match. So just find who you can to face us." Then he laughed manically; yep he's evil alright.

Well, my options were limited. Rosa is a master so she's out. Maya is staff to them, as are the twins. So that leaves Nia, and last time I checked, she was a student.

I shouted into the stands. "Nia, get down here!" Using my sight, I could see her expression and it was hilarious. A mix of horror and excitement. She flew down to me and perched herself on my shoulder. I turned back to the red-cloaked primus. "My team is ready."

He burst out laughing again. "That's your teammate? A pixie? What's a pixie going to do?"

Nia was pissed. "Pixies were using magic when your kind was still swinging from trees!" she hissed, baring her sharp teeth.

He continued to chuckle. "Is that 'bug' even a student?"

The Earth Tower primus stepped forward. "Yes, she is. And I would recommend you show some respect. Pixies are not limited to single elemental disciplines as we are, she will be a worthy opponent I think."

I was grateful to him; it seems that at least the Earth Tower primus likes us.

"Whatever! The pixie can be your 'team', but you're still against five fire wizards. Naton, collect your team!"

Naton stepped forward. "My team is ready to burn some Enchanter butts." And with that, the other four fire wizards entered the ring. This was going to be fun. The idiot then sneered at me. "I'm going to squash that pixie of yours like a stinkbug!"

Nia stood up on her stand. "You have no idea how much I have wanted to kick your ass. You don't threaten my friends and get away with it."

All of the fire wizards pointed and laughed at her. "What's the bug going to do, hit us with pixie dust?"

She was really mad now. "I'M NOT A BUG! I'M A COMBAT PIXIE!" Saying her keyword activated her stand. The enchanted metal turned to liquid and quickly ran up her legs and arms hardening as it went. Only ten seconds later, she was in full combat gear. She unsheathed her twin swords and pointed them at the fire wizards. They insulted her more by doubling over in laughter and pretending to be frightened.

"Nia, I'll make a deal with you," I said quietly, and she looked at me, puzzled. "If you promise not to kill them, I'll sit this one out."

I didn't have to see her to know she was happy. "Hell yes, Mr. Alex!" She redirected her attention to her prey. I took a seat on the ground and leaned back wearily against a boulder to watch the show; I really was pretty tired and sore.

The second the match started, a large fireball launched from the tip of her swords impacting one of the still laughing fire wizards. The boys in red had no idea what had just happened; one second there were five of them, and the next, four. Her fireball hit with so much force that the guy was propelled so far out of the ring that he hit the wall a hundred feet behind him. All fire wizard robes are spelled to resist fire, but it appeared to my mage sight that Nia put a little something extra into her spell.

"What the...!" one of the goons screamed, doing a double take, but it was too late. Another wizard was hit and was also blasted cartwheeling out of the ring. Now with only three left, they woke up and finally started to fight. Naton and one of the others started throwing fireballs at Nia but didn't have a chance of hitting her. The third one opened a summoning circle and brought out a flesh golem, which is basically a reanimated dead body, sewn together. They are pretty strong and dangerous, but not very smart. It struck me that it was an exceedingly odd thing for a fire wizard, considering that flesh golems are generally associated with necromancy. The crowd picked up on it, too, and the booing and cries of outrage intensified. The golem trotted out dragging a large wooden club and headed for my pixie.

Nia just shot farther up into the air, smiled serenely at the golem, and pointed her swords at it. A blinding green ray shot out of the tip and the golem glowed brightly before becoming a pile of ash. I clapped my hands. "Disintegrate, nice!"

She displayed a dazzling smile. "Thanks, I love that one, too; it's just that I could never get it to work right for me before!"

The wizards took notice of that one though. The one who summoned the golem grabbed the front of Naton's robe and shook him frantically. "It turned my golem to dust! Dust! We need to give up!"

Naton slapped the kid. "Shut up and use a fire shield. We're not losing to a pixie and a stupid Enchanter!"

He did as he was ordered and, in a few seconds, a thick wall of fire was now stationed in front of them to block spells. Nia just smiled again and pointed her swords to the sky. Dark, ominous clouds appeared on the horizon streaked with tiger stripes of orange and green wind lines, and settled over the arena. The previous light breeze puffed experimentally a few times and then was hammered by a shrieking gale-force wind, centered and directed at the fire wizards in the middle of the stadium. It didn't so much start to rain, as a waterfall appeared out of nowhere and gushed sideways into the maelstrom, the blades of wind slashing the water into sharp shards of high-velocity projectiles. The fire shield drew back, wavering and bucking almost like a frightened living organism. The resulting collision with the angry maelstrom snuffed it out instantly, revealing the red-robed caster cowering on his knees in the mud with his hands over his head. With a malevolent tearing metal shriek, the storm descended on its target and snatched him up like a hawk skewering a mouse. It quickly formed a spiral cloud that spun him so fast that when he vomited, the stream hit him in the back of the head! Finally, the fire boy passed out and the storm seemed to lose interest. It casually tossed its victim into a now wet manure pile outside the ring, before it dissipated leaving only a heavy rain in its wake.

The other fire wizard had seen enough. He screamed as he ran for his life out of the arena. I didn't think he would stop until he was under his bed in his room. Fear the pixie!

This left Naton by himself. He desperately fired off a few more fireballs at Nia. She didn't even have to dodge; his aim was just that bad. The rain stopped abruptly, and Nia hovered and sheathed her swords. She then cast a minor enchantment which mimicked the loud speaking spell the Headmaster used and addressed the entire crowd.

"So the all powerful, big, strong, very scary fire wizard Naton wants to see some pixie dust from the poor, helpless little bug, does he?" she roared.

Naton's eyes grew wide and he redoubled his efforts to throw a cohesive fireball. Nia, meanwhile, went from hover mode to I-can-barely-see-her mode in less than a blink, as she bore down on him. The sound of a million enraged hornets filled the arena, and the younger spectators dived for cover under their seats.

"No, stay away!" Naton screamed, waving his hands, slapping himself and ducking down like he was under attack. Nia flashed overhead and at the end of her strafing run, released a huge cloud of sparkling dust that surrounded and coalesced around the fire wizard. Suddenly trapped in a shimmering soap bubble, Naton floated off the ground and rose above the floor of the arena. It was hard to be one hundred percent positive with the pixie dust effect in force, but it appeared Naton was turning a particularly unattractive shade of green inside the bubble.

Panicked that he was now thirty feet up in the air, the fire wizard tried another approach.

"Alex, please, call off the pixie! Call off the pixie!"

"Sorry, Naton," I called out lazily, "I'm just watching this one. I'm enjoying the show just fine sitting here. Thanks for checking on me though!"

Then he tried begging for help from the Fire Tower headmaster, who looked at him in disgust.

"You are a disgrace to your robes and the Fire Tower if you lose to a mere bug!" he growled, turning his back on Naton.

Nia, in the meantime, completed a wide lap around the arena. That got the crowd excited and on their feet. Then she pulled up in the middle of the ring, and still using the amplified voice effect, gestured at Naton. "Have you ever picked a dandelion puffball and held it up in the air? And then taken a really, really big breath?" she asked the arena crowd. They responded by going wild, jumping up, whistling and stomping their feet. The effect was deafening.

Naton was trying anything to tear a hole in the bubble or find a seam. He looked remarkably like a trapped rat in a ball high above the ring. Finally, he gave that up, and with my mage sight, I could see that it looked like he was going to try one last massive spell.

Nia spun around once for the crowd, displaying a huge innocent smile.

"Bye-bye, pretty puffball!" she tinkled in her best fairytale pixie voice, and then her voice changed and took on a scary tone that even gave me shivers. "This is for all the children you have bullied!"

She pulled her swords out and unleashed a green vortex of air that twisted and swirled, then gained momentum and drove up toward the bubble like a striking viper. At the same time, Naton's spell triggered. Fierce fire lashed out from his fingertips as he grinned in triumph. The triumph was short-lived, however, as his spell failed to breach the bubble's pixie magic shell. It swelled ominously, but all the fire stayed contained and trapped within the orb. The vortex struck and hurled the ball high into the sky where it exploded with an enormous sonic boom that shook the buildings below and created a dazzling pyrotechnic display of burning flower petal designs. The crowd was instantly mesmerized by the sight and watched with a multitude of oohs and aahs. Few people noticed the smoldering, rag-covered wreck of a fire wizard plummeting onto the roof of a stable across the street.

"By now, everyone should know! Don't mess with a pixie!" Nia boomed out over the crowd.

I was pleased to notice with my mage sight that she had sent a gust of air to cushion Naton's fall just before he impacted.

Cheers erupted from the stadium as Nia sheathed her swords. I stood up and walked over to where she was. She landed on her perch as we both waved to the crowds. I spoke up so at least Nia could hear me. "That was fantastic! I didn't know you knew all those spells."

"Like I said, I'm not very good pixie."

"No, you're an amazing pixie!"

She was beaming under her helmet. I looked up at the dignitaries' stand and noticed that the fire primus had stormed away in disgust, and even the Headmaster was standing and clapping for us.

"Well done Enchanters, well done, indeed. As the Headmaster of Xarparion, I declare the Enchanters Hall the victor of this year's tournament." More cheers. "And as the victors, they win this year's party for their hall, paid for by Xarparion. Enjoy the party, Alex, and umm...Combat Pixie, you earned it!"

A horde of people suddenly flooded the arena around us. Soon we found ourselves trapped in a mob of people congratulating us, asking to touch our armor, and begging to come to our party. I looked around for someone I knew, but I couldn't see anyone, even with my massive height advantage. My attention was drawn to the stands where I spotted all the girls and Darroth cheering from the stands. It felt good to have their support for us. Things were starting to get a little crazy; some of the wizards in the mob were using spells to either move others or to get closer to me and Nia.

One of the girls closest to us tried to grab Nia off my shoulder. I swatted her arm away and placed Nia on my left forearm so she was safe between me and my tower shield. Slowly, I forced my way through the crowds. Weighing in at over three tons helps a lot. I sent a mental message to Rosa to have everyone meet at the hall as the tent would be overrun by now.

Nia clung to my arm as I continued to gently force my way through the mob. Reaching the edge, we finally had some room to move. I took this chance to look down at Nia. She had her visor up so she could see better and was sitting upright on my arm. "Hold on tight, I'm going to run the rest of the way." She looked unconcerned for a second before realizing what I meant. With a hilarious look on her face, she wrapped her arms and legs around my wrist as best she could and held on for dear life.

I took off down the path; it felt good to let loose a bit, even if I still felt a bit weak. I haven't run at these speeds just for the joy of running before. Of course, at these speeds, you don't get to run long before you reach where you're going and I just did. Skidding to a halt in front of the hall, I relaxed; convinced we had some time before the others arrived. I sat down and leaned my back against a wall. I looked down again at Nia, who, like me, was shaking off the dizziness and effects of the run.

"Nia, you can let go now, we stopped."

"Not for me, we haven't." She covered her mouth with her hands. "My head is still spinning and I feel like I'm going to blow chunks."

I laughed, "You're going to be just fine. You did a great job on those guys by the way."

"Thank you, but to be honest, that was the first time my spells worked like I wanted. The swords you made me did all the real work. I never tried using a wand before, looks like that's all I ever needed. All that time of being hated and alone and all I needed was a wand!"

"I'm so sorry, Nia."

Her eyes shot wide. "What? No! Alex, you guys are the best thing to ever happen to me. You and Maya are so nice to me, unlike my real parents. If I hadn't been sent to you, I don't think I would have survived the winter."

"You won't ever have to be alone again."

A small stream of tears ran down her face. "I know, that's what I'm so happy about."

We sat in blissful silence for a few minutes before we heard the sound of horse hoofs rapidly approaching. Looking up, I could see that everyone was packed on the backs of our horses. Maya, Rosa, Lin, and Julia were riding on hers, and Dawn, Dusk, and Darroth were on mine with Dawn at the reins. Darroth, alone, didn't seem to be enjoying the ride. They slowed to a stop and everyone jumped off to join us, beaming proudly.

"You were outstanding, Nia!" shouted Julia as she scooped up the pixie into a hug.

"Too tight! Too tight!"

"Oops, sorry!"

Nia gasped for air when she was released and flew to safety on my shoulder.

The others gathered around us. "You guys are the best. Everybody's talking about you, and we're practically celebrities just for knowing you!" Lin gushed.

"Yes, truly a heroic feat," said Dawn.

"I knew they would win," Dusk chimed in, not to be upstaged by her twin.

"I can't believe you armored a pixie! Really, have any of you ever heard of putting armor on a pixie?" Maya was obviously looking over Nia's armor as she spoke.

"I'm not surprised. If you think her armor is good, then you have no idea what he is capable of creating. Compared to his current project, Nia's armor is a candle to a forest fire." Everyone stared at Darroth as I made a frantic hand signal to get him to stop. "Um, never mind, I never said anything...do I smell ale?" he mumbled and wandered off.

"Well, anyway, you both were great and may have saved Xarparion from a very bad situation." Rosa gave us both a hug. "So, right now, you go inside and get out of that armor. Servants will be here any minute to set things up. By the time you're back, the party will be starting."

Reluctantly, Nia and I went to our room to get changed. When I got there, I found a formal outfit, similar to the one I wore for the dance, on my bed. Nia also had a new dress laid out on her pillow too.

"Rosa has been busy."

Nia landed on the window sill and started to hold up the clothes. It was a lovely purple fall silk dress, complete with a sash for a belt. "Yeah, just look at this dress; it's so cute!"

My outfit was the same design as for the First Day dance, but the shirt had a splash of red and gold mixed in as if it was a glass marble. Nia went behind the divider that I had installed so she could change with some privacy and I could do the same. I used one of the new features that I added to the hall. My closet opens to a lift that raises an armor stand up to my room for my armor. Once everything is on it, I can lower my armor and gear down into my secret armory under the lab. I have a feeling Rosa may know there is a room down there, but I don't think she knows what's in it. The Hall's enchanted walls had to work extra hard on that one.

With both of us dressed, I decided that my war hammer would be a wise precaution, and go great with the outfit, so I slung it across my back. We headed downstairs and back outside. We were surprised to find that the entire area around the hall was a buzz of activity. There must have been over a hundred servants running all over the place setting things up. There were row upon row of tables with food on them, tons of candles on stands, and magical light orbs hung from lines stretched between the hall and nearby buildings. Potted plants and dividers were scattered around to define areas. They even got a water wizard to conjure up a spring and create a small burbling brook to wind through our gravel courtyard making it into the most elegant garden I could ever imagine.

The only person I could see that I knew was Darroth sitting at a table getting a head start on the drinking. With Nia on my shoulder gawking at all the shiny interesting things around her, I headed over to him.

"Quite the sight, isn't it? And they even have real dwarven ale!" He held out a tankard to me, but I passed, and Nia wanted nothing to do with alcohol ever again.

"Where is everyone?"

He snorted and lifted the ale. "They're women, where do you think? They all went inside to put on dresses and brush their hair. I'm actually surprised Nia isn't still with them."

"I'm small and don't have that much hair to brush," she said quietly, still intimidated by all the commotion.

I looked around again as more tables were set up and a new group of servants in formal attire showed up. Leading the group was the Headmaster himself outfitted in the most ornate of his official robes. He stopped and barked a few orders before spotting us and heading in our direction. When he got to us, I extended my hand and he took it. "Congratulations, Alex. I knew you were special, but I would never have thought that an Enchanter would win the tournament. And to make it better, it's your first year still."

"Thank you, Headmaster."

"But I must ask where you got that armor of yours? It truly is a wonder."

Darroth slammed down his empty tankard on the table. "The kid made that armor."

The Headmaster was skeptical. "Truly you don't think that, Darroth?"

"Don't need to think it, I know it. I watched him forge that armor with my own two eyes. Nia's armor as well." The dwarf belched and squinted up at the Headmaster belligerently.

He still didn't seem to be buying it. "Well, I do have that report of a sword you made killing a man just for touching it. I suppose if you could make something that could do that, then you could make a suit of armor. But do tell me what enchantments you placed on it."

I didn't really like the tone of where this was going, so I decided not to give him much. "Well, it's nothing too exciting, just some defensive ones to protect me from spells and the like."

He looked me over and spotted the hammer on my back. "I see you are carrying your war hammer with you now, why is that?"

"Well, as you know we Enchanters can't cast spells like you can, so I need to rely on a weapon for protection seeing that there have been assassins on the campus and all."

His expression darkened and he paused as if to retort to that comment, but then went back to digging for information on the hammer.

"May I see it?"

I was hesitant to show him anything; he was acting strangely, and I still didn't know what he was trying to do. Something was definitely wrong. Normally, my mage sight isn't able to penetrate illusions, but standing right next to me at zero range, I could perceive the weak flow of magic working to disguise the man. On a whim, I allowed my other senses to venture out, and my nose picked up the faint scent of smoke, the same smoke that Naton and his crew reeked of! The man before me was not the real Headmaster, but a fire wizard, as must be the servers who came here with him!

"Rosa, we have fire wizards using illusions to disguise themselves as servants and the Headmaster!"

"I see the ones you're talking about. Stall as long as you can."

"Of course, Headmaster." I unsheathed my war hammer. It

was similar to Winya in color, but longer and didn't radiate beauty. Instead, it had an aura of barely-contained destructive fury. The Headmaster let out a whistle.

"Very impressive! But tell me, what is it made of?"

"I don't know." And that was really the truth, Dad still hasn't told me.

"Then where did you get it?"

"My father gave the metal stock to me."

"Who is your father?" Yep, definitely not the real Headmaster, he had met my dad.

"I don't know."

He was getting restless. "How can you not know who your father is?" I smiled, but not at him. Behind him, Maya had shown up with a large group of guards and started arresting the fire wizards that Rosa was pointing out. And she was doing it all in a stunning party dress. I forced myself back to the situation at hand.

Extending the war hammer effortlessly, I grinned disarmingly. "Does it really matter where it came from, Headmaster? Here, why don't you test the heft of it yourself?"

He reached for the weapon greedily, and I dropped it into his outstretched hands. Now to either Maya or me, it would have felt like a four- or five-pound weapon. The false Headmaster, however, had unexpectedly grabbed hold of something equaling three times his own body weight. The expression on his face was priceless as it drove him to the ground in an instant with zero resistance. I'm pretty sure from the snapping sounds that it easily broke most of the bones in his wrists and hands on impact, and it was currently pinning him to the gravel courtyard.

He fought back a scream and instead gritted out, "What are you doing? I am the Headmaster!"

Darroth spoke up. "No, you're not. The real Headmaster doesn't even know my name! And you should know that magic doesn't work so well around Enchanters." He punctuated his words by dumping the remainder of his ale over the head of the now thrashing fire wizard. Two of Maya's guards arrived and efficiently clamped irons on him so he couldn't cast spells. The impostor was dragged off sputtering and swearing.

Maya hurried over to me; she was in a purple silk dress with a low cut front showing off her neck and shoulders. It also had gold lace that crisscrossed on her back and what looked like a corset. She was very lovely tonight, and I caught her eyeing my outfit as well.

"Well, look at you, handsome. Party hasn't even started and you got into trouble already."

"What can I say, I attract dangerous types."

She placed her arms around my neck and brought her lips close to mine. "Well, lucky for you, I'm a dangerous girl."

"That you definitely are!" I agreed and started to wrap my arms around her. But before anything else could be said, one of her guards ran up to us. "Ma'am, we found vials of poison with the false servants, but it looks like they didn't have time to use them. I called for a healer to check for poison anyway, just to be sure. We will take them to lock up and start our investigation."

Maya snapped back into her stern personality. "Very good, Corporal, carry on."

"With your permission, Ma'am, I'll be leaving a few men here to watch over things. Don't worry, they won't interrupt unless they're needed. Besides with you, Sir Alex, and especially the Combat Pixie here, I don't think there's anything you can't handle."

Her voice was stern, "Thank you, you're dismissed, Corporal."

"Ma'am!" He saluted and rushed off to join the other guards.

Maya sighed as she turned back to me. "I really wish they didn't have to see me like this."

"Why not? You're gorgeous tonight."

She smiled with a little tone of regret in her silky voice. " Remember, unlike you, they still see the illusionary Maya. As usual, it's bad enough that I have to conceal my true self from people I respect; it makes me feel dishonest somehow. But what I was really referring to was that I don't want them to see the softer side of me."

"But that's the part of you that I like best."

She smiled and teased me with a quick kiss.

Rosa came over to us; she was in a red version of Maya's dress and actually looked really good out of white for a change. "Well, that's one way to start a party." We all laughed. The next ones out of the hall were Lin and Julia; they were wearing the same dresses they wore at the First Day dance. Rosa nearly had kittens when they told her that they only owned the one dress each. Now Rosa was excited about all the new dresses she was going to make. The twins had on yellow dresses that were wide at the bottom, almost like a ball gown. They seemed happy and a little dazed just to be here, and as usual, didn't appear to care much about what they wore.

Rosa cleared her throat to get our attention. "Well, this wouldn't be much of a party with just the nine of us, so I invited some more of our growing circle of friends."

At that, a servant waved his hand in the air dramatically and a bunch of people came around from the side of the hall. Right away, I could see Hons and Alera. Behind them were several Earth Tower wizards and healers. In the back, I could see Ranny and his sister as well. Everyone was dressed up and ready to party.

Rosa put her arms around Maya and me. "I'll leave you two alone now, so have fun. And just remember that I am proud of both of you."

"Thanks, Mom!" Maya grinned.

Rosa just laughed. "Believe me, if I could, I would take both of you as my children. I would in a heartbeat. Come on, Nia, let's go enjoy the party!"

Rosa left with Nia, leaving me with Maya. Immediately, people started coming up to us and congratulating me. The women also kept telling Maya that she was lucky to have the tournament winner as a boyfriend, but I saw it the other way around. Some time went by and the people around us started to thin out. We were about to grab some food when one very formally dressed servant came up to us.

"Master Alex, Mistress Maya, your table is ready."

We looked at each other in confusion. "Our table?" I asked.

"That is correct. You are the guest of honor so, naturally, your lady is as well. The pixie has also been given a place of honor this evening. So if you will please follow me..."

Not really knowing what else to do, we followed him over a small bridge that crossed the temporary stream to an island. There, a small round table at the center of the area was set for two. Temporary wood walls surrounded the table on three sides giving us a view of the dance area as well as the musicians. Plants and candles were arranged around us giving the feel of a romantic setting. He pulled a chair out for Maya and seated her and then did the same for me. With us both seated, the servant vanished around the wall and quickly came around the other side with two wine glasses and a bottle.

After wiping both glasses with a clean cloth, he placed them in front of us. He popped the cork and poured the light yellow liquid into our glasses. "Tonight's vintage is a sixty-three-year-old full-bodied wine to complement tonight's wood grilled salmon with potatoes and lemon. Your food will be here shortly, please enjoy!" Then he bowed and quietly left.

Maya lifted her glass and smelled it experimentally before taking a sip. "This is excellent. And this whole evening seems to be planned just for us; I can't believe the transformation in the courtyard."

"Yes, but I'm looking at the best transformation of them all."

She beamed, "It's not every day you get a free romantic evening with your betrothed. I'm starting to like the sound of that."

Our food arrived shortly, along with more wine. The salmon was perfect and way better than anything I could cook. Maya and I just enjoyed our meal together; it was getting much harder these days for us to spend time alone. With our meal done, the servant cleared our table, wished us an enjoyable evening, and escorted us back to the party.

I bowed to Maya. "May I have this dance?"

She smiled. "About time you asked. I thought I was going to have to find another knight in white shining armor!"

Laughing, I set my war hammer next to a very sleepy-looking dwarf, who tried to cuddle it like a teddy bear, and followed Maya.

We went out on the floor and started to dance. Looking around, I spotted Lin and Julia teaching the twins how to dance. Hons was with a girl from the Water Tower who I didn't know. Ranny was with his sister and Alera was dancing with her nebulia. The song abruptly switched to a slow dance, and Maya happily pulled me closer so she could rest her head on my shoulder. "Tonight has been perfect. I couldn't dream of a better evening."

"The night's not over yet." We danced happily entwined in each other's arms long into the night.

Chapter 17

Alex

Almost two weeks passed and winter was almost here. Thankfully, Xarparion was in an area that had very mild winters compared to dreadful stormy winters in Foalshead. The party was still fresh in the students' memories and everyone had a wonderful time. The morning after the party, we had been surprised to find a box outside our hall with a large sum of money. It turned out that Rosa had placed a bet that we would win and the odds were fifty to one, so the Enchanters Hall was going to be getting some new upgrades after all.

Today, though, I wasn't in the mood to work so I decided to make good on one of my other promises. I grabbed my normal leather training gear, as well as my hammer and shield, and set out for the training fields. As I got closer, I could already hear the sounds of armor clanking and swords clashing. Rounding the last corner, I could see Maya in her beat up breastplate barking orders at the men. There were about fifty guards, all in full gear, training. Some were working on sword forms, others were sparring, and a few were running laps. No doubt they did something wrong to deserve that one.

I quietly approached Maya from behind, knowing that sneaking up on a dark elf wasn't going to succeed, but you never know.

"Nice try, Alex, but that's not going to work," she intoned, without turning to look at me. "What are you doing here anyway?"

I smiled and closed the rest of the distance so I was standing next to her. "I seem to remember making a promise that I would help you sometime, so here I am."

Her helmet blocked me from seeing her face, but even in her armor, I know how to read her, and she was taken aback. "I didn't think you took that seriously. I honestly said that as a joke."

"Well, here I am. So you're the boss, what do you need?"

She brushed off the rest of her surprise and stood up straight again. "Follow me." I trailed after her. Off to one side, six men were sparring with swords and small shields. "These men are practicing how to get around a shield." She turned her anger toward the men. "And their ability to do so is appalling! You six now have a new goal, you have to get past Alex's defenses, and I'm only giving you ten minutes or it's fifteen laps for all of you."

She turned and marched off to the center of the training grounds. She didn't have to speak to tell me what she wanted from me. I turned to my six opponents, unsheathed my hammer and readied my shield.

....

Maya

I could tell he knew what I was asking from him; these days we don't even need words to communicate with each other. I know having those men fight Alex would never work, but I hope they learn what I am trying to teach them from all this. Corporal Higs broke off from his group and jogged over to me.

"Ma'am, is that really Alex?"

I turned and looked at how he was doing. He was dancing effortlessly around the six of them like they weren't even there. "Yes, it is."

"But why would you pair them up like that? You know they can't win."

"I know they can't win. Even I wouldn't be able to get past that damn shield of his. But that's not what I am trying to teach them with this. Those six are the most arrogant and headstrong of all of you. They never back down and they never retreat."

The corporal was confused, "I'm not following."

"In an army, their attitude would be a good thing, making them fearless on the battlefield. But as guards, they need to know when to ask for help and when to retreat. Alex represents something that they can't handle by themselves, and they know it. But they still throw themselves at him again and again without a care for their lives. For them to pass this training duel, they need to realize that they need help."

He thought it over for a bit before nodding. "I see what you mean. But how would we beat him if we needed to?"

I laughed. "Out of his armor you might have a slim chance with crossbows. But in his white armor, I don't think anything you've got will touch him."

I would have loved to watch Alex more, but I still had a job to do. A half hour passed before I could check on Alex and his group again. When I got over to him, I found five guards sitting on the ground in rapt attention as Alex demonstrated what they were doing wrong with the sixth. To my surprise, they actually seemed to be paying attention to what he was saying. One of the sitting guards noticed my approach and called the group to attention.

"Well, Alex, how did they do?"

He smiled. "Well, they didn't do all that bad, but they still didn't hit me."

One of the guards, Randez, stepped forward. "Ma'am, we were unable to get past his shield, but he explained to us that the real lesson was to know when to ask for help. We all now see that you have been riding us, not because you hate us, but because you don't want us to get killed. We are truly sorry for fighting you at every turn these last few months."

I was shocked and very glad that I was wearing my helmet so they couldn't see the wonderment on my face. These men have been a thorn in my side for months, and a half hour with Alex turned them into well-disciplined men who are willing to learn. Sometimes, I forget that that man can still surprise me every day.

I regained my composure. "Glad to hear it, private, but you still owe me fifteen laps."

"Yes, Ma'am!" All of them fell into ranks and started their run with smiles on their faces. With them out of earshot, I turned back to Alex.

"I can't believe what I just heard; I should have brought you along months ago!"

He laughed, "I'm free anytime."

"Well, time is almost up for today but the men have been working hard and we still have a half hour. So if you don't mind, I would like to give them all a treat."

"What did you have in mind?"

"Oh, I think a duel between two warriors who actually know how to fight would be entertaining."

I had everyone gather around in a circle for the start of the contest. Alex had his shield and his new war hammer. I think this should be fun. He has reach and defense, but I have skill and Winya. "That stuff going to stand up to Winya?"

He smiled. "Don't worry; both repair themselves when they take damage so she can pound on it as much as she wants."

We did just that. The duel was a lot of fun, but I would have to say that Alex was probably going to win this one. That giant tower shield of his was almost impossible to get around. I would also have to say that his combat skills are as good as mine now, and I grew up as the most skilled swordswoman among my dark elf clan.

The guards around us were having a great time and cheers and praise were being shouted at us. They loved that every time our weapons clashed, there was a flash of light and a spray of sparks. Our duel was cut short by someone calling the group to attention. Both Alex and I stopped to see what had happened. The guards parted as the Captain of the Guard trotted up to us.

"I am sorry, Mistress Maya, but I must cut your class short as you both need to return to your hall."

What in the world is going on? "What's happened, Captain?"

He clenched his fist. "Dammed portals opened right on our doorstep and undead are flooding through. I'd say we have two hours, three at most, before we're surrounded and under siege."

Corporal Higs stepped up and saluted the captain. "Corporal Higs of the east gate, sir. Two hours isn't enough time, we still don't have the gate fixed yet."

The captain was shocked. "What?! I have reports on my desk

saying that it was done two weeks ago!"

The corporal shook his head. "No, sir! We received orders from your office saying to hold off due to lack of funding."

The captain was furious. "I gave no such order!"

Alex stepped up. "Captain, if I may. We believe there is a traitor in Xarparion who has the ability to falsify orders."

"And who might that be?"

"We believe the Fire Tower primus is allied with, or at least funded by, Duke Pharmon."

He thought that over for a minute. "That would make sense. It would take a primus or higher to open a portal like that. But, damn, I can't be in two places at once. The main body of the undead is already positioning to hit the main gate the hardest, but I can't leave the east gate without a commander."

Nor could I. The east gate is where these men are from, and they're my responsibility. "Captain, I will lead the men at the east gate. Most of these men are from there and I trained them all. I know them best and they know me."

"Maya, I can't ask you to do that."

"That's why I'm asking you."

"I don't know..."

Then Alex did something I never expected. "Sir, the Enchanters Hall will hold that gate for you."

He eyed Alex sharply. "You're going with her?"

Alex nodded.

"Fine, but you're keeping all the men from here and the ones at the gate. Corporal Higs, you're her second-in-command." He raised his voice so everyone could hear. "I expect every one of you to follow Maya's orders to the letter. In fact, if any of the Enchanters, who are supporting you, tell you to do something, then you damn well better do it. Do I make myself clear?"

"Yes sir!" shouted each and every guard. The captain saluted us and hurried off in the direction of the main gate.

I turned to the corporal. "Get everything ready and get the men to the gate. I want oil, fire arrows, and the ballista prepped and ready in one hour. And do what you can to set up a barricade where the gate should be."

"Yes, Ma'am!" He started barking orders to the men and got them into formation. Then Alex scooped me up and threw me over his shoulder. "Alex, what the hell are you doing? Put me down, I have a command to oversee!"

He ignored me. "Corporal, we will be back in less than an hour, so get everything ready."

The stupid man even saluted him! "Yes sir!"

Then Alex started running away from the gate, where the hell were we going? "If you think for one minute that you are going to keep me from fighting, then you've got another think coming!"

"Wouldn't even dream of it, sweetheart. But I won't let you face an army of undead with only a banged-up breastplate."

"Then why am I up here?"

"It's faster this way." Looking down, we were moving at an incredible speed. Within a minute, we were back at the Enchanters Hall. He quickly put me down and dragged me inside where the others were franticly running about.

"Nia, find Darroth and tell him to prep for battle, then get back here," Alex barked. She nodded and flew out the door. "Dawn, Dusk, go to your room, open your closet, and put on what you see. You too, Rosa."

"No time for me...too much to do." Rosa disappeared up the stairs with an armful of things.

Alex grabbed my hand and dragged me down the stairs to the lab. On the far wall was a lever that he pulled to open up the wall to another set of stairs that I didn't know about. As we went down, magic torches on the walls burst into faux flames, lighting the dark passageway below. At the bottom of the stairs, the hall opened into a huge well-lit room. Looking around, I could feel my mouth hanging open. There were row upon row of armor and weapons stands. There were so many weapon stands that I don't think every sword and dagger in Xarparion could fill all of them.

"What is this place?"

"Welcome to my armory. As you can see, it's a bit larger than I really need. I only have enough weapons to fill one stand, yet I have over thirty stands." He paused as if deep in thought. "I might have overdone it a bit." He walked over to an armor stand that had a leather suit on it. He removed the leather and handed it to me. "Time is short, so please go into the side room over there and put this on."

I took the leather and went into the side room as directed. This room turned out to be a storage room, but I didn't really care.

Not having an intact undersuit with me, I was forced to strip down my underwear, but it turned out that this leather was very soft and felt good. Now suited up, I went back out into the main area to find that Alex was already in his and had half his main armor on. Seeing that I was done, he quickened his pace. Outfitted completely except for his helm, he came over to me.

"Maya, yours is in there." He pointed to the only closed cabinet in the room. Nervously, I walked over to it and opened the doors, only to have my breath taken away in disbelief. Inside was an armor stand with the most beautiful armor on it that I had ever seen. It was white and silver like Alex's, but it wasn't near as bulky. Instead, plates were only used on the larger areas that weren't required to move much. The chest, thighs, calves, forearms, and upper arms were the only areas with large amounts of armor. The joints were either chainmail or had very small plates that didn't overlap sitting on the silver chainmail. The helmet was also a masterpiece; it was sleeked back and appeared to have room built in for my ears so I wouldn't have to bend them like I do in my old helmet. There were also feathers along the back of the helmet giving it the look of a bird of prey. It was gorgeous.

"Nia designed it just for you. As you can see, it doesn't have as much plate armor as mine, but you get to keep your speed and flexibility. That's not to say it won't protect you; in fact, Winya couldn't even pierce that armor. It will also grant you speed and strength to match mine outside of my armor."

I could feel myself tearing up, it was just so beautiful! "I'll be able to run like you did on the way here?"

"Yes, and much more, but to show you the rest, we need to get you into it."

Alex

Maya was ecstatic with the armor I made for her and was very excited to suit up. Thankfully for her, this set didn't require the user to have the ability to shape metal. The chainmail went on first, and then all you had to do was snap the plates in place where they fused themselves in place automatically. We got her fully armored in half the time it takes me. With everything positioned, she looked in a tall mirror and was surprised at her appearance. I thought she looked best in a dress, but I had to concede the way she looked now was incredible.

"How does it fit?"

She smiled, "It's perfect, no pinching or rubbing. So what now?"

"Now look at your left arm." She did and found that all the plates on her left arm and shoulder were much thicker than on her right arm. On her forearm, there was also a round hole set into the surface. "As you can see, the armor is a lot thicker here so you can use your arm to block. It's made the same as my shield, so you don't have to worry. Also, that slot is for you to put Winya in." She placed the bracelet in the hollow and with a flash of light, the metal filled in around it and smoothed out making it look like nothing was ever there.

"Well, this is strange. I feel like I have a real full body back." Winya said as spikes shot up out of the suit's arms and shoulders. "Oops, sorry about that, Mistress!"

Maya looked at me questioningly. "Winya now has control of your armor in some ways. She can shape it as she just did, make light pass through you to make you very hard to see, assist you in climbing walls. You can also make use of all her forms at the same time, like having a dagger in one hand and a crossbow in the other. She will even be able to learn other things on her own, the enchantments in the armor follow her will."

Maya didn't say anything, just wrapped her arms around my neck and kissed me. A minute passed before she released me. "Come on, handsome, we have an army of undead to kill, or re-kill...you know what I mean."

I took her hand and searched her face. "Are you going to be ok with this? I mean with the undead nightmares and all?"

She paused to evaluate and then squeezed my hand and nodded. "Alex, I know this sounds weird, but it is as if those horrible dreams were a training exercise of sorts. Night after night, I fought them or," she blushed slightly, "we fought them. Anyway, I probably have more experience fighting the undead than anyone on the planet. I know how they move, react, fight, and best of all, die. And with you and Winya by my side, I will never fear them again. Now I really need to get back to my guardsmen."

We got back upstairs to find that the twins were ready in suits of silver scale mail that I made for them. I had already given them the rundown on how to use their suits this morning after getting them done the previous night. Basically, the armor changes with them when they change forms. So as dragons, it protects their heads, necks, and undersides which don't have the same amount of natural armor as the rest of their body. They appeared to be eager to try it out.

A few seconds later, Nia charged in and flew right over to us. "Darroth is on his way, and he says that his project is completed and on its way, as well."

"Good work, Nia."

She looked Maya over from head to toe. "Looking good, Warrior Princess!"

"Thank you, Nia. I'm told that you designed this set for me."

She was beaming. "Yep, and I say I did an excellent job, too!"

Rosa came charging down the stairs with a bag full of scrolls. She was about to go right past us but stopped when she saw Maya. "By the gods, you look hot!" Then she went right back to what she was doing. Old elves...go figure!

Ten minutes passed before Rosa was ready to go. We all went outside and found that Darroth was there in traditional dwarven scale armor, wielding a large two-handed axe. With him were both of our horses, armored and armed to the teeth. They both had large scale mail coats running down the back of their necks flowing all the way down their backs to their tails. The chest plates were nearly solid with just enough joints to maintain mobility. The equines looked like they could run over a hill giant without slowing down. Their legs were armored with built-in joints and had full movement, but the most noticeable thing was the massive plate with a foot and a half long spike on their heads making them look like unicorns.

Maya gasped and covered her mouth when she saw them. She turned quickly to me and whispered, "Silver and white armor, riding a unicorn! Alex, the dream!" I shrugged, not really having time to think about all the ramifications right now. As we approached the stallion and mare, they seemed to know what was about to happen. Both of them were tense and ready to fight. I turned to Darroth, "Excellent job with the armor."

He snorted, "Took a bit longer than I thought. But the thing that really got my beard in a vise is that they put that armor on themselves!"

"They what?" How could they do that if they don't have hands?

"You heard me. I don't know why I'm surprised by this crap anymore. Ever since I met you, it's been one episode after another of things that shouldn't be possible!"

Time was running out so we all mounted up on the two massive warhorses and rode off for the east gate. We arrived just in time, the first wall was completely overrun, and the guards had already fallen back to the much stronger second wall. We got as close as we could before I dropped the twins off on the ground, but I stayed on my horse. Darroth and Rosa got off Maya's horse and joined the twins.

The soldiers were in formation at the gate and saluted us as we approached. Corporal Higs marched up to us. "Ma'am, thank you for volunteering command."

"My pleasure, Corporal."

"That's not all, Ma'am. Well, the men talked and with a battle of this size coming, we may not all make it out. We feel we should clear the air. Ma'am, we know you are a dark elf, we've known for quite a long time."

Maya was totally floored. "But how? I was extremely careful!"

Higs smiled. "True, you never showed your face, but sometimes we would catch a glimpse of skin at the top of your gloves or through a break in your armor. We never made an issue of it and, in fact, we all helped guard your secret from the other troopers."

"Why?" she stammered.

"Because we didn't care by that time. We already knew the kind of person you were, how much you cared about giving us the best possible training advantage to keep us alive. Hell, you even volunteered to go out on several patrols with us and ended up saving some of the boys when they got in over their heads."

"I don't know what to say."

"We do have one request, if it's not too impertinent, Ma'am. We've seen your illusionary face at the dance and the tournament, but with this being the last battle for some of us, could we see your real face for once? It would mean a lot to us."

She paused a moment, and I knew she was choked up and stalling for time to compose herself. Slowly, she reached up and removed the helmet and smiled at her troops. Their jaws all dropped. I know how you feel, guys; she's stunningly beautiful. Rosa sent me a mental message, apparently their respect for me just shot up even more.

"I...um...wow!"

She leveled her gaze at the troopers and raised her voice, "And as far as this being the last battle for some of you, I won't have that! We have trained too long and hard for that to even be considered. So do your jobs, watch each other's backs, and we will make them pay dearly for attacking Xarparion! Your report, Corporal?"

He snapped out of it. "Sorry, Ma'am. The first wall has

already fallen, but it was never really meant to do much anyway, just to keep siege towers at bay. But it looks like all they brought is ladders thankfully. Reports coming in say the main force is about four thousand strong."

She thought on that. "Four thousand is ok; we should be able to take on four thousand. How many are left?" Maya queried as she placed her helmet back on.

"Reports say fewer than three thousand, but we have about five hundred at this gate alone."

She looked around again before turning to us. "Ok, here's what we're going to do. Darroth, I need you and your axe on the wall. Chop down any ladder they set up."

He grinned. "You got it!" And ran up the ramp to the wall.

"Dawn, Dusk, I need you two to do what you can to limit their movement, keep them here, where we can see them."

"Yes, Mistress!" They hissed in unison, already transforming into dragons and launching themselves up and over the wall. Their demeanor was drastically changed from the shy awkward girls who lived with us. In their scaled form, with wings and claws extended, and fully the fierce dragons of legends, they caused a visceral chill to run down the spine of every human there. It was easy to see why dragons were so feared; their keening screams washed over the walls.

Corporal Higs was flabbergasted by what he just saw. "Those two are dragons? Some of the men were working up the courage to ask them out!"

Maya laughed. "Yes, so make sure none of the men shoot

them, like right now." He stumbled as he ran off and those of us remaining shook our heads. She continued, "Rosa, you said you had things to do?"

She snapped out of it. "Oh yes, I was going to enchant the walls to burn ladders, it should affect the entire second wall but it will take time, so keep them off me."

Maya nodded as Rosa ran to the base of the wall and got to work. She then assigned two guards to protect Rosa as she worked. That only left the three of us.

"Alex, I have a fifteen-foot-wide hole in my door that I need you to plug. Nia, I need you to go with Alex. I'll also have five guards and five reserves for you two as well. Too bad this isn't an open battlefield so we could make full use of the horses. Those two would crush these undead into dust."

"You can count on us." I started walking to the gate.

"One more thing, Alex." I stopped and looked back at her as she quickly murmured, "I love you."

I took a couple strides back and took her hand, bringing it up to my faceplate. I leaned in and whispered, "I'm but a simple blacksmith, and I do not have the words for a queen, but I have loved you long before seeing your face." And with that, I dashed to the gate. Once there, I checked that my guard support was ready; they were, but a bit scared. Nia was also ready and in her armor on my shoulder. I looked out at the sea of undead before us. Most still wore clothes and armor that appeared to be from faraway lands, as I didn't recognize their gear. Many of the "older" minions must have been in multiple campaigns, as they were ragged and missing various parts, but were still mobile and deadly. Their weapons ranged from rusty swords and pole arms to merely sharp rocks. Some of the fresher looking corpses still had a semblance of coordination and carried better gear; a few were even still capable of loading and firing crossbows. Mixed in with the common foot soldiers were a handful of wights and ghouls. Great, there's never a paladin around when you need one. One thing was missing, however; there didn't seem to be any officers or other trappings of command structure. The scary term "hive mind" came to my thoughts immediately.

The undead were approaching steadily when Dawn and Dusk leapt off the nearby guard tower and breathed ice along both sides of the horde, funneling them to the section of wall that had the most guards on it, and also where I was. Nia fired off a few fireballs that destroyed many in the front lines but still only managed to break them up a bit.

As soon as they were close enough, I sprang into action. I activated an enchantment in my hammer that made it glow with a white light. The first few were no problem for me, but as more and more approached at the same time, some started to get past me. The guards behind me were doing ok for now, but I could tell they weren't going to last long. Seconds later, one of them went down with a ghoul on him. But before I could help him, my horse kicked the ghoul off him and then stomped on its head busting it open like a rotten melon. The guard was very fortunate not to have been bitten and was able to continue fighting with a warhorse watching his back.

From the ground, I couldn't tell how the others were doing, nor could I tell how many were left. If I had to guess, though, I would say that between the seven of us on the ground, we had taken down about a hundred. The battle continued for over an hour, I was still doing okay, but Nia was almost out of spells and I had lost three guards. Then I heard Maya shout out my name, and a sharp pain pierced my head. Forcing down the pain, I called for my reserves to cover for me and ran to find Maya.

I found her next to Rosa, who was laid out on the ground. She had taken a crossbow bolt to the midsection and was losing a lot of blood.

"Rosa! Hang in there!" Maya was already putting pressure on the wound. The only other thing I could think to do was to use a healing enchantment, but that would be too slow to save her. Then from behind me, I felt a hand on my shoulder.

"Out of the way, please."

I looked over my shoulder and, much to my surprise, found Alera. "Alera, what are you doing here?"

"I told you that I would come when you need me, so here I am. Now move, both of you!"

Maya and I took a few steps back to give her space. After one quick look at Rosa, she took hold of the bolt and yanked it out, quickly placing her hand over the wound. Seconds passed, then a minute, and then finally Rosa opened her eyes. "What happened?" she said groggily.

Maya was crying now, but they were tears of joy. "You got shot, you stupid, old lady!"

We pulled Rosa to her feet, and we were about to return to the battle when the Captain rode up to us. He looked shaken at the blood covering Rosa's robes. "Headmaster Rosa, I have urgent news. Another portal has opened at the top of Central Tower and orcs are flooding the tower. Regrettably, the Headmaster was critically wounded, and all other tower heads were killed in the first wave, leaving you as the only functional high-ranking faculty member left.

What are your orders?"

The Headmaster is badly wounded and Central has been taken? "What else can you tell me, Captain?" she asked shakily. I was reminded how debilitating recovery from near death was, but Rosa had the strength of three men, and if anyone could power through the pain and weakness, she could.

"The Headmaster doesn't look good. He managed to make it to his old office in the Wind Tower before he collapsed, but the healer I spoke with said to expect the worst, so you are to assume command. As far as Xarparion's situation, our spotters are saying there is another wave of twelve thousand undead two miles away."

"We can't take on that many, not with an open portal inside the walls!"

There was silence for a few seconds. "Your orders, Headmaster?"

Rosa's face was hard and her eyes were cold. "Save as many as you can, Captain Jarsin, we're evacuating Xarparion!"

The way she said that was like someone driving an icicle into our hearts, but we all knew that it was the only thing we could do. The Captain looked both relieved and disappointed at the same time.

"Yes, Ma'am, I'll start the evacuation. Where do you want them to go?"

Rosa thought about this for a second. "Portal fourteen, it's out of the way and that area should have almost no undead. That portal also has a lock so we can't be followed."

"Understood."

He turned to leave, but Rosa put a hand on his shoulder. "One more thing, Warehouse Thirteen has twenty crates marked 'Enchanters Hall' on them. We need those crates captain; get as many as you can through that portal."

"That's awfully close to the main gate." He growled.

"I know, but we won't last long without them."

He sighed, "I'll do what I can." Then he backed up his horse, spun and spurred off.

Rosa then turned to Maya and me; Alera had already disappeared again. "Alex, we need to buy some time, see what you can do." I nodded. "Maya, round up your men and get them ready to move."

The two of us put our helmets back on and ran back to the failing temporary barricade. When I got there, only four of the seven guards I left there were still alive. I pushed back the feeling of guilt in my mind and turned it to determination. I looked around, the walls of the stone gatehouse weren't looking so good, and there was a lot of heavy stone above it, enough to block it even.

I shouted up the wall. "Maya, get everyone off the wall!"

I didn't know if she responded, but as I smashed a few more skeletons, I saw men jumping off the walls and down the ladders. Nia was still firing away at them from a piece of rubble she was using as a perch.

"Nia, I need a bigger boom, clear as many of them away as you can!"

She must have been getting really tired by now, the number of fireballs she had already cast was easily ten times more than any human could do. "I'll try, Mr. Alex!" I could see she was putting everything she had into one spell. When she was ready, the fireball was several feet wide and burning blue. She fired it into the center of the swarm of undead, vaporizing the ones closest to the blast. The walls around me shook, breaking loose clouds of dust as the shockwave and bits of bone hit us. Through the dust, I could see that she took out almost all the remaining undead in the immediate area, but more were coming our way now.

Nia had collapsed from exhaustion. I scooped her up and placed her on her perch on my shoulder, shaping the metal to protect her and keep her in place. Then I readied everything I had as well, activating an enchantment in my hammer to increase force. I slammed it into the wall, breaking off massive pieces of stone and brick. With the weight of this armor, my own strength, and the enchantments in my hammer, I was able to blow out five foot chunks with each strike.

After a few more massive blows, the arch above me was ready to give out. One more hit was all it took to send it crumbling down towards me. Suddenly I was jerked backward and thrown clear of the rubble. I landed on my back, looking up at the sky as Maya hovered over me.

"Just so you know, you might not count them, but I do; you owe me one now!"

I laughed, "What about those other two times I saved you?"

"You told me I didn't owe you anything, so the way I see it, you owe me one." She pulled me to my feet. "Come on, handsome, I returned the guards to Jarsin's command so it's just you and me. By the way, great job collapsing the wall, but it's really stupid that we can't have an earth wizard on hand to just make a new wall."

"Yeah, where are all the wizards anyway?"

"School rule, students can't fight."

"Well, that's stupid!"

"Yeah, good thing no one told you! Now, come on already, we have two angry warhorses ready to go and a lot of filthy undead in the streets. So let's have some fun!"

Sure enough, both warhorses were ready to crush some skulls. As soon as we were mounted up, they both took off down the road towards the center of Xarparion and the largest number of undead.

The horses took the hint and came to a full charge. The skeletons weren't that smart so they didn't even raise a spear to protect themselves. The heavily-armored horses impacted the first few so hard the bones were shattered against their heavy steel chest plates and then crushed beneath iron-clad hooves.

Maya was laughing as she swung Winya at skeletons that got within reach; I found myself laughing with her as well. I don't know how many we destroyed, but we soon found ourselves in front of the Healers Tower. Skeletons were attempting to force their way into the tower through the main door. From my vantage point, it would seem that the only thing stopping them were two guards and Alera's nebulia, all three of whom looked totally exhausted; they couldn't have much time left.

"Maya, we have to get them out of there!"

She nodded. "I'm right behind you."

Without us even pulling on the reins, the intelligent horses seemed to know their new objective. They rammed a broad path to the main door, and then did a circle in front of the door clearing away the rest of the undead in the spot.

I quickly dismounted and rushed over to the guards, who were fighting the last few skeletons that had made it into the entry area. I grabbed the last two that were fighting the guards and crushed their skulls in my armored hands.

The guards were stunned; one even thought I was another undead for a second. But as I pulled them to their feet, it sank in that I was there to help them. Maya and the nebulia both came over to me; the nebulia looked like he had been fighting even longer than Maya and I had.

As always, I couldn't understand what he was saying, but he did bow to me again, and that I was able to understand.

"He says thank you for saving his life a second time." I turned around to find Alera, tired looking and covered in other people's blood. "And I would like to thank you, as would all the healers, for your timely assistance!"

Maya stepped between us, probably not liking the attention I was getting from Alera. "How many are trapped inside?"

Even faced with an irritated dark elf warrior, she didn't flinch. "Almost all of us, there were only a few who were in other parts of the school when the attack hit. I have gotten everyone ready to leave with what they can fit in a backpack, as well as all the portable healing equipment in the tower. They're waiting on the second floor."

"Why are they so interested in you guys?" I asked.

"We took out all the orcs in Central, they have very weak minds. Anyway, the skeletons noticed and concentrated on us. Since they are not alive nor have a brain, we can't do a thing to them."

"But healers can't throw spells...can they?"

Alera flushed slightly and corrected me mildly. "Well, most healers can't, it's true, but some of us can adjust the flows of energy through the heart and brain at a distance. Normally, we use this power for weal and not woe, but orcs are filthy degenerate creatures with a lust for evil, so the gloves came off!"

Wow, remind me never to tick off a healer.

"Get everyone moving, we will get you to the gate," Maya said probably thinking the same thing I was.

"Thank you!" And she was gone in a flash.

"I really hate it that I'm starting to like her," Maya complained with a growl.

Outside, only a few undead had moved in, but I knew there were thousands more on the walls by now. We had maybe half an hour until they were on us. We dispatched the few that were around, and then mounted our warhorses as the first healers came out the door. Just like Alera had reported, they all had backpacks. They also had pairs of healers carrying large crates.

As soon as the first group of two was close enough, I asked, "Are you sure you can carry all that to the portal?"

The boy and girl smiled at me. "The fear of death is a good motivator; besides, we all know what we need to do."

I nodded to them; I supposed they were right. We watched as the rest of them came out of the tower; there appeared to be about fifty healers and about twenty crates. Alera gave us a thumbs up that we were ready to go. Maya and I took the lead leaving the two guards and the nebulia to bring up the rear.

Oddly, we only came across a handful of undead as we approached the halfway point to the gate. The reason soon became clear as we rounded a corner and plunged right into battle. Our friends, the earth wizards, had made their own convoy and seemed to have attracted the bulk of the undead's attention.

I looked at Maya and she just nodded back at me. "Shall we?" she asked.

"Lead on, my lady!"

With the wizards formed into a circle, it was very easy for us to finish off the remaining undead with their help. I scanned the earth wizards, most of them were tired and I spotted quite a few wounded. But I could also see Lin and Julia were ok and so was Hons. I even saw Reggie, Julia's pet earth elemental bashing skeletons to pieces at the back of the column. The two druids and Hons ran over to Maya and me.

"Holy crap! Maya, that armor is super sexy," said Lin, and Julia bounced in agreement.

"Um, thank you...I think."

Hons moved over to me as I dismounted. "Thanks for the help, Alex."

"No problem, how many did you get?"

He sighed tiredly. "We got most of the earth wizards together right away and tried to help the Water and Wind Towers, but most of them refused to leave, saying their primus ordered them to stay. So we sealed their towers in stone; they should have enough supplies for about a year in there. But a few of them came with us when they heard you Enchanters were in charge. We have about six of each. Sadly, many of my people were badly hurt getting this far."

"Don't worry; we got the healers out so we can get everyone fixed up when we get through the portal. Any word from the Fire Tower?"

He shook his head. "None, I think they were the first tower to fall. Take out the heavy hitters first, you know."

"Yeah, I know. Sadly, I think many of them would have been good people without their corrupted primus." Hons nodded and ran his fingers uneasily through his hair as he surveyed the carnage.

Maya strode over and interrupted curtly, "We need to hurry to the portal; we have less than ten minutes before the undead get here."

"You're right." He turned and shouted to the healers and earth wizards. "Let's double time it, people! C'mon, move it"

They rushed the rest of the way as Maya and I helped clear the road. We made very good time as we rounded the corner to the portal. The portal looked just like the one we had used to go home, but this one was glowing yellow instead of blue. There were about twenty guards there who immediately started sending the people through.

Maya pointed out Rosa near the portal talking with the captain. She spotted us as we approached and rushed over to us as we dismounted, wrapping both of us in a hug as soon as we were on the ground. "Thank the gods you're both alright! When you ran off, I thought you wouldn't make it back in time!"

"We had to save who we could."

She squeezed some more. "I know, but I was still worried." She released us. "We've been doing the best we can here rounding up staff and their families and shuttling them across, pretty much anyone else we can grab, as well. So I see you got the earth wizards and the healers, no one else?"

"We have a few water and wind wizards, but most of them voted to stay. Their towers have been sealed."

She nodded slowly. "I understand, but that complicates things for us down the road. I sent most of the guards through first to secure the area on the other side of the portal, along with most of my survival boxes as well as most of the staff who aren't golems. If I recall, this portal opens into one the unaligned areas, but they say it's safe so we need to hurry. That yellow color means there's less than five minutes left before it closes for good."

"Where are the twins and Darroth?"

She smiled. "They're all fine. They volunteered to go with the guards when I first opened the portal." She tapped me on the shoulder. "Alex, don't worry about the Foalshead portal. I knew you would be worried about your family and friends. I changed the end route parameters for any transfers from Xarparion to there. Any undead that go through are going to come out on the surface of the sun," Rosa said grimly. "And with Foalshead's geographical isolation, it will be a very long time before any undead walk there."

I gave her a heartfelt hug. "Thank you, Master, you are really the best! Or should I call you Headmaster now? We both hugged again and Maya linked up as well.

We waited and watched as the last of the students made it

through, leaving us and the guards. I checked on Nia on my shoulder and she seemed to be doing just fine sleeping off her magic hangover, which was a relief to me.

As the portal turned blood red, it was time for us to go. The guards went through first, followed by the captain.

Rosa stayed with us as we watched the undead slowly moving our way from the end of the road. She placed a hand on each of our shoulders. "We'll be back."

"You know, I don't think we will," I said, deep in my own thoughts.

Maya took my hand, squeezed it gently, and we walked through the portal together and said a final goodbye to our home.

End of book 1

Look for book two 'Return to Sky Raven.'

60849414R00224

Made in the USA
Lexington, KY
20 February 2017